A Cradle in the Rain

George R. Swaniker.

Dedication

To my lovely wife and best friend. Vivian, your love is a gift.

Table of Contents

CHAPTER 1

The cooling effort in the offices was no match to the unusual late April heat in Southern California. Judge Brooks had fallen into a routine of wiping her sweaty palm with a white handkerchief that lay beside her gavel. Her perspiring palm continued to draw attention, not only to her hands, but rather to her sweaty scarred brow. She wiped it and resumed gazing at the thirty-three-year-old lawyer, Richard Troy Bridges, and Bridges sensed it.

He knew he was posturing between the predispositions of Judge Brooks and his client, Stan Eavesderry. Unfortunately, Eavesderry was a client who'd burnt his bridges of public sympathy behind him. He sat expressionless. His charges had bridled him. 'Mighty Eavesderry,' as he was once dubbed in a local newspaper, looked very subdued. He wore the semblance of a heart-broken little child. His wet eyes showed his broken spirit. His fear was the foreboding of a likely five-year imprisonment for an alleged horrid charge of rape. Earlier, three accusers in a previous harassment case testified against him. His prosecutors had been ruthless and had gone to every length to unearth any material they deemed useful in building their case against him.

It'd been a long hard afternoon. Eavesderry wasn't perspiring, nor was he shivering. He was simply an image of insipidity.

"Counselor Bridges, what do you have for this court that we don't know about?" The judge announced him quizzically. In response, Bridges whispered a word of cheer into his client's ears as he got up to assume the floor.

"Your Honor, with all due respect to your office and this court, I'd like to make a quick reference to a remark by our first Chief Justice of the Supreme Court, Justice John Jay on the prudence of Trial by Jury."

Richard Bridges started his address in a deliberate submissive tone. His goal was to solicit an empathizing ear from the rather assertive Judge Brooks and an audience who had pre-condemned his client.

"Your Honor, according to Justice Jay, I quote 'The jury has the right to judge both the law as well as the fact in controversy,' unquote." He continued "The question now is: what is 'the fact in controversy' in this case? The reason is the reassembling of this jury."

Richard's mind reeled fast to his first meeting with Eavesderry. He saw the tears in his eyes and remembered the words of his broken client; "My son, if I did it I would confess it - to you. I – did – not – have – sex – with - that lady. There wasn't any sensual contact, discussion, no, nothing. I wasn't drunk then, and I'm not now. Please, believe me."

Richard Bridges believed him.

He turned to face the jury. They had endured days of stringent deliberations and had returned to their seats at their own request. They wanted further testimony on the theory that had been planted in their minds during the closing arguments of Defense Attorney Bridges. Bridges had contested how the defendant's DNA was collected. He argued that the DNA results shouldn't be admissible because of questionable procedural approach. He maintained that the way by which the hair of Mr. Eavesderry was discovered and collected from the collar of the blouse of Ms. Kim was imprudent. He argued that a more admissible DNA sample must not be a one that could be potentially transported by hands onto any blouse. In view of this, he maintained that the hairs of Eavesderry could be easily accessed by Ms. Kim from the hairbrush in Eavesderry's bathroom and those could easily be transported, especially for framing purposes. He argued that it shouldn't be the hair, but his saliva or some other discovery on the plaintiff especially so in a case of rape. Bridges perceived that the accuser could easily pick the hair of Eavesderry's and plant them all over her body and clothes. In response to that argument, the jury felt compelled to reassemble for answers to the query by the defense to avoid a hang-jury or, a seeming ultimate jury nullification.

"Your Honor," Bridges continued, as he paced confidently towards the jury. His eyes panned across the faces of the audience, then instantly froze on the jurors, whilst he intentionally and spitefully kept his back against the prosecution, and then derisively sputtered out his line of action. "Defense would – like – to – call – the - plaintiff, Ms. - Kim – to – the - stand."

The quiet audience murmured into life. Judge Brooks dropped her gavel, and roared above the muttering, "Silence!" She asserted her place. "Counselors, what's going on here?"

"The truth would unravel before your eyes, Your Honor." Bridges declared.

"This is nothing new, Your Honor." Prosecutor, Ms. Cromwell shot back. "I am her voice. And Ms. Kim has already declared her intent to not take the stand."

"Then you take the stand. I formally request the prosecutor to take the stand, Your Honor." Bridges asserted with vehemence.

"Your Honor, the Counselor is out of control."

"Stop it Counselors!" Judge Brooks yelled authoritatively. "Any more word from any of you will be considered contemptible." She interjected as she tried to regain her breath.

"Counselor Bridges, you may continue. But you'll have to stay within the boundaries of this court and the profession. What backs your request to put the plaintiff on the stand?"

"Your Honor, please, I apologize for our joint conduct." Bridges played softly to the bench. Judge Brooks liked it; she smiled and nodded.

"I crave the indulgence of this court to allow me to exhaustively prove that we're about to hear a perjuring plaintiff, and if Prosecution would like to stand by her claim, which I believe they strongly avow to, then may I refer to the Supreme Court's stand on the Brady versus Maryland case which mandated, and in this case that Counselor Cromwell removes herself from these proceedings to avail herself to take the stand for her client, thus allowing another counselor to assume her role. The precedence in the Brady versus Maryland case supports this. The prosecution may choose to avoid this angle by allowing Ms. Kim to testify, and O – yes to make her case. And, Your Honor, defense promises without any badgering, to syphon the truth for the hearing of these walls."

Prosecutor Cromwell shot back. "Your Honor, it sounds to me that the defense failed to exchange some of the evidence with us. If they have any, then we request for that evidence before our client, Ms. Kim takes the stand. If they don't have any, then there are no new answers or explanations that the defense needs from my client and may this bluff end."

The insinuation, however, didn't deter Richard Bridges. He kept his gaze on Ms. Kim. It was a rather deliberate ploy to intimidate her.

"Your Honor, defense doesn't have whatever evidence prosecution may be requesting for. What we have, and are willing to exchange, is called Truth; the voice of truth. Why is it difficult

11

for the prosecution to take the witness stand? After all, that's why the Jury returned to this room, is it not?"

Judge Brooks cleared her throat. "I would like to warn the defense that any physical evidence which has not been furnished to the prosecution or this court will not be admissible and is tantamount to contempt of court. Am I clear?"

"Very, very clear," Bridges replied in a triumphant tone while defying his own strong hidden fears. Nonetheless, his obstinate and defiant approach had driven the prosecution into a more worrying position. That audacious confidence was shooting arrows of discomfiture to both sides that even his own Co-Defense Attorney stood up to claim his attention in order to discretely dissuade him from his risky pursuit. Bridges turned to discretely acknowledge his co-defense attorney's concern. However, against Richard's character, he gave his co-defender a strong fiery glare that sent him cowering back into his chair.

Incidentally, and rather imprudently, Bridges had withheld his strategy from his co-defense attorney. He had reasons to believe that his colleague would discourage him from his risky and unpredictable pursuit. Bridges had often believed and said: "Sometimes you've got to take risks – worthy risks - if it would help a good cause." His colleague never subscribed to that. He often would dot his i's and cross his t's and promote formality even on a trivial whim. Richard Bridges was a different material, and his gamble this time had rendered the prosecution uneasy.

"Your Honor, we, the prosecution has assembled every recognizable mountain of proof of guilt that this court wants to hear. Defense is simply dilly-dallying, and theirs is an effort to wear off the patience of this court. We've seen enough of the defense's theatrics."

Richard smiled and countered very softly, but confidently. "Your Honor, resemblance of truth is not the truth, the natural truth. It's the look-a-like of truth. It isn't the same, the real truth. Defense intends to reveal the real truth, to prove beyond any shadow of doubt that there was no physical bodily contact between Mr. Eavesderry and Ms. Kim, apart from a regular, normal handshake."

The audience sighed in disbelief, but Richard continued, at this point, rather firmly; "No – no bodily contact. However, absurd it may sound, it's the truth and the truth has to be heard. The prosecution cannot silence this truth. Truth is a voice and is begging to be heard. May I request Ms. Kim to take the stand?"

After some moments of jostling in the prosecution corner, Ms. Kim stood up. She looked shaken and was in tears. Her emotion moved the audience, but not Richard. Ms. Kim was sworn in and eventually walked very feebly to the box.

Strangely, Richard began to dread the moment, the moment he had created. He'd hoped he wouldn't have to confront the accuser. He simply wanted an easy, early confession and to be spared of the legal wrestling with the accuser. He realized he'd begun to sweat. He'd hyped the tenor of his argument that he was afraid and had literally forgotten his next line of action. He wiped his brow. His co-attorney walked to him and while handing him a bundle of folded facial tissues, whispered loosely, "I hope you know what you're doing." Richard Bridges received it with shaky hands. He wished he could take off his jacket, perhaps his tie, his shirt, if the court would allow it. But then he remembered that; whenever he felt stressed, what had often been therapeutic for him was to capture beautiful sceneries into his mind's eye. He fell on that and within moments, his mind catapulted him to a beautiful white sandy beach where partial nudity was not offensive. He saw people basking in the sun and envied them. He relished that thought and beamed a promising sunny smile to his co-defense corner. His corner didn't smile back but, Bridges then walked to the plaintiff in the witness box.

"How are you, Ms. Kim?"

"I'm fine."

"I'm going to ask you few questions and I expect you to answer them as close to the truth as you can. It would help you, it would help me, and it would help us all."

"Yes, Sir."

"Do you know Mr. Eavesderry?"

"Yes."

"Is he here in this courtroom?"

"Yes." She pointed to him.

"What is he to you?"

"He was my employer. I worked for him."

"You claim he had sex with you, right?"

"Yes."

"Please, sorry, I will rephrase that question. You claim he forcibly had sex with you, correct?"

"Yes."

"What time of the day was this sexual encounter? Was it in the morning, afternoon, or at night?"

"In the afternoon."

Bridges paused for a moment and turned to the Judge and the Jury. "Your Honor, I will be a little graphic in my line of questioning here. Again, I beg the court to allow me to be very exhaustive. It may be very uncomfortable, but very necessary for us to establish this."

"Go ahead, but don't be too long." "Ms. Kim, how did you know Mr. Eavesderry was approaching you for sex?"

"He was wearing only his briefs as he walked towards me "

"No shirt?"

"No shirt."

"So, you might have seen the birthmark on his right shoulder."

"Objection," Ms. Cromwell countered. "Your Honor, the counselor is putting words in the witness' mouth."

"I'm sorry, Your Honor. I'll rephrase the question. Ms. Kim, did you see a mark on Mr. Eavesderry's shoulder?"

"Yes, I did." She answered very confidently.

"What was it?"

"I am not sure what it was."

"Was it a tattoo, birthmark, or something strange?

"It looked like a birthmark."

"Was there something else you saw?"

"We were struggling, so I couldn't see much."

"I thought so. But did you see his chest?"

"Yes."

"Was there any hair on his chest?"

"It was slightly hairy, not very much."

"What else did you see?"

"...on his chest?"

"Yes, on his chest."

"Nothing."

"... Nothing that got your attention?"

"Nothing."

"Are you sure?"

"Hmm – nothing." Ms. Kim answered after a brief contemplation.

"Ms. Kim, this is your last chance to tell the whole truth to this court, because what you have just claimed are all lies, and we can prove them. You wittily fabricated these lies to extort money from Mr. Eavesderry, to disgrace this innocent man and to ruin his life. I'm telling you, you didn't see Mr. Eavesderry's nakedness. And you didn't see his bare shoulders. His shoulders carry no marks as you just claimed. He couldn't have had sex with you." He declared firmly.

Ms. Kim became jittery and fell silent.

"Your Honor, please, we've had enough of the defense's willful badgering." Prosecuting Lawyer Cromwell expressed angrily.

Ms. Kim began to sob in the witness stand. Her emotional posturing was validating the prosecutions' argument of badgering, and Richard Bridges began to sense that he was losing even more of the public favor. He spoke softly.

"Your Honor, please allow me to prove this. Mr. Eavesderry, please take off your shirt." Eavesderry stood up slowly, and rather reluctantly began to take off his coat. The courtroom was in ghostly silence. He began to unbutton his white shirt. The process was taking long; he was feeling betrayed, and Bridges was restless.

"Mr. Eavesderry had a very rough childhood. As a child, any prank from young

Stan Eavesderry was met with strong, violent punishment. His abusive stepfather would use a hot metal to burn his chest like a cattle owner would employ hot iron branding to mark his cattle. The scars are on the defendant's chest; he, therefore, hardly takes off his shirt. He does so only when showering; even then, he cringes at the sight of those marks. He loves beaches, but he won't bask bare-chested like anyone else. Stan Eavesderry carries these scars and hurt with him. Mr. Eavesderry, allow the court to see your chest." Bridges implored him again

Stan Eavesderry hadn't anticipated that his attorney would employ that approach. His chest was a forbidden territory, a tabooed subject in thought and in speech.

He finished unbuttoning his shirt and began to slowly take it off, but for the sleeveless singlet that he wore underneath. He revealed a pair of plain shoulders. There was no mark; not a birthmark or anything to suggest a previous activity on any of his shoulders. "Ladies and Gentlemen, please see the shoulders' of the defendant. I implore the jury of this court and the Prosecution to take a closer look." Bridges announced his temporal triumph.

Satisfied with what the court had seen so far, Judge Brooks ruled to ask Mr. Bridges to continue with his witness. However, Mr. Eavesderry was rather reluctant to reveal his naked upper frame, which was worrying. Bridges hadn't physically seen Eavesderry's chest as he'd claimed in their earlier client-attorney discussion. Bridges simply believed his moving childhood story. However, he was also aware of many accused persons who sometimes had come up with strange lies to drum up a plea for sympathy. Incidents of lying clients were rife, and in this case, it didn't augur well for Bridges, especially when the accused wasn't willing to comply with his request. Richard Bridges gave a quick glance once again at his gloom-faced co-defense lawyer.

"Mr. Eavesderry, take – off – the - undershirt." Bridges commanded, clenching his teeth. Stan Eavesderry looked up, suppressing a tear that wanted to run down his partially unshaven face. He drained his wet eyes with a finger, and then cast a disapproving but emotional look at his attorney. Eavesderry wasn't a lone crier. Some in the audience were moved too.

Slowly and painfully, he lifted his sleeveless undershirt over his head. Behold a scarred terrain of wickedness. Eyes couldn't go there, but the eyes that did, gasped in disbelief and sympathy.

The truth had silenced the lie.

Bridges cleaned his nose. He felt a little disconcerted, "but who cares," he thought aloud. He had won.

Ms. Kim eventually gave an emotional and disgraceful confession and Richard Bridges heaved a sigh of relief. It was over.

The scars had saved the day.

Judge Brooks dropped her gavel and eventually announced with relief, "Court is adjourned." Again, she wiped off the perspiration on her brow as the jurors began to file out.

Bridges took few strides to Eavesderry and hugged him. As they hugged, he felt a tap on his shoulder. "Congratulations. You were brilliant" a voice said, the voice of Ms. Celia Cromwell, the Prosecutor.

"Thank you. That's the highest compliment I've ever received in my career, especially coming from you." Bridges acknowledged.

"I am equally flattered. Take care."

They shook hands and she turned to leave at the sound of a cellphone. She thought the call was hers. It was Bridges' phone. "A party is waiting for you." An unidentified caller said. "A party…?" Bridges frowned.

CHAPTER 2

Richard arrived at his office later in the afternoon and was met by his secretary Sally who had organized a warm welcome for him. The atmosphere was warm buddy, buddy and hi-fiving. Sally was more jubilant; she cocked out champagne and rang out the words, "You can't silence the truth." Richard had won a number of trials within the few years of his practice at the Milo, Grady, and Strong Law firm, but this was a watershed triumph, and everybody wanted to know how he'd pulled it off.

"Thank you, guys. Please, what, what - what I really need now is a breather, a - a good rest." He stuttered his appeal. He felt mentally and emotionally drained. However, on occasions like this, especially when surrounded by colleagues and friends, it was difficult to suppress a whimper, especially when kind sentiments began to fly. Amidst the sentimental words, the Managing Senior Partner walked in. "I have come to congratulate our hero." The Senior Partner had to swallow his compliments when the telephone on Richard's desk rang. Richard picked up the receiver and gestured to the group that he had to take that call. His colleagues began to disperse when they saw his face lower into a purposeful formality. He used his hand to cup-cover his phone and moved towards the door where he could see the offices of his colleagues through his partial glass door.

"Hello! This is Bridges."

"Heh, Richard, it's a rescue call. Don't mention names. Just pretend and play along until they all leave your office."

"All right, Sir, I will take note of that." Richard played along. "Let me grab a pen and a note pad. Please hold." However, Sally lingered and with her typical index-finger- wave, she tried to solicit her boss' attention.

"For a second; the refreshment is at the Bienverido Hotel. It's at six. My intuition is; the press will be there." She expressed that under her breath and stealthily trod out, closing the door softly behind her.

The trick had worked. He picked back the receiver. "Hello!" The caller was gone. He got to the door opened it, and Phil, the caller, the rescuer, was about to walk in. "I could see from my office that they were leaving eventually." Phil explained.

Phil had been routing for him since the inception of the trial. Like Bridges, he was a presentable young man and commanded an athletic bearing. He exuded a very confident demeanor. The girls liked him. Richard appreciated him.

Upon walking in, Phil noticed the unusual look of Richard's indoor plant that had been sitting at the corner at the back of his desk. Richard's preoccupation with Eavesderry's case had deprived the plant of care and consequently had stunted its development. It looked water starved. Phil emptied the left-over water on Richard's desk onto the plant. "You got to take care of your plant, m-a-n. Remember, it's a living thing and don't overlook the other lives in your life." Phil chided. "Give me the juice before we leave."

Richard was careful about sharing the intricacies of the event, especially his agony with Kim while she was in the witness seat. He knew he could confide in a few of his colleagues, including his friend Phil.

Five years before, a young law school grad walked into the law offices of Milo, Grady, and Strong. He was very quiet and reserved. The staff wondered if he was lawyer material because he talked very little. He was reading a book on his lunch break when a lunch delivery for two was directed to his office. His immediate reaction to the delivery was, "You have the wrong office." But a colleague who had then walked into his office corrected, "No, the delivery has your name, Richard Bridges, and it's by the courtesy of Phil Sawyer." They shook hands and had remained friends. However, their professional assignments had kept them away from the office walls. They hardly even ran into each other.

"You know it's at six. We won't have enough time." Richard countered.

"Then, synopsize it. How did you know the lady was lying? After all, the entire DNA report was in her favor."

"You're right. But that's where we sometimes err - when we allow the essence of lawyering to outweigh the emotional dispositions of our client. I believed Eavesderry. I took a chance. It's called faith, and in this case - in what he told me."

"But clients sometimes lie."

"Yes. Many times, they do, but not when Eavesderry's story attacked the very core of the charges against him. He strongly denied there was any bodily contact apart from a normal handshake. That's when I realized how crucial the absence of bodily fluid was to this case."

"I would find it hard to believe such denial," Phil expressed.

"Not when a sixty-year-old man looked you in the eye tearfully and said, 'my son, I did not do it,' and pleaded to be believed."

"He could have played on your emotions." Phil persisted with his reasons.

"Listen, Phil, a man of Eavesderry's caliber could be more discreet with his sexual overtures. You see, the lady called his office to tell him about his fresh, newly delivered laundry. So, she knew he would come home and change or collect few fresh clothes for his trip that day. She trapped him into her scheme."

"I thought the sexual harassment testimonies could nail Eavesderry."

"Well, it did sway some jurors, I would think. However, truth has a way of rearing its pretty head. One should know the facts very well before they rush to opinion. You see, Eavesderry used to live in a rustic society where men approached women crudely. That's where he picked up those very crude and less-flattering approaches to women. Don't let his affluence fool you, he's actually naively raw. He's kind-of bashful, but many times, he hides behind his bashfulness, and by trying to impress, he comes across with a jolt of raw and ugly bluntness. I feel for him. Heh, I wish him well. We should be leaving now."

"We'll meet by the elevators." Phil got up and stepped out.

The towering high-rise buildings that had always impeded the rays of the setting sun, was declaring evening in downtown Los Angeles. Some street lights were up, but the moving crowd and the hustle and bustle were still brisk. To stop and chat would be an eccentric's endeavor. However, Richard and Phil continued to make their way through the crowd. Phil, the swanky attorney, was very protective of the waft of fresh cologne fragrance on him, a concern so pronounced that he walked like he was avoiding human mines that would blow him up upon any bodily contact He would go every length to simply avoid a sweaty contact in the moving crowd.

"Man, let's pick up the pace a little bit. We're getting late." Richard urged.

"It's all right. We have few minutes. They'll wait." Phil, with little care assured Richard.

As they turned at the intersections of Wilshire Boulevard and Figueroa Street, Richard slowed down and turned abruptly. "Huh" He sighed. He made three more paces up. Sharply and abruptly, he turned again. "S-e-th N-a-than!" He yelled out. A tall, black man, about twenty feet away from him, froze in the crowd. The man turned, looked to his left, his right, and then quickened his pace. Richard started shouldering hurriedly his way through the crowd. The man, more aggressively, tried to speedily make away. Richard doubled up, pressing harder. He yelled again, "Seth, STOP! Stop and wait for me." Seth's pace slowed. He was giving up and Richard caught up with him.

Before Richard stood a very haggard man, hair unkempt, clothes dirty with an unwelcome odor. Richard looked shocked, but the excitement of seeing his old friend dismantled the hygienic barrier between them. Richard attempted to hug him, but Seth was very indifferent and less enthusiastic. He moved back.

"No, don't touch me. I'm dirty."

"Why? Why are you dressed like this? Are you shooting a movie or something?"

"Yeah – yeah – a movie," Seth lied.

"Seth, are you a-l-right? Come; come let's move to the curb." Richard directed.

They moved to the curb; there was momentary silence as they sized each other. Seth allowed a wry smile on his face, but Richard's face wasn't smiling. Richard's was more like "What's going on with him?" His curiosity eventually betrayed his thoughts. "Come on ma-n, Seth, what's going on? Something isn't right. What is it? Tell me."

"Bridge," Seth, eventually declared; "I have sores all over me. I couldn't let you hug me."

"O, oh. Sorry to hear that. What is it, chicken pox or something?"

"Yeah, chicken pox. Chicken pox, yeah." He was nodding to discourage his friend from further prying and to discourage any revealing lengthy discussion.

"Seth, you're lying to me." Richard declared matter-of-factly. "You're lying, Seth."

"Nice seeing you, Bridge." Seth turned to walk away.

"You don't walk away – just walk away like that." Richard was upset.

"What do you want me to tell you? You didn't believe me." Seth turned to leave but was held up by the traffic light.

Richard stood tongue-tied and in utter disbelief that the excitement of seeing his closest college friend, someone he'd longed to meet would treat his excitement with a less-gratifying response. With a suppressed hurt, Richard watched Seth Nathan cross over to the other side of the street. While he watched, Richard was joined by Phil who had walked back to find out why he'd been abandoned. Phil looked at him curiously, but surprisingly said nothing.

"Phil, please, I need a huge favor from you. Go to the refreshment without me. Apologize on my behalf, let them know I'm indisposed - not feeling well. Please, pull up something. Just do something. I really have to go home."

"You're going to miss this, are you serious? Free great publicity for you and the office? Huh, the partners won't like this. Think again."

"Please, you must do it for me, Phil, if you call me a friend."

As Phil tried to make his way to the hotel, Richard chose not to go home, but to discreetly follow Seth. *What was Seth trying to run away from; was he really sore all over as he claimed?* The thoughts raced through Richard's mind with every step.

Night had arrived and it provided a good cover for his amateurish undercover effort. He walked several blocks away from the kempt streets of downtown Los Angeles. He'd noticed he'd entered a different zone. The streets were quiet but rather unkempt. He could see a shadow emerging from a neglected home. Richard crossed the street to another structure, also with banes of neglect. Few faces could be noticed and even the bright redness from the inhaled cigarette tips couldn't glow bright enough onto the faces of the inhalers who lurked around the corner. A huge rat had just made its way through a small bush - Richard observed. He wasn't hearing any clatter of horses, so it wasn't after all a live western town, as he was driven to hallucinate.

He could hear emergency response sirens from the distance. The sound became louder with every passing second. Then he saw the flashing red and blue lights speeding past by. "I'm no cowboy hero. I'm Richard Bridges and I'm out of here," he expressed to himself with conviction.

CHAPTER 3

As the smell of food and wine wafted across the bar to the doors of the restaurant, one could sense the uneasiness of the few guests who were yet to be seated. A waiter walked past to a Reception area where a gentleman in a dark suit had his head seemingly buried in a magazine that he'd picked up to read. The waitress announced to the man; "Mr. Eavesderry, your guest is here." Richard was escorted to a reserved table where the guest had been waiting. Mr. Eavesderry extended his right hand with a light-hearted insinuation to "the gentleman who exposed my artistic chest for the world to see."

They laughed off the joke loud enough that they drew the attention of other customers. Knowing Eavesderry for his social persona, Richard had anticipated a joke from him that might crudely sensitize a retrospective moment at the trial. He was right, very right. "It's good that you don't allow those memories to shape you."

"They don't."

"I thought I would lose your friendship and trust." Richard remarked.

"Why? Because you exposed my chest?" Eavesderry went a-laughing again.

"The world needed to know the heart behind that chest." Richard remarked graciously. "I felt the world owed you the correct appraisal of the flawed image they had formed of you." He said in a more formal tone as the conversation was interrupted at the arrival of a waitress. Within minutes, she was done, and Richard and Stan were back at it. "Son, I came to know myself, I mean to know me more than I have ever thought of myself. I am extremely grateful. You've reshaped Stan."

"It's gratifying – the pleasure is mine."

"I have a gift for you. It's not my legal fee. I've already settled the fees with your office. This is for Richard Troy Bridges."

"You know I can't accept a gift from you. It's against MGS policy."

"I know. That's why it won't come from me, but from an admirer, a fan."

Richard smiled. He knew Eavesderry meant well with his offer, but he wouldn't want to be ensnared into doing something stupid by the very person he had saved few days ago from going to prison. He stared at the spread before them. His appetite begged: Food, food, food, whilst Eavesderry was waiting for an answer.

"Let me think about it." Richard assured him.

"Don't think too hard - about a real estate property." Eavesderry hinted.

Richard lit another cautious smile on his face. Midway through their meals he thought of Seth Nathan and his flooding appetite began to regress to total oral drought. He sipped his water. He was no actor; his countenance was an open book and it posed very easy reading for Eavesderry.

"Are you alright?"

"Yes, I am. It was a short interruption by something on my mind."

"Is everything alright at home?" Eavesderry was pressing. He hoped his generous gesture hadn't flown into his face, for he meant well and highly respected the young attorney. He would hate himself if he were to be blamed for the sudden sour development. It was one friendship he wouldn't allow his indiscretions to ruin. "I hope is not me."

"O – No! Please, I appreciate the lunch. I appreciate the time." Richard allayed Eavesderry's concern.

"Richard, the offer still stands," Eavesderry appealed to him again.

"I will be thinking about it and will definitely let you know," He replied with a reassuring smile.

They got up, shook hands, and Richard patted Eavesderry's back before stepping away from their table. Richard led the way through an exit door into a waiting seventy-five degrees sunny Los Angeles outdoors. He would've been a better guest if he'd resolved the dissonance on his mind; Seth Nathan. Yes, Seth. The questions kept multiplying. Was he doing drugs? No. Not the Seth he knew. Was he, for some reason, mentally not well? No. What could have caused that? Did he have anything unfathomable? No. Seth is no philanderer. No. He couldn't stretch his imagination that far. Why would he? His girlfriend, Erika – No – She had never been that type. No – no – no!

His noisy garage door began to open, and its noise was a welcome reminder. Richard was home, in fact, he was beginning to wonder how he'd gotten there. The door closed behind him while Apphia waited by the inner. She'd won the bet. The anniversary had been forgotten again by her husband who'd betted on his forgetfulness and had complained about the nagging reminders from her. He couldn't go back.

"Richard, what's going on?" She asked.

"Apphia, I'm sorry – very sorry. I had lunch with my former client, Stan Eavesderry and drove around few places......"

"And your place at home never dawned on you?" Apphia interrupted softly. There was a burden on her heart. "Richard, what is it? Is it me?"

"No-o-o-o!" Richard's yell rang through the house. Apphia was shaken. What had come over her gentle husband? She wondered inaudibly. His jeopardy had inflicted another wound– more self-distraught. He paced forward like a wounded gladiator tottering to his fall at the feet of his villain foe, himself. With gentle inclination he held his wife, yet very gently, and yielded to his emotions. After few moments of emotional strain, he composed himself. "No, Apphia, it's not you. There are things in life that probe the human spirit that sometimes we don't have answers for. Life has more to offer than this, than you and me."

"I agree, and I'm willing. Let's adopt again."

"O - That's not what I am talking about. A bird will still fly if it doesn't have a song, but it cannot fly with broken wings." Richard's riddle hit a familiar note to Apphia. It was like a plaintive tune – a tune which wouldn't come from him. Her world came crushing. She sank to her knees, feeling crushed with grief. Richard was surprised at the grief he'd caused her. "What's wrong with what I said? I didn't mean to hurt your feelings." He helped her up to her feet. She jerked herself away from his hold and proceeded to the bedroom. Impulsive compliance urged his feet to follow her but halted upon seeing her surprise and elaborate decorations in all the rooms. His guilt was becoming clear.

"Wow! Apphia, I am sorry again that I totally forgot the anniversary."

"Don't worry, when the bird becomes fertile, she will sing and use her broken wings to cover her young – even if she can't fly." She insinuated.

Richard had marched his steps of ignorance into his wife's world of open propriety. He had been a fool. Apphia's actions became clearer; much clearer. He realized he was left with no choice if he wanted to save face. What he'd planned to keep away from her had become unavoidable, more unavoidable that it fell from his lips. "Apphia, it's not at all about you, it's about our friend, Seth Nathan. I saw him today. I talked to him. Seth is sick, and I think he's dying."

Apphia stopped and turned to check the veracity of the statement on her husband's face. His face was solemn. He couldn't have made that up to cover up his unsentimental response over their nuptial anniversary. Her husband had never complained about her inability to have children. She realized that she'd once again stood on a scaffold of insecurity to decorate their relationship with such platitude. She held his hand, looked into his eyes and she what she saw – the eyes of an honest, selfless man. Richard was still Richard.

CHAPTER 4

Sally Sanchez arrived by taxi at the Canary Village Community gates to see her boss, Richard Bridges. Clearance for Sally at the gate had stalled because no provision was made for a taxi to drive into the Canary Community where he lived. She was carrying two boxes of files which he'd requested to be delivered by Sally. He needed those files to work from home. Eventually, he arrived at the main gate to validate Sally's access to the Canary community and to officially introduce her to the security personnel. He'd never been pleased with what he felt were unnecessary protocols for visitors since he moved to the community two years ago.

"Sir, what was holding up my visitor?" He inquired.

"Canary has rules and you didn't follow the rules." The Security person declared in stoic tone.

Richard loaded the two boxes onto his car and drove off with Sally. They talked very little on the way, but Sally intimated that Phil had asked her if she'd had heard from Richard.

"I told him I was hoping you would call. It's been two days. Someone remarked, she saw you talking to a guy who might have been asking you for money."

"Yes, I did stop to talk to a friend I bumped into." The reference triggered yet another reminder of his meeting with Seth Nathan. Since that meeting, he'd hardly been able to take his mind off him. The Seth he knew eight years ago wasn't the Seth he'd met; dirty, unpresentable and haggard.

His car pulled up onto his driveway and a voice greeted Sally. She was about to meet his wife for the first time.

"Now, I can match the face with the name and the voice."

"Yes, me too, although I've seen family pictures, it's different when you meet them in person." Sally expressed warmly.

"Come, come on in and meet our son, Josh."

Josh stood by the front door and with his small outstretched arms was attempting enthusiastically to relieve his father of the box of files he was carrying into the house. Sally, noticed Josh's enthusiasm and child-like endeavor. It drove her to remark, "O how cute! That's a strong man right there."

Like many mothers, Apphia couldn't suppress her pride in her son. "O – He's too much. Don't let him start with his questions," she remarked. Apphia hardly discussed him outside her walls, but she would open up occasionally when she felt comfortable with the company. She did with Sally. Sally's sincere compliments about the Bridges' home and decor delighted her. After an excursion around the house, Sally parted with Apphia to rejoin her boss in a room that Richard had converted into a home-office.

"Sally!" Richard was monotone and solemn. "Again, I'm sorry for the unnecessary problems at the gate, and I want to thank you for bringing these files over." Sally partially lowered her head in bashful but assuring smile. "Mr. Bridges, you know I am here for you - anytime."

His words took a tone of anxiety. "I want to share something in utmost confidence with you. I know I can trust you." Sally blushed as she found herself being rushed into a seeming hard vow of confidence.

"I plan to work from home for a week after which I intend to take a vacation. I will be working on a project which I don't intend to discuss with the office. Mr. Eavesderry will call; please don't let him leave messages on the phone. Please, I would rather like him to talk to you. It's more assuring to talk to a live person than a machine. Get this phone and please, to reach me, call me on this number." He handed her a new cell phone with a new number. "Chances are, I may not be in a position to take your call, but I'll call back upon recognition of the number."

"Mr. Bridges, is everything alright?"

"Yes, Sally, everything is alright. I simply have to make some hard decisions which will demand some time outside the office. I'm fine. I don't want the office to pry into my concerns."

After elaborating precautionary instructions, Richard returned with Sally to the "Canary Community" gate where a taxi was waiting to take her back to Milo, Grady, and Strong offices. Sally waved as her taxi made a turn and evanesced into the speeding highway.

Richard checked his wrist watch, and after a brief contemplation sped off – onto the highway. No, he wasn't following Sally; he was following his reasoning.

After covering some tens of miles, he exited. He suppressed the sound of the engine after a few turns and turns, and allowed his car to taxi to a stop, quite a distance from his marked destination. He was about fifty yards away from the gates of the Stan Eavesderry estate. He began to walk the rest of the way towards the tall trees that lined the stretch of the landscape outside the gates. He didn't know what to expect as he stood behind the walls that towered above him. He chose to try the prospects that awaited him. With his shoulder he nudged a side of the metal gate and it opened noisily and surprisingly, rather very easily. He interpreted that as a positive omen about the trip.

Richard Bridges had no appointments with him and wasn't sure if the protocol and security-minded Eavesderry would be home. The trip was unusual and he was anticipating the typical Eavesderry fiendish outbursts. He knew Eavesderry never welcomed surprises and was known to react to a surprise visit with fierce volcanic virulence that often sent the rest of his household recoiling into their sheltered shells. However, Richard in a casual pair of blue jeans with a white T-shirt was determined to be a guest – an uninvited guest who must be welcomed. His instincts had given him that elevated level of self-assurance.

Eventually, he stepped on to the graveled portion of the driveway that led to the forecourt of the house. The stony soil wasn't friendly; each step was loud amidst the ghostly atmosphere in the windy orchards of the estate. Richard repulsed the noise. He wished he could opt for another route. A worthy option for him was the path of the luxuriant green lawn that would take him to another wing of the house, and to the informal guest gateway to the estate. It was a path more-winding, less-trodden, and presented the least attractive choice. However providentially, Richard fathomed that he'd just figuratively discovered an untrodden pathway into the life of Stan Eavesderry.

He pressed the doorbell and heard the chime faintly inside. Having prepared himself that he would be in for the long haul at the door, he resignedly leaned on his shoulder against the wall by the door. A test of his fate again and yes, the door opened readily and Richard was greeted by a very well dressed, young man, presumably in his early twenties. His face lit with delight as he extended the width of the open-door space much wider for a more generous warmth of welcome. The young man led the way. He knew Richard as the famous lawyer, but the lawyer knew him not.

"I guess you're here to see Mr. Eavesderry." The young man expressed as they climbed a flight of stairs to a huge loft that discreetly overlooked the main gate to the estate.

"Yes." Richard's response was abrupt with a tone that gave little room to gratify his escort. He settled in a chair and waited for a word about his former client and his new unofficial host. Seconds turned to minutes; minutes to very long minutes, and to very, very long minutes. The silence was haunting. The doldrums of unproductive long sitting were beginning to take a toll on him. He had to keep his mind alert and he chose to engage it on an expedition, perhaps more consequential than what he'd found himself in. He sent his mind on an imaginary prowl in some quiet woods somewhere, where it was worth it to appreciate howling canines as great ecological friends. However, he still couldn't keep his head up for long. He was near slumbering. Eventually, he yielded and slumbered in Eavesderry's waiting couch whilst still encumbered with saving citizen Eavesderry like a lost hiker in his business woods.

After a few minutes sleep, he was startled by the return of his young escort.

"Mr. Bridges, my Dad will see you now." He announced and led him to the bedroom of Stan Eavesderry. Richard was quite acquainted with the large vicinity area of the bedroom. He was remembering and picturing the scene as the perjured plaintiff, Kim, tried to describe and to convey in her testimony against Mr. Eavesderry. That was his second visit and it seemed to bring the whole incident alive again, but there was something different. The whole area reeked of liquor and perhaps vomit. A man lay on his stomach on the floor. The size of the physical frame, his long legs and his big head, revealed a composite figure that gave instant match to Eavesderry. Richard was horrified. A variety of speculations were flying through his mind. He turned and gave a good look at the young man who had just surprised him with his filial relationship to Eavesderry. Eavesderry had never discussed he had a son. The blinds and the drapes were rendering the room dark and were offering little help for Richard to fully behold the face of the young man.

"I may choose to open the blinds for more light and fresh air, but he doesn't want me to." The young man spoke.

"Who didn't want you to?" Richard asked sharply, revealing an anger spawned from his anxieties. Then he heard a groaning from the figure on the floor. He turned sharply.

"Richard, my son, I did." It was the same voice that carried that note of plea, "My son if I did it, I would confess it to you." By reflex response, Richard gasped out his relief. It was loud. He knew he'd heard the voice of Eavesderry, but he struggled to reconcile the kempt and exuding Eavesderry with the sullied-looking and subdued Eavesderry.

"Open the drapes, Lawson, but be gentle. Don't flood the room." Eavesderry instructed his son. His cautionary instruction was to prevent damaging his eyes from any surge of blinding beam. A measure of light rushed into the room. Richard could now, well, see the faces of the red-eyed, tavern-cheery Eavesderry, and his handsome conservatively dressed son, Lawson.

Lawson didn't do a good job at cleaning his father's mess during Richard's brief slumber in the loft couch. He couldn't have; the room was dark, and he had limited time to carry out the directive of his father to usher Richard upstairs into his presence and into an unsoiled room.

As his father pulled himself off the floor, he revealed a yellowish stain on one of the sleeves of his white shirt. It was clearly a semblance of drying vomit, but it was the smell of the regurgitant odor that drove them out of the room. Richard requested a move to another room. The situation of the abjectness was portraying a squalid persona unlike the Eavesderry that Richard had held any claim to knowing.

Lawson led the way, and they settled in a smaller room few yards away from Eavesderry's regular bedroom. Richard recognized it. It was the room that Kim had alleged that she was assaulted in by Eavesderry. Since then, Eavesderry had never stepped his feet near the door, even after court orders on the room were lifted. The memories were profound. He loathed everything about it.

Eavesderry settled in his chair and lowered his head in a resigned and pensive mood. For a protracted period, with his head still bowed while Lawson and Bridges looked on, he said nothing. When he eventually lifted his head up, he presented a face deluged with tears, and a pair of eyes as scarlet as the intoxicant that was debasing his personhood. His room companions were seeing a wounded and broken man.

"Lawson bring me a damp towel. Your father needs it to freshen up." Upon the request, Lawson left to fetch the damp towel and returned in no time with one. Richard received it and attempted to apply it, but Eavesderry restrained him and assumed the responsibility himself. He wiped his face and made quick rounds with the damp towel around his neck and his partially exposed chest, and then handed the towel back to Lawson.

"Bridges, I am not a happy man."

The words lanced at the ears of his former counselor. It was an expression with candor rarely declared by a person of Eavesderry's make-up. Richard had no response. He was not overly surprised since the condition he had found Eavesderry in seemed to convey that emotion. Richard was moved but felt very empty to command a meaningful word of empathy to him. Nonplused by the development, he sought to explore what had culminated into Eavesderry's strange statement. He turned and gave Lawson a look that conveyed a demand to be alone with Eavesderry, his father. Lawson heard the silent request and walked out gently.

"Mr. Stan Eavesderry, that's a very candid statement," Richard remarked.

"Yes, it is. And by making this admission before you, I count it an act of valor on my part. Please, don't ask me why I'm unhappy, because I don't know."

The unexpected remark left Richard with no peg to hang on for any further thoughtful discussion with him. There was a long silence, perhaps about a minute. The drapes that earlier had curtained off the light from the room were beginning to admit a cooler flow of breeze from the swinging trees outside. The breeze was soothing and was quietly bringing Eavesderry out of his hangover stupor. He got up and wobbled his way to the open window. A more generous flow of breeze greeted his face. He saw the ecstatic trees dancing. He wished he could dance with them. He smiled; he only knew why he smiled. His sanity was returning.

Richard was even more perplexed at the sudden fluctuations of Eavesderry's mood. Eavesderry smiled again; this time, more at Richard's distinctive expressed facial puzzlement. That yielded another trend of perplexity while Eavesderry tried to suppress his simmering smile. The reality was, every good display of Bridges' smile rolled into a grin on Eavesderry's face; it stretched into a smile. The smile grew and Richard's confusion chagrined into broader ripples of amusement and into a shared result of rippling laughter.

"What's funny?" Richard asked himself after his exhaustion from laughing.

"The medley of confusion and the anger on your face was amusing," Eavesderry replied. Then a solemn countenance suddenly took over his face again. Richard observed again the sudden emotional fluctuations and wasn't pleased with them. He was convinced that something more complicating was eating his client up. He felt there was a seething anxiety in the behavior of Eavesderry as divulged by Sally when she brought in the boxes. He was beginning to believe Sally. Eavesderry's actions had started to reveal some concerns Richard had had about him. He'd begun to wonder if there were more to Eavesderry's sexual assault case than he'd known.

"Mr. Eavesderry," Richard addressed him. "Please, tell me something you otherwise wouldn't want to tell me, but you know I would like to know."

"I've just told you, Bridges. I am an unhappy man." After a rather lengthy silence again, Eavesderry, who stood by the window, chose to open the drapes wider for a greater flow of the fresher breeze from outside. He then reached out and pulled his chair to a seating advantage by the window. He needed it, and it helped. He was more awake, but his memory travelled to his childhood years.

After his father's death, young Stan Eavesderry who was then seven years old met Sid. Sid used to pay regular visits to the widowed mother of young Stan Eavesderry. On many occasions Sid's truck would pull up at the front yard and would holler out to young Stan and they would then drive off to their favorite fishing site. It was always an exciting time for young Stan, especially when the day was crowned with a good catch. That was among the many early weeks with Sid. Those were wonderful times for Stan.

Young Stan naturally developed a close bond with Sid. He loved Sid. His mother loved him more. Soon they were married, Mr. and Mrs. Sid. Sid moved into the late Mr. Eavesderry's home, home of young Stan's father. However, the once bubbly-spirited happy home became a nightmare for kiddy Stan Eavesderry. With his mother's blessing, one day young Stan went on a trip with the neighbors' children. The trip, however, was the ultra-unpardonable violation of Sid's rule and the consequence marked the inception of Stan's hot iron branding, the charring marks on Stan Eavesderry's chest. The incident left Mrs. Eavesderry with a cold comprehension that she'd married a monster. She feared her new husband; her son feared his stepfather more. For three years, Stan lived with multiple episodes of the hot iron branding. He bore the torture in silence and for the rest of his youthful years the protracted trauma caused him to have total distrust for anybody who was not a relative.

Although it dawned on young Stan several times to escape the wickedness of his stepfather, he shuddered at the thought of the grave consequences that fleeing would bring onto his mother. He feared the worst.

One day, when Sid was at work, Stan's mother packed a lunch of sandwiches for his son and sent him away to his maternal grandparents. Stan was ten. During his stay with them, he took interest in his grandma's cooking. He learned how to cook from her and developed his own special recipe. It was a flavor for grilled onions especially for hotdogs. When Stan turned fourteen, his grandfather saw in him qualities of entrepreneurial acumen and supported him in developing his gift. He surprised Stan when one day he pulled home a used hotdog cart.

With the help of his grandfather, he refurbished the hotdog stand and got it in operation. Young Stan Eavesderry proudly named it: "Stan's Stand." Within a year he'd acquired three more stands. By his twenty-first birthday, Stan became the owner of Stan's Stand Hotdog Holdings, a hotdog franchise that was serving his signature Stan Hot Dogs and Stan Burgess. Every Stan's Stand Hotdog Cart and Stan's Stand Joints - vending his hotdogs and burgess all fell under his Holding. Stan's Stand became visible at every boardwalk, stadiums and every popular American recreational event.

"I'm a proud millionaire with an asset worth of about twenty-one million dollars, twenty-one at twenty-one," Stan Eavesderry once boasted at a celebration with his mother and grandparents. Success had begun to smile on him. "I've been lucky; not everybody has. My biological parents taught me to always remember those who are less fortunate. My father was and so was my mother." Mr. Eavesderry continued his story, and in a flash, memories of the times with his late biological father overwhelmed him.

"Four years ago, I met a young teenager on the grounds of a small shopping center. He had at a corner many bouquets of flowers. He approached me and impressed me to buy some flowers from him. To please him, I did. In many ways, that kid reminded me of myself when I was about his age. I had a conversation with him, and he told me about their hard conditions since they'd arrived here from Panama. I was moved by his story and he invited me to his house. One day, I drove to his house and met him and his parents. It had been rough for them. I could see; the parents had prematurely grown old. I advised the kid to go back to school; he was thirteen years old then. I decided to employ his sister as a housemaid who was then about nineteen and encouraged her to enroll in a night school. Her name was Kim. Two years later, I promoted Kim to a housekeeper position. She had access to my home office and to this room. My bedroom was solely handled by Lawson's mother who was my girlfriend then. I don't know why I haven't proposed to her all these years, perhaps, my fears." Eavesderry admitted loosely.

He continued. "One day, Kim introduced a young man to me as her boyfriend. She said she depended on him for a ride home. Christmas was coming. I gave her and the other workers in the house bonuses but yes, I gave her more. The idea was to help her purchase a used car. You know the story; she used that against me in court that I was trying to lure her."

"Did she purchase the car?" Richard asked.

"I'm not sure she did; I simply wanted to help her. Two days later, the police arrived here with the ridiculous charges." Eavesderry was silent for a minute as he tried to regain his emotional composure.

"The closest physical contact was a handshake. As a principle, I don't hug people for the sheer concern that a hug would reveal the scars on my chest. Absolutely, I never had any close physical contact with her. No thought of an affair even crossed my mind. There was never any form of fraternization or any subject that may encourage such thoughts. I never imagined such wicked lies could ever be formulated by her. I helped her, her brother, and her parents. I'm still in disbelief that she could scheme such wickedness."

"Bridges, after my court encounter with her, I lived in fear and doubt. I pretended all was well for few days, but in reality, I don't know how to trust and to trust anybody again. As you can see, my house is quiet; it's empty. My girlfriend, Lawson's mother had to leave. She gave me no cause to distrust her, but I failed to get along with her. I lived in fear of all the attendants in my house. My business is suffering. Yes, the court exonerated me from all the accusations, but the harm has already been done."

Richard listened keenly and began to perceive the nature of Eavesderry's journey so far. He drew closer to him by the window in a show of empathy.

"I'm sorry for what you've been through and are going through. The effect on you is unimaginably terrible. I hope you'll get through this. There are many out there who need to know you. They don't know your kind heart and what you're going through right now. However, in this world of interdependence, trust is very crucial."

Rather impatiently, Eavesderry cut in. "How can I trust anyone?"

"Trust is a rare find. It's no commonplace commodity. It's a breed of sincerity and the silent sibling of faithfulness. Love breeds them all."

Softly, the heart of Richard spoke. It revealed his yielding empathy even more for his marooned client, who was still groping his way out of the stormy life of treachery created by Kim, his former housekeeper. Eavesderry's cloud of doubt remained dense. However, with Bridges, the reality that a person's life's events and exposures often shape the character of the person is a profound truth.

"And who breeds love?" Eavesderry asked again; this time in a clearer tone of frustration textured with arrogance; and perhaps, in discreet anger.

"Love breeds love," Richard breathed out slowly in an endearing and assuring tone.

Silence fell. The much softer rendition of Richards's heart pervaded Eavesderry's dusky world, and the skeptical opinions about the frosts of life. Eavesderry grinned. His twisted lips showed a bashful resignation of his pride. The power of warmth began to melt the built-up icy consequences of Kim's treachery in his heart.

He rose from his chair; attempted to make a comment but checked himself. However, that was enough to warn Richard that there was still a looming frontier. Eavesderry was restless and he showed it. He ran his fingers through his hair and deployed his other fingers to a repeated scratching of his partially unshaved and rough beard. He continued very broodingly. Eventually, he unpacked his mind.

"Bridges, do you believe in the existence of God?"

"In fact, I do. I choose to. I'd rather permit my mind to adapt itself to the good things I read and hear about God. Somebody made us; we didn't make ourselves. Mr. Eavesderry, you do not need to go far to fetch this truth. Every time you look at yourself, you must see yourself as a work of a creator not by an accident or a thing of chance, but by God. Stan, please, please, if you miss this truth, you miss life.

Please, Mr. Eavesderry, I also want to share something with you.

Now, as matter of fact, again listen to this and think about it.

Every woman has two bottles in her chest. And anytime she is pregnant or about to have a baby, her bosom bottles or what we know as breasts, gets filled up with milk. Where does the milk come from? The creator simply got it ready for the mother so as to provide milk for her baby when the baby arrives. Even so, when the woman is not pregnant no milk is formed in her breasts.

Every part of our body is designed for a particular function, for also, at a particular time. We are a piece of marvel – a created masterpiece by one who knew what he was doing. It's a simple premise. I would rather believe that than be told I morphed out of a monkey. I also believe there's a bad one out there who deceives with lies, sweet, and good talk, and sometimes with actions, but full of sinister motives. One may not have to swallow what he offers. You may ask, 'how then can we distinguish between the deceiver and the real good or truthful one?' That's the battle. I believe the true one shows selfless love, love without conditions; that's the willingness to die for what one loves. Your stepfather,

Sid exemplified a deceiver. Kim showed greed. She totally betrayed your trust. Your world shouldn't revolve around them. Their deceit and wickedness shouldn't dictate your future. Otherwise, they win. You know better than that. Mr. Eavesderry, I believe the only way out is to learn to shift to another level of trust."

"What do you mean?" Stan Eavesderry asked.

"I mean, to forgive them; close the pages of your memory of their wickedness." Richard answered sharply.

"It's impossible. I'll forever live with these memories."

"It's possible. You can if you want to." Richard shot back. "Otherwise, you'll be living your life like a tech machine with a memory chip full of harms done to you, overshadowing reminders of happy moments. Otherwise, how can you look forward to and celebrate happy moments when they show up? Because you may not recognize those moments of happiness in your life; because you simply do not know them. Mr. Stan Eavesderry, you are feeding yourself with doubts and platers of negatives, everything negative. You won't like a poisonous memory with a daily dosage of poisonous or hurtful reminders – very terrible. Mr. Eavesderry, you have to move on. It may not come easy, but you have to."

"How can I do that? How can I trust anyone?" Stan asked nervously.

"We can trust God." Richard replied. "Man is prone to failures because of man's weakness and because of man's dependence on himself in spite of all his frailties. Develop a sense of pity towards them, all who have abused your trust – in fact, they're pitiful, for they chose to neglect the imbued nature of God's goodness in you which always comes with a quiet blessing."

"Bridges, how can I do that?"

"Well, I know it's not easy, but I still believe you can. Try to learn from someone who did that. That's a good start; it can help you." Bridges expressed softly. Then a long silence sharply pervaded the atmosphere. Eavesderry, however, broke the lull with a whimper. "To learn to forgive - where do I go from here?"

"I guess where you can learn or from whom you can learn. The source must be a forgiver, one who practically forgave his enemies. And I know he did because he prayed for them. You know what, I think you should pray for them, really pray for them. It will give you an inner peace by expressing well-wishing thoughts about them and for them. A new level of trust begins here. Trusting him, him who you don't see, and also who isn't tangible for you. That's obviously to trust God." Richard Bridges expressed.

"How?" Eavesderry asked.

"I don't know. Get to know him and try to know him enough." Richard responded.

"Why 'enough,'" Eavesderry asked?

"He was here before we came. He'll be here when we leave; he'll always be. He created us. We did not make ourselves. We must know this, it's the paramount truth. He's infinite. How can we, the finite ones, fully comprehend the infinite? My wisdom is very limited regarding the deep mysteries of God and about God. I'm also trying to know him, yes, to know him enough too."

Eavesderry heaved deeply and sighed loudly. "I believe you'll get to know him, Bridges, I believe you will."

Eavesderry turned and directed his attention to the trees outside. They were still swaying to the wind while the open fronds continued to wave an equivocating gesture, goodbye or welcome to him, who enjoys the breeze. Eavesderry watched contemplatively, a captive of his own imaginations. Eventually, he turned to face his room and his devoted legal counselor.

"Thank you. You're a good man. It's been very rewarding. God sends people like you. Bridges come with me."

Eavesderry led the way back to his drab, liquor-vomit smelling bedroom. He threw the drapes open, wider, for the smell to escape his bedroom. Richard was dragging his feet; the room wasn't inviting. He wished for instant disappearance but, unrelenting Eavesderry urged him to step in. He obliged. The quiet room was quieter. Then he saw it. He saw the brandished pistol; in the grip of Eavesderry. Its shiny barrel was staring at him. *Is he insane?*

The question raced frightfully through Richard's mind. A gun in the hands of Eavesderry was a grand stand of irony. Eavesderry took few steps forward. Richard's heart jumped.

"I was going to use it this morning. My parting words are under my pillow. I didn't want my mother to observe it, nor to hear it go off. The house workers have the day off. Lawson was about to run errands for me; I was simply trying to keep him away. Then you appeared. What drew you here - God sent - perhaps. Please, take the gun, please destroy it. Destroy it." Eavesderry stretched out his arm to hand the gun over to Richard who stood frozen, shaken up with fear and cold disbelief. Then, Eavesderry placed the gun on a table and initiated a move for a hug. With the gun resting on the table, Richard hugged him and felt the rough, scarred chest.

"Once again, you've made me see hope in life, even with my scarred chest. I'm sure there are many out there who can use you, Mr. Bridges." Eavesderry expressed appreciatively.

"I felt the rough treasure chest. What's in there?" Richard joked.

"A trove of life's lessons," Eavesderry joked back.

CHAPTER 5

Richard's escapade to Eavesderry's home led him into thinking and wondering about the fleeting span of everything. It led him into thinking about his friend, Seth Nathan. Richard paused and chuckled at the thought.

There was a strange man with a rather unusual bearing. The sun had tanned him quite a bit and his sight seemed to be failing him. Sometimes the stranger would be found at a different street corner and would often strike a conversation about news events and news headlines with anyone who passed by. A friend of the stranger, an older lady, would often bring him breakfast at his usual bus stop while he waited for the bus. The older lady called him, "Sonny" and he called her "Mommy."

One day, after Mommy had driven off after her routine breakfast supply, he was joined by another neighbor. This neighbor and Sonny were getting acquainted when Sonny noticed from few blocks away, that his friend, Mommy, with her old yellow car, had made a U-turn and was approaching them. Mommy's car pulled right in front of Sonny and his new-found friend.

"Sonny, come home and share a real breakfast with me," Mommy pleaded with her friend, but Sonny showed no thrill about the offer.

"Not today, Mommy, perhaps tomorrow."

"I have baked some muffins. Come on over."

Sonny turned and looked at his other friend for approval. Sonny nodded: "I will come if my friend here can come with me."

"Yes, yes, yes, he can come too." Mommy was excited, but Sonny's friend wasn't keen. "It's a mother and son thing and I don't want to be a bother." Sonny's friend expressed, having formed the opinion that Mommy and Sonny were a mother and son relationship.

"No, you wouldn't be a bother at all, absolutely not." Mommy explained to Sonny's friend.

"If I was clean enough, I would, but not the way I'm looking right now," the friend explained.

"You look alright to me. I promise you; I'll bring you back after you've had something to eat. Come – on. Jump in – eh – eh." Mommy kept the door open in a silent persuasion effort for Sonny's friend to hop in. "What's your name?"

"Sena."

"Nice name. Well, come on in Sena. 'Sonny and Sena' has a nice ring to it; the way it sounds, you know." They jumped in and soon they were on their way.

Sena wasn't comfortable and Mommy had observed that. In his mind, he'd been baited into a cage. Eventually, it dawned on him, the folly of his apprehensions. *O – How foolish of us to allow our fears to dictate our assumptions,* he thought. The silence in the car was broken when Mommy began to hum a tune. Eventually the lyrics took over.

"Many are the questions floating in the sky

Many are the answers, but little truths to fly

Many are the choices hovering all about

Many are the decisions that shut all wisdom out."

Sena was moved by the words, especially hearing the rendition from Mommy. Her voice was not spectacular, but her rendition emanated from her inner recesses, her soul, Sena thought. Identifying with the spirit of her singing, Sena soon found himself caught into duetting the refrain with Mommy.

"Why should the skies cause our days of drought

O teach me to understand what's this all about

There's a flowing fountain in a dry desert rock

It takes the believing heart to take in the pleasant shock."

Sena was feeling even more comfortable and got carried away. He found himself singing along. He had a great tenor, but he hardly unleashed those pipes; not that day, the song had awakened something in him:

"Many are the achievements, boasting our skills to survive

Many are our gains about how to truly thrive

Many are the influences testing our human will

Many are our tendencies that pride our strength and zeal"

Sonny tried to join in the singing, but the words were strange to him. He sounded like a person rolling a lump of hot food in his mouth and was faced with the dilemma of swallowing or spitting it out. Mommy came to his rescue. "Sonny, please don't force it." He obeyed and they all celebrated his instant obedience with laughter. Sena, on the other hand, was enjoying the singing.

"Can we dare to lay claims to things we did not create?

Can we dare make changes led decisions led by fate?

Oh, tell me – Can we even change the spots of the leopard's scan?

Do we know the wonders that mock the minds of man?"

The words of the song were still in Sena's mouth when the car eventually arrived at its destination, Mommy's home. "Please give me a different chair; I don't want to ruin your furniture." Sena sounded rather odd with his imposition as he stood by the door and with no desire to move or look around at his environment. Sonny returned with a rattan chair with a disposable plastic covering. As he walked in, Sena had his back towards the house and so didn't see the arrival of his requested chair. In his unflinching stance to stay outdoors of their home, he reiterated his request. However, his strange behavior didn't surprise Sonny. He knew Sena was in good hands. Sonny took off his bearded guise and moustache and announced to his friend: "Seth, it's me, Richard."

Seth was in awe. There was a long silence. Mommy had brought a chair, and this time, she didn't look gray-haired as she'd previously disguised herself in. She looked younger, and was very much like Apphia Takis who used to be the girlfriend of Richard. Apphia smiled, her signature warm smile lit on her face. Seth knew that smile. He recalled instantly how he'd often teased Richard that it was "Apphia's smile that mesmerized the Bridge." Still in shock, Seth stood there like helpless prey, frozen at the sight of a menacing predator. Apphia picked up the rattan chair and settled it at the back of Seth; her way of inviting him to sit down. Seth turned around in grateful acknowledgement of the gesture. Apphia then noticed the tears in Seth's eyes. She squatted, cross-legged on the lawn, and Richard joined them with a box of facial tissues.

"Now, may I have some of the baked muffins?" Seth asked humbly but jokingly. To his surprise, Apphia indeed had baked some muffins and brought in a tray- full. Then she returned with a jug of orange juice. Richard brought a bowl of water with soap for Seth to wash his hands. He smiled gratefully.

"Hygiene means nothing to me now. I'm going to die anyway."

"Don't say that, Seth. There could be a cure for your sickness." Apphia affirmed.

"Apphia, it will take more than hope. Now, let's discuss something light-hearted," Seth remarked.

"You matter to us, everybody matters. How is Erika? Did you guys continue ----?" A brief silence greeted Apphia's question. Seth struggled with the answer. He looked up and heaved a deep sigh as he turned his head to look away from them. The question had struck a nerve. He breathed in hard and then exhaled his answer.

"I married her – six years ago; I buried her – a year ago." He said softly.

Richard and Apphia were in utter shock. Apphia regretted having exhumed a buried history. It was too late to rebury the story she'd just unearthed. If she had her way, she would rather avoid the discussion of the Nathans. At best, she would prefer something more light-hearted, her husband's dry jokes. In her opinion, Richard would be a good candidate for a comic relief. Although Apphia had no furtive motives, the flap over her question about Erika instantly incarcerated her into her shell. Apphia feared any family matters' might break into the walls of her guarded gynecological problems. Often, she would shy away from any leanings that might remind her as a biologically childless mother, and which was anathema to her heritage. Her husband knew her very well, so he charged into those walls with a humane tongue of wisdom.

"Life is a gift; we must appreciate it in whatever way it's wrapped. Sometimes we receive the gift when we least expect it. And that's always a pleasant surprise."

Apphia succumbed to her kind rescuer.

She narrated how she and Richard had had a beautiful wedding and how they'd looked forward to having children, but hadn't been blessed with one yet. She spoke about how she adored her adopted son Josh, and how it would please her and her parents even more if she had her own biological child - a challenge that had also made her more socially withdrawn from her Greek parental circles.

Her narrative was long. Richard was getting bored. He broke his silence with a lawyer's typical question line to Seth.

"What happened to Erika?"

"The doctor said she died from complications of allergies but couldn't narrow it to a particular allergen; which I didn't believe. Rumors were flying that it was AIDS, frankly Bridge, I don't know."

"What did she tell you? Something might have caused her sickness."

"She was on a long trip that took her to Australia, China and India. When she returned, she complained of being tired, which was normal. I suspected jetlag, but she grew weaker and weaker by the day. So, we went to see the doctor."

"Who was her doctor?"

"Dr. Appleworth of Pledge Health Insurance Services."

"You do remember his name very well." Bridges remarked interrogatively.

"The doctor is a she, Marlene Appleworth - Easy to remember by thinking apple."

"Is that her married or maiden name?"

Seth laughed. "Bridge, how would I know? It's not a question I could have asked her?" Richard laughed back and conceded, "I guess that was a dumb question. You're right. Anyway, do you know who Erika's insurance carrier was?"

"Yes, I had the same insurance; it's PHIS, Pledge Health Insurance Services."

"Seth, let me ask you, do you think your situation is an infection from her?"

The question threw Seth into a pensive mood. He wished Richard hadn't asked that question. It brought back memories. He was quiet and the silence began to rebuild a sense of guilt in Richard.

"Seth, I'm sorry. I didn't mean to." He didn't finish his statement when Seth cut in. "No, no, no, I'm fine with it. After her visits to the doctor, she started getting better, but was very weak. Her appetite was poor, and she was losing weight. She felt very delicate and tender. One evening, when I returned from the High School where I worked, I jumped straight into the shower because I was sweaty and dirty. Erika came and stood by the shower door and complained that I didn't care about her anymore. She went on to say that I didn't find her cuddly anymore and I should remember that she was once beautiful. Bridge, that complaint was like a stab into my heart."

Seth paused for a moment. He choked back his tears and tried to regain his composure.

"I knew Erika. She said those words because she felt insecure. But she shouldn't have been, because I loved her even more. My problem was that I didn't know she was interpreting my caring as a regular patient care and not a lover's care. I never viewed my home as a hospice; it was a home that love built. I was broken. I picked her up just as she was and brought her under the shower. I carried her as I sang softly for her above the noise of the shower. I saw the twinkles in her eyes scintillate across the steady crystal shower. Her drenched clothes held tight on her thin and feeble body. I felt the silent rhythm of her pulse; I knew she was feeling mine. I carried the once vibrant and audacious Erika out of the shower. I told her how much I loved her. I took off her wet clothes and tried to dry her up like a baby with a towel. That was when I saw that her thighs and portions around her abdomen were riddled with sores. She saw the shock on my face. I was moved with sympathy. She looked dewy-eyed and I sensed her question: 'would you still love me?' She died the next evening. Did I get infected? Perhaps! I don't know. I'm still trying to find out."

Apphia heaved a sigh. It was loud enough to imply that Erika's story might have influenced her contrition. However, Richard's concern was less audible, though it carried loud anxieties. He wondered why there were multiple versions of Erika's diagnosis. It would take a physician to answer his queries, not Seth Nathan, the ever-grieving husband. Richard heard his phone ringing, but ignored it. The answering machine beeped. It offered no attraction either to him. Apphia, who had briefly stepped away, re-emerged, and was looking like Mommy. Seth saw the transformed Apphia and chuckled with an incredulous headshake. Richard was yet to emerge; he eventually did, and he looked very much like Sonny. "Sena, I have to take care of that call, if you don't mind, Mommy will drop you off. I'll be coming to see you very often. Just look for this yellow Volkswagen."

Seth smiled again. "You guys went through a lot of trouble for me and I appreciate it. You overwhelmed me. Bridge, I mean Sonny, I'll look for you."

Richard watched Apphia and Seth drive off in the yellow jalopy onto the main street. He reached into his right pocket and fetched a pair of plastic gloves, and having worn them, unwrapped the plastic covering on the chair that had been used by Seth and released it into the discarded empty computer box that sat by the entrance to the backyard of the house. He rid his hands of the gloves too. As he re-entered the room, the home phone's red flashing light caught his eyes.

"Hi, Mr. Bridges, this is Sally Sanchez. I've been trying to reach you on the other phone. I guess it's either turned off or has a low battery. Please, I must speak with you. Call me, please."

Richard picked up a second phone on a coffee table and dialed. After the third ring, he heard: "Good afternoon, this is Mr. Bridges office." It was Sally, but Richard anxiously interrupted her greeting. After settling in an immediate chair by his coffee table, Sally unfurled a bundle of developments in the office. Then she added: "So, this new hire who will be starting tomorrow, will be using your office until you return." Richard frowned. "Thank you, Sally. By the way, did Mr. Eavesderry call?"

"Yes, he did. He plans to contact you at home."

"Thank you. You will see me tomorrow." Bridges hung up.

69

CHAPTER 6

The office had a new fragrant smell. It was uncomfortably strong for Richard. He threw his coat on the visitor's couch and just when he was about to settle in his chair, he heard the sound of approaching steps. His intuition drove him to act busy. The sound of the steps ended at his door. The partially opened door widened and she walked in. She was very attractive.

"Oh, I'm sorry. I didn't expect to see anybody here this early. I'm Evelyn Hedge, a new hire and I believe you're Mr. Richard Bridges."

"Yes, and how did you arrive at that?" Richard asked with a relaxed tone.

"Well, I guessed."

"No, you said you 'believe' and that narrowed your expressed implication to absolute indication."

"I mean it's your office. And I wouldn't expect any other person in here."

"Any other person would otherwise be you if I waited ten minutes before showing up."

"You aren't suggesting I'm trespassing, are you?"

"No, on the contrary, I'm expressing the magnitude of the shock that would be mine if I walked in here and found a pretty lady behind my desk. I would naturally be wondering if I were a worthy target of her espionage."

"Wow. I heard, I saw, now I believe."

"Ms. Hedge, relax. It's my way of translating the courtesy of opening the passenger door to a very important guest who I may have the privilege to be riding with on this collaborative journey of the legal profession."

"Well, you jolted me with your sense of detail mindedness."

"If it's from me, it's harmless." Richard opened up for a handshake. Evelyn smiled and felt at ease. They shook hands and he moved from behind his desk and offered a chair behind her to settle in.

"Thank you." Grateful, she sat down but very discomfited by his presence and her shattered plans for the day in the office. She wished she knew when he would leave the office.

"So, Ms. Hedge, you heard, you saw, you believed. What did you hear?"

"I knew you wouldn't rest that statement. Frankly, I hear you're smart, I saw your last case victory on the news and have witnessed your sharp sense of ascertainment and I believe it makes great lawyering, but it makes people nervous around you."

"Wow, that's unflattering"

"It's the truth. You're prone to dissect words, even in a simple, social, ordinary dialogue. It's good in a courtroom, but not in a social casual setting."

"I didn't intend to offend you." Richard submitted graciously.

"Mr. Bridges, you have not." Evelyn replied.

"Have I made you nervous around me?"

Evelyn burst into raucous but controlled laughter. She was unaware that she was in an office environment. She laughed so hard that it rendered her eyes wet. Richard wasn't amused.

"What's funny?" He asked with a sense of regret.

"I anticipated your question and it's funny you hit it as I expected."

Richard thought it was a wry response. He felt he had been a fool in keeping his guard up. After all, he should have been the relaxed party if he devoutly wanted to siphon the motive behind her association with his office. Ms. Hedge composed herself, blotting her wet eyes as she smiled.

"Richard, o-oh I am sorry. Mr. Bridges, I didn't intend to sound too informal." Evelyn apologized. However, Richard interrupted to set her at ease. "No, it's fine. Call me Richard."

"Back to your question, Richard, in all sincerity, you haven't made me nervous around you. If you did, I wouldn't laugh this loud, but I felt you lost in this exchange. You lost something to me."

"How did I?"

"You brandished your best weapon, so I knew how to defend myself, I mean, what to use from a professional standpoint as a lawyer."

"My best weapon - and what was that?"

"Your analytical mind, your sharp sense to screen any hidden implication to a tepid jury or audience, which prepares an opponent to weigh his words around you, so he or she comes, prepared to be very evasive with his or her choice of words."

"Wow, I didn't know I was that good. If I could make a litigant more concerned about words and fails to dwell on the issues and facts of the case, then I must be very good, I mean very, very good. My folly is that, I don't know I am."

Richard smiled, very confidently. He'd had the last laugh. Evelyn felt bruised. She wished she could expostulate with him on another issue, but her cannon was empty and Richard had resigned his fire power. He didn't want to fight.

"Come on let's go get some coffee. It's on me. That's how nice I am."

Evelyn was ready to retort his claim but checked herself. She shook her head, but not in disagreement. She smiled. She liked him - for his intellectual abrasiveness. "*No-o-o!*" Her conscience screamed. "*I like him. I like him because I just like him, a lot. '*

Richard settled that he and Evelyn had to share the small office space. In an attempt to get up, because of the tight leg-room of the desk, Evelyn grabbed the top edge of the desk, braced her arms and shoulders to leverage her chair backwards, and in the process, her upper frame projected forward across horizontally which resulted in her revealing a firm, but not an overly-covered cleavage for wandering eyes. But, Richard's eyes were not roaming. Eventually, she successfully gained more leg room, stood up, and girlishly threw back a few strands of hair off her face to reveal her perfectly cured brows. She smiled again; a smile that conveyed her unconscious boast; 'I am a pretty face.'

Evelyn's steady but relaxed gait dictated the pace to the elevators. Her legs bore the elegance usually displayed by models on the catwalk. She commanded poise, a quality that justified her training while preparing for the Miss Michigan pageant. However, she withdrew from that contest because she felt indisposed due to brewing relationship problems between her parents. She adored her father and when she learned about her mother's infidelity to him, it shattered her. It was hard for her to forgive her mother. Among the few wall pictures in Evelyn's living room, there was one that often brought fond memories – a man in his thirties kneeling by a little girl who was holding a beach ball on a beach. That girl was Evelyn Hedge; the man was Tom Hedge, her father.

The coffee moment was brief. Evelyn returned to Bridges office and Richard Bridges walked alone to the small conference room where he had been scheduled to meet with Mr. Milo the Executive Partner of the company, Milo, Grady and Strong law firm. Evelyn could see from her position in Richard's office the going-ons in the conference room. She saw Richard walked in and a ready outstretched arm of handshake from Mr. Milo welcomed him. There were smiles, seemingly some jokes, and also cordial warm taps on his shoulder from Mr. Milo. The Managing Partner at the local office gestured an invitation for him to sit down. Shortly after, Mr. Milo became aware that the glass door was still ajar. He got up in the middle of his delivery and with two long strides reached the glass door and closed it.

Any opportunity to eavesdrop the exchange was closed, but it didn't matter to Evelyn Hedge. She was already aware of the subject of discussion. She knew Richard would be formally told to professionally mentor her and more importantly the two of them would have to handle the "P-Plans" which constituted crucially viable cases for Milo, Grady, and Strong. This was a high point in Evelyn's professional career, and she relished it. There she was working side by side with the most celebrated attorney in the office, Mr. Richard Troy Bridges. She'd come to conceive a stronger predilection for him and it wasn't only for his presentable physical bearing, but for his general genteel demeanor. She liked what she'd seen so far.

After about ninety minutes, the meeting was over. Evelyn saw the individual parties gather their papers and stack them into their various folders. She saw parting handshakes, but they weren't as cordial as those that preceded the meeting. Richard was yet to walk out. At least Evelyn was sure of one thing, he wasn't smiling. It bothered her. However, she couldn't muster the courage to ask him how the meeting had gone. Sally, the admin assistant for Mr. Bridges walked in. She was as usual, the buoyant spirit on the floor. She giggled over the silliest thing and her giggling had always been infectious.

"Good Morning, Ms. Hedge." Sally greeted Evelyn gleefully. "It's very beautiful outside." Evelyn smiled back, but her response was interrupted by the stealthy entering of Richard.

"Is everything alright Mr. Bridges?" Sally was quick to notice the sullen countenance of her boss.

"I'm fine." he mumbled. Clearly, something or somebody might be the problem. "I'll be in the office if you need me." Sally suggested as she made her way out to her office leaving Richard and Evelyn behind to share their thoughts on whatever was brewing. They looked at each other in silence. Evelyn was more cautious. Her earlier encounter with him had narrowed her dialoguing parameters, especially under such cloud of silence.

"Ms. Hedge, I'm sure you are aware of our joint commitment to the 'P' clienteles of MGS." he eventually spoke.

"Yes, I do. You don't seem to be enthusiastic about it. Is it I or the 'P' commitments?"

"No, no, no, it's not you. Don't feel that way. I hold some reservations about the size and scope of the clients under the P-commitments. I will leave and allow you to settle down."

"Are you saying you're leaving the office – for the rest of the day?" Evelyn was curiously surprised. "Richard, you don't want me to be here alone." She expressed interrogatively.

"You'll be fine. Get acquainted with the files. We'll have much to discuss on our next meeting." He grabbed his coat, his file roller, a quick look at Evelyn, smiled, and she heard him say, "Have a nice weekend."

He also hoped he would have a nice weekend. Why not? He'd just been offered a new salary proposition, a half-million deal with great fringe benefits, but he still wasn't smiling. He wasn't pleased with the clientele that he and Miss Hedge had to deal with. The P clients included Pharmaceutical companies, Physicians, Patient Safety Issues, Politicians, and hordes of clients that fell under the "P" category. He'd just handled the Palanquin Incorporated case in which Mr. Milo held a vested interest.

Richard had surmised that the publics of the P group were large and moreover were more prone to litigations than other categories.

He recalled a deposition incident during which the recording had to be interrupted several times because of numerous frequent visits to the bathroom by a testifying nervous nurse. The more he thought of the P group clients, the more he deluded himself into thinking that perhaps nobody wanted it. Think about the five hundred grands. "Nah! I can use that." He thought aloud and drove off; where to, he didn't know, but any thought of walls outside the walls of MGS was liberating enough.

However, that relieving thought was short-lived when the busy streets reminded him of Seth. He often wondered what Seth's surviving chances would be from his strange illness. He wondered even more what he could do to help save his friend. He needed to think. He remembered how he'd rescued Star during those desperate trial moments. He began to sweat. His air condition in the car couldn't help. The beach! The beach! He didn't think; he already knew it and he sped off; Seth, a good lunch, the beach.

Richard was commanding a great view of the sprawling Pacific Ocean below his hilly perch point, a few yards away from where he'd parked his car. He was seeing very few people, partly because it was still morning, and partly because cooler temperatures were beginning to move in. He felt a little cold and realized that very soon he might need a jacket or a sweater to ward off the chilly sea wind. He hadn't any; after all, the beach wasn't on his itinerary. What had drawn him over was the desire to escape the tedium of office demands and his concern over the health of Seth. He walked back to his car, risking losing his advantageous sea-view perch. He checked the trunk and wished he would find a towel but found none. He walked back to his perch, but with a greater determination to endure the winds while he allowed the serenity of nature to calm his rumbling heart. As he got closer, he realized to his disappointment that his spot had been taken. He walked on with the hope of discovering another.

"Mister, Sir!" He heard a voice, seemingly from the space he'd just lost. Involuntarily, he turned in reaction. "I'm sorry; I didn't know you were planning to return to your spot. I kind of thought it was open for grabs. But since you are here, I guess, it's all yours."

"Sir, that's nice of you. I think you deserve it. I abandoned it and you claimed it. Legally, it's yours." Richard conceded as he walked closer to meet the gentleman.

"Legally, it's a public spot and no one has any claim to it. First come, first serve, I guess," The gentleman remarked with a smile.

Richard discovered the sincerity of his gentle acquaintance and suggested that they share the space since the size of it could even accommodate a family. The gentleman agreed and he offered to introduce himself.

"I'm Patrick."

"I'm Richard. Again, it's very kind and very civil of you. Do you visit here often?"

"When it's possible, yes. I try to take in the awesomeness of God."

"Of God …?" Richard couldn't control his surprise.

"O- yes, as much as I can." Patrick spoke with a sense of calm assuredness. "Feed my mind on his creation. They speak in resounding tones of his greatness."

"I see. You mean, you meditate."

"Well, you could say that, but not like chanting or evoking a spiritual power to fill me. I simply ponder on the creator's gift, the beauty of the waves, the strength of the waves and tides, and yet how peacefully they splash their touch of coolness on the weary feet of those out there." Patrick pointed to some couples on the banks of the sea; how they playfully welcomed the surf on their feet, but child-like kept running from it.

Richard laughed. "You sound very poetic. But 'weary feet' – you don't mean from long walking?"

"No, I mean the feet of the physically or emotionally drained or tired persons."

"Interesting." Richard sounded derisively cynical.

"The majority of people who visit the beach want to escape the heat or the toils of life, to unwind and refresh – a feeling of renewal."

There was momentary silence. The two strangers kept their gaze on the water then Patrick heard Richard heave heavily.

"You know, I have a friend who, in his moments of stress, or when he feels his blood pressure is shooting up, will simply allow his mind to travel to a beach scene."

"Most people do that. In fact, I do, sometimes." Richard admitted.

"There you go!" Patrick remarked cheerfully. "It's like therapy. Imagine the waves, the flying birds, the strolling lovers – O-that's something. Richard, isn't that true?"

Richard nodded in agreement. "But Patrick, you forget there are people who don't have beaches, consider those living in inland countries and even here, the inland states here in America."
"That's a fair observation, but they have their own coping ways. Actually, I won't be surprised if they find the sea as a very monstrous and frightening spectacle, the very thing you and I look on for recreation. Imagine the butterflies, they cannot survive this

windy environment. But they're quite a sight outside the beach. Imagine, how with their wings with numerous colors, they glide from one colorful flower to another beautiful flower, from one pretty petal to another."

Richard was beginning to capture the picture in his mind's eye as Patrick painted the scene in a calm serenading voice.

"Has a butterfly settled on your finger before? Perhaps not - Richard, the color and the artistic design, the detail of the loud colors and the fading kaleidoscopic glow as they spread their wings, wow, it's quite a sight. And do you know, they leave a tangible smear of their physical colors on the finger? It's like telling you 'Painting is in progress.' That's how close and beautiful you get to touching the creator's paint brush."

Richard smiled and wondered if he were talking to a naturalist freak. Patrick was a captive of nature.

"Lest we forget, the hinterland people have their everglades, the forests where they are in touch with nature, the chirping, singing birds, and wow, the sound of rain, the coolness, the freshness of life that it brings."

"Hmm," Richard sighed. "I've never met a person who is so taken to environmental philosophies like you do."

"Richard, it's life, the life around us." Patrick expressed with controlled excitement. "A wise man once said, 'As cold water to a weary soul, so is good news from a far country.' How true that is; a person with arid conditions pants for water and gets a cool drink; so, it's also to the restless and worried person, who yearns for peace and eventually receives the good news that all is well. The choice to drink the cool water is like the choice to accept the provision of the provider. It's like the willingness to accept the assurance that the one who made this vast sea is more than capable to handle any problem. Wow! A view like this, this vast sea, points me to the great creator. And that's refreshing. It's assuring – unless you don't believe his ownership to creatorship."

Richard was impressed with Patrick's short oratory. He was hearing nature revealing nature to him. He felt captivated and lost his awareness of the prevailing cold breeze while Patrick unveiled nature's picturesque painting in words. The minute Patrick was silent, Richard's awareness of the cold breeze returned and that spurred his desire to leave, but an inner impulsion kept him glued to the company of Patrick. He hadn't met a person with such unparalleled passion for the regular, natural and simple things of life. He realized how those things which he'd slovenly ignored were the pearls that adorned the emblem of life he tried to reflect. For him it was a way of life, yet he knew not how to mirror it. That was the grist in the mill for Richard. His pursuits were noble, but at the expense of his wife, Apphia. Apphia continued to struggle with an issue that wasn't normal, but the issue was becoming ignobly normal for her because she was gradually accepting her husband's sense of resignation to her need. Her sister Febe, however, never suppressed her empathy for her; she showed it.

CHAPTER 7

Febe, the only sister of Apphia was in the crowd but very absent from it. Her eyes were on her son Brady, as he ran amongst other screaming children in their yard. She nearly lost him from food poisoning a few months ago, so Febe had her reasons to give him a very special birthday treat.

Among the children was Josh, son of Apphia and Richard. He would always return to his mother, panting and sweating after a few accomplished runs to recharge his mother's attention on him. The relatives were also present, but visibly missing was Apphia's husband, Richard. Richard would always find an excuse to stay away from Apphia's flippant grandmother who liked to inject unnecessarily into any discussion, that Apphia must have her own biological child to add to her adopted son Josh. To Richard, she was an enigma to anything prudent. For two years, he'd been avoiding his grandmother-in-law simply to prevent any irreverent response to her glib unhealthy comments, after all, it was Febe's son's party.

However, nothing could dampen the spirit, the excitement, and mirth of the party as the children continued in their activity of jolly physical tiring experience. The humming noise of the inflator machine was no-much to the glee, the giggles, laughter and merry cries coming from the colorful bounce house that stood on the fore space of Febe's house. A neighbor's child dared her mother on the tarpaulin bouncing competition and soon they were at it. The mother, a more gracious competitor, was allowing her daughter to achieve a feat by allowing her to out-jump and out-bounce her to higher heights on the outdoor tarpa ulin bounce house.

No doubt, the life of the party was the children, but periodically, the roar of cheering men would burst into the air from the den of Febe's house where her large television screen could feed the eyes of about fifteen people. The outburst often startled the old grandmother; it was loud, enough to attack her weak heart. She withdrew to Febe's bedroom. There, she still had a commanding view of the children at play outside. She observed them as they assembled together for what seemed to be prep for a new game. She was right; the children had just decided to play hide and seek. They scattered amongst the crowd and hid at various nooks, whether convenient or not as long as it would meet the cleverest hideout choice for the wittiest kid. Anytime a child uncovered another's hiding place, a rousing noise of celebration of the gleeful children would greet the atmosphere. It was a more welcoming noise to the female adults of the party.

Grandma, the matriarch of Apphia and Febe's, watched on as the children inhaled and exhaled the vibrancy of their youth. She longed for her youthful years and disdained the sure futility of the effort to retrieve those years. Her most prolific claim at best was to only address the quiet years that awaited her in the rest of her sentimental journey. Her children and grandchildren were reminding her. And she could see them.

The sound of another happy yelp erupted again as Brady, the artful hider, came crawling from under the big decorated table that carried the birthday cake. However, Febe wasn't too pleased to see her son so covered in dirt. She didn't want to see him wearing dirty outfits in his birthday pictures. She restrained herself from openly rebuking him and rushed him into his room to get changed. Apphia, who had suspected that her sister's countenance was foreboding a strong reprimand for Brady, followed them to the room.

"Febe, that's what children do. They create the mess; we make them see the result of their mess and we help them correct it. It's from the mess that they learn. That's what parent's do; otherwise the child won't explore and learn new things for fear of being messy." Apphia's remark was firm. Febe knew her sister was right, but she hated to be corrected, especially before her child who needed her discipline, and that discipline had been undermined by the overzealous big-sisterly act.

"I won't do this to you, when you're ready to discipline Josh." Febe protested.

"Febe, what I'm saying is: it's okay. He can take the picture in his dirty clothes. It's part of the fun; the picture brings the memory of the incident."

Apphia explained and Febe grudgingly let Brady off the hook. Brady immediately flew out of the room like an escaped bird flying to rejoin his feathery friends. Surrounded by sweaty children, Febe's husband Joe announced that although the winner of the Hide-and-Seek game was Brady, the prize would go to another participant because Brady was the birthday-boy and must play a good host to allow someone else have the prize. It was getting late, so he suggested a raffle draw amongst the participants to determine the winner. To be sure that every child had a chance in the draw, there was a count of heads to match the number of names submitted by the parents. It was almost dark, and the count had failed to match the number on the registered list. A child was missing. The child was Josh.

Uncle Joe, as Febe's husband was referred to, gathered all the children into one room and questioned them about where they last saw Josh. The questions yielded nothing. Their gibberish answers failed to squash any of the fears the parents were beginning to form. Febe was left in charge of the assembled children in her living room. Uncle Joe led the search and was supported by Apphia. "Josh, where are you? Mom is looking for you. Jo-o-o-sh, Jo-o-o-sh," the cries went on. No response – Apphia began to panic. It was dark. The neighbors' outdoor lights were on. The search turned into house to house enquiry. Apphia was near fainting, as thoughts and fears of the worst began to assail her otherwise calm mind. Upon Uncle Joe's advice, she returned to the house and regrettably into the company of her grandmother.

"Don't worry they'll find him. That's why, I always tell you: 'you need a child with the sap of the Takis in him.' The Takis don't behave foolishly." Grandma's mouth was as usual, very insensitive, unthoughtful, and cold. The remark was a new low blow to the already walloped image that Apphia had always seen herself in, through the eyes of her grandmother. She walked out of her presence and joined her sister. Apphia was shaking. Nonetheless, her shaking mouth couldn't erupt the pent-up volcanic feeling in her. She wondered why her grandmother was so evil. Yet Apphia knew her place; she wasn't to whisper any irreverent word about her.

Josh had always kept away from her. There were incidents where Josh refused to hug his great-grandmother when she had spuriously requested his hug. A child could sense love and where it exists. Josh had grown rather repulsive to her spurious hug invitations.

The men returned empty-handed. Their faces looked sullen. They gathered around again, this time to deliberate the next line of action. There was a suggestion for a prayer and Joe offered to pray. After the prayer, weary and worrying Apphia asked in a rather shaking voice if the neighbors were helpful and offered suggestions. She thought they would know more about their area, and naturally about the residents of the area – their suggestions could be helpful, she thought. Impressed by Apphia's question, a man remembered being asked a series of questions by a neighbor. He remembered being asked if the children were playing hide-and-seek, and if the missing child tended to be withdrawn.

The neighbor had suggested that if the children were playing hide-and-seek, and the missing child habitually was the withdrawn type, he might see the hide-and-seek game as an opportunity to shine or to be a hero and get all the attention that he'd always wanted, but rarely had. "The child may go to greater lengths to do something stupid. If I were you, I would check the clothes dryer machine, the garage, all the trunks of the cars, and even check all abstract areas." The recapitulation of the neighbor's words was loud enough to get the whole searching gang attention.

Instantly, something kindled in the man who reiterated the neighbor's suggestion. With greater confidence, he felt spirited into action. He assumed the leadership of the search mobilization.

"Guys let's do it. Ms. Febe, please check your dryer. Guys check your cars, the trunks. The little guy must be panting for his last breath. Do it. Do it. Do it. Let's go." He clapped his hands as he exhorted them into action for the mission on hand, and all the men spirited into action once again.

"Apphia, give me your car keys." Joe requested imperatively.

"It's not locked."

"My goodness," Joe exclaimed and sprinted to Apphia's car. Apphia unconsciously found herself sprinting behind him as if they knew something was awaiting them there. With very nervous hands, Joe opened the trunk. An object moved. Then the object tried to shield his eyes with his hand from the beam of the pair of flashlights that were focused on him. An extraordinary surge of strength came upon Apphia as she bent to lift Josh up from the back of her car trunk. Josh's eyes were a mixture of fright and relief.

"I swear, you'll never leave my sight again, never." Apphia vowed.

They returned home to a worried husband who had been waiting for them. Their rehearsed cheery spirits gave no hint of what they'd been through. Josh was excited to see his Dad. Richard wanted to hear all about the fun they had, but he had to make one more call and later would have all the time for Josh. Then Dad Bridges remembered. Ms. Hedge was a candle saver. She might already be in bed.

CHAPTER 8

Evelyn tossed restlessly in her bed as she wrestled with sleep. The night lamp was beaming its presence. It irritated her. She turned it off. She began to hear a howling dog in the distance. It brought back a childhood mythos that when dogs howled it was because they'd seen a ghost or spirit. This childhood fear had lived with her. She immediately chose to reemploy the night lamp. A partial ambience cast its soothing presence in her room. It was sleep-lulling and her frame was giving way. Then she heard her grandfather's clock chime once, then a second, a third; and she knew her night was over.

Her mind was reeling from one thing to another; her office encounter with Richard to the loose comment that he'd made during their chat at the coffee shop. He'd said that one of the worst regrets of a person was when that person failed to make peace with a dying friend or relative due to unresolved sentiments between the two. His remark was a subtle foreboding about his friend, Seth and his situation. However, a shadow of the remark fell on Evelyn and her checkered past. It soon asserted its unwanted place in her mind, and it haunted her. It exacerbated her continued pensive scuffling whilst she tried to fend off the rush of conjectured inklings and presumptions about that remark. The thought wouldn't leave her. Sleep O – elusive sleep, she moaned.

Sleep that soothed even the beastly brow to rest was ruffling this beauty's brow to test.

"Enough, I've had enough." Angry Evelyn crawled out of her bed, turned the rest of the lights on, walked to her coffeemaker, turned it on and proceeded to brew herself a coffee. She caught a glimpse of herself as she went towards her closet. She didn't like what she saw. Her eyes looked sleep-shot and wore the look of a freshly birthed baby. She heard the distant howling of a dog. She heard the howling again. This time it sounded closer and became an orchestra of dogs. They might be the neighbor's dogs. Those howling hounds might be seeing something closer to her home, she thought; a travelling spirit maybe. Evelyn paced softly to her living room. The main switch light was within reach. As she reached out with her left arm to turn the lights on, a haunting figure with a long-extended arm nearly laid hold of her. She startled and screamed. And the haunting image on the wall startled and screamed soundlessly in simultaneous reaction with her. She dropped into her couch in a synchronized action with the haunter on the wall.

A feeling of uneasiness crept over her. It overrode her sense of paranoia. She turned the living room lights on and picked up her phone. She dialed a number she hadn't dialed for a long time and heard the phone ringing at the receiver's end. She hung up. Her grandfather's clock chimed again, once. It was three-thirty in the morning. She vowed to see her mother first thing at dawn. Until then, the fury of her mental storm raged on. It was flooding every vessel of doubt on her mind. She sank back into her couch and pillowed her prayerfully clasped hands to await sweet repose.

"No – O – No. It's not true. It can't be true. She's not dead. No. No-o-o-o!" She screamed. There was loud banging on her door, and it jolted her from her nightmare. She trod softly across her rooms to the main front door. She peeped through the pinhole and without hesitation, opened the door. He walked in looking rather distraught.

"D-a-d! Why so early?" Evelyn's greeting was an unusual question.
"Six-thirty on a Monday morning is not so early. Why did you call her so early - at?

three-thirty in the morning?"

With her left hand loosely scratching her head in a contemplative posture, she questioned herself, "I did?" After a brief recollection Evelyn admitted. "Yes, I guess I did."

"Your mother needs her rest. You know she's very sick and your early call has driven her more worried. Eve, what's going on?" Mr. Thomas Hedge asked, sounding very weary.

"Yes, yes, I did and I'm sorry. How is she?" Evelyn yawned as she led the way from the main door to her living room.

"She's hanging in there. I don't think she's getting better. You'd know more if you visited her." Tom diverted his course to the kitchen and tried to help himself with the coffee Evelyn had brewed earlier only to discover that it wasn't hot enough. He suppressed his disappointment and walked back to Evelyn.

"Dad, you know what she did, and as a child, I've lived with that picture in my mind."

"Please, sit down." Tom implored his daughter. "You're a very angry young woman and you have the right to be angry, very, very angry. There are some things that time teaches. Some are excusable and some, very inexcusable." Tom withdrew once again to the kitchen, very bent on making a fresh pot of coffee. He could hear Evelyn mumbling something. He ignored her until his coffee was done and returned to her. "You will be late for work; let's have this discussion later, this evening may be."

"I don't know. I'm not sure. I'll try to find time."

"Eve, you still haven't told me why you called her." Hedge sounded impatient.

Evelyn heaved heavily and sighed slowly as she tried to suppress her feelings. "Dad, I'm trying to feign to be receptive to someone who treated my father with utter disgust. I can't come to grips with that. It's driving me crazy and last night was another sleepless night."

"You haven't forgiven her. And it frightens me because it means, if I happen to offend you, I run the risk of being despised by you. You can't live your life like that, because in this imperfect society – called the world, people will offend people, they will trample upon the kindness they once pleaded for; you may even offend yourself one day. And let me tell you, be careful. It's a grave betrayal; very grave betrayal of self when self cannot forgive self." Feeling relieved after addressing her daughter very pointedly, Tom decided to leave.

"You make it sound like I'm so evil and full of hate, but I know I'm not." Evelyn broke down and sobbed. Her father reached out to her, extended his long arms around the emotional, heaving and jerking frame of his daughter. His left shoulder was drenched with tears. And as she held him, she heard his usual comforting voice; "It's all right, Honey, it's all right." Then she heard the grandfather clock chiming. Upon hearing the seventh chime, she relinquished her embrace of her father. She was sure if she hurried, she would make it to the office before nine o'clock.

Richard stood by his office window watching the busy street live its life. A growling grouchiness seemed to be dictating his day. He was actually lamenting his day, his day which was rather young - about only nine hours old.

Richard Bridges was feeling very grumpy and grouchy. He could survey from his aerial view the white-collar elites walking back to their various office buildings carrying coffee in one hand while the other hand held a mobile phone that sheepishly accepted its role to channel ostentatiously the speech of the empty barrels, who with convincing tongues, would promote and sell a cow-dung as the most fragrant nutrition for man. "O - the sheer callousness and mischievous ploys of men." Then came by some blue shirted men, who with their mechanical minds, craftily machinate the diagnosis of a broken machine, and issue underhanded claims to fleece the fiscal strength of a desperate client. Why? Has it ever been a crime to have money? What an outrageous and callous way to spin the wheel! Then came a young ambitious student who was rushing to catch the waiting and engine-running public bus to school. O - he missed it but, he dared not slouch; he would have to wait for the next bus. He was yet to receive life's lemon; and must be ready to juice up life's lemonade.

The grumps, the grumps! It was the mind of Richard on a Monday morning. It was venting its silent frustration to no one else other than the ardent but passive ardor in him. Seth was on his mind. Seth would die if he failed to help. Richard was seeing himself a flaky friend. Lost in those thoughts, he startled when his office door opened behind him, and Evelyn walked in.

"Good Morning, Richard."

"Good Morning, Evelyn." Richard noticed her obvious sleep-shot eyes and wondered if those eyes were communicating something else apart from insomnia. He couldn't hazard any guesses, if he did, he didn't have the courage to even declare them. Yes, professional barriers had drawn the lines. Nonetheless, with his eyes fixated on her eyes, Evelyn surrendered.

"I had a rough night. I couldn't sleep." She set her purse on the rolling file cabinet next to the chair of the temporal desk which the law firm had furnished her in Richard's office. Her eyes welled up and she threw her head back repeatedly in an effort to subdue an apparent imminent emotional burst. "How – uh - about you?" She stuttered her greeting, trying to shift the focus off her to Richard. However, the cadence of her unusual melancholy couldn't hush his observation.

"Evelyn, what's going on?" The question blew open the emotional flood gates that had already been weakened by the weekend sleepless night of torrential blame and guilt in her family. The tears sent her into spasms of helplessness and eventually into a pair of ready arms which she had to lean on for support, the arms of Richard. Rattled in shock, he started gently to pat her back. "It's all right." He said repeatedly, while wondering if he were blamefully part of Evelyn's blues.

After countless use of facial paper tissues, she eventually regained her composure and was ready to speak. "I'm sorry, Richard. I haven't been able to grapple successfully with some issues that keep bothering me. You know, when you made that remark, you remember, the remark that one of the worst regrets of a person was if the person fails to make peace with a dying patient due to unresolved sentiments before the patient's death that - spoke loudly to me."

"I was actually thinking aloud about a friend of mine, Seth. And I fear the worst - his health – he… I think may be dying." Richard cut in sharply to allay Evelyn's burden of guilt.

"I know you meant no harm, but it sent me thinking about a situation I found myself in. It's about, about - my mother."

"O – I'm sorry. Sorry to hear that. Are you saying …?" Richard checked himself as she nodded to complete his unfinished thought.

"Richard, I'm not sure that I really know you enough. I mean, I don't know you well enough for me to acquaint you with my personal issue. But strangely, I feel comfortable airing it to you. Do I have your ears?" Richard looked puzzled, but she looked up into his face and smiled. And he smiled back reassuringly. Evelyn started her narrative in a very soft voice.

"My mom, dad and I lived in a fairly middle-class neighborhood in St. Troy, Michigan. I was about eight years old. My father owned a shop, a general store stocked with all sorts of items. I used to take my friends to my father's store after school. I took pride in seeing my dad offering candies and little goodies to them. Apart from my Dad's generosity, it gave me a sense of acceptability and a level of importance among my peers and friends. On many afternoons my mother would also pamper my friends with snacks any time they stopped by our house. Incidentally, it was my mother who supplied the home-baked pastries and the confectionery items to the store. My friends' parents knew my mom and my mom knew them. You can call it closely-knit kind of community."

"Your school was within the vicinity, right?" Richard cut in as he tried to imagine the setting of her story."

"The school was about; I may say a mile and a half or two away. Megan was my closest friend and her mother would sometimes give me a ride home or to my father's store if my parents would not be home. One day, school let out early and Megan's mom picked us up. She had a doctor's appointment so she'd decided with my father's consent for Megan to stay with us until she returned from her doctor's appointment. She dropped us off by the street and we excitedly raced to the backyard to proudly show Megan the new small puppy my Dad had given me. I opened the backdoor which led to the den and the kitchen. And I, I – I – O I can't, I can't – say it."

A new wave of emotional brokenness swept over her. She dropped her head on the upholstered pad on her desk and with her arms dangling loosely towards the floor, she sobbed touchingly. Her helpless spirit was crying out, but it was only audible to her yielding will and her newly found confidant and friend, Richard. She was hearing his repeated whisper, "Eve, it will be all right." It was comforting for her and very assuring to hear him uttering her name affectionately.

She felt comfortable and he sensed it, immediately reminding himself to be careful and to not send a wrong message of over-congeniality.

"Eve, if you aren't comfortable to continue with the story, please, you don't have to tell me."

"No, I must tell you, I must tell someone. I can't keep it anymore." There was another quiet moment; it helped her catch her breath before she resumed whimpering the rest of her life narrative. "We, I mean, Megan and I saw my, my, my mother in a se-se-sexual condition with another man. My mom was in her robes, but he had his pants down.

"O' my …!" Richard cringed.

"And O – Richard, they were so lost in it that they didn't hear us coming through the open door. Richard, perhaps I could deal with it if I were the only witness."

The story shocked Richard. There was silence. Eventually, he spoke. "Did you tell your father?"

"My mother might think I did, but I didn't. I thought I would be taken as the guilty party. I'd been an impudent child with wandering eyes that roamed to witness such a thing. I was traumatized. I lived in fear of my mom and the eventual retributions from her. Megan's mom was very supportive. I lost my friends. I was rather withdrawn and cold with guilt. I was never the same. I believed my father eventually heard about it. If he did, he didn't show it. I never saw the man again, but I was sure the affair didn't end that morning."

"Any retribution?" Richard asked.

"I wasn't sure. My mom tried to be extra nice to me, but I became afraid of her. Richard, I hated her. When I got to high school, I didn't want to have anything to do with her."

Richard was surprised she considered him to be privy to her less-savoring experience. Throughout the narration he felt catapulted to a live event of her mother's incident and it made him empathize more with Evelyn.

"Where's your mother now?"

"They separated when I was in college, eight years ago. I haven't seen her since then. We all moved to Southern California." Evelyn confessed with little pride.

Richard wondered why Evelyn would suddenly thrust herself into nostalgia about the mother she hated. "Do you miss her now?"

Evelyn's response was flatly blunt. "No, I don't." In the prevailing sullen atmosphere, she whispered; "She is sick, very gravely."

Richard reached for his phone and dialed Sally's office. "Sally, I am going to route all my direct calls to your desk. Ms. Hedge and I won't be available to take any calls at this time. Please confirm my appointment with Dr. Appleworth for tomorrow morning at nine when her office calls."

Richard turned to Evelyn and announced; "We're going to see your mother this afternoon."

"I don't plan to." Evelyn protested.

"Yes, you do. You simply lack the courage to take the step. I am taking you there this afternoon. We'll handle the files, as many as we can, and we'll be on our way.' He grabbed the phone again. "Sally, please order breakfast for three; that includes you. Thank you."

Evelyn felt spirited into the moment. "The time has come. I'm going to see my mother." She thought loudly and was surprised at herself that she hadn't contested against Richard taking the lead. She liked it; she liked being obedient, no, cooperating with a benevolent absolutist. Until then, they had work to do. They plunged into the files and an hour later, the phone on Richard's desk rang and Sally announced, "Breakfast is here."

CHAPTER 9

The housekeeper courteously escorted Richard and Evelyn through a rerouted course to purposely avoid the freshly mopped wet floor and to the newly constructed wheelchair accessibility ramp that led to a den by Dorina's bedroom. The atmosphere presented a feeling of being ushered into a hospital admission ward or a hospice. The difference was the absence of nurses and the natural residence setting. The home environment was typically Dorina's way, very clean.

Upon the request of the housekeeper, Evelyn and Richard had to wait and be cleared by Dorina's nurse. After a few minutes the housekeeper returned with the home-health nurse.

"You can go in and see her, but she can't speak with you. She's heavily sedated and sleeping. A late-night phone call interrupted her sleep last night and she hasn't been able to sleep well after that. The pain came back. You can go in now. Please turn off your cell phones; don't stir her up." After the nurse's briefing, Evelyn and Richard trod in softly.

"Here she is." Evelyn's eyes addressed Richard's and he looked upon Dorina with sympathy. He would be a fool to argue that her one-time stand with that unknown man had not, after all, deprived her of her pound of flesh. That thinking would be from the infected tasteless constitution of a desensitized mind who fed on fruits born from years of immoral philosophies about life If life ever defined itself as a blitz of few minutes of pleasure, regardless of the merits and the demerits of it, then how would life fare with the rest of its minutes and hours - without pleasure?

Evelyn couldn't read the expression on Richard's face. His face was a puzzle. She couldn't tell if Richard's unexpressed righteous indignation was a judgment over her indifference towards her sick mother. Then suddenly, the sleeping figure began to loom before her like a live apparition of a dressed body in a shroud garment, and the face was her mother's, and she looked peaceful, but she was sad, very sad. However, while wallowing in her ephemeral dream, she felt an arm tapping her shoulder. That exited the trance and nudged her into reality. It was Richard saying, "It's time we left."

The home-health nurse emerged and realized that Richard and Evelyn were about to leave. She hastily tried to correct any impression that her return to the room might tend to wrongly communicate a signal notice for them to leave. "I simply want to perform routine repositioning of Dorina so that she doesn't develop bed sores."

"And how often do you do this?" Richard asked.

"Every two hours." She replied.

"I do notice sores and seeming rashes on her neck. Are those results of her extended positioning on one side?"

"No, not-at-all!" The caregiver replied nervously. "And we have dated pictures to prove that the sores were there before I took this assignment."

"I'm sorry; I didn't mean to alarm you." Richard moved closer to Dorina's bed and as the nurse turned her, he saw more sores on the other side of Dorina's neck and was alarmed at the sight of those fresh sores and her badly stained pillows.

"Nurse, please do you have those pictures of the sores with you, which you're saying were taken on your assumption of this assignment?" Richard inquired.

"Not right here with me, but Dorina must have copies with her. In fact, her boyfriend, Mr. Hedge has copies. He's here every afternoon at four, if you'll be able to make it here at four you will meet him."

"Thank you. I appreciate it very much. Let me ask you - your professional opinion. What do you make of these sores?"

"Professionally, I can tell you, these aren't bed sores. If they are, you'd find them more around bony areas or generally, areas with little fat, especially the heels, hips and lower back and the spine, but not on her neck. What you are seeing are bruises from excessive scratching of the rashes on her."

"Thank you very much for this schooling, Ms... uh" Richard smiled off.

"Thelma." The nurse mentioned while directing him to the name on her badge.

As they walked out, forlorn and very dismal looking Evelyn was surprised at Richard's sudden interest in sores and bed sores and she couldn't contain her anxiety.

"What's up with this new interest in sores?"

"I don't preempt my suspicions until it's a firm conviction." Richard replied. "Moreover, what I'm trying to learn has nothing to do with the files or any case you and I are working on."

"Wait a minute, you found sores on my sick mother and you feel I shouldn't be concerned about your opinion or suspicions about the sores on her?" Evelyn retorted.

Richard froze, gave her a quick stare at and then shook his head. He resumed his walk towards the car without a word of response to Evelyn's query. He approached the front passenger door and as his typical courtesy was, opened the door for Evelyn. She sat down in quiet profound remorse. His quiet kindness and care had subdued her loud abrasiveness and pugnacity. "Evelyn, do you really want to know?" He broke his silence softly.

"Yes, please." Evelyn sounded like a child acceding respectfully to her parent's request. The events had taken a toll on her and he saw how much she needed him; not by the call of prudent professionalism but by the summons of the gentle human spirit.

"Brace yourself." Richard advised. His car taxied around the cul-de-sac of Dorina's residence as Evelyn looked back in tears with the unanswered question on her mind, *is this the last time I'm seeing her alive?*

The homes were in sharp contrast to Evelyn's expectations. She saw abandoned ones and largely dilapidated structures but with echoes of life; merry voices and laughter that could still ring in the air. And yet there were few that harbored daily street-life retirees. Richard's car slowed down as he approached the intersection where he once played "Sonny" and his wife, Apphia played "Mommy." The air reeked of liquor and urine. The car pulled to a stop. Evelyn turned and looked at Richard in surprise.

"Why did you stop?" Evelyn inquired.

Richard smiled again. "I told you to brace yourself. We're going to that house." He pointed to a house near the curb, a few yards away from his parked car.

Evelyn was appalled at the volume of litter along the sides of the streets. However, the small front patio inside the fence offered a different spectacle. It was modest, but clean; small but creatively designed. The garden flowers were in beautiful bloom and so was the hanging ones. A small streaming fountain easily boasted of the hands that built it. The water that was gushing from a rock ran down to an earthen pot that dispensed it in a downward flow through twelve differently shaped faucets to a small rippling lagoon below.

Standing akimbo by the other end of his room, Seth saw them walk into his yard but didn't budge. Richard called out gently, "Seth, are you home?" And he heard a soft response from the first room that led to the main front door.

"Come in, Bridge, it's opened." It was the second visit of Richard to Seth's house. The guest couches were still in place and quite distant from Seth's regular chair. With a wave of his hand, he asked his visitors to sit down. Feeling quite disconcerted, Evelyn smiled wryly and opted to stand. She saw Seth smile, but it wasn't a reciprocally gratifying smile and she wasn't pleased with his reaction. Seth lowered his head in another smile, but in a lip-biting and confident smile. He knew his nonverbal reaction had made her very uncomfortable.

"Miss, I implore you to sit down; everything here is very clean. The exceptions are this chair and my bed."

"Seth, I have mentioned you to Evelyn, but we haven't discussed you." Richard remarked in anticipation of any wrong impression Seth might be forming from the unannounced encounter with Evelyn.

"It doesn't matter. I would be equally cautious to share the same walls with a very calamine patient like me, and especially so if I didn't know the nature of the sickness or infection."

Richard allayed Evelyn's fears with an assuring look and that convinced her to sit down. He observed that Seth had grown thinner and Seth admitted that he hadn't been eating well and regularly.

"You eat when you have the appetite for food, right? I don't, and sometimes I had to force myself to eat." Seth explained.

"Seth, you must try to eat for sustenance. You can only draw that from eating." Richard then turned his focus to Evelyn and tried to formally introduce. Seth smiled and bowed his head to accord Evelyn his respect. Richard drew in a long breath and said: "Evelyn, this is a very, very dear friend. We attended college together and both married our college girlfriends. His wife died last year and since her death he hasn't been the same."

"I'm very sorry to hear that." Evelyn's regret and sympathy were profound and Seth sensed that in her choking voice. He saw her sincerity and gratefully acknowledged her sentiments.

"Seth is very sick with a strange illness." Richard continued. "And his doctor is trying to determine the cause of it. Incidentally, his wife, the late Erika, showed similar symptoms of the illness before she died, but it wasn't clear whether that disorder was her killer. Erika did have rashes, but for how long, it wasn't known.

Seth discovered that on the eve of her death. Erika's doctor won't discuss her records citing her compliance with HIPAA, the Health Insurance Portability and Accountability Act. I'm sure you know it. It is the law that sets the standard for protecting sensitive patient data. That is, the patient-doctor confidentiality."

Evelyn began debating within her whether it would be an inopportune timing to ask questions and wouldn't be considered insolent. But she was surprised and relieved when Seth directly asked her for her opinion about what might have killed Erica.

"Much will depend on what the doctor says. But, do you experience fevers?" Evelyn expressed.

"No, I don't. And if Erika did, I wouldn't know because I didn't observe that or perhaps, she didn't show it." Seth answered confidently. "Erika talked very little when she returned from her trip. She complained repeatedly of tiredness. She hardly ate and grew weaker and weaker until she died." Seth paused for a moment to retune. He didn't want to show emotions, especially in the presence of Evelyn.

"I lived with that look in her eyes, especially when I carried her frail figure from the shower, and as she planted that interrogative look in my mind, She simply wanted me to affirm my love for her, if I still loved her even in her frail outlook. I cried with her, and I kissed her. The expression was deep in my heart and in my mind; I didn't verbalize it. I thought that was a standing understanding. An afterthought told me I should've verbalized it. I still live with the regret that I didn't utter the affirmation of my love for her."

He got up and walked towards the other end of the room. He slipped on a pair of rubber gloves and asked his friends to follow him. He was leading the charge towards a dark room door that was in their direct view. When almost at the door, Seth turned around and noticed that Evelyn was holding them up by trying to slip on some gloves too. "Ms. Evelyn, you won't be needing them. I'm the one who has to be careful to not contaminate things around here. Please, believe me; you won't need them."

"I'm sorry; I thought you expected us to." Evelyn explained. When she caught up with them, Seth turned on the light for the room.

Richard and Evelyn were in awe. A spectacular gallery of different paintings of Erika Nathan in mesmerizing glamor greeted them. The middle section of the room was the central attraction. It hosted a life-sized painting of a wet and drenched Seth carrying in his arms, assumedly from a shower, his soaked, frail and thin wife, Erika. Their eyes were also drawn to the walls where ambience lighting revealed a serenading glow on beautiful different paintings of his beautiful wife.

"Seth, you hid this room from me." Richard complained.

"I didn't want you to think I am obsessed with her. Bridge, I would rather spend my time on this productive venture of painting the woman I loved than painting flowers, which, of course, I live with and have them around me every day. But Erika, she isn't here. She isn't - a - alive around me." Seth became emotional and struggled with his words.

"I can't reproduce her in my dreams; I can only reproduce her memory within my walls. Glorifying her would diffuse the guilt on my mind."

"Mr. Nathan, I'm overwhelmed and very touched with this." Evelyn remarked. Seth nodded in grateful acknowledgement and requested to retire to his chair in the living room. He couldn't endure staying long on his feet. He'd grown leaner and emaciated; any boast of his former athletic look wouldn't just be a wicked flattery, but slime from a lying tongue. He smiled as he turned towards the door.

Each artwork carried a date of completion and Seth's signature. There was a piece of an unfinished work, undated and yet framed. It was a portrait of Seth and Erika but the paint work on Seth was conspicuously not completed. It also carried an incomplete signature of Seth. It caught the attention of Richard, but he silenced his anxieties to accommodate Evelyn's continued interest and patronage of the paintings. He quietly left the gallery and joined Seth.

"Seth, what's going on with that framed unfinished painting?" Seth smiled and turned looked at his friend and leveled up with a comical line.

"Richard Troy Bridges, nothing escapes your attention. Ma-a-an you were born to be a lawyer and a lawyer you'll always be."

"Eh, I'm looking out for you." Richard replied.

Seth attempted to lift himself up from the chair but changed his mind. He gasped and spoke softly.

"Bridge, if you walked further, you would discover another unfinished painting. It was also undated with an incomplete signature and framed like the unfinished earlier painting." Seth sighed again. "Erika completed me. When she died, part of me was gone. The distance between the paintings reflects the separation."

Seth's eyes welled up again, but he checked himself as Evelyn walked in to rejoin them. She overheard the dialogue and had been drawn back to join them by the fervor of Seth's sentiments. She'd observed enough, heard enough, and had learned enough; not from the pages of a textbook, but from the lessons in the unfolding pages of the haps and mishaps that continued to shape her. She could no longer question that her appreciation of her colleague and neo-personal friend, Richard was beginning to test her candor about the growing bond between them.

Within a few days, Evelyn had heard Richard's fiery voice and how it melted the cold lies of a felonious fraud in court. She'd seen him define the defiance of a devotee's faithfulness in friendship, and was beginning to experience his kind heart transforms her obstinate nature to a tender personality. She knew she would need his chaperonage again for her impending trip back to her mother. Richard's support for his grieving friend continued to echo the anthem of friendship. Why couldn't Evelyn's parents have that? The question was haunting. The answer was within Evelyn. Why could she not be forgiving? Evelyn pondered over them, over and over again, and her mind landed at the bedside of her moribund mother.

"It's time we left." Richard declared after checking his time. Evidently, they'd overstayed, considering the avalanche of files they had waiting for them in the office.

"Bridge, where is your yellow Volkswagen?" Seth asked.

"Well, I have it home, it still runs good. Why do you ask?" Richard wondered.

"Could I buy it from you if you would sell it?"

"It's yours. Apphia and I will drop it off tomorrow." He replied without giving it a thought.

"Please, I would need it today if it wouldn't be too much of a hassle for you."

"I have some pressing appointments to handle. Let me see what I can do." After a brief contemplation, Richard promised to bring his yellow Volkswagen to Seth's house later in the evening.

Evelyn, on the other hand, held a feeling that her night would be unpredictable. She could only hope she would sleep better after her father's visit. She had to keep her lights on to dispel the shadows she thought had kept the neighbor's dogs howling. She would prefer to hear them barking; that would be a more tolerable nuisance.

CHAPTER 10

It was a rainy night, and Evelyn could see through her living room misty glass window, the shimmering rays of the headlights of an incoming car that was attempting to park. Hastily, she tried to put things in order before her father stepped under her roof. She anticipated he would find something to complain about as he so usually did. She fluffed the pillows and set them in place on the couches. She was ready and waited for the doorbell to ring. It didn't. She sensed that the headlights of the parked car had gone off, and so was the engine. She was beginning to be apprehensive about what might be looming behind her door. Eventually the doorbell rang.

"Dad, you got me worried. It took you so long to get off the car." Evelyn's greeting expression was poignant, but she regretted it when she saw the weary countenance of her father. "Are you okay?" She asked remorsefully. Tom walked in and went straight to the kitchen hoping to get a cup of coffee.

"Yes, I'm Okay. I was on the phone with Thelma, your mother's nurse." He explained. "She was discussing your mother. She was refusing her medications."

"So, what do you have to do?" Evelyn asked in an earnest concerned tone.

"I think she could do without it for tonight. I'll go and see her, first thing tomorrow. Thelma told me you were there with your boyfriend. You haven't introduced him to me yet."

"It's because he isn't my boyfriend; O I wish. He's married. He's my colleague and mentor in the office. I'm surprised at how she, I mean Thelma, rushed to that opinion."

"I guess, in her eyes you make a lovely couple." Tom teased.

"You know, Dad, one thing you hardly talk about is your romance with mom. You don't have wedding pictures; no romantic event pictures. Why is that?"

There was a long silence. Evelyn was getting uncomfortable. She'd hoped for a ready answer. It began to dawn on her that she'd struck a sensitive nerve. "We tried to be less ostentatious with our romance."

"Why, don't you love her?" She continued to probe.

Her father smiled. "The law school has spoiled you. Am I on a witness stand?"

"Seriously Dad, you hardly discuss it." Evelyn pressed on.

"When you saw your mother, how did you react?" Mr. Hedge's aim was to simply evade. He was aware of Evelyn's cold relationship with her mother and her father hadn't been pleased with it. He knew his passivity had done more to foment the crisis than to quell it.

Evelyn was silent. As an attorney she was seeing all the signs of witness evasiveness. Her dad was flagrantly dodging the answers. A change in his voice inflection, and the absence of eye contact with his daughter suggested an obvious escapism. His eyes were traveling around the room. His concern for the windy conditions outside also shared the blame of his inattentiveness. It was still raining, and it was beginning to get colder. Suddenly the lights went out at a sudden surge of a very strong wind. The cracking noise of a falling tree was more audible above the noise of the rain.

"Eve, do you have any flashlights?"

"Dad, I don't care about the darkness, I don't care about the flashlights; please answer my question."

Their eyes were yet to get adjusted to the darkness in the room. He was seeing her as a figure in a chair and she was seeing him as a restless figure leaning on the open kitchen counter. The silence was long.

"Get me a flashlight and I'll answer your question." Evelyn got off her chair, paced a few steps towards the drawers of the very counter her father had been leaning on, and brought out two flashlights. She turned one flashlight on. The rays weren't bright enough but were sufficient to help identify visible objects in the room. Her father assumed the couch on the other end of the living room space closer to the window.

121

Evelyn had dressed warm and was comfortable. The faint light dictated more of a romantic setting than a setting for the arduous task of handling a domestic rivalry. The city was sleeping on this cold night. A feeling of anxiety and a sense of apprehension filled the room. She didn't know why, but a cold feeling of uncertainty had seethed through her guarded sense of self-assuredness.

Mr. Hedge lifted up his head. His right leg rested crossed on the other. With his left arm resting on the armrest of the couch, his fingers were in drumming frenzy on the edge of the armrest. From his end, he could see the light shining partially on the side of her daughter's face; he was seeing a frown, and not a child's look of curiosity about a strange story, the outcome of every dad's usual exaggerated stories of war heroism. Then he saw sadness mulling over his daughter's face. It crushed him and he yielded.

"Evelyn, I love you and I always will. Since you asked, I might as well tell you. After all, it's better from my lips than from a fool elsewhere."

There was silence – a long one. His expressive anger was visible but rather quiet. He clasped his hands together and began grating his palms fiercely against each other. As he firmly wrung his left wrist with his right hand, he yielded to his self-inflicted pain with a loud cry, "Why, why, why?" His much winded agony didn't prick up Evelyn's sympathetic ears nor did it texturize for softness on her face. She simply wanted an answer from her father. Eventually, it came poignantly. "Evelyn, I'm not your father." He uttered softly. "None the less, you're the only child I have, and I will always resist anybody coming between us."

Evelyn got up from her chair. Without a word, she walked across the stretch of her living room to the kitchen refrigerator. She opened it and the escaping cold air hit her face. She closed it and reopened it. She wasn't hearing the usual quiet humming of her functioning appliance. Then she realized her sudden unusual display of short memory. In reaction, she turned to look back disconcertedly but chose to peep through the dark walls of that vertical six-foot cold storage again. She discovered contents of emptiness in the grocery laden refrigerator. Her appetite was amiss, no, her essence, her person.

Evelyn's refrigerator had lost its sustaining light of life except for the chill in its white walls. O – What a cold but, potent symbolism of unsolicited reality, she thought. Indeed, the storm had rendered her home without power, and without the shining metaphoric bustle of life. Strangely awful, she thought.

Evelyn wasn't different, she was superstitious. And superstition had always had a way to superimpose its lame frame on the feeble predispositions of the paranoid. To her, the abrupt absence of light in her house was predictive of the absence of the light of hope, and of the elusive truth from her father. It was foretelling the absence of the light of promise of a warm tomorrow.

She walked back to her chair with her head dangling down off her shoulders. The weight of the disappointment had crushed her. Twice she sniffled, yielding to a cloudy sense of betrayal that had gloomed the glowing portrait of the man she'd adored.

"I feel like I'm an orphan." She declared softly. "Please leave." Tom wasn't sure he heard Eve's assertive request well.

"Eve, it's been difficult trying to break this to you. If you'll allow me, I'll explain everything to you, please."

It had been emotionally torturous for Evelyn. The words were hardly coming out of her mouth. She couldn't even fight. She was losing her voice and didn't have the strength to even postulate her feelings. The thought of destroying her pictures with her father crossed her mind. She remembered the flattery "you look just like your dad." Now it sounded like a poisoned compliment, a lie pronounced by an idiot full of husks of sycophancy signifying the treachery of hypocrites. Whatever the resemblance might be, the pride in that claim had been fouled.

"If you aren't my father then what am I to you, a hostage to a familiar-face kidnapper? I think you have overstayed your visit." She declared again while looking away from the direction of where her father was sitting. Evelyn was totally and helplessly convulsed by her emotions. She buried her face in the blanket she had on her shoulder as her body repeatedly jerked convulsively. "Why have you kept this from me all these years? Why?"

Tom was beginning to see that his fatherhood merit was beginning to lose its credence. He got up, walked over to her and knelt beside her. He wrapped his arms around her as the loving dad he had always tried to portray.

"Please, leave me alone."

"Honey, I can't. I just can't." He protested feebly. "Evelyn, Evelyn, Evelyn, if there ever is a day that I feel so broken, that day is today. It's like part of – of – of - me has left me." He broke down, stuttering his lament. "I was touched hearing you cry helplessly and couldn't do anything to pacify you. You were a baby then – barely six months old."

The word "baby" arrested Evelyn's attention. She cautiously angled her head towards him for a furtive glance at her one-time hero. She'd never seen her so-called father in tears before, not even in tears of joy. For the first time, she was seeing her father's masculinity meltdown and was hearing a broken man. She slightly pulled off the blanket which she'd partially buried her face in to verify the face behind the sobbing voice she'd been hearing.

"Eve it's a long story." he declared. His stretched legs were sprawled on the floor as his back leaned vertically against the empty side of Evelyn's couch. That was a better and convenient posture for him, and he exhaled in relief. Evelyn wasn't impressed by his demonstrative show of contrition, however he had her attention. She adjusted herself to catch the side-view of this pride-beaten and reluctantly compelled narrator.

"I was thirty-one when I returned home after five years of national service abroad. Before I was shipped out, Aunt Betty, Megan's mom, used to be my girlfriend. Betty and I had plans, but when I returned, she was already engaged and few months later, she was married. Of course, we kept our distances because Betty wasn't single. I was hurt and disappointed, but I had to move on.

One summer afternoon, I was visiting the St Troy county Fair at South Bend in Indiana. Among the hundreds of booths at this fair was a confectionery stand where a lady was handing out different pastry samples. She was beautiful. She was Dorina. I was drawn to her stand not because of her samples, but because of her person. I tasted her pastry. It was great. I also saw how overwhelming it was for her as she attended to the customers while keeping an eye on a foldable small crib discretely placed in a corner behind her. Concerned and curious that I was, my eyes travelled with hers to the crib, when I heard a baby's cry. It was the most adorable sight I ever beheld - a beautiful baby. That was you, and barely four months old."

Evelyn chuckled, restraining a gratifying smile to imply that she wasn't a won-over, at least, by what she was hearing. However, her attention was still keen.

"I had the audacity to request if I could carry the baby. I thought I could pacify the adorable bundle. I must admit, Dorina immediately dropped waiting on her customers and gave me a fiery glare. Never, ever, in my life have I been so browbeaten with a look? I was like 'O I simply wanted to help!' I think she saw my innocence and changed her stance. She was like 'You sit down here, and I will give you the baby.' I sat on a stool, a tall stool behind her which I later realized she used periodically whenever she got tired from standing. The baby continued to cry while she was holding her but, a strange thing happened. The baby ceased crying immediately after she placed her in my arms. I guess you and I bonded right away."

Evelyn gave a very short wry smile. It wasn't very conciliatory as Tom had craved for. However, he still had her ears.

"The baby fixed her eyes inquisitively on my face. I guess she was wondering in whose arms she was. Suddenly, she lit up with a beautiful smile. Well, Dorina and I became friends thereon. I knew she was a native of Romania and sometimes I mimicked her Romanian foreign accent jokingly. She loved it anytime I tried it. We dated for months, but I feared I would be shipped abroad again and that it might affect our relationship. Dorina hardly discussed the baby's father, and I was afraid he might show up one day. It wouldn't be a pleasant encounter. I was reluctant to make commitments. I later got to know that as an accomplished violinist and ballerina, Dorina would have to go on tours twice a year. I wasn't comfortable with the touring aspect, although I knew the profession demanded it. Eventually she moved in with me. No, it wasn't right. We weren't married but taking care of you helped her with her travelling commitments."

The trend of the unfolding events in the story had arrested Evelyn's interest. She repositioned herself to a more comfortable posture on the couch and extended the blanket to cover her feet, particularly, her toes. She was all ears. Tom continued.

"The touring really bothered me. She would sometimes go for months and our world was only you and I."

Evelyn launched her face into a dubitable frown. "Well, did I …"

Tom read her thought with a complement ready answer.

"Yes, you did miss her when she was away, but she made up for the lost time by returning with gifts for you and taking you to places. However, a greater bond developed between us than it did between you and your mother. She noticed that, and there were occasions she felt estranged from the family."

Tom cited few incidents. Evelyn remembered a particular incident. It was a fight that ensued after Tom sided with her as she'd cried in protest against her mother's forceful demand that she must eat her food at a time when she was feeling sick and had no appetite.

The flashlight was beginning to dim and very soon Evelyn would have to employ the other unused flashlight. Tom had become tired from his sitting posture. He got up and stretched. His mind read "coffee." Evelyn knew it, but her mind mumbled, "Sorry sir, I can't help you, no electricity. Just finish your story."

Tom settled beside her on the couch and continued. "The relationship between your mother and I took a complicated turn. She'd complained earlier that her only escape from the tours, according to the contract with her sponsors would only be, if she was pregnant or a six-month notice to quit. Eventually we found a common ground. She would quit her musical tours and we would start a joint-venture business, something that would involve her pastry making. So, I took a loan and we opened the store. The store was doing well, but with our personal lives - we weren't. No, O – No we weren't happy."

There was a long pause. Tom got up. He held his head up to avoid his welled eyes from shedding a tear. He walked to the door and gave a strange, dismal look to the baby he once knew, the teenager he chauffeured to prom, and the college grad whose boyfriend once called him "Mr. Cool".

"I must leave." He said. His mirthless tone spoke volumes. His prolonged disconsolate look was worth the confession of the brush of a painter. He was planting a lasting visage. "I'm sure your mother will tell you the rest of the story. I'm sure she will tell it truthfully."

Evelyn was in shock. The tables had turned against her. She needed him. He needed to tell her the rest of the story. She knew she could no longer accommodate the platitudes that had often left her with more questions, and it might be sheer callousness to remind a bed-ridden mother about what had constituted a bane in her life. Evelyn feared she might never have the opportunity again if she didn't press Tom to unfold what he'd been withholding from her. It would take the wiles of a loving daughter. And she knew that.

"Will you leave her hanging? If truly, your professed love for the crying baby you held in your arms on that hot and humid summer afternoon at the St. Troy County Fair has not changed? Please, tell me, what has changed you?"

"I will never change towards you, Evelyn. And you know that."

Tom stood by the door, his right hand still on the door knob while he struggled with the dilemma of leaving or staying to simply appease her. He knew he hadn't told her everything and she knew as a trained attorney, her dad was being tight-lipped about something. Tom leaned his head forward on the door, entrapped by his loyalty of love for his little girl who used to cry a lot. It was her melancholies that touchingly drove him to vow to always make her laugh. In the spirit of that vow, Tom turned and headed back towards Evelyn's couch. He sat close to her and she took his hand. She smiled to him and he smiled back.

"There were few reasons for our unhappy relationship." He spoke softly. "I'd always hoped I would get some answers from your Mom. One of them was about your biological father. I've never met him. I don't know him, and your mother wouldn't discuss him. Anytime I brought him up in a simple conversation her response was, 'I love you enough for you to stop worrying about him.' Her answer had remained the same."

Tom failed to meet Evelyn's expectations. While she pondered over their discussion, he cut in. "On second thought, there's something else you have to know. I find it very intriguing. After several attempts, arguments, and persuasions - I didn't forget this, because the response bothered me. Dorina once said, 'Evelyn is my joy, and that's enough. I don't want to remember what I'm trying hard to forget.' So, I asked her again what she meant by that and she simply replied, 'Someday, someday.' That's it, so I stopped pushing it."

As fate would have it, the time to chase those parochial moments of gloom out of Evelyn's house came - and rather unexpectedly. The lights in the house came back on. Evelyn wasn't very expressive with her joy, but the simultaneity of Tom's last words and the suddenness of the return of the electricity, ignited an intuition of hope and encouraging prospect for her.

Tom went on to describe to her how much her mother loved her and had invested her happiness in her. "She loves you dearly. She named you Eveline; to the Romanians it means light. To other cultures and languages, Evelyn means life. And so, you have been to us. Your mother has never been the same since you began to shun her."

Evelyn began to envisage better prospects ahead. She had the materials to build her bridge back into her mother's life. However, her sense of guilt resurged. She lamented over the mother she evilly loved. How could she have loathed the sight of her mother who she once loved dearly? She still had to grapple with her inner conflicts and the unsettling questions about what she and Megan witnessed - the anguish of it all.

She whirled herself back to a regular sitting posture on the couch, stretched her arms horizontally forward to relax the muscles of her upper frame and shoulders, and then got off the couch. She walked across to the kitchen to meet her father's unuttered request for coffee. She then realized that she didn't have a single coffee filter to prepare his coffee.

"Dad, sorry, there's no filter, no coffee, I tried."

"How did you know I wanted coffee?" He smiled.

"I have lived with you long enough to read my dad and know my dad."

Tom heard it. She'd still called him, "Dad." He got up and proceeded towards the door. In his full view was the damage caused by the brief storm. He didn't care. For in his rear view was the damage caused by his patriarchal storm, or perhaps, his non-

132

patriarchal repairs. And that, he cared about more. The challenge was still before him. Evelyn held the door open as he walked out into the subsided storm. Her father smiled gratefully.

She smiled reciprocally. "Goodnight."

CHAPTER 11

Richard walked the stretch of the atrium confidently to join the waiting few for the next elevator. In no time, a bell chimed to announce the arrival of one of the elevator cars. As the doors opened on the first floor, a redolence of liniment balm or lab smell greeted the new passengers as they boarded. It wasn't pleasant, neither was it odorous. The third floor came up, and to Richard's surprise, the balm smell was confined only to the elevator. He got off, and made his way to the door that carried the plate Dr. Malini Appleworth, MD.

Among the multiple rooms in the suite was a fairly large reception area. The receptionist was quick to perceive that she was face to face with the special guest of Dr. Appleworth.

"Mr. Bridges?" She asked.

"Yes. Is she ready to see me?" Richard asked.

"Yes. This way, please." The receptionist led the way to an eight-seated size conference room. Richard opted for water in response to the receptionist's courtesy drink offer. Immediately after his first sip, Dr. Appleworth walked in.

She reached out her hand for a handshake whilst Richard tried to settle his glass of water back on the table.

"Malini Appleworth. You look surprised to see me." Dr. Appleworth introduced herself.

"Honestly I am, for two reasons." Richard smiled it off.

"I can guess one. I'm not a Caucasian as the name may suggest, and perhaps not Marlene, but Malini."

"You're right." Richard conceded. "And the second one is ..."

"I'm beautiful." Dr. Appleworth took the words out of his mouth.

Richard was impressed. He hadn't met anybody who would own up to her beauty, and still declare it non-boastfully.

"I'm originally an Indian, divorced, and I still carry my married name. Mr. Bridges I have heard these comments many times from guests and visitors to the clinic. So, your reaction is by default. Now, that said, how can I help you?"

"I'm a friend of your patient, Seth Nathan and his deceased wife, Erika Nathan. As you know, Seth's situation lately has been deteriorating. How can I help him - knowing that his situation doesn't seem to be different from his late wife's?"

"Mr. Bridges, lawyers don't normally word their questions this long. What's your motive? I can discuss Mr. Nathan's, because he authorized me to by phone yesterday, but Mrs. Nathan's, I can't. Professionally, ethically, morally and legally all will contest my attempt to even discuss it with you."

Richard smiled. He realized he'd met a woman who wouldn't bend her principle to appease a needy friend. He wasn't new to this. He softened his appeal and buried any measure of bull-dozing masculinity in him. Otherwise the assertive approach might normally turn off some women. He adopted a more congenial stance.

"Dr. Malini, I'm not here as an attorney, no I'm not. I'm here as a man in dire need to help a dying friend." He spoke softly. "We were college friends, Erika, Seth and I, well, including my wife. I need your help."

Dr. Malini also softened her stance. "Mr. Nathan came to my clinic when he realized he was beginning to develop the sores on his skin. He noticed he had rash which hadn't been healing. As the husband and well acquainted with his wife's situation, Mr. Nathan was alarmed. Based on the signs and symptoms he exhibited I started a psoriasis treatment. He said he itched all over, which generally is quite normal with dry skin, so I put him on a prescription of moisturizer creams and retinoids which are laden with vitamin A and hoped that would solve the problem. I didn't see him for a long time after that visit. My natural assumption was that the treatment was effective. However, a few weeks ago, I received his appointment to see me, but again he failed to show up. I wouldn't know his condition now."

Dr. Appleworth's response failed to resolve the growing dissonance on the mind of Richard. He knew Seth's condition was getting worse; from his perspective as a layman.

"Doc, did you request any lab work on his first visit?"

"No, I did not. It wasn't necessary from what I saw. All the signs of psoriasis were evident, and it didn't look very bad then. There was no visible swelling or any emerging swelling that is normally felt from touching – none. I will, however, on his next visit, if the condition warrants that, which I think may be necessary from what you're telling me."

Dr. Appleworth couldn't come up with any prognosis, and that worried him. He felt the doctor was still not forthcoming with what she knew.

"Well, you're the doctor; I'm not. What are the side effects of Erika's medication?"

"Mr. Bridges, I told you, I'll not discuss Erika. Don't try to cajole me into the levity of forgetting my professional ethics and to breach my late patient's confidentiality."

"Please doctor, I'm crawling you know. Suppose it wasn't psoriasis as you suspected, what else could it be?"

"Well, I would be simply speculating and as a doctor I don't like to participate in speculations. However, I can tell you this. There's no cure for psoriasis, but treatments can greatly control and reduce the symptoms even in very severe cases. It isn't contagious."

"Wait a minute. Did you just say it isn't contagious?" Richard asked excitedly.

"No, it isn't, unless it's something else." The doctor assured him.

"What is that 'something else?'

Dr. Appleworth laughed. "I knew you would ask that." The laughter lingered on their faces. "Mr. Bridges, I told you I don't indulge in speculations. That's why Mr. Nathan has to come and see me. I won't bite him." She joked.

"Thank you, doctor. It's been a pleasure."

Richard returned to his office to an unwelcoming busy office activity. Behind a closed-door Evelyn had been trying to peruse every single file in the box that sat beside her desk. The huge undertaking was taxing her resolve and strength. Sometimes discouragement and cynicism would drive her to launch a spate of audible discouragement, "I wish I wasn't a lawyer."

Unfortunately, Richard walked in and caught her last words as he opened the door.

"Ms. Hedge, have you been talking to yourself?"

"Obviously, as you can see, I'm frustrated. I'm not making much headway with these files."

Richard walked over to his desk and hung his jacket behind the shoulders of his chair. "What? You need a rescue?"

"Yes, yes, come, my hero. Come rescue me." Evelyn intoned clowning along in a shrill pleading voice.

"Well, the mood is better than it was few days ago. I'm wondering what made the difference." he remarked.

"I talked to my father. He came over and we had a good talk. There were few things I didn't understand, but with time, I will. I'll get to the bottom of it."

"Good. I also had the chance to meet with Dr. Appleworth. I think Seth has to go and see her. I think it's very necessary and I have to convince Seth to do that."

"And how are you going to do that?" Her question was challenging, and Richard had no immediate answer.

"I will talk to him; I will try - any ideas?"

He waited for response from her, but none came.

"Evelyn." He called.

She didn't hear him. Evelyn seemed captivated by the file she'd opened before her. Her reaction was like a person practicing deliberate self-absentmindedness or perhaps the reaction of a person with a jaw-dropping live discovery. Richard got up and covered the opened file with his right hand. That got Evelyn's attention.

"Richard have you seen this?" She handed him the folder when he withdrew his wide palm off the page.

The document revealed an indictment of Poce Laboratory Pharmaceuticals for clinical trial malpractice. Richard drew the document closer for a pensive closer look.

"It's the 'Posi Laboratory' scandal." Evelyn's excitement was at a yelling level.

"Yes, I heard about it. The pronunciation is 'Po-ke Laboratories.' They haven't retained us yet, although we serve their legal needs."

"Are we going to do anything about it?" Evelyn asked.

"No. We can't go fishing in foreign waters if we haven't received permission to do so. Who knows; they may decide to not contest it? Sometimes long litigations carry a trail of lasting messy and negative publicity which is always very difficult to clean."

Evelyn chose to not pursue the discussion further. After few minutes her cellphone rang, and she walked out to take her call.

She was yet to get used to the limited privacy that she had. Until then she had to enjoy the privilege of working with the reputable Milo, Grady and Strong law firm and particularly under the guidance of Richard. Many times, a person's reputation would demand living up to the elevated level the public held of the person. Richard was aware of that. He called Sally's desk.

"Sally, do you remember the Poce Laboratory files?"

"Yes, I do. What's come of them?"

"Do we have duplicates of them?"

"Yes, we do. They're among the set of files I brought over to your house the other time. They're in the red folder."

"Thank you." Richard replaced the phone receiver speedily but picked it up again and redialed a different number.

"Honey, it's me."

"O, Hi! Sorry it took me long to get to the phone. What's up?" Apphia asked.

"Please walk to my office, I have a red folder sitting on my desk; please tell me if the papers are intact. If they are, restack them back into the folder."

Richard continued to hold the line. Two minutes passed. It turned to three minutes; then four. "Talk to me Apphia. I can't lose those documents." Richard whined to himself. Then she heard Apphia's voice.

"Sorry, Honey. I had to take care of Josh. Yes, everything is intact."

"Whew! Good. And what about Josh?"

"I was about to get him in the shower and I've just discovered that he has rashes over his body, and apparently he's been scratching it over the night."

"What's the nature of the rashes?" Richard asked.

"I'm not sure. I don't know."

"Apphia, you sound worried."

"You know the excessive scratching is leaving sores around his stomach."

"Are you sure?"

"I don't know what to tell you, but the other time he was looking for his toys; I discovered them in the box by the garage among the plastic coverings we used over the seats for Seth."

"Are you sure?"

"Stop asking me am I sure. I have him right here and I'm telling you what I'm seeing."

"Because I met with Seth's physician and she explained that Seth's condition wasn't contagious, and I believed her. I'll be home early and we'll try to take care of that."

Evelyn walked in. She discovered Richard's change in countenance and suspected something was amiss. He hardly discussed his private affairs, and Evelyn wasn't the prying type. To her, her stand-offish stance was prudently sound, and she'd often kept herself that way.

Richard took a look at his watch. He was convinced he could make it home early enough to rush his son to the nearest Urgent Care Clinic. The news about Josh's rashes had rendered him more confused. Questions, reasoning, rationalization and fear began to convene on his mind. He had to act, but not brashly. Apphia could take Josh to see the doctor, Richard thought, after his unnecessary fretting and overt display of impetuosity. "Why not?" He reached the phone again and dialed.

"Honey, what's Josh's temperature again?"

"Temperature? Josh doesn't have temperature. He's out here playing."

"The rashes aren't bleeding, are they?"

"No, Richard. Josh is fine. Why would he bleed? It's just a rash."

CHAPTER 12

The Bridges' visit to the Urgent Care clinic was very brief. Richard had anticipated disturbing news about his son's condition, but he received a good disappointment. Josh was fine. His skin was a sheer result of excessive scratching. The severity of the cases of Erika, Seth, and Dorina had pushed him to suspecting that the doctor's prognosis was wrong. He, therefore, hoped nothing would offset his planned second trip to Dorina with Evelyn, for it would avail him the opportunity to compare his son's rashes with Dorina's.

He checked his wrist watch. He was five minutes early than his agreed meeting time with Evelyn. From his parked location on the street, he was positioned to see the traffic of personnel in and out of Dorina's house. He could also see Evelyn's car emerge from where the streets adjoined. After waiting for ten minutes, Richard got out of his car, walked a few paces up and down the block, and returned to his seat in his car. He began to wonder if he was at the right address. He reached his cellphone and dialed Evelyn's number. The phone rang five times, and her recorded answering voice came on. That was strange. Evelyn would notify him if she wanted to cancel the visit. He thought. Nervous, Richard drove off, abandoning his visiting plan.

It wasn't a warm day, but Californians' typical habit of dressing for summer all-year round was evident on the sidewalks as cold-feeling Richard drove by. "Not every California cranny could boast of sunny coastal conditions everyday so why make shorts a regular, even on a fifty-degree Fahrenheit day?" As Richard grumbled his reasoning, he imagined he would be the only visitor at the shore. He was convinced that the beach would hold the quietness, and the get-away atmosphere he wanted, and would allow him to figure out a solution for Seth, Dorina and his only child, Joshua. He remembered his last visit and his meeting with Patrick, the gentle eccentric who adored nature, and had lines of poetic attributes to them. This day might be different, he thought.

Richard was right. It was colder and breezier and very few braved the conditions to be there. He found a good spot, about hundred yards away from the location of his last visit. And this time he came prepared with warmer clothes. Practicing what he picked up from Patrick during that visit, he searched his heart to reflect and appreciate the strength in the waves and the power that was buoying a distant liner afloat in the horizon. His eyes journeyed across the length and breadth of the vast ocean and began to wonder what was beyond the parapet. He wondered why the tides retreated after their splash at the banks. And he found himself romanticizing the action of the waves. He allowed his thoughts to play on words, and then he tried to compose a rhyme.

"When their work is done,

And their journey, fully run,

A wave of new life springs;

Splashing joy to all things,

And seasoning the times for all creation,

In humble respect and adoration …. for, for, for …""

"For whom," a voice a few feet away asked. Richard turned to seek the face behind the voice. The voice was familiar, as was the face.

"Hi there, my friend, what brings you out - to sea-viewing in this weather?" Patrick exuding his usual warmth drew closer while Richard inched away to create space for him.

"Hi Patrick, I just want some quietness and enjoy the beauty of nature."

"Well, it's a good place to be when noisy atmosphere distracts and drives us away from our courses. However, with time you may discover other interesting places." Patrick assured Richard. "So, what has drawn you here, if I may ask?"

Richard hesitated and then sighed deeply. "Sick friends and a sick son and the mystery of an elusive cure, even some issues I want to unravel. I am still searching for answers."

"O sorry to hear that. I'm sure your search will be rewarding. What are the doctors saying?" Patrick asked.

"All three seem to display a common symptom, rashes. And that's what killed my friend's wife. And now, my friend has the same rashes over his body, and it seems my son has it too."

"It sounds like a looming epidemic outbreak. But if the doctors aren't alarmed, you shouldn't be."

Richard turned and looked at Patrick questionably. However, consoling his statement tried to convey, he felt it was insensitive.

"You see, people wind up with rashes under different conditions. Hot weather, heat rashes; cold weather, goose skin, blisters or rashes; stress renders the skin very reactive with hives, blisters, acne: fear creates rashes; lack of sleep, rashes; food reaction creates rashes; of course, not forgetting that vitamin deficiency can course sores and itching skin conditions. So, rashes are the external picture of an inner dissonance, biological, emotional, psychological or whatever. Many times, rashes are a prelude to something or they're simply the underlining cause of a condition." Patrick pressed his point and rendered Richard ambivalent about his pursuit. Richard was quiet and Patrick sensed he'd struck a nerve.

"Friend, I hope I wasn't offensive."

"No, you weren't. I was wondering if I've been a fool." Richard deprecated his own actions rather surly.

"No, my friend - the mark of good-naturedness is rarely found in people these days. I salute your spirit. Don't stop caring. You're a rare breed." Patrick joked.

"Thank you. Patrick, do you live around here by this beach?"

"No. I don't, but I come here quite often. Why do you ask?"

Richard reached into his pocket and brought out his office complimentary card and offered it to Patrick. "I'd love to help if you ever need my services. Please, do not hesitate to call."

After a grateful remark, Patrick decided to move on. It was getting colder and Richard was feeling the need to share his new seemingly relieving discovery with his family. Nonetheless, the question of Evelyn's no-show still weighed on his mind. He couldn't fathom any reason, and he knew better to not to question it. In three days, they would meet at the office, but would it be an encounter or a coy welcome?

The alarm beeps on the car that was parked a few spots away from Richard's car startled him. The office building parking lot was almost full. Richard turned involuntarily in response and saw

Evelyn. Her quick artless strides towards Richard didn't suggest a friendly approach, but a gait of anxiety. Other cars drove to and from the parking lot, and a less-cautious driver nearly ran Evelyn over because Evelyn's eyes remained fixated on the object before her and was carelessly oblivious of the traffic in the parking lot. She walked on, and as she passed by Richard, she discreetly uttered a cringing expression.

"Meet me at the lake, the ducks-park at nine. I can't be in the office today." Evelyn proceeded on to a yellow car which Richard recognized was his old car that he'd given to Seth. He wondered what Seth might be doing in the building. He was even more curious about the clandestine nature of the rather unusual and unlikely meeting between Seth and Evelyn. He watched with surprise as an elbow with a gloved hand emerged out of the window and rested halfway on the pane. Richard chose to ignore any guessing or any remote inference that was beginning to build on his mind. He proceeded to the lobby-bound garage elevators and promised himself to meet with Evelyn later. He wouldn't retaliate for her failure to show up at her mother's three days ago.

The park looked typically quiet on a week day morning. It hadn't totally lost its former setting for romance, although it had been abused by alleged drug peddling activities. Only a few of the web-footed birds were swimming in its small artificial lake. The benches that lined along the festooned walkways on the park had few occupants. Richard was punctual.

He seemed intrigued by the actions of a duck. He was watching a duck chase another duck away, probably trying to deprive its rival duck of mating advances. Richard was so very amused that when he saw Evelyn coming, he tried to control himself, but he couldn't fully compose himself and burst out laughing again at the replay of the scene of the fleeing lover duck ran through his mind again. He tried to catch his breath while expressing his reason for his hilarity. Evelyn was not amused, and Richard sensed that.

She rolled up the sleeve of the blouse she had on under her jacket and revealed fresh mushrooming rashes over a large portion of her right arm. A portion indicated an open skin, probably due to excessive scratching. Richard was alarmed. He beckoned Evelyn to sit down, but she shook her head in refusal. She feared she might spread it.

"I'm sorry, very sorry. Was that the reason of your meeting with Seth?"

"Yes, I wanted to compare his with mine." Evelyn answered.

"And what did you find?"

Evelyn was silent. She fixed her gaze on his face in a mute expression of, "What do you think?" She rolled down her sleeve to cover her rashes, and then she sat down at the far end of the park bench. Acting more cautiously, Evelyn's eyes travelled along the length and breadth of the park and suddenly she flashed the back of her legs for Richard's eyes. He noticed another spread of rashes behind her left leg. His face signaled bewilderment, and he was troubled by the irreconcilable visual reality of rashes against what he'd heard from Dr. Appleworth and Patrick, his beach bench acquaintance. Momentary silence prevailed in the shock. First, it was Erika, then Seth, then Dorina, then Josh and now Evelyn. There was no need for them to vocalize their feelings; they formed a mutual pact to pursue the cure for this strange sickness.

"There's something I don't understand. My son has the rashes, but none of us seem to have it, even after weeks of fondling and interacting with him. That makes Dr. Appleworth's point, and even Patrick's, who logically argues that many physio-sociological conditions could be responsible for rashes manifestation."

Evelyn's response was mute. As a young lady she pondered over the depravities she would have to deal with as a result of her skin condition. She might not be able to show off her legs in swimsuits, she imagined if she were married, what a horrid expression her husband's face would reveal if he were to see it for the first time, and worse still, suppose the rashes crept up on to her face. The thoughts haunted her. She felt the urge to blame Richard for her condition because he brought her in contact with Seth, but something kept suppressing that urge. What it was, she did not know. She knew that was unlike her, prone to impetuousness and combativeness.

Richard was equally surprised. He had braced himself for Evelyn's fury, and the absence of that had touched him. Where is your sting, Evelyn? He wondered. She had lost it to her humanness, the reality of human vulnerability. She was realizing how ephemeral the budding joys of the flower of her youth were, and what the fluctuating fortunes and misfortunes of fate could be. Evelyn picked up her purse and was ready to leave. Richard wanted to hug her to cheer her up, but she restrained him.

"I don't care, Evelyn; we're in this thing together." he declared.

"No, Richard. Your family needs you. Apphia and Josh need you; there are innocent victims of the law who have no voice who need you. I can't bear their loss by a selfish claim to your emotions. Please, don't let me deprive them. I'll be more at peace if their misfortune will not be traced to me."

"Evelyn, listen to me. I have a friend in whom I confided Seth's and your mom's condition. And he explained that rashes are mere outward show of an internal situation and moreover, Dr. Appleworth says Seth's rashes aren't contagious. If they are, then I should have them, but I don't. Did your mother get it because of her contact with Seth? Of course, not! Let's see what's out there that can help us all. There must be something we're overlooking."

She smiled. She smiled hard. And she smiled again. That was contagious. She knew Richard was right. He smiled back. He didn't know why she was smiling, and she didn't know why he was smiling. They both just smiled and smiled into laughter. And they just laughed. When the laughing was over, Evelyn allowed Richard's hug on the side of her body which was rashes-free.

"I just witnessed Mr. Richard Troy Bridges making closing arguments on the case between the rashes versus the Seth Nathan club." Evelyn teased Richard. She stood up and readjusted her purse on her shoulder for a parting hug again on her rash-free body side. Accidentally, some of the contents in her purse fell out in the process onto the park-bench and on the grass. Richard stooped in attempt to help retrieve the items, but Evelyn playfully and remonstratively slapped the back of Richard's hand gently.

"Items in a lady's purse are only for the eyes of the lady." Evelyn counseled. She picked her hand moisturizer, her pen, and a folded piece of paper which she assumed, was also from her purse. She wondered what it was. She knew she wasn't keeping any paper in her purse. "See this, Richard," she drew his attention to the piece of paper. The scribbling read:

"What's for sure

Is what is pure

It's not a lure

To what you endure

An herb for cure

No procedure

And that's for sure"

What is good

May be crude

It's good food

In Lily's hood

From the roots to the shoots

Just a hen's hood

For its brood

It's all good

A nook to bear the fruits

Right for every breed.

Heh, take heed

Follow my lead

It's good indeed."

Upon noticing that the last line was underlined in red ink, Evelyn got petrified. "Richard, let's get out of here." Evelyn demanded. She knew she'd stumbled upon a gang message and she wouldn't want any association with that world. Her car was parked about a block away, so she was very pleased when Richard offered to escort her. Having covered a few yards away from their park-seat, she sensed a young teenager - a boy was following them. He was brown and looked sixteen. He had an arm tattoo that was close to his shoulder. It revealed a graphic art of a hen with its brood under its covering. Evelyn couldn't take her eyes off the image on the young man's upper shoulder.

"Do you like it Mam?" He addressed Evelyn interrogatively.

"Yes – yes – yes, yes, I do." Stammering in fear, Evelyn responded.

"No, no, no, I don't mean this artwork. I mean what you read – I mean the paper on the bench seat." The youth, speaking softly yet confidently, corrected Evelyn.

"O that – No, I don't understand it, but it's nice. It's interesting." Evelyn complimented him nervously.

"I'm sorry if I made you guys nervous. I understand. By the way, they call me around here, 'Eloquenter,' 'Street Eloquenter' or simply 'Elo.' I wrote those lines. It's a message for anybody who visits this park and uses the seats here. Some say it's a riddle. I leave it for the reader." Elo smiled and extended his arm to solicit a handshake with them. "Guys, have a nice day."

Richard and Evelyn watched Elo walk away. With their fears almost allayed they wondered what a character they had just encountered. Richard was cautious in his opinion of him. "When one hears words like 'herb' and 'lily', one is tempted to infer marijuana or a drug, but I'm struck by his intelligence in spite of perhaps - a rough background."

"I simply want to get away from here." Evelyn remarked. She gave Eloquenter's paper to Richard and joked, "Perhaps you'll help avoid a gang war."

CHAPTER 13

It was a different atmosphere in Dorina's house. The cheery personality of Thelma always glowed around her, even in the performance of her duties. She perceived that the health needs of Dorina were beyond the shelves of the pharmacist. It was her silent conviction. Thelma had grown used to hearing her groan, heave, and sigh until one day, she decided to win Dorina's trust by sharing her personal story with her. She hoped it would help Dorina open up. It did to a measure.

Thelma told Dorina how her husband, who she'd supported him fiscally during his college years, had left her for another woman barely three months after his graduation. The story resonated with Dorina. They were on a common ground, but it also silently defined the emotional gulf between their worlds, Thelma's and hers. Dorina realized that the gulf across, which was the gulf of Thelma's, always beamed radiance of sunny emotions amidst the overhead of lurking clouds of disappointment and loneliness. However, Thelma always came up with something. Quite often Dorina would find herself in a recreational vaudeville initiated by Thelma.

Dorina took a sip of the apple cider which sat on her bedside table. It didn't taste very sweet, but that was how she wanted it. The foam at the top revealed a measure of fermentation and Dorina's facial expression showed an alloyed face of grim and okay, but it was her repeated sharp clucking sound that drew Thelma, her nurse's attention.

"Dorina, does it mean you like it, or you don't?" Thelma asked.

"It means both. Not very sweet because of the fermentation, but at the same time it makes it hard to swallow." Dorina's frail facial muscle could still hold a chuckle. "I'm not complaining." She said and smiled to confirm her remark. Thelma walked stealthily over to her with a mirror, and eventually she brought the mirror out closer for Dorina to have closer view of her face. Dorina burst out laughing at herself as much as her strength could allow; upon seeing the residue of the foam that had lined across her upper lip. She looked like she was wearing a white moustache and depicting an image in a milk advertisement. There was another round of laughter as they tried to deride the woman in Thelma's mirror by declaring in unison, "Got Juice?"

Dorina always appreciated Thelma's attempt to inculcate humor into her life, and Thelma knew that. Her warm approach to her duties always kindled a wishful imagination. Dorina also imagined an elusive mother and daughter relationship she had longed to have with Evelyn. Thelma wiped out the juice foamy mark off Dorina's lips.

"You know what, next time we'll try using a straw, how about that?"

"No. I prefer the touch of the glass on my lips. To use the straw is like kissing." Dorina joked with a smile. "And I don't remember the last time I kissed someone."

"Don't say that, how about Mr. Hedge?" Thelma asked.

"O Bless his heart. He's a wonderful man. I competed with him over the love for our daughter. He won. He won because I was travelling and he was taking care of her. Evelyn didn't like me much because I was strict – little or no television, especially when I returned from my concert tours and tried to enforce my values. Do you have a child, Thelma?"

"Yes, I do. He's six."

"Don't let him watch too much television. Tom was always busy in the store, so the TV kept Evelyn company." Snippets of cough interrupted her statement and Thelma realized she had to give her a break from talking. Her day's work was almost done and as she walked out of Dorina's room to get ready, she heard her straining her weak voice to call her back.

"I have a favor to ask of you. Would you bring your son, one day? I'd like to meet him." Dorina requested.

"Certainly, I will. That will be on a weekend when there's no school." Thelma assured her. Dorina's request didn't come as a surprise to Thelma. She noticed how Dorina liked to watch her neighbor's children play in their backyard. She even knew those children by their names. To some extent, Dorina identified herself in Joan. Joan reminded her of her childhood years – not giving in to Felix who always wanted to boss her about. She was so thrilled to see Joan stand up against her overbearing brother. On one occasion, she called out Thelma to share in her quiet spectating or perhaps, her peeping mischief. That was how far Dorina had come when Thelma entered into her life as her caregiver and nurse. Dorina would often> see Thelma kneel and pray, and sometimes would also hear her name, "Dorina" mentioned in Thelma's prayers. Each night, as Thelma looked forward to returning to her family, Dorina's crested spirits would drop. That night was no different.

Then the doorbell rang. The guest stood there. She was no ordinary guest, but Thelma couldn't recognize her. Thelma opened the door partially and sized her up. She responded with a glare to express her proprietary rights to the house she was being screened to enter into. Thelma stood her ground.

"How can I help you?"

"I'm Evelyn Hedge, Dorina's daughter."

"Oh, it's you. Come on in. Ms. Hedge I am sure you'll understand that I have to screen Dorina's visitors to avoid unwelcome ones."

"Well, at least you knew me." Evelyn asserted.

The two stood in the living room during their exchange. Dorina was hearing the dialogue and she was not comfortable with it.

"No, actually I don't."

"I met you here on my last visit with the gentleman who queried about the sores on my mother. So, it's a little surprising you expected me to accept your pretenses. Now, could I see her?"

"You may have to wait while I get her ready to receive you. And Ms. Hedge, that was a long time ago, about three weeks – hairstyle, makeups - people change, you know."

"Cha-a-n-ge?" An insidious word that charged the ears of Evelyn at a time when she felt her rashes had dethroned her charm. "Cha-a-n-ge!" The yell froze Thelma's steps as she headed back to Dorina's room. She turned to face a much-bruised Evelyn.

"Ms. Hedge, 'Change' is not a bad word." She spoke softly. "People change to look better. I'm sure you didn't have this hairstyle on your last visit, and you look great. There are things I want to change about me and around me, and I mean it in a good way."

Astute-thinking Thelma had avoided a firestorm; she had to face her soft employer. Dorina looked perplexed. She'd moved from her chair to the bed.

"You'll be okay. Your daughter is here to see you." Thelma turned and realized Evelyn had been standing by the doorway and was overhearing her discussion with her mother. Dorina looked frightened as Evelyn walked in.

"I'm here. Mom, I'm here. It's me, Evelyn."

Fear had completely engulfed the entire frame of Dorina. She seemed to be afraid of her daughter and had recoiled to her low-spirited and ailing self. She began to tremble and greeted her daughter's advances with fear, especially when Evelyn tried to reach to and touch her mother's hair.

"Mom, what's wrong? It's me."

Evelyn couldn't bring herself to understand her mother's reaction. She hadn't anticipated such a cold reunion. She never gave it a thought that her visit would blindside the very woman who once cradled her. Evelyn had forgotten that she once thundered the words, "I hate you." That was ten years ago. If time really heals, in their case, it'd ironically morphed into virulence. Dorina didn't expect that the baby she once held in her arms to her heart would one day be a villain to her. Time hadn't healed Evelyn. Dorina felt. She did overhear Evelyn's exchange with the kind and caring Thelma, so she even wondered if she could survive Evelyn's claws as she advanced them to touch the hair on her face.

Evelyn saw the fear in her mother's eyes. Indeed, the grim paralysis on Dorina's face communicated the reality of Evelyn's overbearing persona on her ailing and vulnerable mother. "Mom, it's me, your daughter, Evelyn," but in Dorina's ears, she was hearing: "Woe, behold, it's me, the, the, Evelyn."

Evelyn dropped to her knees in tears. "O, she thinks I'm a monster. She's afraid of me." While Evelyn wept, kneeling by her mother's bed, Thelma rushed in and gently tucked Dorina in. Noticing how broken Evelyn was, she helped her to her feet and out of the room.

"Ms. Hedge, if I knew you were coming, I would've prepared her, your mother, I mean mentally to be more receptive of you. I think she'll be okay on your next visit."

"Thank you." Evelyn appreciated Thelma's assistance this time and walked quietly to her car. She'd made a fool of herself. If Bridges had been with her, the faux pas would've been avoided. She started to take an introspection of her life. She questioned her behavior and the more she thought of it, the more she wanted to know about her biological father. Sadly, her only resource was her mother, but she continued to burn her bridges to her.

Settled in her car, Evelyn flipped down the sun visor and checked her face in the vanity mirror attached to the sun visor. She cleaned up her make up. "Well, time to go," she whispered to herself. She rolled back her sleeves to achieve a more comfortable and convenient arm positioning on the steering. Then she saw it. She saw them. Up to her wrist the rashes had spread. It was a very slow drive home.

CHAPTER 14

The burden of the condition of Seth continued to weigh daily on the mind of Richard. The days turned to weeks; the weeks to months; and the months continued to exist as an empty conveyor, conveying nothing, nothing to the health and life of Seth. Seth's state of despondency had worsened. He'd grown leaner and was beginning to label himself with the worst attributes. He was becoming more withdrawn from society. Richard couldn't figure any hope he could convey to his friend. He tossed and tossed in his bed. It was two in the morning, and Apphia felt she had to get off the bed.

"I might as well keep vigil with you if you don't want to sleep." She robed herself and headed off for the kitchen. Then the phone rang. "I guess we might be disturbing our neighbors." She concluded. The phone continued to ring. She picked it up and muted the speaker. "It's Evelyn. Why would she call so early in the morning?"

"I can find out if you hand me the phone." Richard yawned as he received the phone from Apphia.

"Hi Richard, I'm very sorry for calling your house so early in the morning."

"That's okay, but what is it? Are you okay?" Richard asked.

"Richard, I'm desperate. I can't sleep. I have to talk to you."

"Okay. You know, its two am, right?"

"Yes, and I'm sorry. Do you still have the piece of paper we found at the park?" Evelyn asked with a measured excitement.

"I – I – think so. It's some - where. What about it?" Richard stammered his response.

"Well, I've been thinking about the riddle on the paper. I think I can decipher what it was trying to say."

"Evelyn, that can wait till later in the morning."

"I know, but you don't understand. We have to contact him …"

"Who is 'him?'" Richard asked.

"The guy, Eloquinto, I guess that's the name, right?"

"No. The name is Eloquenter. But how are we going to start looking for him at two am?"

"No, no, no, not this very moment, but I want to ask you to kindly include that in your itinerary today before other plans override it. Please."

"You got it, Evelyn." Meanwhile Apphia had to withdraw herself to Joshua's room

"Thanks, Richard. We have to see Lily tomorrow."

"I thought we were to see Eloquenter. Who is Lily? You're confusing me."

"No, no, no, sorry for the confusion, the Elo guy will take us to Lily. Lily is the real deal. She's the one who cooks the herb. Richard, I told you, I've got everything together. I didn't tell you - my rashes are spreading to every part of my arm It's up to my right wrist, and about to take over my right hand. I won't allow it. I must resort to a desperate solution at this moment."

The conversation was over, and nothing made sense to Apphia. Richard narrated their encounter with Eloquenter. He mentioned the riddle.

"The riddle, the riddle - O – where did I put it?"

Richard threw everybody in the household into panic and that triggered an obligation to look for the paper with the scribbled riddle. Everyone including little Josh searched every nook and cranny of the house for the riddle without avail. A few minutes later, after abandoning the search, Apphia heard a snoring sound by the couch. It was Richard. Apphia would have the bed to herself. She wondered who Lily might be; perhaps someone in Richard's dreams or perhaps a discovery in Evelyn's dreams.

Evelyn was first to arrive at the duck lake park. She preferred a different seating location to the one they'd previously used on their last visit. From her location, persons from various walks-of-life passed before her. She pondered what impression she might be conveying to them as a lone visitor at a park – a park with a notoriety for a gang activity. She faintly remembered the face of Eloquenter. She craved the presence of the person she once feared. She saw a young man seemingly in a phone argument with another party. The sight frightened her when she imagined probable outcomes from such arguments. Then she saw Richard accompanied by Seth.

"Our first task is to see if we can find a copy of that piece of paper." That was Richard's indirect confession about the missing original. Evelyn's ballooned hopes were instantly deflated. Richard decided to ask the arguing young man on the phone about Eloquenter.

"Yes, I know Elo, the smooth rhymer. He'll be here, but I don't know when."

Richard turned his attention to Evelyn. "Don't worry; I believe he'll be here. We know he's here most of the time. That's what he said, right?"

Except for Seth who looked very sickly and very casual, Richard and Evelyn looked white-color conservative professionals in formal suits. The young man suspected that Richard's request about Elo might be something positive. For he knew they wouldn't be in the open if they were law enforcement personnel. They would rather watch from their cars. Moreover, they'd earned his respect with such impressive wardrobe command. The young man turned, approached Richard and his friends again. He looked at his watch and, nodding his head confidently as his finger drummed on his wristwatch, he remarked: "Prison time at this time."

The new development had shocked them. Evelyn's hope was totally dashed. Seth seemed like he didn't care. Only Richard held up hope if indeed Evelyn's interpretation of the riddle was right.

"Do you know Lily?" Richard asked the young man.

"No. I don't know no Lily."

"Does Elo have a Sister called Lily?" Richard pressed.

"O – I get it. Man, the only person to talk to you about Lily is Elo. Man, I got to go." The young man departed with the mystery of Eloquenter and Lily still in the air.

"Do you think we can visit him in prison and ask him about Lily?" Evelyn inquired from her friends. Richard was silent. He felt Evelyn's question was latent selfishness at best. Richard's mental resolve was to find out what help he could offer to get Eloquenter out. Seth cut in and cleared their clouded perceptions.

"You know, you guys totally misunderstood what he was telling you. You're allowing your perceptions about this place or about him to shape what you hear or better still, the meaning of what you hear. That guy was pointing repeatedly to his watch to emphasize the point that around this time or about this time, this

Elo guy may be at the prison grounds – may be visiting or something. Which prison grounds? We don't know. Remember his words were 'at this time.' Richard, I thought you'd catch that."

Seth was right and Richard realized that. He wondered why that had escaped him. After all, the young man did say Elo would be at the park, but he didn't know when. Richard wondered if he was losing his analytical mind or if he'd been ineffectually applying it. He remembered his first argument encounter with Evelyn on her first day at work when she'd enviously tried to demean his gifted flair to unravel the thoughts of a litigant. Where is that Richard? What had reduced him to an average lawyer? If he were Richard, Eloquenter's riddle would be no match. The thought challenged him. The reality awoke him. The paper must be found. The riddle must be solved; and must be solved by him.

"I think we should leave." Richard suggested. Evelyn didn't welcome it, but she had no choice. She felt she wouldn't be safe on the park alone. Her eyes traveled around the park again and she hastily acceded to Richard's request.

Evelyn had formed a habit of returning home late in the night. As a single, she reasoned that the lateness would spare her the awareness of the reality of her singleness in a large four-bedroom house. She'd silenced the illusions of happy children running noisily across the rooms and the frenzied loud cheering husband in the couch who would bellow his excitement and call out his imaginary wife Evelyn at sundry times to join him to watch games on the TV together. She thought she'd overcome that, but when she arrived home and saw her father's car parked and waiting for her, the fantasy resurged. "That should have been my husband's car."

"Hi Dad! What brings you hear so late without calling?"

"I need to talk to you. Can we go in?" Tom suggested and Evelyn led the way to her living room. Tom's eyes were drawn to the items on her center table. A half-filled bottle of liquor and an unfinished glass of liquor had betrayed her concealed newly formed habit. She noticed her fathers expressed facial disapproval and was surprised that he suppressed his comment. That bothered her. With a sense of betrayal of her father's trust, she quietly cleared the center table.

"Your mother wants to meet with us." Tom announced.

"Both of us?" Surprised by the message, Evelyn was cautiously curious. "I thought she didn't want to see me."

"Well, she wants to see you this time, and wants to speak with both of us at the same time."

"Why the change of mind, do you know?"

"I don't know. It shouldn't surprise you. She's your mother; a mother wants to talk to her daughter. That's it. I think Thelma might have impressed upon her to do that, I guess."

"Dad, it's scary – like she wants us together to hear her parting words. I hope she's okay though."

"She's by far much better than she was few weeks ago. I mean much better. I'll meet you there tomorrow evening." Tom left on that note.

The same night when Tom was parting with his daughter, Richard was being welcomed with news at home. Josh walked in with an unusual smile. He was advertising a strange smile with an apparent invitation for Daddy's comment or inquisitiveness about why he was smiling strangely. When Josh realized his dad wasn't questioning his obvious display of being mump, he volunteered a clue.

"I'm not telling." He expressed that with a triumphant smile of a kind blackmailer. "Huh, huh, I'm not telling." That arrested dads' attention; something was amiss. He decided to play along and spoke in a hushed tone. "O – please, tell me, pretty please." Josh's giggling went loud, enough to notify Apphia that her son was giving away their secret.

"Jo-o-sh!" Mom called. "What are you doing?" Josh's giggling grew louder. "Re-mem-be-e-r." Apphia sounded a cautionary note. Richard couldn't take it anymore.

"Honey, what's going on? Please tell me you've found Elo's paper."

"Please, just come in and see." Apphia yielded.

Richard walked into his small home office. Apphia sat in the visitor's chair with a plastic covering over the chair. She lifted her blouse to uncover a portion below her right armpit. Apphia had become the newest member of the rash enigma. She'd been scratching it during Evelyn's two o'clock morning call, and she couldn't conceal it anymore. A small portion of open skin confirmed the level of Apphia's excessive scratching. Richard was in shock.

"Do we see the doctor, tomorrow?" He asked.

"Let's wait and see. Let's give it probably a week. If it's not gone then, we will see the doctor." Apphia suggested.

"Are you sure?" Richard pressed.

"Don't worry - no fevers, I'll be fine. I'll use the floor tonight."

"For goodness sake my wife is sleeping on no floor. We'll be sleeping on this bed together and even tonight we will, we will uh … uh." Apphia understood that.

"Richard, behave yourself."

"Regardless, nobody is sleeping on the floor. We shall both share this bed tonight. I dare this rash." Richard declared confidently.

"Please, Richard, don't say that. Somebody must survive it in the family."

"It's not going to affect my skin, and even if it does, a cure is coming." With this stalwart conviction and declaration, Richard bent over and picked his wife from her chair as his left arm literally brushed over Apphia's rashes.

She looked into his face in utter consternation. Then she smiled.

"O – Richard, I love you."

It was a different atmosphere within the walls of Seth's house. A mountain of books towered up to the armrest of his chair. Any convincing literature about his ailment was a must-read for him. He'd even become an authority on nutritional facts and could command vitamin solutions to any vitamin deficiency health issue. The self-made "Dr. Seth Nathan" had just completed his routine volume of readings for the day. He walked to his kitchen and to the far end to a table, burdened with the weight of various types of herbs. One of them was a jar filled with chopped roots of plants from South America. He'd been told it could cure all kinds of diseases. Name it; it cures it. Seth believed it.

The root which had a red sap enjoyed a strong bias by virtue of its prank worthiness. Each night Seth would pick a root and chew it dry and would wake up each morning with a frightening scarlet red mouth. His tongue, his lips, his teeth, everything would turn so red that it could even dare any menacing vampire. On his first day of using that herb, Seth had walked drowsily to his bathroom and stood before the sink. He watched the tap run while he routinely dispensed the toothpaste onto his toothbrush. When he lifted his head up to start brushing, a haunting apparition of a bloodied mouth of himself fiercely glared at him. He screamed at his own open-mouth image in the mirror. His repeated opening of his mouth aggravated the horror of his image even more. He learned from that experience to practice rinsing his mouth thoroughly each night before going to bed. In spite of his condition, Seth had a great sense of humor. He often joked about how he scared his neighbors off his door who were out treat-or tricking with their children on a Halloween night. His trick, he opened his mouth.

However, Seth was no werewolf; he was a man seeking a cure. The elusive cure was taking a toll on him. He heard rumors that his condition was due to generational curse, a curse which was pronounced on his grandfather for defrauding his neighbor of a huge sum of money. Another story was that he infected his wife with his condition, but the medication and the curative measures were more effective on Seth than her. The measures failed his wife; the result was her death, and that theory had rendered Seth to live with the guilt. Many subscribed to the later theory that even Richard at times had found himself very tempted to believe it. The ostensible theories were eating Seth up. Richard knew it, and it bothered him as much as it bothered Seth.

CHAPTER 15

Tom and Evelyn shared a ride in Evelyn's car to Dorina's house. Thelma noticed their car as they pulled up and following an earlier instruction by Dorina to have her driveway blocked with orange cones, the Hedges were compelled to park their car by the street. Dorina's reason was to create a more convenient emergency access through the driveway to her, due to her failing strength. This directive had compelled her visitors to enter her premises by the backyard. Evelyn hadn't seen that side of the house before. She observed that the garden had been left fallow for quite a time. When Dorina moved in she used to tend the garden herself, but when her health issues began, she abandoned the garden into the care of James, a kind young student who volunteered to help her.

James used to be Dorina's neighbor until he and his family moved to Colorado. James had met her one summer afternoon when he went after his football which flew over to Dorina's yard. The catcher on his team missed that throw and a kind friendship began upon his attempt to retrieve that ball. He was touched to discover Dorina's lonely state so he tried to help her with basic chores and to tend her garden whenever he could. She called him Jimmy, and he called her Maunty, his coined-up acronym for Mom and Aunty.

One morning, as James worked in the garden, he heard a beautiful violin tune. He knew the sound he was hearing was from an accomplished fiddler. He traced the tune to Dorina's living room. Instantly, James dropped his garden tools, rushed to his house, picked up his guitar, and the string sounds of a duo filled the air.

Her friendship days with James were also the very high moments of her life. Dorina was bubbly most of the time, although there was also an obvious lingering burden that weighed upon her spirits. Quite often, James would hear her heave and sigh, but she never discussed it.

"Mrs. Hedge is everything alright?" James one day summoned courage to ask her. "Jimmy everything is fine. Everyone has some regrets in life and sometimes I think about mine." James discovered that one way of cheering her up was to engage her to play their music together.

As Tom and Evelyn approached the house, the sound of a distant familiar tune lit a smile on his face. Evelyn noticed that her father's facial expression of pleasure might be from the tune they were hearing. He smiled again.

"What's making you smile?" She asked.

"The music." His tag response wasn't enough for Evelyn, but because they were almost at Dorina's door, she decided to suspend their petty idiosyncrasies. Dorina turned down the sound volume of the music as they walked in and greeted them. Tom stooped to kiss her. Evelyn also followed in the same fashion with a delicate hug and a cheek kiss.

"E-ve-line, you've grown more beautiful than I'd imagined you in picture." Dorina remarked. She knew she had to choose her words well to avoid her sensitive daughter's displeasure, and not to ruin the day for everyone.

"Thank you, Mom. It's been a long time."

"Your dad tells me you're a lawyer now. Who knows, I may need your service one day." Dorina stammered her joke. Her voice was still frail as she turned to Tom.

"Do you recognize the music?" Dorina asked him as she turned it up a little bit more.

"Yes, I do. That's you and James, right?" Tom answered confidently, and Dorina smiled while nodding to deride his unexplained confidence in his answer.

"Where is he now?" he asked, but with a resigned tone of guilt. Dorina was still smiling, but this time she was shaking her head in response.

"I don't know. You chased him away. How would I know? You should know."

Evelyn was totally at sea as to what they were discussing. "At the appropriate time I will tell you that joke." Tom tried to make light of the issue.

Evelyn couldn't keep her eyes off her mother. She was observing her better than she had in her previous hyper-frenzied visiting moments. She was seeing how the once strong and energetic young Romanian woman had become so feeble and small. Her agility had faded away and the strength in her voice had fizzled into a whimpering monotone. Her eyes dim and watery had never been engaging like the strength she used to have in her gaze. Even then, surrounded by her family, Dorina struggled to maintain eye-contact with her daughter. In a way, she still feared her.

The gravity of Dorina's fear of her daughter was unascertainable, but Evelyn could appropriate the fear that she'd put into her mother, to be a lot. She hated recollections of her yelling tantrums. She remembered she'd even gone far to call her mother "infidel" because of the live scene of her mother's promiscuity with another man. It was a traumatizing experience for her then, as a child.

There was a knock on the door and Dorina invited Thelma in. She came in with bottles of water and left, shutting the door behind her. Dorina solicited Tom's help to twist the lid off her bottle. She then took a sip and reclined more comfortably in her chair. She heaved and sighed again, this time, more deeply. She spoke softly and in her characteristic Romanian intonation.

"I've looked forward to this day. I thank you for deciding to come. It was on a short notice; I'm very grateful. I want to start first by telling you the story of a woman whose life has had a remarkable influence on mine. In fact, without her I wouldn't be sitting here today. Her name is Vanda."

She paused for a moment and looked up to study the faces of her listening guests again. She was convinced she had their rapt attention. She continued.

"Vanda and I were childhood friends. We were very close and so were our parents. Our parents fled Romania when we were in our late teens because of the oppressive rule of the Romanian communist regime. We were very poor, and our parents worked many jobs to make a living for us all. With my little knowledge of English, which I studied while in Romania, I could interact better than my parents did. I also knew how to play the violin and how to perform as a ballerina. It was actually Vanda who encouraged me to take the lessons in violin and ballet in Romania. However, Vanda was a better performer than I. She took up jobs to play in English pubs during a few years stay in Europe. The money she earned helped pay our trip to the US. With our parents off our backs in Europe, we felt free to do whatever we liked."

As Dorina continued with her narrative while her home-made music recording with James played in the background, a sense of sentimentalism pervaded the atmosphere. She tried to check her emotions and to maintain a discipline of self-restraint from breaking down, for she was very overwhelmed with nostalgia and regrets.

"Vanda decided to play in the night clubs and bars again. She came home each night with huge tips which we lived on. That helped to pay our bills. There were times I became jealous of her and felt I should abandon my quiet nature and follow her to the clubs. I decided not to do that. She often teased me and joked about what I was missing out on in life. I realized I had to find a job and stop giving her the chance to ridicule me. I took a janitorial job. I liked it until she started following me to work. Vanda eventually took over the job. I was okay with that because she stopped her night life.

"Vanda became pregnant. I wasn't sure when the pregnancy began to show. She always complained about a family that lived in a home, like an abandoned home, with a trailer truck, and how she would often hear them fighting as she passed by their house on her way home. It wasn't a clean house. She said what made her sad more was their baby, about two months old, who she often found left outside and many times fighting off flies from a wooden box cradle she lay in. One time, Vanda was so angry; she felt like going in there to tell them her piece of mind, but she didn't. That was when she made up her mind to have a baby and determined to give her all the love and care that she could offer to her future baby. It was her way of celebrating life with and for a baby and closing her mind on what she'd been seeing every day as she passed by that house.

"The janitorial work was very helpful. Its sobered Vanda, but there was a problem. One morning, Vanda's supervisor wanted to know when she would have her baby so that she could find a replacement for her during her maternity period. Vanda was due the next month. A day after her supervisor approached her, I saw a change in Vanda. She brooded a lot. She was troubled about something, something she kept to herself. One night, it was pouring rain and Vanda hadn't returned home. A week passed by, and no word from Vanda. That wasn't unusual with her. She could go for days and then show up unexpectedly. However, on the second week, Vanda came with a baby. The baby was big like a three-month-old, but that's how big Vanda's belly had been.

"That night, when the baby was sleeping, Vanda went to her car and brought in a belly pack, yes, a belly pack. They were rubber foam with a second layer of sand padding which gave it the hard touch feeling from outside like a pregnant woman's belly, and two layers of nude color panty hoses. They faked the pregnancy that Vanda was carrying all this time, until – until – until she had her delivery by stealing the baby from the yard of those fighting couple."

"Huh!" Evelyn exclaimed. "What …."

Dorina hushed her instantly, and Evelyn checked herself.

"Well, Vanda shocked me too." Dorina continued. "You see, she had it all planned. In her mind, she thought she was going to save that baby and care for her. If they didn't like their own baby, or didn't care about her, she would. She was going to steal her away, anyway.

"On that rainy evening, when Vanda was walking home to catch the bus, it was very windy. She struggled to keep her partially wet skirt onto her body from the wind, and as she tried to do that, the wind at the same time, was turning her cheap umbrella inside out. Eventually, the umbrella flew from her hand and landed by a table which held it up in the yard. She ran to get it to prevent it from flying farther away, but as she picked it up, that wooden box which was the cradle for the baby crossed her eyes. She thought it possible that the couple might have forgotten about their baby and left her in the box in the rain. And behold, shockingly, very shockingly, there she was, almost - (pause) - drowning. The – the – baby - was crying but the sound of the rain was drowning her cries."

Dorina began to choke with emotion. Her voice was shaking as her chest throbbed heavily trying to restrain the sorrow that the crystal imagination had brought her. Then it overwhelmed her. She cried uncontrollably. Tom knelt and held her, completely

184

oblivious of the restraint imposed by the rashes over her body. Evelyn cried with her. Tom continued to dab his running nose and his flooded eyes as well. The pack of tissue that Evelyn carried in her purse was empty.

After that emotional whirlwind, there was a moment of calm. Evelyn reached out and held her mother's hand. Tom suppressed his expression of shock. Nonetheless, he liked what he'd witnessed. He was pleased to see something he hadn't seen for years. Dorina smiled reciprocally and continued.

"You see, Vanda had actually planned to steal the baby, but there was no greater opportunity than what the situation offered her. She held the shivering baby tight to her body and hoped her body temperature would keep her warm. She knew she was holding a stolen baby, so she didn't want to risk going to any stores to buy anything to cover the baby. She took off her pregnant belly pack, the foam and all those belly padding to cover the baby and to keep her warm.

Strangely, and I say that again, very strangely, there was no news about a missing baby, even weeks after - nothing. However, Vanda found herself living in the shadows. Her janitorial co-workers threw a baby shower for her, but she couldn't attend the function. She had to pick her gifts from one of her friend's house with the excuse that the baby's father's mother was baby-sitting her sick baby. Vanda and I realized that we had to move a quieter suburb. So, we moved to Michigan. We liked Michigan. It was hard, because we continued to live in the shadows. I envied Vanda and I wanted to also have a child as beautiful as her child. She promised to help me."

At this point, Evelyn's eyes widened. Anxiety had overthrown her calm composure. Her thoughts were going wild, exploring how she came in the picture as Dorina's child. Dorina had also sensed Evelyn's anxiety. There was silence. Dorina was holding everyone in suspense. She looked up as if she was praying or just about to. Her feelings were mixed with fear, rejection, and an unchained conscience. She dabbed a few tears from her eyes and eventually Dorina declared in solemn poignancy.

"I am Vanda. Vanda is my middle name. I carried the name with a different character and behavior to hide my identity. Evelyn, the baby in the box, the improvised wooden cradle was you."

Evelyn's jaws dropped. She began to shake as she slowly dropped to her knees and slowly wrapped her arms around the degenerated, small frame of Dorina, mother Vanda. With tears streaming from her eyes, Evelyn continued to grapple with words; words that she'd never uttered to her mother before. With no power to control her emotions she left the room. Tom followed her and after consoling her for few minutes, they rejoined Dorina. Evelyn was now uttering those words, but her tears were choking them. She went on uttering them, but they were failing her mother, because her mother's unbelief could not validate what Evelyn had said; at least what she was now hearing. Evelyn said it again and this time with a firmer conviction. "Mom, I love you. Thank you, thank you. Yes, I love you. I'm okay. I'm okay."

The music was about to end. Tom reached the cassette player to stop it, but Evelyn requested a replay. When Tom was about to rewind the tape, Dorina interrupted. "There's more, more of my music with James, and even so, I still have more to tell you."

The next music began. The song was different. When the first note hit the air, it absorbed the moment. It revealed the hidden extra fingering mastery, and string works of Dorina as her beautiful melody played on. She waited for few seconds to allow the music to seethe into the atmosphere. It did, and it siphoned a remark from Evelyn. "What's the name of this song?" Evelyn smiled in appreciation as she waited for her answer. Dorina smiled back, but her eyes went wet again. Evelyn sensed that her question had evoked another sentimental moment, but Dorina smiled again in her tears.

"It was Vanda who originally named this song. She called it 'Arrival.' You see, the melody came to her when one day she was rejoicing and celebrating that she'd brought the 'Crying Baby' home. I remember her words when Vanda held her to her bosom, and looking into her eyes, she said, 'Baby, you have arrived home, and the crying days are over.' Yes, they were over, but that was when another chapter began.

"You see, back home, Vanda was an easy-going, happy-go lucky person, and never took life seriously. When I was a child, I was the favorite of my grandmother, my father's mother. I could get anything I wanted when my grandmother was around. I remember throwing tantrums just to get what I wanted. You can say I was spoilt by her. She affectionately called me 'Vanda.' The rest of the family called me Dorina. There was this 'go-getter' part of me that was the Vanda who was aggressive and always wanted things her way. As I grew older, I became more matured, and became more responsible, and that was when Vanda faded out and quiet Dorina appeared again. Amidst all this, my biggest wish was to get married and have a child. As I grew older and became more matured, I knew I had to be more Dorina. It also became necessary for us to leave Romania, because of the political problems.

"When I came to America, the political problems still continued in Romania. You see, when I arrived here, and eventually the baby also came into my life just at the right time, I had the chance to name her in my Immigration asylum papers. For the first time, I gave her the name 'Eveline,' but the lady spelt her name the American way, 'Evelyn.' Eveline means light or life, and my baby was giving me light and a hope for future life.

"I taught myself how to bake and began selling and delivering pastries. My big moment was at the St Troy County Fair at South Bend. I received so many orders. My biggest order was when a handsome young man approached my stand. At first, I was afraid of him. He was wearing sun glasses and I couldn't see his eyes. I thought he was from the police because he kept looking at the crying baby behind my table. Well, he gave me the biggest order, the request of friendship. I'm sure you all know that man. He's a wonderful man. I'm surprised he still loves this old lady."

They all burst out laughing and continued to laugh as Dorina continued to teasingly make faces at Tom. The earlier gloom that so far Dorina's narrative had brought, left the room. The smiles were back again. However, the thrill was short-lived, for a shadow of dread and apprehension returned to cloud Dorina's countenance again. Nonetheless, she decided to continue.

"I moved in with Tom. He cared very much for us. We became comfortable and Vanda decided to return, but I tried to keep her away. Vanda persisted; she didn't want to get rusty with her violin so after many practices she decided playing at clubs again. Tom didn't like the Vanda of me, and I knew it. To stop Vanda's activities, Tom adopted the baby and we came up with the store project. Though Dorina and Evelyn were safe, Vanda still lived in fear.

"One morning; Vanda had returned from the store and was getting ready to shower when she heard a strange noise in the backyard. Vanda knew Tom was at the store so she thought it might be Evelyn's little dog trying to get attention to come in. Vanda opened the back door and strong hands grabbed her, and pushed her helplessly against the opened door. The man kept uttering under his breath, 'I have been following you.' Vanda concluded at that moment that she'd been caught, but when the man tried forcefully to take the robe off her, and pushed her against the broken washing- machine, that was when she knew she was in a different kind of trouble. The man gagged her with his elbow so she couldn't scream for help. That was when the children walked in, Evelyn and Megan. In fact, Vanda was afraid the man would even do some harm to the children, so Vanda started kicking the air with her right leg as a sign to tell them to leave and if possible, get help. In fact, she thought she would be killed. She had the chance to bite the man's arm, and that was the time she screamed hard and freed herself. The neighbor's dog began to bark, and the man fled.

Well, help didn't come. That morning, Vanda faded out of my life. Her days of wandering ended. She left, disgraced, and humiliated. She never returned, and Dorina never missed her. The incident had a lasting effect on my relationship with my daughter. I couldn't explain my situation since I would have to explain my fears, the suspicion of being arrested, the baby situation and all that. For years, I wondered why it didn't dawn on my daughter that her mother was hurt, but her daughter rather thought her mother delighted in what was going on. The thinking stabs my heart every time. I'm like: 'have I given her any cause to make her believe that I delighted in that kind of a thing?' My heart has been bleeding for years because of this.

"Well, Dorina did not, and could not report to the police about the incident, because she feared the man knew about the stolen baby. Evelyn, I told your father about this incident. He was angry and hurt. He felt for me, he believed me; I am very grateful."

Evelyn, who had remained on the floor, and with her back inclined against her mother's bed through the second half of the story, turned around and hugged her mother. She apologized to her repeatedly. "Mom, you've endured so much for my sake I don't have words to express my sorrow for my actions against you. Again, I'm very, very sorry." She hugged her again and dabbed her mother's eyes off the tears. "No more crying. The crying baby must cease crying; that's why we moved to California. She's home with her mom, Mother Dorina."

There was silence. Evelyn's conscience had been on trial during Dorina's narration. She'd seen a lot about her daughter's contrition and willing heart for reconciliation. She strained her voice to call Thelma, but Thelma didn't hear her. She tried again, and Thelma showed up - with an explanation. "A man came to ask of you. I told him you were in a family meeting and you wouldn't want interruptions. He looked disappointed as he turned to leave."

"A man – who could he be?" Dorina remarked worriedly, but soon dispelled that bane of worry.

"Well, Thelma I want you to meet my family. We haven't been like this in a long time." Thelma shook hands with them after the formal introduction. She joked at the turn of every handshake. With Tom, "Are you sure we've met before?" Her joke on Evelyn drew much laughter; "This lady nearly got me fired, and I promise I'll be on my best behavior on your next visit."

The music stopped playing. It was time they left. Evelyn was dragging her feet to leave, but she had to, because she carpooled with her father who had pending plans before the close of the day.

"Mom, I'll come again tomorrow, and we'll have a talk. I have much to tell you."

Indeed, she had much to say; what had filled her time from High school years to a career practicing attorney who had been rubbing shoulders with versatile lawyers like Richard. Evelyn relished that reference; especially when the outcome of a legal case brought her also into prime attention. However, Richard was yet to solve, perhaps alone, what had been staring him in the face, the hunt for the cure for the strange rashes on Dorina; Evelyn, Apphia, Josh, and Seth. He felt obligated and would not relent.

CHAPTER 16

Seth was surprised to hear a knock on his door at an inopportune time of his weekday morning. It was around ten. He'd had an unusual, but regular practice of entering into his art studio at ten each morning and pursuing his acquired hobby of painting. His paintings were the portraits of Erika. He claimed the unusual practice always gave him a sense of fulfilment, a measure of closeness to her.

He wasn't expecting anybody. However, he wasn't surprised at whom the guest turned out to be. Richard brushed the sole of his shoes off on the outdoor doormat. He walked in while Seth held the door opened for him. The unannounced visit instantly aroused Seth's excitement about imminent news on Eloquenter's missing piece of paper, the paper with the rhyme or riddle. Intuitively, Seth believed that their fruitless visit to the park would one day be atoned for by a crucial and positive omen, particularly if ever the paper was found. So, he didn't spare his breath and Richard walked in.

"Please, tell me you've found that piece of paper." He expressed excitedly.

"Actually, no, but I hope I will, one day." Richard expressed nonchalantly his failure to recover it. Then he approached and settled in the famous chair. From previous visits, Richard knew it was the exclusive chair for the guests of his ailing friend. Seth's life, a life in a quarantine in his own home was a common knowledge to his few friends. He wore his gloves as he pulled his disposable plastic-covering chair closer to Richard. Then he rested his head in the palm of his propped left hand that had elbow support by the armrest of his chair. He was all ears for Richard to announce the purpose of his mission. Richard was tongue-tied. He was losing the courage to dissect his friend. He was no slouch at this. He had the lawyering artillery to invade the conscience and rescue the obscured truth that was being held hostage by the stubborn will of his eccentric friend. Do it, he pressed himself.

"Seth, do you have the most current pictures of Erika, before she died?"

"I'm not sure. They aren't dated. I can bring you a set of pictures we took two years ago; that's a year before she died."

"Yes, please, if you can do that."

"But why do you want the pictures?"

"Seth, I want to help you. I want to determine a timeline between the probable time that she took sick and the time that she died. It will help me determine the length of time of her sickness."

"I don't know how the pictures can help you, but Sir, at your word, your honor, I'll be obliged." Seth left for the pictures deriding his friend with utmost obedience. Richard's eyes began to travel around the room. He was looking for anything that would serve the purpose of his trip. He had little time to accomplish that; Seth's exit was very brief. He returned with quite a pile and spread them before Richard. Most of the pictures were group types - taken at parties, and few were exclusive Erika and Seth portraits.

"Seth, I may be blunt on this. Do you have any that reveals the rashes on her skin?"

"What! Let me be blunt with you. Are you requesting for nude pictures of my wife? I don't go about taking nude pictures of her. I was seeing her nudity live, why would I have to be taking pictures of that?" Seth retorted angrily.

"I'm sorry, Seth."

"You must be. You've insulted her; you've insulted me. I once told you; the spread was on her thighs, stomach areas and her butt side. You don't go there. You have insulted her; insulted me and questioned her moral principles. Mr. Richard Bridges, please, the door." Seth pointed the door to his friend. Richard was in shock. He did not anticipate such response from Seth on what he thought was a simple request. He got up in subdued compliance and walked towards the door. He turned for a last look and a word for his friend.

"Again, Seth, I'm sorry. I simply wanted to establish that there's hope for your situation, for if it had taken this long for these rashes to take your life, or positively thinking - to disappear, then your infection, if supposedly you were, the infection might not even be traced to Erika - at all. Scrutinizing Erika's infection and comparing it with yours would help establish similarities, and or differences, that is, if there is any at all. Seth, I simply wanted to help." Richard declared quietly with a very hurt spirit, he turned and grimaced. On that note, he left.

Seth had to face his world alone. In his mind, he'd disarmed a fellow combatant on the frontlines of his struggle with his health. With his impatience, he'd lost a listening ear and probably the voice of panacea to his ills. Seth tried to shove his pride aside and to call his friend back. He got up; walked to the door, and while his hand was on the door knob, he heard a motorbike engine driving away. It was Richard's.

Richard riding a motorbike – that was something new. Perhaps Seth was yet to know his friend better. He hadn't been pleased with the disruption of his ten o'clock morning routine portrait painting of his wife. However, he'd always known Richard to be a nice person. He recalled an incident of him with a foreign student.

It was a Thanksgiving weekend year before, and the campus was very quiet. Richard had returned to the hall to pick up a gift which he'd left on his bed. It was for his grandmother's eightieth birthday. He had to rush back quickly to be able to catch his flight, but he ran into Moro, an African new foreign student, who was sick with a high fever. Richard sacrificed his Thanksgiving trip to help Moro to an Urgent Care Clinic. As a show of gratitude,

Moro, who was a talented artist, presented Richard with a polished wooden portrait of him.

Seth wouldn't mince words to confess that his idea of expressing sentiments to his beloved Erika was a borrowed template from Moro, the sick lonely African student. The landmark of that incident had been a stamp on Richard's character. The towering reminder was once again reminding Seth that the actual roots of his sentimental paintings were by virtue of the outcome of Richard's kindness and caring nature. Even so, however egregious the disruption of his routine passion was, he shouldn't fail to see Richard's intent in a better light. Seth knew he had to go back to him. He also knew that his friend's persistent nature would drive him looking for Eloquenter's rhyme or riddle, and the recreational park posed a more plausible place of interest for Richard.

It took no time for Seth to arrive at the park. He assumed he would find Richard at the park by the bench where they discovered the famous rhyme and riddle. However, not all the benches on the park were occupied. His eyes caught a fleeting glance of a person who he assumed was his former student, chatting with an older lady. Not willing to be noticed, Seth artfully disappeared behind a small crowd that had gathered around a hotdogs peddler's stand. He heard a customer address the peddler "Lily" as they attempted their purchase. The name rang a bell. He recalled that the name "Lily" was in the riddle. Could she be the "Lily?"

Seth attempted hysterically to withdraw from the crowd to a quieter place and to make a call to Richard. Again, he felt he didn't look presentable enough to be seen and even be noticed by his former student. He hadn't shaved for a long time; looked very lean, and even with clean clothes, he still looked haggard. He was aware of his uninviting appearance and that had often translated into his coy demeanor. Seth turned and looked again in the direction of where he'd first observed his assumed ex-student in a chat with a lady. The student had parted with the lady and she stood there alone. Seth felt relieved. He tried to call Richard, but after hearing the fifth ring on the receiver's end, he hung up. An urge to talk to the hotdog seller began to brew in him. After some time, the customers dissipated to various directions on the park and Seth made his move to the hotdog stand.

"Miss, please is your name Lily? Do you live around here?" Seth inquired.

"Yes, my name is Lily, but I don't live around here; why do you ask?" Lily answered.

"My name is Seth and I'm looking for Lily. I'm told she lives around here."

"Whoever told you that is stupid. This is a park; no Lily lives on this park. Is she homeless or something – the house that is close to here is over there. I don't live around here. I don't know no Lily around here." Seth felt humiliated.

"Thank you." He turned to leave. After a few strides away from the hotdog stand, he heard Lily yelling him back.

"Heh! Come, come and have some hotdogs. It's on me." Seth didn't look back; he moved on. That hope on Lily had crushed him – had crushed the last vestiges of the self-worthiness in him. With feeble steps, and a sagged spirit, he walked on. On - to his yellow jalopy he walked. In that carriage, he sat. And to his home, he drove. There, his walls would re-echo the welcome voice of Erika. There, the axiom of Seth's heart was revealed. Erika lived there; she lived there with him, the queen of his domain. He believed.

On arrival, he walked straight to the far end of his kitchen to the table with the spread of various types of herbs. He began to carefully select certain types of herbs. He was well acquainted with the effect each herb had on him. He heaped a jar with his preferred roots which included his favorite, the red sap roots, and settled the jar on top of the mountain of books by his chair. The selected roots were the most potent of the lot in his collection.

Then he embarked on the venture that he'd often been attracted to but had shuddered away from - to chew all the potent roots. He believed he would benefit from each side of the result, cure him or kill him. A root at a time he began. The average length of the roots was two inches and in several minutes, he chewed five, only five for a desperate chewer. His jaws ached and his tongue, all sore.

He was still alive.

His phone rang, and he reluctantly got up and picked it up. Seth sounded like a person fighting hot food in his mouth. Indeed, his sorely tongue was hot, and it took the keen caller greater keener ears to identify the voice of Seth Nathan.

"Hello, Seth is that you?"

"Ye-e-ls, it's me."

"Hi, it's me, Apphia. Is Richard there with you? Can I speak with him?"

"No-ol. He-l is not he-e rel." Seth replied drowsily.

Apphia realized her futile effort to reach her husband – wherever he might be, and hung up. To avoid lateness for her appointment she had to talk to Richard to pick up Josh. She could not afford to blow the opportunity which her sister Febe was offering her. The appointment was so crucial that she would upbraid herself if she missed it. It was a favor from Febe.

CHAPTER 17

"Congratulations!" The doctor walked in confidently to break the news to Febe. Then she turned to Apphia with a more ecstatic greeting. "Well, well, well congratulations, Mrs. Bridges! Well, you can count on your sister's very healthy eggs for your treatment." She announced enthusiastically.

Her sales pitch to get Apphia excited about her fertility treatment paid off. Apphia in a grateful mood, hugged the doctor and her sister. The doctor proceeded then to basic preliminary questions. She explored her health lifestyle, about smoking and drinking, none of which were a regular indulgent. She also wanted to know if Apphia had experienced any premature ovarian failure or a recurrent miscarriage.

"Are you taking any medication to stimulate your ovaries to release eggs?"

"No." Apphia answered.

"Very well, we'll be good to go as soon as the sperm donation procedures are complete. By the way, do you still stand by the idea of keeping your husband out of the loop?"

"Yes, I do. I'm doing this for him; perhaps for us. I want him to hold his head up among my relatives who think he's not man enough because he's never been a biological father." Apphia tried to explain, but the doctor had determined from her answers that Apphia might be the problem, and that Apphia knew very well, and that actually drove her to the clinic.

"You know, it's a big thing if a woman is not biologically disposed to having babies. They have all sorts of names for her in a circle of Greek relatives and friends." Apphia maintained.

"Mrs. Bridges, it's my role professionally to let you know that you might not have to completely blame your husband. Seemingly, yours outweighs his, but that's why I'm here and I'll do everything possible to help you. I have a package prepared for you which the nurse will present to you before you leave. Please read them carefully before your next appointment."

Febe hadn't been happy about the discrete and deceitful intent of her sister. However, she found herself trapped in trying to please her sister who might interpret any cautionary counsel from her as unwillingness or reluctance to cooperate in her scheme. She'd always held her brother-in-law, Richard in high regard and it was agonizing for her to acknowledge a hand in Apphia's desperate indiscretion. The thought frightened her, but she didn't have the courage to confront her older sister.

It was about nine in the night and Apphia was still waiting to hear the garage door open. It would be music to her ears, but so far, it hadn't opened. There was no imaginary music for imaginary ears. Her husband was still not home. He hadn't returned any of her calls. It was a new agonizing experience for her. There had been occasions when Apphia had tried to reach her husband when he was in court and on all occasions he'd made a deliberate effort to reach her through his Administrative Assistant. This long silence was, therefore, very unusual. She wasn't sure if Richard was getting the calls at all. Then the frightening thought of being widowed crossed her mind. Josh heard her deep-drawn sigh and it prompted him to ask questions like any child would do.

"Mom, are you sad?"

"No, I'm not. What makes you think that?"

"You're very quiet and you're not talking to me." Josh's observation was an obvious indication of a prevailing somber atmosphere in the house. To suppress him from further questionings, Apphia decided to send him to bed. As Josh laid comfortably tucked in bed, he expected a story from his mother, but she was ready to retire to her room and to ponder over her fears. She'd never felt that way before.

"Mom, please tell me a story, Jesus story?"

"Do you know any Jesus story?" Apphia asked, having been surprised by the question.

"Yes. One day, a little boy went to see Jesus at the park, and there was plenty of people there and – and – there was no food, and the little boy gave his little food to Jesus and – and Jesus made the food become plenty, lots of food for everybody on the park. Everybody was full."

Apphia found herself applauding for the story, and then it struck her. How did Josh come by this story?

"Who told you this story, Josh?" Apphia asked.

"Andy. His Mom tells him the story every night, lots of Jesus stories. You want me tell you another one?" Josh asked rather excitedly, but for a boy being prepped for bed that was absurd.

"Yes, but you have to make it short. You must sleep. It's late far beyond your bed time."

"I will. Long time ago, very, very long time ago, before Jesus was born; there was a woman who lived far away. The woman had one son, but the boy's Daddy was dead and so every day it was hard for her to get food. So, what she did was go to a neighbor to ask for help and said that she would pay the neighbor back someday. One day, they didn't know what to do so, they knelt down and asked God to help them."

On impulse, Josh tossed off his bed covering, and tried to demonstrate to his mother how to kneel and pray.

"Mom, do you know how to kneel? This is what you do. You kneel, and you look up to heaven, that is where Jesus lives before, He came down, so you look up and ask him."

"Ask him what?" Impressed by her son's excitement about the story Apphia became curious. It seemed Josh had captured her attention.

"Ask him. Just ask him anything you want. You just talk to him when you look up to heaven. You just tell him in a nice way what you want. So, the boy and his mother, they were kneeling down and they looked up and they talked to Jesus. Mom guess what happened. Jesus sent somebody the next day. This is what happened, they had little flour and oil to make bread. Then a weak-looking and old man came and knocked on their door. That man also wanted food because he was also very hungry, so he begged them to let him have the bread when they finish baking it. Guess what."

"What?" Apphia asked, as a keen participant.

"They gave him their food." Josh replied with a yielding tone of a compliant benevolent.

"Why? They would go hungry." Apphia asked, testing her son's conviction.

"Yes they would, but you know what, Mom, the man, he looked old and was very weak and he might have died soon, but you see, the boy and his mother, they were young and not as weak, so they could wait a little bit more for some food somewhere. So, Mom, they just sat there and watched the old man eat their last bread. But guess what, when the man finished eating the food, he told them there would be plenty of food for them always and they would never be hungry again. Mom, that's just what happened. They always had lots of food and were never hungry again."

"Josh, that's a beautiful story. Now, did you say Andy told you the story?"

Josh nodded confidently. "Yes, you know Andy. Miss Brew says he's always shy. He's my friend. Tomorrow, I'll tell you about the little boy who played in the hot sun for a long time without drinking enough water. Do you know what happened?"

"No," Apphia conceded. "I promise I'll tell you Jesus story tomorrow night." She kissed her son good night, and quietly withdrew to her bedroom in pensive reflection over her 'good night' chat with her son. Apphia was beginning to see how she'd been depriving Josh's wholesome mind of the seeds of value which were usually nurtured by the peace and quietness of the night, when there was no corruptible sound of electronic violent toys and games of heroism, but the peaceful voice of nourishments from stories of virtue, love and kindness.

The night was still young, but to Apphia it had been a long night. She continued her wait in hope for her husband's call. Every minute was a reminder of her lonely night. Then the doorbell chimed. She flew down the stairs and peeped through the peephole. Richard was behind the door. Apphia opened the door hastily.

"I chose to park the car outside just for now. How's Josh?" Richard asked.

"Fine; must be sleeping now." Apphia replied. Richard threw his coat on the nearest couch and proceeded to the bathroom. He came out after a few minutes and settled in one of the dining chairs by its table. He looked weary and was quiet. Apphia perceived he was hungry. She hastily tried to assemble items together to warm up a meal for him.

"Apphia, I'm not hungry. It can wait till tomorrow."

"Richard, are you alright?" Apphia asked concernedly. Richard remained quiet – no response. He wished he could unload his mind and spread it before her, but that wouldn't help and neither would it improve the situation. His silence spoke volumes, particularly to Apphia. To her, it expostulated how their marriage had been a failure and how she'd been unproductive. The silence was questioning if she merited any right to be the mother of their child since she, a daughter of a gambling mother who knew not how to cradle her young. Who could stand this daughter of a woman whose breath every moment reeked of alcohol and smelled like chimney? "Could any good come from that home?" Silence screamed in Apphia's mind. A sense of low self-esteem began to cloud her perception and without subscribing to a second opinion, she uttered the words which got her husband's attention. She spoke softly.

"Richard, are you seeing another woman?" Richard wasn't sure if he heard her right.

"What did you say, Apphia?"

"I wanted to know if you're seeing another woman." She reiterated, softly.

"What?" Richard was in shock. He wondered what he'd done wrong to encourage an unwarranted question from his wife. He shook his head in disbelief.

The banes of life many times aren't as clear like a speeding arrow clearly sees its marked target. Richard thought, and no, it wasn't the arrow of Cupid. No, Richard wasn't a target.

He'd hoped to fly into the comforting arms of his wife, and even without glamour and fanfare, he'd expected the coddling cheer of 'honey, honey, honey' even while he was still failing to buzz a word of cheer to pining queen bee, Apphia. Weary Richard, craving for empathy after his day's futile expeditions, had ignorantly set a tone for coldness with his pointless silence.

He was still ignorant of the potential consequences that his silence had created. It had created room for huge conjecturing and doubts.

"Richard, do you think you waste words and time on me when you speak to me?" Apphia blurted out angrily. She felt it was time she proved she was not a walk-over. Her words had rendered her husband confused – more confused and frustrated than ever.

If he couldn't find peace in his own home where else would he find it? Richard hammered his left arm to the dining table and then followed it up with his forehead. It was painful but his frustration absorbed it.

The day's dreary events began to unfold in his mind's eye. He saw how he'd humiliated himself to the amusement of Evelyn as he fell off his office colleague's and friend, Phil's motorbike as an inexperienced bike rider, before getting the hang of it and riding off to Seth's house. He saw himself seeing Seth pointing the door to him as he was ordering him out. He saw himself at the beach alone, hoping his beach friend, Patrick would show up, but did not. He saw himself waiting in the office for Phil to return his car and while waiting Evelyn was trying to flirt with him and was almost tempted to kiss her when Phil showed up. He imagined that Phil had been watching them from a distance; he saw his moral vulnerability and believed Phil had seen it too. He imagined an eruption of a scandal that would mar his otherwise clean profile. Now his home, the haven he had longed to fly to, was also less cordial and according him with little or no warmth. Apphia had assertively questioned his coldness towards her.

"Richard – O – Richard what a failure you've been." His mind mocked him.

It was a banner headline on his forehead. If no one could read it, he, Richard could. He knew what he'd been through and what he found himself subscribing to, failure. The events had headlined it on his frontal billboard above his eye-brows, and perhaps that was what Apphia saw. She'd uncovered the mettle of his heroism and that her husband was simply a man like any other man with lots of flaws. She was questioning his choice to be silent, and Richard disdained the thinking that he was losing the influence he had among his friends and even, in his own home. His entitlement to be silent had even come into question. More deprecating was the scorn and contempt he'd received from Seth for Seth's disregard and lack of interest in him and his efforts to uncover the illness that killed Erika. Undeserved humiliation with unappreciated tendencies was mocking his selfless motive to save the life of his dying friend.

Richard had been an exciting legal drama persona to watch as he would often pull a legal trick up his sleeves. People loved him, not only for his courtroom drama and his mastery of the law, but also for his good-naturedness. The praises and accolades which had shaped him had also shackled him with a commitment to live up to that merit. Richard began to reflect and eventually opinioned, perhaps wrongly, that he'd tried to enact a performance of first aiding where and when actually there were no bruises or unwholesomeness for treatment. "Richard O – Richard, what is wrong with you?" He thought aloud. He was now a casualty of what he hated and dreaded, failure.

He'd won almost all his court cases, and those cases he knew he couldn't win, he gained out-of-court settlement. In a way he failed to make his case and to convince the one-man jury, Seth. Also, by his actions, he chose to abandon his despairing client by acceding to client Seth's request to leave. In fact, he fled; he thought. He left vanquished with emotional injuries.

Richard's action tended to support the axiom that endurance was often the test of man, and failure always lurks by in wait for any opportunity to test a person's endurance with a ploy of muffled emotions or with self-pitying. Richard was succumbing to his endurance test, the wile of perfectionism.

He got up and grabbed his jacket that he'd thrown on the couch, and with three long strides he was at the door, and out of his house. Apphia looked on with bewilderment. O what had come upon her Richard? She wondered. "What have I done to him? I have driven him out, but what did I do?" She introspected. Her hero was leaving - her. No later, she heard the car engine running. Richard was ready to leave into the darkness of a night supported by few street lights, to where it was described "anywhere." His haven would soon be behind him.

Suddenly, the voice of Apphia rang out by the door where she stood. First, it sounded like derision, and then it sounded like an appeal, the voice of emotion, different emotion, the emotion of guilt.

She began to see the reel of her day's events spin before her mind's eyes. She saw herself being congratulated by the doctor for a successful egg match, and also her sister, Febe as a donor. She saw the doctor correcting her that Richard wasn't to be blamed for their infertile results. She saw the anguish of unwillingness that countenanced Febe's face. She remembered her fright when she saw Phil, her husband's friend, arriving at the clinic in Richard's car, and was wondering why. She remembered Phil's explanation that he swapped his motorbike for it because of previous break-in attempts. She remembered Phil telling her at the clinic that he wouldn't be her sperm donor unless she first discussed the arrangement with her husband. In her disappointment, Apphia saw Phil driving off in Richard's car in a symbolic imagery of being the new potential single and being left in her own lurch.

The fear and shock from the scenes of her day's events did break the specter of her imaginations and ushered her into reality. Her man, Richard was still her hero, but a wounded hero. She had to bind his wounds and pour into his drained vial a new balm of courage perfumed with her love and support. If she failed in that, she'd failed her call to be a helpmate, and Richard had failed his call to recognize her needs and hear her cries.

"Richard, are you leaving because I, your wife, queried your actions? I didn't marry a man who couldn't endure the sharpness of truth. You reveal a weakness, Richard. You do. What are you fleeing from?"

The words assailed Richard like fiery stabs from a traitor. He'd heard them before.

"I don't expect anger from you, because you're gentle enough for that, but where is your will? Where is your zeal? What has crushed those bones of the Richard in you?" Apphia lamented.

"Perhaps it takes more than you, Richard; more than a physical will." Apphia's voice began to crack. "Don't leave, Richard, don't."

Richard allowed the engine to run as he looked up. He saw the agony in the eyes of the woman he'd always loved. He collapsed his head and shoulders on his steering wheel and broke down. While in his brokenness, a shadow lurked by furtively. It partially covered the driver's glass window. It tried to open the door. It couldn't. Then it spoke. "Daddy come home. We're waiting for you." The voice of Josh was above the sound of the engine and cut through the still night, and through the hearts of those under his voice.

CHAPTER 18

Richard noticed, as he walked into his office the next day, that the small plant that sat at the back of his desk was reclining against the wall as if it had been partially knocked off at its base on a small tool. It awoke his memory to the illustration he shared with Evelyn that a tilting object shouldn't be counted out until it hit the ground. The reminder spoke volumes to him, but he tried to shove it aside to address the compelling emails that had been waiting for him. He read a few, got up and headed straight to the breakroom for some coffee. He seldom drank coffee. He thought in that rare situation that the coffee that morning would be the instant panacea. On his way, he heard the ebullient and cheery voice of his admin, Sally. Her voice rang out with laughter while she was on the phone. She saw her boss and she hastily wound up her phone chat.

In a deliberate gesture of avoiding disturbing Sally on her call, he offered a passing greeting nod and paced with few strides into the break room. The brew was done, and he tried to pour himself a cup when Sally walked in. She observed that his hand was shaking as he tried to reach the pile of the Styrofoam cups, and in the process, knocked the pile off its weak holder. Richard was embarrassed at his clumsiness. He knew the night had taken a toll on him. He offered apologies and tried to clean his mess. Sally quickly stepped up and assumed the responsibility of clearing the mess her boss had created. Richard thanked her and walked back to his office. He barely sat down when his phone rang. It was a familiar voice.

"Hi Bridge, it's me, Seth."

"Hi Seth, what can I do for you?" Richard's reaction was formal with little enthusiasm.

".... To please, accept my apology. I was ungrateful. I need your forgiveness." Seth submitted with a sincere contrition that came clearly through his tone. The phone was silent at Richard's end. He was reflecting. He was hearing a very noisy background on Seth's end of the phone.

"My action was shameful." He continued. "You've always proved to me that you're a great guy. If I should die today, I would be at peace because, at least, I knew I made peace with you."

Seth's words did not sit well with Richard, but Richard suppressed his anxiety.

"Seth, where are you? Are you driving?"

"No, I'm not. Bridge, have you accepted my apology?" Seth appealed again.

Richard felt a sense of responsiveness towards his friend again. Strangely, an overwhelming intuitive concern descended upon him. He was discerning a foreboding from Seth's statement that despondent Seth might be contemplating suicide. In the light of that, Richard sensed that a conciliatory response might rather fulfill Seth's wish for a gratifying ending of his life. In a sense, Seth was in jeopardy and Richard was in a distant fortress.

"Seth, tell me where you are. I'm coming - for us to have breakfast together."

"Not here - where I am right now ..." Seth replied ambivalently.

"No, no, no, I'm bringing breakfast; I'm picking it on my way to you. I'll meet you at your house; just wait for me."

"Do you have to do this, Bridge?"

"Hey, don't worry about it. I will be there in no time. Just wait for me." Richard assured his friend and hung up. A calm composure settled on Richard. He knew he'd spoken to Seth and hadn't heard words and sounds from an illusion. The situation had availed him the opportunity to redeem himself after his previous empty and humiliating trip to Seth's house. He better not blew it; he thought. He checked his watch; he realized he had to act fast before a change of mind dawned on Seth. He picked his bag, forced it into the limited space of the second drawer of his desk, and locked it up. Richard looked up and saw the door before him. Before him, in akimbo between the door posts stood Evelyn.

"Richard, you're not leaving. Are you?"

"Yes, I am. Why?"

"You're not leaving me in the den to face the pack alone."

"What's going on?"

".… The damage control meeting at nine – The Palate Scandal – remember?" Evelyn squirmed interrogatively.

The reminder was very untimely for Richard. If he'd read his email, he would have been informed about the meeting, but he hadn't, and he wished he hadn't been reminded either. The information had set him between his employers, Milo, Grady and Strong and the sudden commitment to his friend, Seth.

"Palate International" the internationally famed consultancy of wine farmers and connoisseurs had been confronted with various allegations of intrigues, bribery and corruption. The allegations were loaded with nuances on varying bribery figures and stories of Palate International being rather the victim of blackmail. The stories were also fraught with hearsays, but they made interesting reading to a gossiping-happy public. Embarrassed by the daily changing rumors, Palate International, however, was yet to issue a statement to dispute or refute the allegations or to admit the company's indiscretions with any form of deep contrition. Nonetheless, news about Palate executives had surfaced again in the morning. Word had it that Palate had sommeliers at some restaurants and hotels that serve Palate interests by pushing some selected vintage that benefit Palate International.

Tough that the choice was, Richard knew that any form of derailment and delay would affect his pursuit to save Seth from hurting himself.

"What's the source?' Richard asked.

"I don't know. Milo flew in last night. I'm sure he'll share it at the meeting."

"Evelyn, you must know something. C'mon what's the story in the house? The stakes seem so high for the office if Milo had to fly in." Richard persisted.

"Richard, please read your emails. The story first broke out in Paris, a French newspaper. Honestly, Richard I don't know much about it as you do. I know one thing though; there will be wine tasting." Evelyn's remark brought a chuckle to his rather serious face.

"So, where is Milo?" he asked.

"Already in the den," her response belied her fear of being in the den without Richard. She'd earlier spoken with Mr. Milo on his way to the conference room which had come to be known as the den.

That conference room carried a stigma of hosting heated meetings. One of them was when a former employee, Daniel Stein challenged staff executives for allowing their political leanings to influence their judgments and lobby interests. Dan Stein was said to have singlehandedly "blasted" the executives – describing them as "starved lions waiting for innocent prey." Dan resigned and opened his own firm. In MGS circles this story had come to be known as "Daniel in the corporate's den."

Richard looked beyond his doorway past Evelyn and saw Mr. Milo on the phone in the den. He had to do something about the timing of the meeting. He brushed his way against Evelyn who stood there like she'd commandeered Richard's doorpost and nothing or nobody could pass by her without her consent but, Richard was in no mood for jokes.

"Where are you going, Mr. Bridges?"

"A courtesy 'excuse me' would do." Evelyn insinuated.

Richard smiled, and followed it up with a theatric wry grin, as he proceeded towards the den. Mr. Milo who had seen Richard approaching the den way, signaled him with a raise of a finger for a minute - more time on the phone. Richard acknowledged it with a nod, and after few seconds he had the chance to walk in. Milo wasn't long on his call.

"Well, son, how are you doing?"

"Very well, Mr. Milo." Richard replied confidently.

"Is the firm treating you well?"

"Very well, sir," he responded.

"By the way, don't forget the extraordinary meeting tonight." Richard wasn't sure he'd heard Mr. Milo right.

"Tonight, on the Palate scandal ...?" He asked with a welcome impulsive excitement.

"Yes, Bridges, tonight at nine ... But I wouldn't call it 'scandal.' You know better than that, son. We call it 'News, The Palate News.' Is the meeting conflicting with other plans?" Milo admonished Richard and subtly queried his other priorities but, Palate News.

"No, no sir." Richard stuttered. Apparently, the welcome revelation of the correct meeting time by Milo, rather immediately took the wind out of his sail. Having been wrongly informed by Evelyn, he didn't anticipate any information that would make his trip to Milo at the Den relevant. Richard had to find a way to justify his mission or to simply suggest a postponement of the Palate morning meeting, to a more feasible evening session that would favorably accommodate his plans to handle Seth's issue.

He had to rewind his agenda for this unplanned meeting with Milo. For, to unrealistically walk all the way to simply say "Hi" suggested the style of a sucker. The absence of any official matter for discussion with Mr. Milo would make him, Richard a grand member of suckers. He had to grapple with an explanation or come up with a relevant speedily conjectured subject of discussion, otherwise the general perception of his action would simply be a suck-up move, and that would be Milo's version as well, he thought.

Richard, in principle frowned on any seeming practice of sucking up.

"Well, Mr. Milo, I hold a different view on tonight's meeting at nine. I have been thinking about it all this morning." Richard submitted a necessary lie.

"Well, sit down, sit down, and tell me what you think." Milo beckoned him excitedly.

Obediently, Richard pulled a chair and sat down. He looked perceptibly into the face of the intently-listening Mr. Milo and saw the weight of his presumptuous action. He saw that his attempt to counter Milo's prescheduled meeting time with his more selfishly inclined, but feasible time was a risky venture.

"Mr. Milo, I must concede that I haven't read the entire story about the news on the Palate International, but so far from what I have read, the alleged incidents make interesting reading for those who want to label the stories as scandals. In the light of this, any of the publics associated with Palate or the interests of Palate will also be under close scrutiny. In fact, they may fall under more stringent scrutiny than Palate International and its holdings, because these observers may speculate that Palate may wisely disperse their operations. We represent the interests of Palate so we mustn't be surprised at the press watching our every move, who goes in and who comes out. I believe the plan to hold our meeting at nine tonight may suggest a clandestine motive which may rather fuel the already conflagrant rumors, lies, perceptions and gossips. Mr. Milo, to meet as late as nine tonight may validate the question; 'what are they hiding?'."

"Huh son, I tell you, you may be right." Mr. Milo was impressed. "You know, the nine pm choice is solely for the wine tasting after the meeting, just like they say, 'wine at nine.' But, the task on hand clearly is more important. What time do you have in mind then?"

Richard saw his opportunity. "Well, I'm being careful to suggest tomorrow evening at four." He was treading softly; aptly floundering.

"Why not today?" In a raised voice, Milo portrayed his disappointment. Richard, however, didn't cower to Milo's vehemence of expression. He'd come too far to waver.

"Sir, if we have to issue a statement for Palate, or let's say, if Palate has to issue a statement, it must reflect the broad stand of the Association of Connoisseurs, and also any recognized body of the Sommeliers, and we are yet to hear from them." Richard commanded the moment in a vivid display of the quality that distinguished him as a smart lawyer, and Milo saw himself with a flawed perception about the whole Palate International saga.

"Very well, four tomorrow evening, it is. I'll send the word out. Bridges, stay in touch." Milo, a little fazed by Richard's superior wits, signed off the discussion and hurriedly dismissed Richard.

Evelyn saw the flying strides of Richard's long legs breeze across the hallway while she silently hoped she would get a word from him, but he was gone. His sudden and hasty departure from the office had left her intrusively wondering where her mentor was heading. She walked to Sally and tried to siphon Richard's itinerary from her.

"Did Richard make lunch appointment reservations?"

"Yes, he did." Sally replied.

"Where?" Evelyn persisted.

"Here... It will be delivered by his wife, Apphia " Sally evened up with Evelyn, her wits.

Richard arrived at Seth's house an hour and a half late. His discussion with Mr. Milo about the Palate International scandal and his effort to purchase the breakfast on the way had impeded his original plan which would have saved him about an hour. He walked straight into the yard and was immediately struck by the changes in the house. The flowers in the various pots hadn't been tended to and were dying. Few were already dead. Seth's water works fountain wasn't functioning, and what seemed to be a lagoon, where the dispensing waters ended up had dried up or had been seemingly emptied. The house looked abandoned. "Se-e-eth, Se-e-eth," Richard called out. No response emerged from the house.

He quietly tried to scout the house looking for any opening that would clearly convey his voice distinctly to his friend, if Seth were locked in. The blinds were closed, and the bedroom window revealed a tattered drape. Richard walked back and approached the front door. He discovered a note and with trembling hands, pulled it, and read it. His face alloyed with uncertainty dropped as he hurried back to his car. He drove slowly around the block with the hope of finding a neighbor who might be acquainted with Seth. After few futile rounds Richard turned to make his way back home, and then his phone rang. The caller was Seth.

"Bridge, I'm here at the ducks park. I waited for over an hour. I thought you couldn't make it." Richard felt relieved to hear Seth's voice again.

"Seth, I'm here at your house."

"I thought you would be. Please, come to the duck park. I'll be here – about a block distance from the hotdogs stand."

Richard drove off; with a hopeful thought that Seth might have abandoned his fiendish scheme about hurting himself for there was nothing to detect and no trace of emotionalism in Seth's voice. Richard hung on to that hope as he approached the vicinity of the duck park.

It was a chilly day and the cold air was partly the reason for the sparse turn up at the park. Nonetheless, few people still roamed the walkways under the trees. Richard passed by the hotdog stand which as usual was surrounded by its avid customers. His eyes were everywhere. In the distance, he saw another group of people; perhaps surrounding another peddler and he hoped Seth might be among them. As Richard drew closer, he sensed the temperament of the crowd; it was embroiled in a commotion. He decided to keep away knowing from experience that Seth would rather avoid the crowd for fear of infecting others with his health condition. Then Richard heard the words: "Somebody please call 911." He sensed a dire emergency situation was unfolding, and that was enough to plug him in - in the emergency affair of a life. He edged closer - drawn by an unrelenting spirit that was challenging his conscience.

It was a spectacle, he beheld it, and it held him in shock.

Richard's wobbling legs became restless as he slowly dropped his weakening knees to the partially graveled and lawny grounds of the park. The sight was a thin man – a very thin man. His partial gray beard covered the bony jaws that had helped shape a very skeletal face of an unkempt hairy head. He lay weak on the grass exposing an arm hairy with mingled rashes and sore. Touching him posed infection risk. Richard's scream stunned the concerned crowd.

"O he knew him." Somebody thought aloud in the crowd.

Richard knelt and lowered his right arm under the back of the upper frame of Seth's shoulders to access leverage for the purpose of carrying him. He successfully elevated his ailing friend's upper frame. The sleeves of his shirt and coat were muddied in the process. With his feeble strength, Seth turned to see the face of the owner of the arms clutching under him. He saw the panic in Richard's eyes; Richard saw the agony of emotional pain in the dim glow of his friend's eyes. Seth opened his dry mouth; it stank, but Richard carried a deodorizing zeal.

"Seth, look at me. You'll be okay. Open your mouth again." Richard administered the water which was part of the breakfast he'd brought with him. Seth swallowed the small gulp in his mouth. Richard repeated the water and Seth swallowed it again.

"Bridge, they've called …the Ambulance. I don't want to die in a hospital. Please take me to my house. I want to die in the studio." Seth appealed to his friend.

"Seth, don't talk about death." Richard countered.

"Please, Bridge; it's my wish, perhaps, my last wish. Will you please do it for me?"

"Yes, I'll take you home." Richard got hold of Seth's keys from his pocket. "Yes, I'll take you home." He repeated.

The anxious crowd could hear the siren in the distance and Seth could hear it too, but with disenchantment.

"Please I can help." A voice declared over the shoulders of Richard.

"Mr. Nathan, it's me, Miguel – the school team – basketball – remember?"

Seth turned in response and acknowledged the voice with a smile. He knew him well. He used to call him "Mig." He remembered him as his former student, the student who was stabbed by his girlfriend's brother, but he also knew him for his singing. The incident of Miguel's injury flashed through his mind and Seth acknowledged Miguel again with a smile.

"Take care, Mig." He said softly.

To meet Seth's request, Richard had to act fast to avoid the paramedics. He tried to fetch his car keys out of his pocket, but with difficulty as it was a one-hand effort. Miguel noticed his struggle but wondered what Seth's helper's noble intent was. He offered to help, for his car was closer.

"I'm parked right over there. We can take him by my car." Miguel offered, and ran to his car. Then Richard got on both knees and lifted his friend into his arms. As he carried him, the weight of the six-foot, lean and thin frame of his helpless friend, dangling down in his arms dictated a tottering emotional walk towards Miguel's car.

Richard's arms were firm. Bloodied by the brown mud and the ruddy gravel, he showed the sheer pride and the dignity in defying white color with a brazen desire to support life, embrace life, and define life with imaginable sacrifice. His wet eyes had no blinkers, but with each tottering step, he followed the straight path towards Miguel's car in honor of his dying friend's will.

The surrounding crowd made way. Their eyes filed straightly after them through the milky, smoggy strip that led to Miguel's car. The closer view was becoming a distant sight of a skeletal figure in the arms of valor. The park stood still. Hearts were moved. The thoughts of the observers froze to a shivery melancholy, and their lips quivered for lack of words to express their emotions. They were witnessing the poetic truth of the human spirit unfold.

The car sped off to ironically escape the approaching help, help from trained medics.

Richard quickly scribbled out his house directions as Mig continued to drive. A few blocks away, Richard eventually adjusted his left shoulder for Seth's slumped weight to rest on it. A fly hummed past Richard's ear and he missed his attempt to swat it down. Incidentally, something caught his eye. He noticed some familiar papers by the hind compartment of the car. He knew he'd seen those papers before. Miguel smiled, for he also knew what had captured his unflinching attention.

"Have we met before?" Richard directed his question to Miguel.

"Yes, we have. I am Eloquenter." Richard stretched his neck in a wide-eyed stare of incredulity at the voice behind the wheel. Also, in a sharp reflexive response, Seth grunted in disbelief, but silently he mused about Mig. Is Eloquenter a myth or a hyped figment?

Richard was even more curious.

Upon arriving at Richard's house, Richard advised Miguel to stay with Seth who had been sleeping the whole way, while he went to prepare a room for their ailing sleeping friend. Miguel became aware that he'd involuntarily conscripted himself to the task of caring for Seth. However, unlike Miguel, Richard had his hurdles to clear.

Richard knew that the idea to host Seth would be hard sell to his wife. Apphia had her sincere legitimate concerns. Josh, their son had been experiencing some sporadic appearances of rashes on his skin, and same could be said of Apphia. Although Apphia had been assured that their experiences weren't a direct cause by bacteria or virus, she felt Richard's judgment was foolhardy; he'd ostracized himself from reality.

"Richard, we all love Seth. You know that, but I think this time you've gone too far." Apphia's voice bewailed the position her husband had placed them in, and to say "no" would portray her as the inconsiderate one.

"Apphia, I went to his house, it looked abandoned. Seth might stay in that house and might be a neglected corpse for weeks without discovery. You and I might live with that guilt. It's the least we can do for him."

"Have you thought of any quarantining steps?" Apphia inquired.

"… Plenty ... Seth will use the guest master bedroom down here with its private bathroom. As long as he's surrounded by his paintings of Erika, he's fine."

Apphia took that in with a pinch of salt. Nonetheless, she got to work to clean the guest room and reformat the furniture arrangements to accommodate Seth's condition and movements. Richard returned, gave Apphia's car keys to Miguel, having contrived with him to drive to Seth's house and to return with all Erika paintings. Miguel left while Seth was still sleeping in the car.

Eventually after few rounds, Richard returned and found Apphia's car parked outside. Miguel had made it back. He met Richard by the driveway and winked at him.

"Seth, wake up." Richard shook and woke him up into a different surrounding. He showed his surprise, but upon seeing Apphia he knew where he was. He smiled. The trio, Richard, Apphia and Eloquenter Miguel smiled back. Slowly, Seth got to his new room. His imaginary Erika-Erika-on-the-wall was waiting for him. He turned around and opened his milky, salivary partially dry mouth. His words were hardly audible but were loud in the hearts of the trio; they heard him. Miguel returned to his car and before Richard realized it, he was gone.

"He's quite a guy." Richard admitted.

"He says you are - quite a guy." Apphia redirected the compliment and smiled.

"It takes Apphia to make Richard quite a guy." Richard remarked with a cheerer admiration. They looked into each other's eyes; they saw their hearts; they heard the throbbing as they inched their lips towards each other.

Seth observed the romantic moment and knew he was in a different home.

CHAPTER 19

Apphia couldn't believe what she was hearing, the sound of unusual whistling. It was a merry melody, and it wasn't from their neighbor's yard, and neither was it from her backyard. She followed the sound and traced it to their guest room. Seth wasn't the sole whistler. Miguel, also known as Eloquenter, Seth's former student and new-found friend, was with him and was also bellowing his lungs through the aperture of his contracted scarred lips. They weren't making great music, but they were a delight to hear for sheer amusement.

Seth had been a guest of the Bridges for three days and Apphia had observed how he'd looked forward to Eloquenter's visit each day. Even more striking to Apphia was the change she'd begun to see in the condition of Seth. She wouldn't want to rush to the perception that Seth's improvement was by and large, due to Eloquenter's great influence on him. The thought was relieving, but it drove Apphia to wonder even more the wand that Eloquenter had been waving. As she held the flyer that Eloquenter had presented her, she sought to uncover that glitter of fascination about the rhyme riddle on the flyer, having heard various intriguing interpretations of it. To her it was sheer exuberance of a youth trying to play on words. "Intriguing" that it was, she thought by reading it contemplatively, she might discover some valence in Eloquenter's words. Ironically, she chose to read it loudly.

"What's for sure

Is what is pure

It's not a lure

To what you endure

An herb for cure

Without procedure

And that's for sure"

What is good

May be crude

It's good food

In Lily's hood

Just a hen's hood

Over its brood

A nook so secure

So right for nurture"

There was silence. The loud reading had hushed whistling Seth and Eloquenter. Eloquenter emerged from the door after listening to Apphia as she read his riddle. He approached her smiling and couldn't hold back his compliment.

"Mrs. Bridges, I wrote this rhyme, but I haven't heard anybody deliver it that well with such feeling. You almost revealed its meaning. Do you understand it?"

"No, not quite, I try to let it make sense to me, but unfortunately – well, not yet."

"Your answer isn't strange to me. Many things don't make sense to us, but we accept them as they are." Eloquenter submitted.

"Like what – we accept things for what they are, their value." Apphia re-echoed the claim.

"You're right. Like the air we breathe, we don't know where it comes from, it has no color, no form, no identity, we don't even see it, but we breathe it in to keep us alive."

"So, what are you saying?" Apphia asked.

"Mrs. Bridges, I'm saying, we inhale that into our system, although we have no idea where it comes from. It has no color, no identity, and it isn't visible, yet we trust what we're breathing in is the right thing, and receiving the right inhalant. Please, allow me to say that there are things we do daily which are simply based on blind trust. Everyone has a level of belief ingrained in oneself;

no one, absolutely no one, can claim to have no belief in anything."

Apphia angled her head to her left shoulder in expression of her measured approval of Eloquenter's claim. "That's a profound statement to make. I'm not sure; a lot of people may disagree with you," Apphia remarked.

"But, do you?" Eloquenter asked firmly.

"I'm am not sure." Apphia replied.

"Please, Mrs. Bridges let me explain myself. Every deliberate action by a person is dictated by the anticipated result from that action. In other words, we drink to quench a thirst. Our belief in the result of getting our thirst quenched drove us to drink the water. Even so is the air we breathe."

"Well, we need the air." She remarked and Eloquenter continued.

"Yes we do, and need makes us to rely on what we need. And it's like wishing to receive the needed item or like wondering how to get the needed item. It implies that the item or the needed provision has to come from a source or party that has the item or knows how to produce the item."

"So, Eloquenter, again, what are you saying, what am I hearing?"

"I'm saying, there must be something that we don't necessarily need evidence of - smell, color, shape and tangibility's before we trust in it. And I'm also saying that there must be a provider who we may not see but still have to trust to provide us with the right provisions that meet our need. If we can trust his provision for what is pure, we can trust his goodness for sure. That provider must be someone who loves us; we must know his love and we'll understand him even more. If he made us, he must love us. Love drives a person to create what the person loves."

Elo's explanation had challenged Apphia's thinking. Initially, she'd considered that the riddle, as a whole, was replete with many abstracts and had maintained it would offer a very difficult interpretation attempt. A change of heart was beginning to form in her and had begun to wonder the food for thought Eloquenter was trying to serve. Elo felt obliged to give a flicker of hint on the riddle.

"Mrs. Bridges, the riddle simply discusses an aspect of life. Mr. Nathan told me something remarkable about you and your husband. He told me how the two of you risked your health to take care of him, disregarding how infectious his condition could be. You gave him a ride in your yellow car and you made him feel loved. Mr. Nathan still remembers the muffin and 'Mommy and Sonny.' You see, Mrs. Bridges that was blind trust. You cared despite the risk of infection. This is a story best described as a story of faith and selflessness. Mrs. Bridges, you've written a story on the tablets of Mr. Nathan's heart." Apphia was quiet. Eloquenter had stirred her heart. She watched him as he walked to the door.

"I must be leaving. I pray I have the opportunity to see you again."

As Seth also watched him leave, he turned his attention to Apphia. He had no regrets for touting the impressions the Bridges had made on him.

"Apphia, I haven't had the opportunity to formally thank you. I'm healing. I know that and I'm very grateful to you and Bridge." Seth turned to walk back to his room. Few days ago, he was allowing his ill health to roll back his tide of confidence. The strength in his voice was sagging to a level of timidity, especially on occasions when he approached the crest-fallen face of Apphia. He hardly chatted with her, but in the presence of Richard, his confidence would often resurge. Seth had marked each day with a desire to return to his house which used to be his parents' property. Home would always be home, and he knew he wouldn't feel the sense of limitations that had shadowed his stay with the Bridges. Lost in his thoughts about this yearning, he heard Apphia calling him.

"Seth, I do see your improvement, what is helping you?" She asked rather calmly. She noticed the quirk of hopefulness that was beginning to thread through his social tapestry. She could no longer hide her own struggles from her husband's friend. She had a warped idea of herself and had always felt very insecure. If Seth was healing, he needed to share with her the healing balm he'd discovered. After all, she still carried with her the rashes which the doctors had pronounced non-contagious. She loathed her own invented thinking that her skin rashes were contributing to her child bearing failure, but she was gradually beginning to disclaim her strange theory.

Seth grappled for answers to Apphia's single question. He thought hard.

"Apphia, would you believe me or believe it if I told you?" Seth asked and he received an absolute 'yes' response from her.

"I've been a teacher, but I've found myself being taught by my student. Is it condescending? Of course not, he knows something I don't know. As the student, or this time, as the person in need, my condition must render me humble; if it doesn't then my needy condition may render me the opposite effect, bitter. My choice is to get well so, I chose to be a humble student. I'm sure you always see Eloquenter's scarred lips; they're healed wounds that left him scars from his street life. We all have scars. His are very visible, but others carry their non-visible scars which can only be noticed by others from their actions. I learned from Eloquenter that I was carrying a scar from the wounds from Erika's death. If my ,wounds aren't visible, then I must perhaps need a non-visible treatment. He said I needed to clean my mind by feeding it with

pure positive thoughts, love, kindness and humility –
acknowledging always that there are people greater than me, and
that every person has need of God."

Apphia listened thoughtfully. She wondered if she also carried
a scar. Perhaps not, she thought. Then it dawned on her that if she
had need, then she might have been carrying an unhealed wound
and as a deprived person, she might have been walking about with
that scar unknowingly. She remembered the years of feeling
unloved by her parents. The memory immediately threw her into
a state of cautious bewilderment. She wanted to hear more.

"So, what treatment has he been giving you?" She asked.

"I guess none yet, until I'm ready for it. In his metaphor, I'm
still drinking milk. The time to eat meat is yet to arrive. He brings
me just for the day each day's reading material which has to do
with a story of hope. He calls it a Daily Devotional

"Elo said there was an ancient army commander for the ancient
king of Syria. His name was Naaman. However, apart from the
many war victories that Naaman had brought for the King of
Syria, Naaman found himself in a fight he was not winning. He
became a leper and his condition worsened. Among the servants
that served in his house was a Jewish slave girl. Out of concern
about her master's leprous condition, the girl audaciously
suggested to her master, General Naaman. She said she believed
that the General could be healed if he went and met a prophet in

Israel called Elisha who was a man of God. The girl believed that the man of God would intercede in prayers for her master Naaman. 'What does a slave girl know?' Naaman might have questioned the idea, but he swallowed his pride and went.

"As a dignitary from the powerful Syrian kingdom, Naaman was expecting a protocol that would herald his arrival and be accorded with a special welcome by the prophet. However, while Naaman stood at the door of the prophet with his chariots and horses, the prophet refused to come out to meet him, and chose to send a messenger to convey to Naaman, a very simple instruction: 'Go and wash seven times in the River Jordan.' Naaman was furious. He felt insulted and humiliated, for many reasons. The prophet didn't treat him with respect for failing to come out to welcome him. The prophet didn't perform any chanting or magical ritual as he'd expected. Naaman felt his plight wasn't taken seriously and to be told to go and wash in the rather muddy and perhaps dirty Jordan River was absurd, and nonsensical. He felt scorned and insulted so he turned and returned to Syria very furious.

On his return, Naaman's servants approached him again and encouraged him to follow what the prophet had instructed him to do. They even questioned his judgement for it was rather easier to bath in the Jordan seven times than to be levied with untold rituals and strange sacrifices which might be harder requests. Naaman swallowed his pride, listened to his servants, and washed in the

Jordan River seven times as Prophet Elisha the man of God had earlier instructed him to do. Upon the seventh attempt of washing himself in the Jordan, Naaman's skin or leprous flesh was completely healed and the skin was restored to a skin of a child.

"Apphia, this true story from the Bible like many others gives me hope. I'm sure you can infer multiple lessons from it. His advice is that I must engage my mind with true stories of sincere goodness and love. I've been reading the story in my quiet time at night before going to bed, and that has been giving me a measure of nightly peace before going to bed. Let me ask you, beyond the reach of human help, who will you reach out to?"

Apphia pondered over the question and what she had heard. How would a daily practice of story reading, simply make a woman fertile? She wondered, and in her confused limbo, she remembered the words 'blind trust,' and 'humble student.'

"Seth, please tell me, what did you read last night before going to bed?" Apphia solicited in a tone uncharacteristic of her matter-of-fact stance. Notably, she sounded submissively interested.

Seth offered her the reading material so that she could read the story directly from the piece. Upon that suggestion, Seth attempted to leave for Eloquenter's story, but Apphia called him back. Her preference was to hear the narrative from Seth.

"You may not understand; I think I need to hear it. I need the narration by a physical voice. You may choose to read it or simply narrate what you've read."

"Apphia, may I suggest, since Eloquenter insisted on the aspect of nightly reading, that I narrate or read it for you tonight, hopefully Bridge will be here to hear it too."

Night came and Seth sat by the reading lamp that Apphia had moved from Richard's home office room. She looked comfortable on the couch which was at a good hearing distance from Seth. She was slouching under the dim light, an opportune moment for good old sleep, but she was determined to hear the story. She watched him observe few seconds of silence, and then adjusted the paper he was holding. He'd barely started to read the story when he decided to rather narrate it. "By the way, this story, what I am about to tell you is not a true story but it's a story that teaches about life's lessons. It's like a parable.

"Life was very normal in the house of Albert, Betty and their daughter, Carol. Albert loved Betty dearly and he showed it. He brought her flowers very often and Betty never stopped complimenting Albert about his goodness and what a wonderful man he was. Carol eventually picked up this wonderful trait of her parents.

With time, David, an exceptional young man, decided to propose to Carol. The engagement went well and few months later, they were married. As it was, Albert and Betty had to share their nest alone without Carol. Carol and David lived about seven miles away from them and they kept in touch with regular visits.

"One afternoon, while Betty was cooking, she heard a knock on her door. She realized it didn't sound like a familiar knock. She left the kitchen and rushed to the door. Behind the door were two men wearing the very noticeable firemen uniform of the town.

"'Mom Betty, I'm sure you heard about the fire on the hill which is travelling fast to our homes. It's consumed some farms and produce. Some of the men who have been on the frontlines include your husband, Albert. I'm afraid they were overtaken by the fire. Their injuries are serious. The county hospital and their good doctors are doing all they can to save them. Please your prayers and all the townsfolk are needed to save Albert and the rest of the crew.'

"Betty was devastated. She abandoned the cooking and began to pray. She waited each day for news about her husband Albert and the other injured men because the men had to stay in the hospital for weeks and were not allowed visitors for fear of getting infected. Eventually, Albert's health improved, but sadly he was confined home and could not work anymore.

"Betty knew how to sew so she began a business of clothing alterations for the townsfolk. However, because the economy of the town was bad, her small business suffered. Life became hard. Daily subsistence was hard to come by and quite often Betty had to seek help from Carol and David. Albert aged fast; the condition also took a toll on his health. It became a practice for Betty to call upon her daughter's family frequent evenings for help – something she was very reluctant to do. There had been days she felt they would rather go hungry than make the long seven-mile walking trip to her daughter's. Was that a wise choice? Well, Betty could hear the stomach of her ailing husband groaning and she knew she might have to do something. She remembered a Bible story about how a starving nation was saved by four starving lepers. She also remembered the resolve of the lepers that if they just stayed there and did nothing, they would die anyway, so they would rather do something and believed in God to mercifully help them.

"Soon, Betty found herself ready for the seven-mile trip, but just when she was about to leave, she heard the loud clatter beating on their zinc roof. It was pouring rain - cats and dogs. Betty had been feeling very weak from hunger, so to make the trip became an actual challenge. Her mind was flooded with imaginations that came with her reluctance, fear, and uncertain outcome. What if she were attacked on the way by a strange animal or person? What if something happened to her beloved Albert in her absence? O surely the rain was a clear shadow of a predictable fruitless venture. These thoughts and many others stormed Betty's mind. What did she do?

"Well, with her hand still on the door knob, right by where her Albert hanged his coats, she turned and found his raincoat; it was good enough to help her make it through the rain. She saw the sad look in Albert's eyes and summoned courage. She grabbed his raincoat, and challenging the doubts on her mind, stepped out into the dark rainy night. Soon, she began to feel the chilly winds from the rain, but she had only covered one mile. The lightning didn't cease from flashing and Betty became very afraid. She realized that she had to walk faster because that would help him to warm up. Immediately she started to speed up her pace, 'ouu-ch' her right foot hit a hard stone on the rocky ground, 'ouu-ch'. The pain was very severe, especially as she was already feeling cold. Betty realized she was bleeding from the bruise, a sharp cut on her toe.

"'O I knew it, I knew it. That's why I shouldn't have made this trip in the first place. I could have waited.' Betty blamed herself and lamented tearfully. However, she felt a moral obligation to move that entrenched stone from the pathway. In her pain in the rain, very drenched that she was, she stooped to move that sharp and firmly entrenched stone to clear the path so that it wouldn't be of further harm to others. Betty continued to shake the dirty wicked stone off its hold in the soil until she finally got it out. Just then, the thunder flashed another ferocious lightning. Perhaps it was a sharp piece of broken bottle that had bruised her foot, she thought. O - How she wished she could deal with whoever was responsible for the broken piece of wickedness that she now held in her hand as the rain continued to pour. As Betty was about to throw it into the rough, a sharp blinding effect from the lightning struck her eyes again. Betty became still; struck by lightning? Oh no! Albert might not be able to handle this. Betty had just been struck by a lightning of providence. Her eyes were glowing. "O – no – no – no," she held her heart. Her hand was trembling. She was not feeling the pain in the rain. She was feeling the weight of the piece she was holding in her hand. She looked at it again as the pouring rain continued to wash off the dirt that covered the object in her hand. It was a piece of diamond. Her hands held the most expensive material she'd ever held, a very expensive diamond. Instantly, her pain was gone. The excitement had driven it away. Strength had replaced weakness and hope had replaced despair. Nonetheless, it came with the goodwill of selflessness, the heart to intentionally prevent others from the injury she suffered. What a remarkable lesson! She could not wait. Betty run back home to share the news with her Albert.

"Sometimes the hunger, the rain, the injury, the hurt and the pain, they suggest the nature of the road for the journey - from a nervous Worryland to a sure Cheeryville. It depends on the traveler. It's anybody's story. Think about it. You have a story, because you're still travelling."

Apphia heaved a sigh of delight and got up.

"Do you have more stories?" She craved.

"Remember, it's a story a night. Good night, Apphia."

CHAPTER 20

The lights were up in the home of the Bridges, and dusk had also emerged in the offices of Milo, Grady and Strong Law Firm. There was excitement in the air, but Richard was in no-hurry to get to the Palate International damage control meeting. Few had already assembled in the den, "the Daniel Stein's den," and the lively chattering behind the glass door periodically escaped out of its confinement as the glass door opened and closed with the traffic flow of the damage control elite meeting members. A roar of deep-throated laughter greeted a joke shared by Mr. Shazzy Spicer, the Vice President for Marketing Affairs of Palace International. It was clear that an aura of revelry was beginning to build up even without a spill or a drop from the vine yet.

An unoccupied chair was notifying the group of a missing member. The missing member was Richard and he barely made it in to hear Mr. Milo call the meeting to order. Richard had compiled a folder-full material which oddly, unlike the rest of the group he discretely brought with him. Mr. Milo formerly introduced Shazzy Spicer to the meeting who further went on to address the session. He extoled the values of wine and touted proudly the health benefits of wine.

"Folks, it shouldn't surprise you that Christians agree that the first miracle performed by Jesus was to turn water into wine.

Don't underestimate the providential attributes to wine." Spicer's attempt to make comical facial expressions while making his remarks got the room laughing loud except for Richard and Phil.

"Is anybody here who is a teetotaler?" Spicer asked.

"Some of us are, Mr. Spicer." Phil admitted.

"O, Poor-Some-Of-You," Spicer derided. "By the way, call me Shazzy. I don't do 'mister', please." Shazzy's remark aroused laughter again. "A glass of wine every night, just a glass, supports a healthy heart, prevention and protection against any grave sickness, and also fosters stronger bones; not forgetting of course, that it makes the heart merry. Don't get me wrong, we all know - that too much of everything is bad, so drinking wine must also be in moderation. However, your 'moderation' may be different from my 'moderation.' That very much depends on the individual."

Shazzy spoke for twenty minutes without addressing the very reason for the meeting, the Palate Scandal. The tedium of his unsolicited exposé on the subjectivity of a person's drinking capacity was beginning to take its toll in the room. Mr. Milo's mental countdown to the wine tasting moment seemed impatiently endless, especially because it was crucial that the damage control discussions assume its prominence over the wine tasting moment. Milo deliberately checked his time ostentatiously to subtly hint Shazzy Spicer on the essence of time for the Law Firm and Spicer discerned the hint.

"Ladies and gentlemen, I'm sure you all know why we're meeting here this late afternoon. I must state that all the allegations labeled against Palate are all false. Palate isn't different from any corporate institution. She endeavors to find creative ways to reward her hardworking personnel and even go a step further to reward and encourage allied institutions that support her commitment to excellence and to ensure that our wines taste good for successful business – nothing short of that. The people at the frontlines of our successes are the sommeliers who rightly recommend brands that they find highly recommendable. These brands in many cases happened to be brands sealed by Palate International."

Spicer's excitement was beginning to dictate his choice of words.

"We aren't (expletive) cheap and will never condescend to any (expletive) cheap stuff. We endorse the best wines, and the world knows that."

He checked his watch. He realized he'd given little room to discussing the response of his company's scandal. It was vital that the meeting heard the full story that sparked the scandal, but he had said very little so far.

"I'd like to invite Mrs. Bruna Dhahl, a seasoned Sommelier to discuss their business operations with Palate International."

Mrs. Dhahl, a brown-haired beautiful sommelier walked in to a courtesy applause from the group. She bowed to the lively audience and introduced herself as a former Portuguese, who had been living as an American citizen for twenty years and had been Sommeliering for five years. Bruna explained that as a Sommelier, she had a very sound knowledge about various types and regions of wines. She said it was her responsibility to help the customers choose the right wine for their meal. She'd also worked with executive chefs; from whom she acquired her extra mastery in wine and food pairing. Bruna articulated her resume with much pride.

"I try to keep up with current trends in the general culinary industry. I must say, however, that my forte is in the wines or the liquor."

Bruna's eyes travelled on many occasions to the corner where Phil was sitting. Phil knew he was listening to a speaker who wanted to flirt, however, he remained expressionless to dissuade her overtures. He also knew that he had been listening to a woman who was not only a good speaker but an adept sommelier.

"Before we start our first round of wine tasting which, of course, will come with some training, the looming question is Palate International's relationship with Sommeliers."

Milo responded with an approval grin, and he looked around the room to see if his staff shared his position. Bruna heaved deeply and allowed a great smile to assume the countenance on her face.

"Someone once said that the difference between a sommelier and a connoisseur is: 'You discuss wine with a connoisseur. They know wine, but they may not know what they like.'"

Bruna's use of voice inflection to highlight her phrase "but they may not know what they like" was an attempt to jokingly mock the connoisseur profession. She achieved it, for she drew laughter from the group. Shazzy Spicer laughed as well, projecting his tongue out to taunt Bruna.

"Regarding a sommelier, 'you buy wine from a sommelier. They know wine, and they will help you find what you like.' In other words, a connoisseur is like a Family Practice physician and a sommelier is like the Specialist Physician, who has specialized in a particular medical field. To put it simply, the connoisseur tells you it's a good and tasty wine; the sommelier will tell you: for your money, or for the choice of food, or for the particular feeling that you desire, like a simple good feeling or if for aphrodisiacal whim, then go for this. Basically, this describes the relationship that exists between Palate and sommeliers."

When Bruna was about to take her seat, a lady wheeled in a tray full of wine glasses and was followed by another lady with a cart of vintage cocktails. Excitement filled the air and a grand applause greeted the arrival of the seeming mobile bar. Everyone except Richard and Phil held up an empty wine glass while they waited for the wine. Evelyn, who was two-seats away from Richard, held up her empty glass and jokingly made a distant wave at him with it. He smiled and lowered his head as Bruna was about to announce the birth of mirth.

"Now this is the fun part," she continued, "Mr. Spicer and I will take some questions from you, after this vintage break. In the cheery time, note that I didn't say in the 'mean' time, because this is not a time for 'meanness,' I will be showing you the simple art of tasting wine. You need to get this preliminary run with these wines before we practice the art on the real thing; I mean the grand stuff and very soon you'll know why."

Bruna assumed her place behind the white-linen draped table that hosted two of the wines which were wheeled in earlier. She uncorked a bottle and invited the attention of the room. "The wine industry dates back several years, ancient times, if I could say about 4000 BC. The industry has grown since then from animal skin containers to bottles. Grapes dictate the quality of the wine, but the quality of the grapes to a greater degree depends on the soil condition, the weather, and how the vines are pruned during the seasons."

Known for her experience as a teacher, who had educated clients on the merits of different wines and vintages, Bruna Dahl was able to captivate her audience with her mastery on the subject. Milo looked keener, but somehow he was beginning to question the prominence of wine history over the wine tasting and the drafting of the response intended to refute the unsavory allegations against Palate. Milo was getting jittery in his chair.

"Ladies and gentlemen, I'm going through the trouble to tell you this because wine has its own world and culture, and wine making involves an elaborate process, and if the process isn't handled well, the result could be dangerously disappointing. Imagine being at a restaurant and you are handed a twenty-page plus book full of wines and you don't know what to do or what you want. It, therefore, means you have to explore the world of wine. Do you want the old world wine or the new world wine?"

Bruna eventually sensed that her audience was growing weary of listening to her lecture on wine. She ordered the bottles to be distributed and each member had one.

"We're going to apply the four "I's" principles, and these are, Identify, Inhale or sniff, Imbibe and Indicate your Impression. Okay, for the start, pour yourself a wine and swirl it, swirl the wine in the glass to aid you identify or look at the wine - for many different reasons. The color tells you a lot about what you have in the glass. If the color is purple or ruby red it suggests that it's a very young wine. If it is garnet, it means that wine has some age to it. I call it maturing; wine undergoes certain organic changes as it ages. Now, after swirling it, you inhale it in; this is very important, if not the most important. There are hundreds of different aromas identified in wine so you must know what you're buying and what you'll be drinking. Your next step is to sip it, to taste it."

Bruna invited the group to watch her approach. She cast a glance at Phil and saw him smiling during the entire session. Richard had stepped out and was chatting on his cellphone. Periodically, he turned back to see if the tasting event was over.

"This is the next "I" principle." Bruna continued.

"Imbibe a bit of the wine, about a teaspoonful or about a teaspoonful and a half. Escort the wine all around your mouth; while the wine is in your mouth; briefly draw in a bit of air, swallow and exhale. Please, follow me." Bruna demonstrated the principle with a smile and waited for everyone to practice her example.

"Now the last principle, indicate your impression that is the evaluation of the tasting – the after-taste evaluations on your palate. Now, relax and evaluate your impression with the wine you've just kissed."

The room broke into loud applause for Mrs. Bruna Dahl. She bowed and left the room while the applause followed her. Milo announced that the meeting would reconvene in thirty minutes and counseled the group to keep a sober head for the pending session and he exited the den, the "Daniel Stein's den."

Evelyn joined Richard by the conference room corridor.

"You missed a lot, Richard. Relax a little." Evelyn teased.

"I do. I do have fun – not necessarily with wine."

"Did you realize there was no drama? We have to debunk that myth about 'Dan Stein's den.' Tell me why you don't drink."

"I will tell you – someday. Someday, I will and I promise you that."

Evelyn sensed the undertone of his seriousness and decided to veer the direction of the discussion to something else that she was struggling to come up with.

The thirty-minute recess flew by and all the members of the Palate scandal response team reassembled in keeping with the directive of Mr. Milo, the Senior Partner of Milo, Grady and Strong law firm. The usual feeling of light-heartedness that prevailed in the earlier meeting was missing, but there were few jokes that went around about the bottle of wine that each member received. Milo's counsel for sober headedness had rather lapsed into an uncongenial boredom. They'd been waiting for Milo,

Shazzy Spicer, and Bruna Dhahl, the key figures in the discussion. Evelyn decided to leave briefly, but immediately settled back in her chair when Spicer and Milo walked in. They entered without Bruna.

"Ladies and gentlemen we would like to apologize for this unforeseen delay." Shazzy went on to hype the tenor of the second wine tasting, and also announced some changes that they had made in other to expedite the evening discussion. The wine tasting would be for everyone, but Shazzy decided that the Palate discussion must be limited to a group of three, and Mr. Milo as an observer. Milo was the obvious choice to choose who would constitute his panel to discuss the Palate scandal. Many cheered the decision as it offered an opportunity to leave after the wine tasting session.

Milo was all smiles as he joked about those who wanted to leave early. "They just wanted to flee from Dan's den. I know, I know, but miracles happen in the den you know. The lions keep their mouths' shut."

Laughter filled the air once again; Milo had unlocked the cheery atmosphere.

"Mrs. Dhahl does not need any introduction." Milo continued. "Ladies and gentlemen, I give you Bruna Dhahl."

Then the lights went low and some colored lights emerged at the corners of the room to depict a sophisticated evening atmosphere. Bruna gaited her way into the conference room with majesty. She looked elegantly resplendent. She'd changed and donned on a black sleeveless evening gown and an expensive-looking necklace to complement her looks. The lights also accentuated the shimmering glitz in Bruna's outfit. A duo sound of keyboard and jazz percussionist played to fill the air.

The setting was once upon a time, an official conference room; it had evolved into a mini banquet hall. The illusionary transformation of the office room into the reality of an evening entertainment hall was a lighting designer's feat.

"I guess, you guys, and especially Mr. Phil Sawyer, assumed you've gotten rid of me, didn't you?" Bruna joked. "Well, I'm still here. Check your time. It's six pm. The night has not been birthed yet. Let us, however, talk about something which was birthed years ago – I mean years ago."

Phil listened intently. He'd been wondering why Bruna had been singling him out as the sideliner character of the jokes. He didn't like to be mentioned in the jokes, but ironically he was enjoying it. Phil felt he represented a paradox; a teetotaler sitting and waiting with others for a wine to be served. He turned to catch a glimpse of Richard's disposition. Their eyes met in a simultaneous glancing attempt.

"It was believed that in the 1870's during the presidency of Rutherford B. Hayes, a temperance movement, an advocacy group urged his office to ban alcohol from the White House. President Hayes being a very temperate drinker himself, supported by his wife Lucy, decided to drop wine and alcohol from their White House menu. The prohibition didn't last long."

Bruna turned her introductory remarks into a comical act. Without words she allowed her body language and funny mannerisms to show her disgust for the prohibition act. There wasn't a dull moment with her. They liked her.

"One of the wine brands that survived the ban and was later found in the White House menu was Medoc Bordeaux, a Jeffersonian era wine, a favorite of Thomas Jefferson. Boy, Prex Tee Jay liked his MB." Bruna got them laughing again.

"History had it that it was until 1919 that eventually the general prohibition of hard liquor became effective. During this time a White House butler was able to preserve some of the give-away banned drinks. Among them was one of the rare Jefferson's favorite. Guess what, because of its age and the worn off labelling, they named it Medoc la Grande." The audience listened keenly as Bruna continued.

"I tell you what, an eighteenth century Medoc La Grande is still in the land of the living. We're talking about two hundred years ago. Currently, this museum-worthy bottle of wine is priced at three hundred and fifty thousand dollars."

Phil couldn't contain his surprise and his audible reaction of "what" was heard beyond his seat area. Bruna smiled as she re-echoed Phil's "what" reaction to affirm her claim to charisma and as a seasoned sommelier and lively presenter. Then she began to walk back and forth through the seating spaces within the conference room like an inspector. The lights in the room suddenly went dim as silence fell in the room for a suspenseful but apt attention. The room waited impatiently for unending seconds of silence. Then Bruna intoned loudly.

"Ladies and Gentlemen, please stand for the oldest and living Medoc La Grande!"

Like the pageantry at a coronation, the sound of fanfare bellowed from the pipes of the keyboard. Lighting effects greeted the air while Bruna was positioning herself to receive from the two elegantly dressed men, decked in French Napoleonic military Uniforms, who were carrying aloft a bottle of wine, beribboned in gold, marched slowly and steadily towards her. Upon seeing the men, Bruna began a recital of appellations for the approaching priced wine.

"All Hail the survivor of the years, the vintage from the finest vine, the juice that makes the heart merry, that makes our bones strong, that makes a man the man, and the woman the lush and plush of the eye, O that which carries the cure to survive, and the will to heal and to live; behold the nineteenth century Medoc La Gra-a-nd-e-e." An ovation received the pricey wine. The conference room electronic screen lit up with clips of fireworks and celebration became the sinew of the moment, not the issue of a dreary scandal.

Richard assumed that the first round of wining was a welcome decoy to sway their minds off the vagary of Palate International. The second wining of the heralded Medoc La Grande would be good enough to seal their swayed senses to revel the moment, their moment with the nineteenth century Medoc La Grande and not the officialdoms of legal chaperoning.

Bruna relished the revelry. Richard hated it.

Bruna went around between the tables serving a spoonful of the priced intoxicant to each ready glass in the room. Richard was the lonely soul in the crowd. He found himself like a strayed lamb surrounded by a pack of wolves. His eyes scanned every nook and cranny for his fellow teetotaler, Phil. Richard found him. He had a smile on his face, a ready glass, and sommelier Bruna waiting on her. Phil had broken the solidarity. Richard was lonelier.

Bruna reassumed her position behind the white-draped table at the front and proposed a toast to "all who want the best out of life, the cure for their brokenness." She toasted: "Drink for a merry heart, and the tenacity to survive." All drank cheerfully except the perceived obstinate anti-social being, Richard. Bruna implored them to keep their glasses as souvenirs while they gradually filed out, high-fiving one another for the privileged participation.

Six faces stayed behind which included, Shazzy Spicer and Bruna Dhahl, representing Palate interests; Milo and three MGS staff, including Richard Bridges. These constituted the deliberating crew. After introductory exchanges Milo requested Spicer and Bruna to avail the panel with any information worth divulging to the panel. Spicer shook his head with a vehement "No."

"Gentlemen, we don't intend to hold a press conference on this issue. We simply want to address the allegations, and refute them as strongly as possible." Spicer remarked and went on to distribute copies of the Palate story press clippings to the panel. They were clippings from two different newspapers and one from a sommelier journal. The panel took few minutes to acquaint themselves with the Palate clippings and Milo opened the floor for the discussion.

"Mr. Spicer, I'm sure you're granting us the laxity to explore the best means to truthfully address these allegations."

"Yes." Shazzy Spicer replied.

"Very well, as a lawyer I must have to tell you that we can't address these without finding some answers from both of you."

"What do you mean?" Spicer asked nervously.

"I mean, we may have some questions for you – it's not like a taped deposition or sworn statements from you, but you must be very truthful to us so that we can construct a sound and clean navigational rout to the heart of your publics and the general public - for you." Milo assured him.

Spicer looked at his watch and declared nervously, "If it won't take long."

"No, I assure you, it won't." Richard hated Spicer's arrogance and impudently charged the throes of his pride. "May we start with you Mr. Spicer?" Richard asked.

"Yes, and you may call me Shazzy. It will make your work easier."

"Thank you. Shazzy, how long have you been acquainted with Mrs. Bruna Dhahl?"

"Why do you ask? This has nothing to do with the Palate allegations." he asked rudely.

"There are mega-reasons that explain your attitude to avoid these questions, and that is what the press and the public are waiting for. And if you don't tell us, they're going to tear you up in pieces to find out."

"How dare you talk to me like that?" Shazzy retorted.

"How dare you jeopardize the employees of Palate International by allowing your arrogance to destroy the livelihood of those who cherished the employ of Palate International?"

Milo was shocked to see the fury in Richard's eyes. He wasn't happy with Richard's attitude to a favored client. He was about to address the meeting with an open Richard rebuke when Richard got up and charged towards the window.

"Shazzy," Richard called firmly, "for your eyes only, come and see."

Shazzy compliantly got up and joined him at the window. To his surprise, they could count four media news vans packed outside. "What do they want from us?" Shazzy's lament aroused interest and it pulled the rest of the panel to join them at the window. Milo rushed from the room to suggest to the lingering staff in the offices to keep the office front doors shut. He was told they had been shut thirty minutes ago upon the advice of Richard. So, Milo returned to join the group with a mildly late reprimand and a measured compliment for Richard.

"Mr. Milo, I suggested we had to wait for you before we continue with the deliberations. Please, may we now continue?" Richard indicated.

"Yes, yes, we may, and thanks Richard for addressing the media invasion of the office."Shazzy Spicer looked subdued, but he tried to not yield to the pressure of Richard Bridges' assertive questioning approach, especially in the presence of Bruna Dhahl. Shazzy's ego was supreme. No one dared touch it, but Bridges dared.

"Shazzy, I'll rephrase the question. When did you first get acquainted with Bruna Dhahl, simply how long?"

"I'm not sure." Shazzy's response was unsatisfactory.

"I'm sure we can give you time, about a minute or two, to think about it." Richard weighed in with a generous but compelling offer. Bruna was very uncomfortable and her blush mirrored her feelings. Milo appreciated Richard, but the two minutes of silence was a sheer effrontery of score-settling with Shazzy Spicer. Milo surmised. Eventually Bruna stepped in.

"I can tell you if you want me to."

"O, yes you can if he wants you to, but you aren't a Palate employee." Richard advised.

"I'll tell you." Spicer eventually gave up. "We met about six years ago."

"Thank you, Shazzy. Bruna wasn't a sommelier then, was she?"

"No, and how did you know?" Shazzy asked angrily.

"Bruna just told us when she introduced herself; that she had been Sommeliering for five years." Donald Dent a panel member and employee of the MGS firm stepped in with a prompt answer. "Shazzy, we're here for you. You're paying us for that. You must cooperate with us. You're the patient; we are the surgeons, and if you don't allow us to take out the outgrowing tissue, then you don't need us."

"Thank you Donny." Richard resumed his questioning. "Shazzy, with this line of questioning, we're attempting to establish a sound explanation to confute the argument raised in this report that Bruna Dahl particularly receives some payments from you. You'll be surprised how much dirt is circulating out there. It's in your interest, Bruna's interest and Palate's interest that we have these answers. Please as surgeons per se, we may have to cut out any tissue of false claims. Your overt defiance bespeaks undivulged information."

Evelyn had chosen to wait for the outcome of the meeting. That driven curiosity couldn't penetrate the closed blinds of Dan's den. From her viewing point in the shared office with Richard, Evelyn could only speculate the spirit of the discussion by the kinetic activity which the partial thin lines between the blinds in the Daniel's den continued to reveal. The panel heard a knock on the door and Donny Dent opened it to admit in Evelyn who had come to provide a much-needed cold water to the group. Evelyn had schemed her way in. She didn't discover much, but was struck by the contrast between the sunny Bruna Dhahl and the now frosty Bruna. Where had the glow gone? Much had to do with the answers being sought from them. Spicer had to cooperate.

"Mr. Spicer, sorry, I should have addressed you Shazzy. Have you at any time paid any Sommelier?"

"Yes." Shazzy admitted.

"Who did you pay – the name?" Richard pressed.

"Bruna Dhahl, our spokesperson for Palate International."

"You did or Palate did?"

"I did – on behalf of Palate." Shazzy answered nervously.

"Mr. Spicer, from whose coffers, your personal coffers or Palate's; were you using to pay Mrs. Dhahl?" Richard demanded.

"Palate's – does it really matter?" Shazzy Spicer's anger was beginning to build up again. Richard, however, ignored his temperament.

"Please, could we take a look at a copy of Palate's pay vouchers for Bruna?"

"Unfortunately, I don't have any with me now."

"Could you request your office to fax us a copy?"

"Not tonight, of course ….. I will try some other time."

Richard cast an interrogative glance at Bruna to prospect a comment from her. Bruna was silent and looked timid. Richard was frustrated and so was his panel; he turned to face his colleagues. Upon Donald Dent's nod, the panel walked out to discuss the limited options they had from what they'd gathered so far. Donald led the way and as Richard was closing the door behind them, he caught a wink from Bruna.

Shazzy Spicer sat expressionless in a deep pensive mood. He turned to look at Bruna; but she turned spitefully and looked away. Bruna jerked her chair backwards and tried to get up to escape the presence of Shazzy Spicer. Shazzy got hold of Bruna's wrist to restrain her attempt to leave, but Bruna jostled forcefully to set her arm free.

"Where do you think you're going?" he asked her angrily.

"To the Ladies room – Why, do you want to follow me there, too?"

Bruna pulled away to set herself free from the overbearing, physically intimidating presence of Mr. Spicer and proceeded towards the Ladies room which was outside the office suite, located behind the bank of elevators of the floor. Shazzy's eyes followed Bruna as she exited the office suite of Milo, Grady and Strong law firm. As she was about to enter the ladies area of the bathroom, Mr. Milo was exiting from the Men's bathroom area. They exchanged surprised glances at each other and they moved on. However, just as Milo was about to key his access to the suite, Bruna called him and discreetly handed him a card which she requested him kindly to pass it on to Richard.

"I assure you, I will tell him everything he needs to know. I'll call him. He shouldn't call me. The card will simply help him to recognize the caller, and that will be me, please give it to him." Then Bruna vanished into the Ladies room.

Milo accessed the office and found the rest of his team waiting for him. Shortly after, there was a feeble knocking on the office main front door. It was Bruna, without access to the suite. Evelyn helped her in as Shazzy looked on from the "Daniel's Den" conference room in anticipation of the return of Bruna to the meeting. Looking worn out from the day's events, Mr. Milo went on to adjourn the discussion for the following morning.

It had been an eventful day. The wine tasting had happened; no statement from Palate International was issued; the pageantry of the expensive Jeffersonian Medoc La Grande - was celebrated, seen, and tasted; Shazzy Spicer - quite a character; his sophistry was very pronounced; but who was Mrs. Bruna Dhahl, the lively, beautiful, sophisticated, glamorous sommelier speaker? Richard took a good look again at the card stuck between his left fingers as he drove home. Eventually, his car pulled onto his driveway. He still had the card between his fingers; it bore the name Terri Bach. "If your wine has the potential to provide cure for various illnesses, then Terri Bach, here I come."

CHAPTER 21

Richard didn't discuss the day's events of his office with his wife. Seth was already in bed. He'd improved tremendously. Eloquenter's regular visits and the literature with stories of hope continued to endear the hearts of Seth and Apphia as well. That night, Eloquenter had earlier shared with them how his day had gone. Apphia had also heard the story of hope about Albert and Betty. Richard, who hadn't been around during the night story session had allowed his curiosity to consume his imagination of the Lily in the riddle, perhaps an unknown Mother Teresa.

Apphia, however, noticed that her husband hadn't changed into his regular home clothes. She'd particularly longed for quiet time with him and to share with him the hope story of Alberta and Betty. She'd derived a measure of hope that one day, fate will heal her years of emptiness and insecurities. Then she heard Richard's cellphone ring. She perceived that Richard had been waiting for that call. The caller was Terri Bach.

"I'll tell you more about this call later." Richard intimated to his wife and withdrew to his home office-room. With the door opened, Apphia who was overhearing her husband's remarks was quietly apprehensive as she watched him from the distant living room. Meanwhile, Richard identified the voice. It was Mrs. Bruna Dhahl's.

"Hello, Mrs. Dhahl! This is Bridges."

"Hello, Mr. Bridges – I'm sorry for calling at this late hour. I want to speak with you – alone."

"Why would you want to, Mrs. Dhahl?"

"In the first place, I'm not married, not widowed and Dhahl isn't my real name. It's my sommelier name. Please, just call me Bruna."

"The voice sounds like the Bruna I heard at the office this evening. How could I validate the voice with the face?"

"I was coming to that. I want to meet with you. Suggest a place, I will come over."

"Mrs. Dhahl, I'm sorry." Richard apologized for calling her by her defunct name.

"Bruna, in principle, I can't leave my family alone at this late…." Then Bruna cut in.

"I understand, but I'm begging you. You need to know this. It could be ugly for me."

"Are you alone?" Richard asked with a concerned tone.

"Yes – I am alone."

"Are you being followed?"

"No."

"Is someone else on the phone?"

"Yes, my sister, but she isn't listening. She had to get a temporal phone registered under Terri Bach to conference the three-way call."

"You aren't in danger, are you?" Richard asked concernedly.

"Right now, I'm not, but I may be if I don't act. It's not only for me, but all sommeliers endorsed by Palate."

"If she's not eavesdropping, I mean your sister, how will she hang up when the call is over?" Richard was very skeptical.

"When we both hang up, a sound will notify the last party on the phone."

Richard wasn't convinced, but he perceived something sinister might be lurking behind the actions of Shazzy Spicer. He wouldn't want to be drawn into the private lives of clients of the firm; however, a feeling of moral obligation to assist Bruna continued to invade his conscience.

Richard returned to the living room and was received by Apphia's anxious eyes. "Richard, I want to go with you." Apphia offered.

"No, Apphia, it's my work. What's your fear?" Richard queried.

"I have a feeling you'll need me. I'm being prudent." Apphia replied revealing her pessimism.

Richard kissed his wife and in no time, was driving out. As planned with Bruna, he drove to a suggested house and parked his car in a garage that began to open upon the sighting of his car; the very garage began to close behind him before his attempt to turn his engine off.

Bruna stood by the inner garage door to welcome Richard. Her home commanded the bearings of an upper middle-class in an upscale neighborhood. The luxuriant front lawn with its lively flower garden would beckon the weary feet and the burdened heart. At night, it still commanded its daylight charm due to great and effective outdoor lighting work. It was a haven of rest for Bruna Dhahl who needed to sometimes, flee the wine balconies, and the dining corridors of loose chatter and vagaries. For Richard, he'd found himself not only within the walls of opulence, but also figuratively an echo chamber of voices of muzzled sommeliers. Her vintage collection was remarkable. He thought. They were quite a spread on one side of the walls.

"How was your drive, Mr. Bridges?"

"Fine, the traffic is normally light at this time of the day or night, perhaps."

They laughed off Richard's play on words and Bruna gestured for him to settle in the nearest couch. Bruna chose another couch positioned by the shoulder of Richard's. She'd changed into a less-glamorous wear.

"What can I offer you to drink? I know you don't drink. I do have here, few non-intoxicants – apple juice, grape juice – may be?"

"Water, please without ice," Richard's eyes began to travel around the room. He saw Bruna in a graduation picture on the wall. There were few other guests in the picture including assumed parents of Bruna.

She took no time to return with Richard's water. It was partially cold, just the right temperature. It was past ten in the night; Richard was eager to hear her, but so far Bruna had said nothing.

"Is your sister here?" Richard eventually led out with a tepid question.

"No, I live here alone. I made the call from her house."

"Now, tell me what you wanted to say, but couldn't tell me on the phone."

"Mr. Bridges, you must know this and must believe me. Shazzy always introduces me to people as Mrs. Dhahl to convey the impression that I'm a married woman, but I'm not. It is his way to keep men away from me."

"What is your relationship with him – mistress kind of…?" Richard was blunt.

"That's the suspicion he makes people create and the impression he makes people form of me. That's insulting if indeed I am a 'Mrs. Dhahl' but no - no intimate contact - none."

"I don't believe you. If you want my help, then be forthright honest."

"You must believe me, please. I try to flirt during my presentations so that I can have a relationship. Shazzy always chases my friends away from me, even girl-friends."

"Why does he do that – jealousy?"

"Not exactly, but about – about …." Bruna became emotional.

"You must tell me if you want me to help you. What is it?" Richard pressed her.

"About the payments to sommeliers …. Shazzy has sommeliers that push his wine, Linvin Rouge, and I coordinate the network. Twice I decided to back out and he threatened me. He's suspicious of anyone close to me, and afraid - that anybody close to me may eventually find out. He always portrays me as a married woman. My life is miserable."

"He pays you well."

"Yes, he does."

"From whose coffers – his or Palate's"

"I think Palate's," Bruna expressed timidly.

"What intimidates you about him?"

Bruna was quiet. She was tongue-tied and Richard empathized with her.

"Is he holding you to ransom about something?" Bruna fretted at the word 'ransom' and tried to suppress her tendency of deep sighing that had earlier characterized her demeanor during the questioning of Shazzy Spicer by the panel in the conference room.

"I don't know. I'm not sure."

"What are you not sure about?"

"Why he does what he does"

"You agreed Shazzy pays you well, who else is paying you?"

"No-one." Bruna answered confidently.

"Does Palate know about this?"

"I suspect one executive. He may know – I'm not sure. But I don't know what he knows."

"Please, let me see any of these, a check stub, a ledger, pay stub, receipt or any document that reflects a payment you've received. One will be fine."

"Give me a minute." Bruna withdrew to her bedroom for the document. Shortly after, a loud exchange of words erupted in her immediate neighbor's backyard. It soon turned into a loud sound of violence, then a scream and the sound of breaking glass – a window, perhaps they thought. Bruna rushed back in fear and clung onto Richard on the couch. He was equally startled by the loud violent noise from the neighbor's.

"That's rather unusual. Sometimes I hear them in verbal fights, but this seems to have gone too far." Then she got up, and walked, almost crouching to the floor, towards a window In a stooping posture, she began to furtively peep through the small aperture of her living room window behind the blinds. "Mr. Bridges, please, turn off that switch." Bruna commanded hysterically, pointing to the switch, and Richard involuntarily obeyed. The result was immediate darkness in the living room except the outside lights and the night lamp that led to her garage entrance. This incidental darkness inside Bruna's house augured well for her peeping Tom operation.

"What's going on?" Richard asked.

"I know they fight, but it's never been anything like this…"

"Bruna, if you don't want to be a witness, I'd advise you to step away from that window." Upon Richard's advice, Bruna stepped away from the window and retired to join him in the living room.

"Could I bring you the documents tomorrow?" Bruna asked, and Richard consented due to the prevailing circumstances that they had to deal with.

"It will make our work easier. It will be for your good, and for the good of the sommeliers and Palate International." Richard remarked with an assuring smile. He got up, picked up his car keys, but then froze in bewilderment. He'd just seen sudden flashes of red and blue lights. They'd plagued the streets like a swarm of fireflies. The spinning piercing blue and red rays had alarmed every house on the block and Richard watched dejectedly as police officers began to cordon the entire area. He turned sharply to look away, revealing his frustration and disappointment, and dropped back onto the couch. He reached his cellphone, called his wife, Apphia and explained his sorry plight.

A loud knock on the door instantly sent colder apprehensions from the outside commotion to the room. They were alarmed. Richard tiptoed to the door. With his eyes on the brass pinhole he saw arms-drawn police officers behind the door. He realized he had to speedily open the door before any attempt by the police to kick it open. The officers entered and their eyes landed on fear-gripped Bruna. After hastily explaining their intrusion as a necessary step in a pursuit of a fugitive, the officers left, marooning Richard and his client in a perfect pool of idling environment.

Richard checked his watch again; he perceived it would be a long night for him.

"I hope you're not getting bored."

"Honestly, I am." Richard admitted.

"Well, that's my world. Shazzy drives away my friends - I spend my nights at restaurants and just come home to rest – perhaps with a little wine."

"Tell me Bruna, that story about the three hundred and something thousand dollars wine, is it really true or a marketing ploy?"

"Mr. Bridges, it's true. It's a rare vintage and it commands all the benefits one gets from wine." Bruna declared with a convincing pitch. The response triggered yet another exploratory prying from Richard. He remembered the acclaimed healing benefits and thought of Seth, but Richard wouldn't be that gullible. His pride imposed its stature over any gullible claims. Too smart - he simply would not fall for that.

"Do you still have the wine?" He asked.

"Yes I do," Bruna admitted. "I'll bring it out if you promise me you'll handle it with care." Richard raised his right hand in a nonverbal accession to Bruna's request. Bruna got up and tried to navigate her way around the center table and eventually towards her bedroom where she'd been keeping the highly-priced wine.

The bedroom night-lamp was enough to shine her path to the drawers of the dresser with that discreet cache. The bottom drawers which were the third drawers, harbored drawer spaces below them which had been obscured by the external downward extension of a well-designed base molding that deceived the eye of existing drawer space below the visible third level drawers. Visibly there were no front external features like ball handles to betray the existence of fourth drawers. Thus, one could only access the fourth drawer per the third drawer.

Bruna gently pulled her third drawer out. It displayed her fill of underwear, some with the price tags still on them. She then reached out to the base level, the subtle fourth drawer and picked up the Jeffersonian Medoc La Grande, like a mother would pick up her little one from her crib, into her arms. She returned to Richard, covering the wine with her robe partially wrapped around it. To unveil the wine would by default, unveil what she had under the robe. Bruna played coy and kept a few feet away in respectful admission of Richard's gentleness and respect. With her back turned against him, she brought out the aged wine and presented it to him.

There wasn't much he could unravel, for the dark living room was being served by a thin ray of light from a night lamp. The wine still carried its vestiges of age, the dusty bottle with a strange corking. Upon noticing the dust, Richard tried to wipe it off, but Bruna restrained him with a gentle deterring slap on his hand. The slap surprised him. He looked up at her face and met a shy, remorseful but playful smile. Wondering how to make up for her uncivil treatment to her gentle guest, Bruna took Richard's hand and playfully kissed it. "It won't hurt anymore," she comforted him.

The act evoked in Richard a childlike feeling of being comfortable around her and felt ushered into a playful moment without conservative boundaries. While he contemplated on why he was feeling that way, Bruna, who had been kneeling on their shared couch, noticed his instant pensiveness. She smiled again to purposely ease the grind for him.

"Permit it to wear its gray hair; it's the mark of its age." Bruna joked about the dusty surface of the wine bottle. To Richard, Bruna's loyal servility to the wine was more of a comical gusto than a display of sheer fanaticism. Richard burst out laughing at her comment while he watched her stroke the celebrated bottle gently. And she laughed loud in chorus with him.

"Do you want a taste?" Bruna asked while looking for glasses in her kitchen.

"Nope!" Richard's response was sharp and firm.

"Why not? You have all to gain, your heart-health, great anti-oxidants and many more."

"I drink grape juice." Richard countered.

"Well, Mr. Bridges…"

"You can call me Richard." He suggested as the moment dictated informalities.

"Richard, do you ever wonder why many people drink wine? Doesn't it surprise you that this bottle I'm holding costs more than a home?" Bruna persisted with her argument.

"Well, that's the irony of it. Have you finished the mortgage payments on this house?" Richard laughed. He was impressed by Bruna's attempt to persuade him to appreciate wine. "Don't you think you can sell this to make payments on your house?"

Bruna shook her head softly in sympathetic disagreement. With the glass in her left hand and the wine in the other, she drew closer, almost in his face.

"Richard, O – Richard you sound like the few I know. There are things of more value in this world than a house. Your health, the peace of mind, even life – these are priceless. My dear Richard, when I drink wine, I imagine all these benefits."

Bruna's words set Richard thinking. A wrestling between philanthropy and principles ensued on his mind, and Bruna perceived his dissonance. It was written all over him. Bruna poured for herself a measure of the expensive wine, and went through the routine of swirling the wine in the glass and following it up by tasting it. She turned her head and with a charm of brow-raising smile invited him again to drink with her.

The possibilities he'd heard from Bruna about wine had stoked the zeal in him to help his friend, Seth. He was convinced that fate had led him into Bruna's circle, and fate had drafted him into the Palate International image rebuilding team. He imagined Apphia holding her first baby in a hospital's Delivery Room, he envisaged a happier Apphia with her head up among her relatives. He saw himself playing basketball again together with Seth. He smiled and Bruna handed him a glass. She poured the wine into Richard's glass and held his hand to aid him swirl it, and finally, they toasted to their friendship. Bruna re-sipped her wine; Richard tasted his. It was a taste of his incertitude.

"Congratulations! You've done it. It didn't bite you, did it?" Richard laughed at Bruna's congratulatory joke. He emptied his glass and looked up at Bruna with a sense of accomplishment. She poured herself another round of wine and did it rather delicately. Her argument about the healing qualities of wine had impressed Richard and he found himself reluctantly compelled to ask Bruna for a take-away in a small bottle or container. Very-willing, Bruna got up and began singing and dancing her way to the kitchen.

Richard liked what he was seeing. He was seeing a happy lady holding the tips of her partially lifted robe, tapped and stomped the floor, whirling and swirling her body in rhythmic movement from shoulders to knees. She sang beautifully in Portuguese, but not a word was understood by Richard. He caught the word "obrigado," and she explained it meant "thank you." Richard liked what he was seeing. Bruna returned, obviously very happy, perhaps slightly tipsy. She set the bottle on the center table and filled it with the celebrated Jeffersonian-age wine for Richard and she heard him whisper "obrigado," again and she smiled to acknowledge it.

"That is for your family, this is for you here." She poured another round of refill and handed it to him. Bruna lifted her glass up for a silent toast; Richard also lifted his in response. They drank merrily. She got up and asked him to dance with her. Without waiting for his response, she began hip-wiggling and singing to the song. He was dragging his feet, but he liked what he had been seeing.

Richard attempted to get up then he realized how heavy his legs were, yet feeble. Richard was drunk. Bruna hip-wiggled her dance back to him, and to help him up on his feet. She noticed Richard's eyes were fixated on her pierced navel and Bruna appreciated what Richard had just fed her eyes on and perhaps was imagining too. In her spinning and playful twerking while in the rhythmic wiggling mode, her robes began to give way, and to gradually reveal a treasured hide under the robe.

Richard's heart began to pulsate in rhythmic throbbing with the tempo of her wiggling. He liked what he was seeing and was beginning to drown in the flood of lust that had engulfed him. His legs began to wobble. Then, his cellphone rang. It was Apphia; he knew it. He ignored her. Apphia was troubled.

Poor Richard tried to swim his way out of the deluge of lust, having ignored Apphia's lifeline. Yet the appeal to gratify his appetite was getting stronger. Another engulfing wave came over him. Richard heard Bruna sing a strange and random romantic lament which she'd just made up:

"Richard, O Richard, let the night be mine;

Hear my song from the vine

You make my heart pine;

It is my heart, Richard, it's my heart;

Don't be heartless.

Don't leave, please don't leave."

She evoked his sympathy, his naïve kindness. Richard's mind began to boggle; his eyes were betraying him. The bait was too good. He began to crawl into the net as an innocent prey. Bruna pulled him up his feet and dragged him to her chamber like a beast would drag its wounded prey to its turf.

It was the next day.

She looked happy, very happy; he looked unhappy, very, very unhappy.

CHAPTER 22

He yawned as he fidgeted with the door handle. He was feeling very cold and could see the column of vapor from his breath vanish into the cold air with every yawn. It was about five-thirty in the morning and he couldn't stop yawning. His attempt to open the front door of his house aroused every occupant of the Bridges household.

"Bridge, is that you?" Seth inquired with a sense of security concern. Before his shivering friend could answer him, Apphia arrived at the door. She recognized her shivering husband and hastily assumed the control to opening the door. Richard stepped into his warm walls and was the cynosure of very surprised eyes.

"Let me get a warm bath and I'll tell you my ordeal." He announced to his anxious audience by the door, seemingly more directed to Apphia. They staggered backwards at his breath, covering their noses, apparently shielding their noses from inhaling what Richard was exhaling. His breath stank; it reeked strongly of alcohol and Apphia was more embarrassed. The Richard that walked in wasn't the Richard she had known. She felt tempted to air her pale opinion of his disposition. She simply watched on as her husband, rubbing his cold hands to generate heat, whisked past them. In no time, he was in a warm shower.

There were mountains of questions awaiting him, but Richard was in no hurry to get out of the shower. Apart from the pleasure of the long warm showering, it availed Richard with the opportunity to reflect and also plan how to face his wife, in the light of his moral image that he'd just undermined. He feared the worst that his night of indiscretion with Bruna might one day come to light and ruin and stain his reputation indelibly. He contemplated that he would rather disclose the incident early to his wife, Apphia before it ever came to light. It was his firm resolve.

Apphia waited for minutes by the dining table with freshly brewed coffee. She decided to check on him, having waited long enough. The snoring noise from the dark bedroom directed her eyes to the sprawled figure on the bed. Richard was fast asleep; the narrative about his ordeal would also have to wait. No one wanted to hear it more than her, but she chose to let her tired husband sleep. He'd just returned from conquest and was yet to count the spoils of his self-inflicted defeat.

Richard's cellphone, however, had had no rest. The calls had been unending since eight in the morning. Apphia, still very concerned, tried to wake her husband up. Her frantic nudging of sleepy Richard rather fueled the hysteria that had traveled with him from his short dream to soberness. He looked panic and panting heavily in fear of his own wife - when he eventually opened his eyes.

"Richard, it's me; it's me; don't be afraid, it's me. You must be dreaming." Apphia tried to calm him. He pulled himself up and sat on the bed. When his panting subsided he checked his wrist-watch and sprang instantly from the bed. As he rinsed his mouth and tried to get ready, his eyes traveled back and forth from the wall clock to his office brief-case that was by his bed. They hadn't been tampered with, and he felt relieved.

Apphia's coffee couldn't disperse the hangover cloud that weighed heavily over his brow. Richard made it safely to work. Evelyn saw him crossing the street in quick long strides to enter the atrium of the high-rise office story building and decided to meet him by the elevator lobby of their floor.

Evelyn's seconds by the elevator turned to minutes, long minutes, and into very long minutes for a one-minute elevator waiting. Then she heard the elevator chime its presence and Richard was first to walk out. Evelyn pulled him out, and aside, and on a second thought, pulled him back into the elevator. Richard was confused. His heart was pounding as they rode the elevator back in silence with other passengers. The arrival chime of the elevator on the ground floor was very deafening in Richard's ears. Evelyn couldn't keep it anymore; she jumped in animation and hugged Richard.

"Richard, what is it that makes you tick?"

"I'm not sure I understand you. What do you mean? "C'mon Richard, stop pretending. It happened late last night; everybody knew it would be you and they were right."

That nailed the coffin for Richard. The mental torture was immense, and Evelyn had no clue that she was driving the nails. She was killing her hero softly with her equivocations.

"Richard, perhaps you haven't heard it." Evelyn went on.

"No I haven't. What is it?" Richard asked hysterically. He feared the worst; he tried to brace himself for his potential calamity. Elated Evelyn eventually pre-empted the news.

"Palate International is offering you a board director's membership. I hear they're voting on it tonight." Evelyn announced it cheerfully to the somber ears of dispirited Richard. He tried to flee from his conscience that he once loved but, conscience would always be faithful.

"Wait a minute, wait, wait; where did you hear this?" Richard was less excited. He'd feared his sin had found him out. In an ironical twist, he had rather won the heart of Palate executives who believed they'd found an indispensable caliber to handle the public relations exigencies that Palate was prone to face. Shazzy's unpredictable humiliating theatrics were the culminating factor and Richard was the right material for erring Shazzy Spicer.

The office was rife with rumors that when the wine tasting event was over, Bruna Dhahl began to champion a Board position for Richard. She smartly engineered an insurrection against Shazzy Spicer, by explaining to the others how Shazzy arrogantly stood in the way of the scandal response team and was the cause of the team's failure to come up with remedial actions. Bruna's actions were aimed at breaking free from Shazzy because she feared she might be implicated in his activities. She'd weighed her reasons. Richard was smart and knew too much. She would rather like to ride with him on his flying carpet in every way. She knew him well, very, very, well. Then it was left with Richard to accept the position.

The evening arrived early; a typical pre-autumn climate. The Boardroom halls of Palate International, the California office exuded the splendor that its stature normally commanded. The walls bore resplendent displays of the Palate International logo depicting a golden gloved hand pouring wine into a ready glass. It had Palate's motto, "Haste to taste, appetite by sight; fine wine, pure pleasure." The other walls had pictures of Palate founding authorities. Pictures of current board members were also on display on the adjacent walls. Very soon, Richard would also have his picture on the wall among the celebrated "Palatians."

Richard didn't seem to be keen, and he didn't hide it. He was surprised, however, to see Bruna. Bruna commanded much confidence in her rather unusual formal role. She did not look like the vulnerable, Shazzy-Spicer-fearing Bruna that Richard had known. Richard had no idea of the rumored intrigues Bruna had perpetrated the hours before they were together on that night. The countenance of Bruna bore a fiery-eyed expression and she looked at Richard indifferently when she passed by him into the Boardroom. Richard wondered if he were seeing the same person he was fooling around with in her home. While he waited in his office to be invited to meet the Board formally, an attendant came and handed him a note. It was from Bruna and carried the inscription, "I hope you're OK. Be strong."

After brief speeches by the assembled Board members, Richard was invited in and was congratulated by every member. He didn't come with a prepared speech. He was brief and expressed his gratitude for the honor and promised to employ every nerve in him to serve Palate and its allied interests and publics very well. The speech was interrupted.

The attendant, who had earlier carried the note to Bridges, had interrupted the session with a courier delivery letter addressed to Board chairman, Mr. Otto Nanseman. Otto ripped the package open and everyone saw sweat building on his brow as he read the note inaudibly: *"Bruna's affair with Richard Bridges is an open secret and it shows how low you guys can go to blame me to cover Palate's shame. Mr. Bridges slept over at Bruna's – what a way to pay for Palate's legal fees; it's no secret."* Otto's face dropped while they passed the note around.

"Whose work is this?" Otto asked in a very controlled fury.

"The answer is obvious. It's Shazzy." Bruna answered sharply.

"I'm disappointed that the scandals keep on coming – something new every day." Otto remarked as he looked Richard's way. He saw a brazen frown of an offended man. That was what Richard communicated, but behind that frown was a conscience on fire. What was he getting himself into? Richard questioned his own judgment – inconceivable that he would be involved in a situation like this.

"Bruna, what do you say?" Otto directed his question to her.

"In the first place, I have the right to entertain whoever I want to in my house. I'm sure you all saw and heard on the news about the murder in my neighbor's house. Richard had come over that night to help me with answers to the press since Shazzy did not allow and neither encouraged the meeting to rehearse that. Mr. Bridges could not return to his family because the whole area was cordoned off. Why? Are we answerable to Shazzy Spicer about our lives? Mr. Nanseman, there's nothing to worry about. Shazzy is a sour loser."

The rest of the members applauded Bruna. None was as relieved as Richard was, but was still apprehensive about the prevailing atmosphere in Palate's world.

"Mr. Richard Bridges, please accept our apologies for this unfortunate incident. Please consider yourself as part of the Palate International Incorporated family." Otto apologized and Bridges rendered a formal nod of acknowledgment with a wry chuckle as he took his seat.

The members eventually retired for refreshments. Music was in the air, and as Richard had expected, Palate refreshments bore their mark of sublime culinary artistry and bar tending par excellence. The aroma from the food commanded a salivating spell while the temporal bar that stood by the Office Reception area offered a teasing choice between teetotalism and the intemperate drinker. Otto Nanseman was enjoying the night and that was very evident in his lively hobnobbing moments with guests and members of his Board. Bruna sat at a table closer by the live pianist; with her twinkling eyes she was almost revealing a latency of fascination with Richard. Her eyes stayed on him. She would want to chat with him, but she was being careful to not nurture the seeds already planted in the minds of the Board members by Shazzy Spicer. So far the evening had played well for her and she would woefully upbraid herself to ruin it.

Bruna observed that Richard had gotten up. To confirm her suspicions she looked down the street from an aerial viewing point. She was seeing a limo trying to pull up to the front of the building. It was the same limo rented for Richard for the night's meeting event. It was easy to spot it out from the other limos, because of its marked beribboned front reserved for occasional distinguished Palate's guest. Bruna hastily caught up with Richard as he made his way towards the elevator lobby. There were no waiting elevator riders save the two. Bruna liked it. Richard hated it.

"Mr. Bridges, have you forgiven me?" Upon hearing those words, Richard turned to face the voice. His rebuke was pointed and it reflected his mood.

"What a way to greet a vested executive?" The frown lingered on his face as he looked at Bruna over his shoulder. "I guess I don't merit a congratulatory word from you."

Bruna was shaken by Richard's prickly-tone sarcasm. She froze, and he saw a girly timidity on her face. The elevator arrived and he walked in. He expected her to board the elevator, but she remained frozen. Richard held it open for her and, with a nod, he gestured for her to walk in. She did. It was a comforting ride for her; still scathed, she hoped Richard would say something. He didn't, but she chose to.

"Could I come and meet your family, Mr. Bridges?"

The question surprised Richard. He was hearing a very outlandish request. While Bruna was hoping to mitigate his anger with a friendly request, he was wondering what he might have done to encourage such absurdity from a woman who should be avoiding his wife. Richard had no immediate answer. Bruna read his bewilderment. The elevator touched the ground floor and Richard summoned it up again. They rode back in silence and upon arriving on the floor; Richard led the way back to the guest room by the Reception area.

"You're very angry. I can tell." Bruna broke the silence.

"You're unbelievable. What's the big idea?"

"I want a healthy relationship with you; forgetting about what happened last night. I know I like you, but you don't like me, and I don't know why."

Richard's attempt to keep his repulsive facial look while fighting to suppress an emerging smile, borne from the ridiculous remark, rather created an explosion of laughter on his face. Contagious that it was, coy Bruna laughed with him.

"I like you, Bruna, but in my own way." Richard replied after the laughter had subsided.

"What's your opinion about me, Mr. Bridges?"

"Why must I tell you? If I told you, you would masquerade your actions to simply prove my opinions wrong."

"That means you have very unfavorable opinions about me, right?"

"That means be yourself and stop acting. Why would you want to meet my family?"

"I have no reason to avoid them. I don't intend to hide my goodwill. My conscience is clear." Bruna said confidently.

"What does Palate mean by: 'Haste to taste' in its policy?" Richard was still a captive of the subtle and indiscernible outlook of Palate's world. He didn't know who to trust.

"It simply means, be quick to taste it. It's as simple as it sounds."

"Why do I have to be hasty with it? The wine is going nowhere."

"It's simple; so the wine doesn't lose its savor. You lose your vigor with age, so you must haste to taste." Bruna responded with a wry smile and Richard was confounded by her prompt and witty response.

"You're devil. Did you tell me you feared Mr. Spicer? It doesn't strike me you do." Richard quizzed her mind again.

"I feared Spicer, yes, until I met you. You were the only person who stood up to him."

Richard got up, paced to the window and looked over down to the street. He realized his limo was making way for another car which was yet to pick another guest. He reached out his cellphone and called his limo driver to pick him up in five minutes. After watching Richard make the pick-up arrangements, Bruna turned her attention to the refreshment area. Richard walked back to her.

"I've been wrong on few occasions with my assumptions. Please, tell me, did the Board know that Shazzy owned Linvin

Rouge? Apart from Linvin Rouge, is there another wine of interest to any other Board member?"

Bruna was silent. Richard waited for few more seconds.

"Mrs. Dhahl, good night." Richard made his way to the elevators and didn't look back.

CHAPTER 23

Richard was up very early in the morning. It wasn't unusual. It was his practice to plan for the day's activities early in the mornings. Apphia knew where she would find her husband. His office light was on and she could hear the typing sound of the computer keyboard emerging from the office in the unusual quiet hours before the break of dawn. She had noticed his unusual groaning and long sleepless hours in bed. He had been also very docile and withdrawn. She knew something was eating him up. She watched from the distance and saw her husband signing his finished document, enveloping and sealing it. She chose to not pry unless Richard decided to tell her.

Lately, he'd been returning home very late and Apphia's suspicions of Richard's sullen withdrawal from his home-life worried her. She tried not to worry, but the corrosive anguish forced her to eventually confide her fears in both Eloquenter and Seth. Eloquenter remarked that he would pray for them and reminded them that many times spiritual truths reveal themselves in physical metaphors. His explanation re-echoed in Apphia's ears: "The germinating seed had to, with difficulty, break through the hard surface of the soil to receive the necessary sustenance from the sunlight. Many times life is like that. It depends on how a person handles his or her germinating experience, which is the encounter with the soil. After all, the person would need the soil to hold the roots of the sprout. But have you thought of who made the soil and who nourishes it?"

Richard drove through the typical fall season morning foggy streets and arrived at his office before seven. It was partially dark and he could hear his own steps echoing behind him in the almost empty second level parking of their building. When he got to the office building and his floor, he was drawn to the lights in "Dan's Den" conference room. He drew closer and heard familiar voices. He debated if he should intrude in the activity; he had his hand on the door handle when he was surprised by a voice from the conference room. "Come in Mr. Bridges."

The eyes were fixed on Richard as he walked in. They were Donald Dent, Milo, and the enigmatic, Bruna Dhahl. Richard was in shock to see Bruna and he did not hide it.

"What are you doing here, Ms. Bruna Dhahl?"

"Well, I called this extraordinary early meeting because Palate had to issue some kind of response to the scandalous allegations today, before the Holiday season begins. I was planning on calling you, but on a second thought, I felt you might need some rest."

"I thought Bruna might need more rest than I do, unless the impression being communicated to me here is: it's Bruna Dhahl's de facto meeting." Richard's face lit with a relieving smile. He'd found grounds to make his case against the shadow of Bruna's influence in the affairs of Palate's and even Milo, Grady and Strong's law firm. "May I excuse you, lady and gentlemen?"

Richard closed the door behind him, ignoring Bruna's hand-beckoning call attempt. He walked back to his office like a relieved celebrant. He hung his jacket, loosened his tie and settled in his leather chair; the upholstery was cold, but he was insensitive to it. He opened his office briefcase that he'd set on his desk and picked up the copies of the letters he'd written few hours ago. He gravitated to the one with the subject, "Letter of Resignation" addressed to the, "Chairman, Palate International Board of Directors." He was yet to submit it but would want to discuss his intent with Mr. Milo. The other letter craved the indulgence of Mr. Milo. It was to find a replacement for Richard among the ad hoc Palate damage control committee members.

Richard wanted the committee to dispense with his role. And as his parting contribution to the panel, he listed some recommendations which he believed would reclaim the image of Palate. Richard suggested among a very unfamiliar list, an innocuous demonstration of contrition by Palate and a commitment to allow Palate connoisseurs and sommeliers rotate their functions in durational capacities – believing that it would render Palate to be seen in a more judicious light. He reviewed the existing ethical standards for the sommeliers, wrote new recommendations, and submitted a suggestion that would originate an Annual Sommeliers Competition with a very high prize for winners. Richard read over his work again. He was satisfied with it, but candidly, he didn't care. Eventually, he saw the three leaving the conference room. Mr. Milo then decided to make a phone call. Simultaneously, Richard heard his phone ring and he picked it up.

"Bridges, come to my office," Milo summoned.

Richard got up, armed with his two letters, but as he stood by his door and was about to exit his office, he observed that Bruna was heading towards his office direction. To avoid bumping into her, Richard resorted to a rather circuitous route to Milo's office. His decision positioned both of them to head in the same direction, but Richard was yards ahead of Bruna. The scene presented a visual reality of Bruna following Richard and trying to catch up with him while Richard maintained a steady pace, trying to ignore Bruna's deliberate hasty strides to fall in step with him. Eventually, they all met at Milo's door.

"Mr. Milo, why is your office representative avoiding his client?" Bruna exploded while panting from her speedy tailing of Richard.

"And who could this representative be?" Milo asked – playing unaware of Bruna's exploits. He turned to lock at Richard. Richard was expressionless.

"Mr. Bridges, I simply want to know what your recommendations are since we met without you." Bruna asked quietly without any blatant wile.

"I plan to discuss that with Mr. Milo and I'm sure he will communicate it to you and the rest of the damage control team."

"Thank you." Bruna said in a matter-of-fact tone and turned to leave in an apparent show of her intentional formalism. Milo stepped into his office and Richard followed him. Milo reached for his coffee on the far corner of the desk. His grip felt a cold cup. He sipped it and it was cold; "it tastes like mud." He concluded.

"If it's cold, it's useless. So it is with life. If one is cold, there's no life in the person. Son, you've got to loosen up and warm up your spirit up a little bit." Milo remarked jokingly.

"I hear you, Mr. Milo." Richard smiled bashfully and saw him in a reciprocal bashful smile, nodding his head as if to say without words 'you son of a gun, I know what you did few nights ago'."

Richard continued to smile to hide his apparent emotional change, but was very restless in his chair. He presented his letter to Milo who opened it without hesitation. After reading it, Milo remained quiet for few seconds. He didn't bother to read the attached list of recommendations until Richard implored him to. Milo read it and a rush of excitement surged through him.

"Well Bridges, this is it. Your argument for Palate's contrition and apology is paramount to reclaiming the fast-eroding credibility and public trust." It was relieving for Richard to hear Milo's compliments. He relished them and he decided to impress him even more.

"And Mr. Milo, as I stated, it must simply be a press statement and no press interviews; any opening will be press scrambling for more information. Time heals wounds especially if we play nice. The holidays are here. Palate must play nice; it's the most opportune time for Palate to save its name by being nice with discounts. It's a way to resound the motto: 'Catering to the appetite is our pleasure'." Richard applied the icing on Palate's already baked cake.

"Brilliant!" Milo was ecstatic. He picked up the phone and dialed. After few rings, Milo heard the greeting: "Hello! This is Otto Nanseman."

Milo informed Mr. Nanseman, Palate's Board Chairman about the development. Nanseman was delighted and agreed to every letter of the draft statement that Richard submitted. Nanseman wanted the statement to be out early enough for it to get coverage for the Evening News. While Milo was replacing the receiver on its base, Richard was placing his other letter of resignation from the board back into his jacket. Second thoughts had set in. It would be worth the while to see how things shape up with Palate; he thought.

Richard was ready to leave when Milo's phone rang again. It was Otto Nanseman.

"Make sure you come with Richard to our refreshment tonight. Milo, Richard must come." Otto insisted on the phone. Richard overhead that and he had a ready response.

"No, Mr. Milo – not tonight. My wife and I have plans and it's difficult for me to change them. Please, not tonight."

"Well, you heard him. If you can't honor it, I won't be there. Wait a minute, bring her with you." Milo suggested.

"No-o I can't do that. She'll be the only 'wife' there. Others will have their wives at home. No, I can't do that." Richard maintained his ground.

"Richard, you heard what I was saying a short while ago. You've got to relax and loosen up a bit. Sometimes you're too cold. Don't be cold to a warm person. Warm up son; life is too short. Think about it."

Richard was confused. He'd been thrown again into the throes of another dilemma. He got up and walked back to his office; that time, no strut in his steps.

The limousine pulled up at Richard's house and the driver watched him kiss his wife, hug his son and approach the car. The limo-driver got up, held the door open and Richard had to bask in the wonderful perfume fragrance that had wafted the entire limo when he entered into the spacious dark car. The lights came on and there she was, the co-rider and the source of the rich perfume, Bruna Dhahl.

Bruna and Richard exchanged formal greetings, but they rode half the distance in silence. Bruna didn't like the climate in the car and eventually broke the silence.

"Our statement went out today and received very favorable and positive comments. I know Richard, you did that single handedly, and I'm very grateful."

"Thank you."

"You are a huge asset to the Milo, Grady and Strong Law Firm. What can Palate do to steal you away totally from your firm?"

"Nothing, I love my job."

"Do you know you can own Palate?" Bruna asked.

"I might, but I'm not and will not be interested in it."

"Why not, Richard? You have the brains and what it takes to run the company more efficiently. I know a lot of people have confidence in you. You'd be surprised.

Richard laughed at Bruna's assuring words. He'd come to know her for having sinister motives behind her drives and was very wary of her and her circle of Palate influences.

"Why not you instead?" Richard countered.

"No, I can't. I'm not as smart as you are."

Richard laughed it off again. The limo taxied gently in front of the hotel and attendants appeared instantly to open the doors for both of them. Bruna held her arm in invitation for Richard to hook his with hers. Richard hadn't anticipated the courtesy; he didn't like the gesture, but he didn't want to embarrass Bruna either. Hand in hand they left.

There were as many as forty guests. The ambience and the music predicted the night that awaited the guests. An applause greeted them as they walked in arm in arm. They commanded the attention of the night as Bruna led the way to their reserved seats. The music was soft and jazzy. There were more ladies at the reception this night than it was at the previous refreshment. He was seeing Milo hobnobbing from table to table with his very young wife and Richard was regretting for failing to invite his wife as Milo had suggested.

"I didn't know we could invite our spouses." Richard remarked.

"Unfortunately not, this is a light-hearted official night. The ladies you see here are either Restaurant owners, Event Planners, Chief Chefs or people in the allied industries of Palate International. The lady with Milo is Milo's personal friend who owns a grape farm here in California. What are you thinking, his wife?" Bruna insinuated her response.

"I guessed wrongly." Richard admitted.

"A lawyer guessing, you surprised me, Richard. I thought you guys only deal with evidence."

"We guess sometimes to get ourselves out of a hole. It's a common practice. We call it 'Gut feeling'." Richard smiled and was feeling relaxed with the kind of conversation Bruna was generating.

"I've got a gut feeling, that sometimes you don't believe me." Bruna said. Richard laughed at her impressive handling of their dialogue, so far. She was aware that she had to confine herself within the boundaries of the dictates of the dialogue. She dared not blow it.

The live jazz quartet struck a familiar tune. Five couples got up to dance including Milo and his partner, and also Otto Nanseman and his partner.

"I've got a gut feeling you want us to dance." Richard guessed.

"Your gut feeling is right." Bruna smiled in response. They joined the rest on the floor in a slow dance. They moved slowly, but Richard hinted that he could still make curvy rhythmic moves even in a slow dance. Bruna couldn't be outdone, but she looked melted in Richard's arms like an effortless dancer. Her dancing legs and feet had given way to her dancing heart. Her head lay on Richard's chest, beaming a physical chemistry through a spectrum of different interpretations. Bruna loved it and didn't care what opinions people would form and what they would say. Richard wasn't comfortable, but he relied on a common alibi, they were all tipsy. Eventually they retired to their various seats. The music continued but some weary executives decided to leave; they included Richard and Bruna.

The limousine driver opted to take Bruna home first. She deserved that courtesy as a lady, and moreover, she was picked first. On the way home Bruna tried to keep Richard awake by telling him some silly jokes. The drive wasn't long and soon Bruna's home appeared in view. Bruna got off the limo and waited for Richard to walk her to her door. Richard partially tottering, walked Bruna to the door, but she returned with a message to the limo driver.

"I think I have to sober him up, before he heads home. It will take an hour or two. Don't worry I'll take care of you." The limo driver smiled in grateful agreement.

Bruna's room wasn't different from the one Richard saw days ago. He recognized his environment and it instantly brought memories of his night with her. It triggered an instant recovery. Bruna noticed it and she was disappointed. The lurking and the toll of weariness, all as rival predators, had scared off her prey, she thought.

"Are you alright to leave now?" Bruna asked.

"Yes, I guess so." Richard replied.

"Your gut feeling is saying, yes." Bruna derided by making reference to their earlier dialogue. Richard smiled, and nodded his aching head.

"Well, I need evidence." Bruna left to brew some coffee. She then walked to the den which was closer to her kitchen and dining area, and turned on her CD player. She began playing the tune that they had danced to at the reception few hours ago.

"Mr. Richard Bridges you are the lawyer. Give me evidence that you still have full control of your feet and legs. Come dance with me."

Richard took the challenge and trying to impress Bruna, he literally jumped to his feet. He was back in Bruna's arms again. They danced softly, and again buttery Bruna was a melting solid in the very hot hold of Richard.

"You surprised me Richard; I did not think you could be a good dancer." Bruna whispered with her head on Richard's chest. Richard offered no response. "I have another confession to make." Bruna continued, but Richard interrupted this time.

"You better make it before the judge runs out of patience."

"I will if the honorable judge may notice the penitence in the heart of a woman who took advantage of a kind man."

"What did the woman do?" Richard asked softly as they continued dancing.

"She-she- she fell deeply in love with him." Bruna stammered her confession tearfully. Richard sympathetically held her closer to his body and wiped her tears. They retired to the couch where the dim light was creating a poetic moment. He beheld the glow in her pitiful eyes and he kissed her. He kissed her again; and again he did. Richard returned to the limo smiling – not a pang of guilt.

The limo pulled up at the Bridges' driveway at about an hour after midnight. Apphia was still up; there was light in her bedroom. Richard noticed it as he got off the car. He wasn't cold and wasn't yawning; he was feeling good. Apphia came downstairs to meet him as he attempted to unlock the front door. Again, Richard's breath reeked of alcohol, but his clothes were profound with fragrance - loud on the shirt and the jacket. Apphia kissed her husband to welcome him home. The glossy spread on

Richard's lips gave Apphia a taste of what Richard's lips had touched.

"How was the reception?" Apphia asked quietly, trying not to give away her suspicions.

"It was fun. I thought you would be sleeping by now. Were you waiting for me?"

"I couldn't sleep," Apphia replied.

"Why not, are you still pondering over Eloquenter's bizarre stories and his strange religio-syncrisis?" Richard expressed angrily.

"Richard, you sound upset. What's going on?"

"Nothing, nothing to be upset about – I've just been made a Board member of Palate International Incorporated and I guess the position is overwhelming. Palate will be paying me about a million a year with fringe benefits – twice what I get from the firm. You must understand how overwhelming it is to me."

"You've just told me; I do now." Apphia explained softly.

"You don't sound excited about it." Richard observed.

"You don't seem to be excited about it either. I guess because you don't, that seems to affect me." Apphia said truthfully. "Richard I want you to be happy, all of us to be happy."

"I may stay late working tomorrow, and the next few days. Apphia, don't stay up late and wait for me."

"Richard, I won't. Be careful. Time is a borrowed item. We don't own it."

CHAPTER 24

Gradually, as the days wore on, Richard settled in the newly created position for him at Milo, Grady and Strong and also as Palate Executive Director for Communications. As new Palate personnel it behooved Richard to know much about the wine industry including knowing how the grapes are farmed, harvested and eventually processed into wine.

A grapes farm became a practical curriculum for Richard's new field. The stretch of the farm was breathtaking and he was taking it all in. His tour guide was one of the workers on the farm and quite versatile in his field. The grape farms in California were the choicest for the farm experience Richard needed and he was ready to embrace it. It was almost harvest time on the farm, and in no time, his guide returned with a ready saddled horse for him. The choice of a horse ride for the farm trip took Richard by surprise. His aching head would not support a steady horse riding.

"No, I haven't ridden - not on a horseback before. I don't know how to; I'm sorry." Richard protested to his surprised guide. In response, the guide left to find substitute means of transport for the tour. The sun was up and its rays from the east provided means for clearer distant visions to the west side.

As he waited for the arrival of his tour guide, Richard allowed his eye to carry him to the far narrowing point of the walkway.

He began to see how the scattered dew drops on the leaves welcomed the sunny rays with a sparkle. The berries on the vines were his sheer delight, revealing the bosom of a vine that boasted of fertile sumptuousness. He noticed also how the trellises supporting the vines were in a discipline of straight line formation.

Lost in what he was observing, Richard began to ponder with a rather poignant interest over "why the path narrowed at the end? Perhaps the further the object is, the smaller it appears to the eye." Richard was caught thinking aloud when his guide eventually arrived with a golf-cart.

"That's so true to life, isn't it? The further we are from the situation, that's how insignificant the situation appears to us, but in actual fact, the situation is still enormous in its size, it didn't change." The guide intruded and stirred up Richard's concern.

Richard was surprised at himself that he'd just revealed his thoughts in a soliloquy. He wondered how often he'd been talking to himself; how much of his inner thoughts he'd given away. Was he still feeling drunk? Was he getting mentally deranged or simply experiencing the effects of bloated stress which was ready to burst? There was no cause to admit any of those notions. He was doing well as a young man, respected, loved and a seasoned attorney he prided himself to be. He would not yield any ground to any delusional fears.

"Are we ready to roll, Mr. Bridges?" Richard looked at his host and replied with a smile to hide his pain. "Yes we are." By attempting to turn his head and catch the glimpse of the expression on his guide's face, Richard's eyes would have to cross the reflecting rays from the bright beams emerging from the east. The process brought him sharp and severe pangs of headache. He felt awful, but was determined to complete the excursion through the acres of vine. He wouldn't want to be counted among those who yielded to the tedium of the excursion.

Their golf cart rolled on through the straight pathway among the pines. He saw how the weighty full harvest grapes had to depend on the support of the firm trellis. He saw the red, the purple, green and white grapes; all looking ripe and presenting a pleasant sight. He'd just learnt that another determining factor for harvesting; apart from color change is the firmness and size of the berries. Larger berries may draw attention to ripeness.

"The most reliable means to detect any sign of ripeness is by tasting it. So, let's indulge in one." The guide invited Richard to pluck a berry and taste it, but Richard looked puzzled. He'd been told that it wasn't a healthy practice to taste the vine if it wasn't harvested. He watched his guide pluck one and tasted it. That encouraged him to follow.

"I'm sure you're getting that confused with the truth that once grapes are cut from the vine, they will never ripe any further. Strangely, among all the fruits and berries, it's only the grape that has that peculiarity. Exposure of the berries to sunlight will not ripen them. It's the plant that needs the light for photosynthesis reaction. Yep, once they are cut from the vine, ripening ceases and the taste remains the same. It's, therefore, very important that the grapes stay ripe on the tree before they're harvested." The guide tried to inject basic lessons and discount the myths.

"Interesting, it's good to know." Richard remarked feigning his interest. His head ached.

"Yes, it is." The guide continued: "We've always considered that as a symbolic adage, one must be ready before he attempts his whim, because the result could not be reversible." However, Richard, in his mind disputed the guide's interpretation. He perceived that his interpretation narrowed it to a farmer's perception. The guide thought it was simply a counsel to not rush the blade on the vine for a rushed quantitative harvest instead of waiting for a patient harvest of high quality ripen grapes. However, Richard felt it carried a broader interpretation. He thought it meant a person or thing if severed from the stem of resource, might remain the same and the prospect of flourishing would cease. Richard's own interpretation pricked his inner conscience. The phrase, "the stem of resource" continued to emerge repeatedly on his mind; it became his quiet convenient conviction.

Richard chewed his berries; they tasted sweet and he liked them. "That meant those are ready to be harvested and will soon be on dining tables in many homes." He remarked.

"Well, you cannot discuss grapes without mentioning their health benefits." The tour guide resumed. Richard's interest again was pricked. "It's one fruit that's so rich in minerals. We're talking about magnesium, iron, copper and calcium. It's also rich in vitamins A, C, E and K. In fact, I chew them instead of drinking them – if you know what I mean." The guide laughed at his own effort to be funny.

"O – Yes, I do. I chew them too." Richard remarked with laughter trying to hide his headache. A feeling of nausea was also beginning to set in for him.

"Don't get me wrong, I drink them too, at the appropriate time. Do you?" The guide continued to talk, much against the wish of struggling Richard, especially when he tried to involve him.

"Yes, I also do, I guess on special occasions." Richard said loosely. The subject instantly triggered a reminder about the expensive wine he received in a small bottle from Bruna. He'd been keeping it in one of the inner pockets of the jacket he wore that night. An instant alarm went off. The drink that would betray him of his clandestine affair with Bruna was in his pocket.

"O - In my pocket, my coat's pocket, it has to be there." Richard was unloading his mind again, that time with hysterics

"You mean you always keep your drink in your pocket." Considering it as a joke, the guide innocently laughed at Richard's monologue. Realizing that he had a problem, Richard sighed concernedly and heavily.

The golf-cart eventually made a right turn at the end of the long stretch, the perceived vanishing point. The end of the stretch was still there in perfect parallel continuum from the starting point.

A feeling of uneasiness began to creep over Richard. He wished the trip was over. He was beginning to experience light-headedness. He yawned repeatedly and thought his sleep-short eyes were playing tricks on him. Finally he conceded that he wasn't feeling well and requested his guide to take him back to the farmhouse. The guide sped his way back while Richard held on firmly to the roof grip of the golf cart. He was seeing the vines speeding extraordinarily faster towards them and he tried to strengthen his grip on the cart.

On arrival, he heard new voices in the farmhouse; one sounded very familiar. His condition had made it difficult for him to sharply ascertain the owners of those voices. However, one stood out from the rest. It was the voice of a frequent visitor to the farmhouse and who was the brainchild of the farm induction tour for Richard. The voice belonged to Bruna.

Acknowledging how Richard was feeling and looked, Bruna immediately offered to take him home, and Richard that time, didn't turn down the offer. His condition craved it. He welcomed the offer. Even so, Richard wasn't disposed to premeditating how to introduce Bruna; it didn't even cross his mind. He must simply get home and reorient himself to "Richard-like." On the way, Bruna tried to turn on the radio, but she realized that Richard was uncomfortable with it. He needed sleep and he slept almost all the way home.

The appearance of a strange car in the drive way of the Bridges drew instant curiosity. Apphia and Seth simultaneously peeped discretely through separate downstairs windows. Apphia had been cleaning and wouldn't want to be seen looking unpresentable. To her surprise, she saw her husband alight from the strange car and began walking feebly towards their front door. While Richard had his focus on the door, he heard Bruna's car drive off. Bruna's decision to leave unceremoniously surprised Richard. He'd anticipated some parting well-wishes, and Richard thought it would also be gratifying to accord his kind guest with a reciprocal warm welcome for her generous courtesy of driving him home. It was the most convenient and opportune moment for Richard to introduce Bruna to his family, especially recognizing that it was something Bruna had looked forward to, and under that circumstance, Richard was sure he could handle the situation more surreptitiously without a shadow of rivalry.

Nonetheless, many times the wheel of fate would spin in favor of the cunning foe, especially when the cunning knew how to spin the wheel.

Apphia had started her day with her routine cleaning that often preceded her other plans and commitments for the day. She'd walked to the clothes hamper. It was heaped with dirty clothes that sat by the dividing door between the bathroom and their large closet. As she tried to separate the white clothes from the colored ones, she noticed unfamiliar stains on the collars Richard's shirts. She concluded that by the nature of the stains, they might also have been on the suits and probably, more prominently on the jackets. As a woman, she knew what had stained her husband's clothes. She immediately abandoned the sorting-out process and approached Richard's long hanging array of suits. By elimination, she arrived at the suit Richard had worn on his first night with Bruna. She noticed face powder stains with scant traces of suspicious lipstick stains on the lapel of the jacket. Apphia's heart sank and with trembling hands, she brought down the hanger with the jacket on it.

Still trembling, her hands felt the touch and weight of a small container. She began to run through the inner pockets of Richard's jacket. The find confirmed her suspicions. It was a small bottle filled with wine. The smell betrayed it; it was the bottle Bruna had filled with the expensive Medoc la Grande on her night with Richard. An unusual chill began to run through Apphia, and she used the little strength in her to scream out to Seth. She had to share her find with him. Apphia's trembling hands couldn't accommodate the menacing sight of spite in her palm that it dropped to the floor. Strangely, the bottle survived the impact on the carpet. But Apphia couldn't hold back her tears. Seth, who had rushed up to the floor, instantly picked up the bottle, opened it and smelt the contents. Rightly, it was wine and Apphia was right, it was not a wild imagination. Seth sealed the small bottle and tried to console her.

He helped Apphia up to her feet, however, emotionally broken and blinded by the wetness of her eyes, she had to be guided back to her bedroom and to the only seat in that room, her bedroom stool. Incidentally, that stool was retelling an event, one she could hardly forget. Apphia's mind reeled back to that event.

Richard had returned from work one evening, and had requested playfully to blindfold his wife. She allowed him to, and thereafter, Richard gently guided her to their bedroom. There he carefully placed a pillow on her lap. And while she wondered what he was up to, he prompted her to open her eyes to a very beautiful golden necklace, hyped against a beautiful blue violet pillow on her lap to reveal the beauty and the slew of golden brightness that the necklace commanded.

Incidentally, fate had brought her back to the same stool, and she would have to open her eyes not to a golden ceremony, but to the subtle reality of this challenging time in their life.

In spite of her devastation by the day's discoveries on Richard's clothes, Apphia still considered it a bit ominous for his early return from work in a stranger's car. When she saw him approach the front door in his feeble steps, she sensed something was amiss. It would be foolhardy to presumptuously confront her husband with her potential evidences of his infidelity. Nonetheless, she abandoned what she was doing and jumped into the shower to clean and freshen up. Apphia had restrained Seth from bringing up the issue for discussion with Richard. It was her fight and she would fight it her way. She was yet to come to grips with what she'd suspected days ago. It wasn't the Richard she knew. Something had gone awry and had to be checked before the unimaginable worst happened.

Having freshened up, she made her way downstairs to introduce her new persona while the perfume on her took hold of the room. She saw Richard with his shoes off and feet up on the center table in the den, but she passed by feigning unawareness of his presence. Then she heard him call. She turned instantly to feign startled by his voice.

"Richard, you startled me. Don't do that again."

"I'm sorry, I didn't mean to." Richard's apology carried the submissive tone of a person in a pitiful state. "I don't feel good, and I don't know what's wrong with me."

"What do you mean by you don't know what's wrong with you? If it's constipation or gas we all know we have to hold our breath at your intermittent relief breaks. Of course, we are used to that, but what is it this time?"

"That's funny. Seriously I don't feel well – it's a strange headache."

"Perhaps all you need is a good sleep since you've been very busy and sleeping so late these nights." Apphia recommended with a tinge of insinuation.

Richard heaved a sigh of uneasiness at her remark. Amidst that exchange, the doorbell rang. She gave her husband an interrogative surprised look. He looked back at her in bewilderment at her show of surprise. However, after the pinhole glance, Apphia held the door partially opened to behold the face of her husband's friend.

"You must be Mrs. Bridges. I'm Bruna Dhahl, Mr. Bridges' colleague with Palate International."

"Palate International," Apphia repeated the name with a skeptical brow. "And you knew you could find him here at this time of the day?" She remarked interrogatively with an assertive drive which reminded Richard that something might be brewing with Bruna.

"Well, incidentally I brought him over this morning." Bruna explained defensively.

"Well, come in. He's here." Apphia invited Bruna in because courtesy demanded it. She recognized the matching colors of Bruna's lipstick with the stains on Richard cloths. Then she remembered the words, once spoken in a story. They started coming to her, the words from Eloquenter's story as was read to her by Seth: "Sometimes the hunger, the rain, the injury and the pain suggest the nature of the road for the journey, the journey from nervous Needyland to a sustaining Successville. It depends on the traveler." The words reechoed in Apphia's ears. Her journey had just begun, she thought about it, but with a frown.

Bruna walked in confidently with an air of unpredictability around her. She sat on a sofa that faced Richard. Still stifled by what was unfolding, he sat there with a transfixed imagination of being the bruised arbiter of a domestic fight. Nonetheless, in reality, he saw an opportunity and seized it. He chose to look sicker to simply solicit their sympathy and to eventually divert any potential feuding intentions to the more civil and humane responsibility of administering help to him, the tapped-out Richard. However, to his surprise, Apphia deliberately moved away from the room, to accord her husband and Ms. Dahl, the terrain of office setting for their official Palate discussions. Her ears however, were an extension of the Palate office space in the house.

"How do you feel - seeing any improvement after getting some sleep?" Bruna asked.

"I still need some rest. It'll help me a lot. I'll see a doctor if I don't see any improvement." Richard conceded still portraying his sicker disposition with facial expressions of the pain he was going through.

"Mr. Bridges, your vote is crucial tonight for Palate's severance proposal with Linvin Rouge. I wish I could lobby for deferment of the discussion, but as you know, I will only be there as an observer. I have no vote. This is a hard one because of my recent past association with Linvin Rouge. What do you think?"

The question hung in the air unanswered when Apphia emerged from her hideout which was within earshot. As she made her way to the kitchen, she volunteered an offer of coffee or tea for the two. Bruna was first to respond with a "No, thank you," and eventually Richard also politely supported it. Bruna, however, sharply interrupted Richard's attempt to explain his reason for refusing the coffee offer. She interposed his reasons with a firm recommendation to get the coffee because it would do him good if taken with something that she had for him in her car. On that note, Bruna immediately got up and headed for her car.

"Richard, I don't get it. Is it a duty of Ms. Bruna to provide you with personal care even in your own home?" Apphia asked amidst the gathering storm in the house.

"No, Apphia. She's just trying to help." Richard remarked resignedly.

"Richard, don't you understand? She literally overrode my offer to my husband, my suggestion for my husband, in my home with no respect and regard for my role as the wife in my house."

"Apphia, she's a professional sommelier, trained to recommend cocktails with various items that are supposed to help a person's appetite and well-being." Richard explained feebly.

"So, you're expecting her concoction with ingredients which she carries on her every time in her car. Something, which I can't offer, nor can be found in this house." Apphia questioned the validity of Richard's argument. "O, Richard you make me sicker." She stormed out, and flew up the stairs to their bedroom. With the words still in his mouth, Bruna reentered the room with a medication in a piece of plastic pharmaceutical bottle.

"Did I hear her right, is she also sick?" Bruna asked rather innocently.

"No, she's alright. It's I who is getting sicker.' Richard replied dejectedly. Bruna moved closer to him and easily opened the bottle, and in his view, she dispensed two drops of pills onto her palm.

"Mr. Bridges, this will help you if taken with your wife's coffee." Bruna displayed to him the pills in her palm while waiting for Apphia's coffee. There was no smell of coffee in the air; but something else was brewing in the air.

"Ms. Bruna, wouldn't it dawn on you that Richard's personal care in this house would be his wife's responsibility?" Apphia was upset.

"Mrs. Bridges, I was simply trying to help."

"You've helped enough. What would you recommend to remove the lipstick stains on this shirt and this jacket? Obviously you've stamped your lip service on his cloths. What other service awaits him now, probably the nightly bed tuck-ins, that is, if you've not run out of bedtime stories?" Apphia was burning within.

Bruna feeling highly embarrassed, got up and was ready to leave. "I must leave." She said, but Apphia wasn't done with her lethal verbal onslaught. She brought out the small bottle that contained the portion of the Medoc la Grande wine, as her trump evidence. The sight of it brought Richard on his feet.

"You would need this for your night-cup. It would make sounder nightly sleeping for a Palate couple." The words dissected Richard. They came as a surprise because Apphia didn't brandish her knowledge of Richard's nightly affair to alert him for cover. The wound was unbearable. Richard got up and yelled a command. "Bruna stay!" The power and the volume of the vibration in his voice froze Bruna with fear by the door. Spirited with rage and with fire in his eyes, he started to approach his wife. Yet Apphia was in no mood to compromise, although she feared for her life, for she was seeing a different Richard. She was beholding a sight of a steady advancing spirit towards her, but a resolved disposition of calmness took over her. Apphia transfixed a calm gaze onto her husband's face: "Richard, Remember, it's me."

The few words flowed like a cool stream and Richard began to see the images of their past flowing before his view. He heard the words again: "Richard. Remember, it's me, Apphia. Our struggles built our strength. We cried together; we laughed together. Remember. It's me. We provided together; we shared together." At that point, Seth showed his face. His presence spoke the volumes that Richard had forgotten. Richard looked at his friend; he remembered the gaunt face he helped to rescue. As he took his eyes off him, he heard Apphia's words again: "Richard, look at me. It's our world. We'll build together."

At that point, Richard's knees began to boggle under the weight of Apphia's sentimental words. His legs also began to wobble and protest against his own fierce and shaking steps; but with settled slow strides, he tottered his advance steadily towards Apphia. At almost three feet away, Richard reached out his right arm in request for the small portion of the Medoc la Grande vintage, and without a sinew of restraint, Apphia handed her husband the small bottle. Richard turned without a word and tottered slowly towards Bruna. Still frozen by the door, Bruna looked on as her secret lover walked feebly, tottering towards her, in both physical and emotional pain.

Indeed, Richard had come to like Bruna Dhahl for what she was and who she was. He resolutely admired her. She was very astute in her craft of scheming for whatever she wanted. Politicians would hail her, the public would detest her, and the press would adore her; she would always headline the news. Richard had come to admire her skill to equivocate. Her tact to defend her lies would render the attempt of a pathological, rather amateurish. Her lies were tasty, fit for the willing palate and many had swallowed them. Richard had. And perhaps, he had just begun to fill the sourness of the tastes from Bruna's boiling cauldron.

Eventually, Richard got to where frozen Bruna stood. He looked at her, perhaps admiringly. He stretched his arms, then his right hand in a seeming attempt to hug her, but rather presented her with the sealed small bottle with the expensive Medoc la Grande wine.

"Open it." He said. She tried to twist the cap anti-clockwise to open it. After two difficult attempts, Bruna successfully opened it. As Richard held his gaze on Bruna with a deeper penetrating search into her eyes, he made a strange demand.

"Bruna, drink it. Let's share it." Bruna was astounded by Richard's strange request and glared at him in tongue-tied disbelief. "If it will ease my headache and my emotional pain as you have often said, then let's share it." And Richard briefly attempted to sip it. He drew it to his lips. With his right arm extended to Bruna in a seeming depiction of an invitation for a hug, Richard rephrased the words he once heard from her: "Your health, the peace of mind, even life – these are priceless. My dear Bruna, when you drink wine, you must imagine all these benefits." Richard slightly lifted the small bottle to gesture a toast or seemingly offer her to take her wine back. Discomfited by Richard's action, Bruna angrily knocked off the bottle from Richard's grip. It created a spill on her skirt and blouse. The sight, however, was a portrayal of a more dismal perceptive outlook. They were seeing a blood-stained skirt with a blouse foreboding a bemoaning graphic of symbolic picture of a woman in blood, the woman Richard had loved to hate, and he hated he loved her.

Bruna Dhahl left without a word and Richard turned to face his family. He watched Bruna close the door behind them. Then it was all quiet. Apphia walked towards her husband. Richard anticipated a derisive comment, but she simply passed by. Her eyes were on the bottle on the floor. It still remained unbroken; it had survived another fall. Apphia picked it up. Perhaps the little wine left in it was worth a cost for contention.

CHAPTER 25

With the exit of Bruna from the walls of the Bridges, her shadow however, continued to linger hauntingly within their home. Within those walls, the pages of time rolled by into the threshold of the less predictable future. Laughter held its peace amidst the painful roar of the wounded in the wilderness of strange triumphs. Seth's healing in the house of the Bridges remained a marvel. His request to leave for his own home had often been met with a quiet appeal to stay on for few days by Apphia. She'd also wished the balm of time would heal her ailing relationship with her husband. The thrill in that relationship was fast on the run. Richard knew it. His power and desire to check that run had been sapped by an overpowering enchantment, the vagaries of Bruna's bosom. And Apphia had always factored them on the renditions of Palate, especially served in the palm of Bruna.

Some new liqueurs were emerging very popular among the Palate board. They were yet to be signed and were being pushed by Bruna but, Richard had been a stumbling block. He'd chosen to press on with an avowed commitment to challenge Palate's penchant for so-called "palatable ideas." Richard, on the other hand, was seeing very unsavory consequences.

The previous night, Richard was the lone voice of dissent from Palate's ambition to introduce liqueurs flavored with various herbs and fruits, noticeably from Africa and Brazil. He recalled how Otto Nanseman schooled him: "Mr. Bridges, may I remind you that this company is called Palate. It has everything to do with appetite, and I mean appetite with pleasure, if you stand against it, then I am afraid, you're simply saying you don't share our values and you don't value your membership." That was Richard's new world.

Apphia had sensed mixed suspicions about his new world for a long time. She had often wondered if she were the cause of their teetering relationship.

Richard had been returning home late from his Palate board meetings. Sometimes he would be gone for a day or two with reasons that Apphia had found difficult to believe but, chose to not question them. Her heart ached. In the midst of the turbulence she was seeing her husband as a very troubled and confused man. There were days he would return home with a feeling of despondency, and nothing seemed to appeal to him. He hardly discussed his mind. But that night was a different night.

It was past midnight at a bar. The bartender signaled that it was time he closed, Richard was unwilling to barge. He looked at his wrist watch. He couldn't read the time and he couldn't blame his failure on the low lights in the local bar. Everything looked murky even the face of his wrist watch. He was drunk, very drunk, and being one of the recent regulars at the bar, the bartender struggled with the cruel option to ask him to leave. He wouldn't want to do that. After all, he didn't really know him. He only knew him as a well self-comporting customer. He watched Richard down the last gulp in his glass and announced his triumph over the dregs in the glass.

"It's pretty late. Is she not going to be mad at you tonight?" The bartender struck a conversation with an undertone reference to customer Richard's wife.

"Who?" Richard asked trying to stall for a quick thinking response. He eventually composed a responsible answer. "I'm sure she will, but I won't argue."

"That's wise. Most people do, though." The barman remarked. He watched Richard struggle to adjust himself off the stool and stretch a leg to touch the floor. "It seems you don't need much to get you going."

"How do you know?" Richard asked.

"I noticed your reluctance and your facial expression always betrayed your struggle, even the way you hold your drink."

"You're right. I don't drink much. I acquired this tendency later in this life." Richard owned up to his new habit. "This habit frightens me."

"You know what I'm am going to do for you?" The bartender had a suggestion for Richard. "I'm going to brew you a hot coffee, but while I work on that, I'm going to put music on to help you dance the booze out of you. I work on your coffee; you work out on your sobriety."

"You're kidding, right?"

"No, I'm not. It works. You sweat off the booze in you."

Richard laughed. He imagined dancing alone and how ridiculous he would look.

"D'you mean I will be dancing all by myself like a – like a clown?" Richard asked.

"I didn't say 'like a clown.' It's your word. I'm simply trying to help you to be sober, by dancing into sobriety."

"I am not a good dancer."

"I didn't suggest that you are. I've never seen a drunken person dance to impress; they dance because they're happy or because they want to forget what they're going through. Hey, do you want to dance or not; you can't be behind your wheels like this? You'll kill yourself or an innocent somebody."

The bartender remarked in a matter-of-fact tone and turned his back towards Richard while he got the coffee machine ready for the brew for his special customer. But then he turned back in response to an audible activity behind him and he saw Richard trying to rehearse his moves. The music of the early years of fast-beat Rock-N-Roll exploded in the bar hall. The Richard Bridges show was on.

His footwork had him contending with the tables and chairs in the bar. Then he settled with one chair which became his dancing partner. He swung it around as often as he could while knocking his knees together and shooting his legs off the floor in keeping with the beat. Richard was in a frenzy and his legs began flying in the air while operating his arms rhythmically like trying to catch butterflies in the air. The lone audience, the bartender, watched behind the bar as he also swayed and moved his body. He clapped with the rhythm and beat of the music until the music ended.

"Man, you are no flat-footer at all. You really rocked and rolled"

Richard was panting for breath, but he enjoyed it. He wanted more and he got it. It started in slow rhythm, the beat moved in, and the atmosphere erupted. A blend of modern Rock with undertones of jazzy Rhythms and Blues refilled the air. This time it was not Richard's feet work only on display; his arms also got busy. The hips were busy while his left hand shielded his rhythmic moving crotch, and the busy hips were moving in steady thrust of back and forth. They were also congruous with the interchangeable gusto of the rhythm and the beat of the music. Then he re-engaged the legs in a sideway motion like they were stepping on hot coals.

A couple of guys walked in; a presumed dating couple also walked in. Richard took off his tie and threw it on the nearest table. A guy reached into his wallet, threw a five-dollar bill on the table by Richard's tie. Another guy walked to the table and left a twenty-dollar bill by the five. Richard was in frenzy. He tried to do the "Moon Walk;" he lost his balance and hit the floor. The applause of the audience of five was thunderous enough; at least it was unanimous for drunken Lawyer Richard.

Richard got up, a little disconcerted; he brushed off any dirt on his pants and joked: "The moon wasn't friendly, as I thought it would be." His small audience laughed with him.

"Let me get 'Smirnoff on Rocks'." One of the newly-walked-in men tried to purchase a drink.

"I'm very sorry; I'm closed for the night." The barman explained to them and they left disappointed leaving Richard and his nightly acquaintance.

"Do you feel better after the workout?"

"In fact, I do. I really do."

"Good. Do you think you can now drive?"

"Yes, I think I can, but I need a shot off that." Richard pointed to a bottle among the wide array of bottles on the bar shelf.

"No, here's your coffee." The barman poured him the freshly brewed coffee. Richard disdained the treatment. He felt he was being treated like a child.

"But, Mr. Barkeeper, if I don't drink, you'll be out of business and out of job." Richard joked trying to hold his recovering drunken head up.

"Not really, I'll be selling milk. There's always something to sell. I don't take advantage of people in their mishap. I help turn the economic wheel and I benefit from it. What's your name again?"

"Richard." He replied.

"Now, Richard, get out." The bartender's face turned into a fiery frown.

"Are you kicking me out?" Richard asked innocently.

"You bet I am and you must leave now."

"I'm sorry if I upset you. I'm not good at jokes, but I was led to that loose comment, because I may lose my job too. I guess by tomorrow. Somebody on the executive board hasn't been kind to me. I won't fight it, though."

The bartender had his back against Richard. He'd been busy cleaning up glasses and trying to tidy up the place. He turned and took a good look at him. He saw a very troubled man. He'd observed that Richard hadn't been approaching his drink in the glass like the others did. He always tended to take a hard look at it as if he were debating with it or with himself before drinking it. Richard's awareness of his drinking approach as pointed out to him earlier by the bartender, had impressed Richard's mind that he was talking to no ordinary barkeeper. He must be the proprietor. His look was firm but this time it carried a more temperate glare.

"I'll tell you this; you leave your car here and pick it up tomorrow. I'll call you a cab. He will bring me the bill tomorrow. It's on me." The bartender offered a conciliatory tone.

"You don't have to do that, but I appreciate it very much." Richard   expressed. In no time, the taxi arrived and Richard picked up his tie and the total of the twenty-five dollars on the table, and was on his way. He arrived at a familiar home which wasn't his home. The host didn't seem to be expecting him and wasn't particularly pleased that Richard showed up unannounced. The host was already in bed, but chose to come to the door and let him in. She was wearing a robe which Richard was familiar with after few nightly escapades in her house. Richard jokingly tried to pull the robe off her, but she clasped it tighter to her body. The audible activity attracted another guest who was already in the house.

"Bruna, who is it?" The other guest asked from one of the rooms. Richard recognized that voice for its familiar huskiness, but Richard refused to accept the recognition until the owner of that voice came out. Sobriety instantly asserted its place over Richard. He saw the man. He hadn't shed off an iota of his pride and still carried the air of arrogance around him. The man laughed to scorn upon seeing Richard and walked to a switch on the wall. He turned on the light to fully assure himself of the sight that was in his view. There was arrogance in his laugh and Richard had always hated that. The images of the meeting at "Dan's Den" conference room flashed through his mind.

"Sit down, Mr. Bridges. What brings you here this early hour of the morning?"

"I was going to ask you the same question, Shazzy Spicer."

"This is my house. I own this house." Richard turned to look at Bruna in shock and in disbelief. She looked coy with shame. Richard didn't know who to believe. He'd feasted on the wanton appealing appetites of lies cooked by Bruna, and the reality was, only Bruna could serve the taste for escape. Richard didn't know what to expect. A Portuguese utterance of betrayal was audible: "Voce tambem, Bruna?" Bruna's Portuguese lessons paid off there for Richard.

"Didn't she tell you? I guess not, sorry, but I wonder why." Shazzy expressed in derision as he shrugged his shoulders.

"Well, Shazzy, Bruna, I must be leaving. Good night." Richard turned to leave with his head down. He heard Shazzy's mocking voice and laughter rang in the air behind him.

"No. Mr. Bridges; you just got here. You have a lot to learn. Don't leave. I could still host you; plenty of rooms here - unless you're just passing by." Shazzy derided his stranded foe again.

"Yes, I'm just passing by." Richard replied and didn't look back. Through the main front door, he could hear Shazzy ordering Bruna back to bed. Richard hoped he could find the cab-driver, but the driver had already taken off. Richard was alone without any means to get home. He boldly stepped into the quiet streets and into the cool night breeze of the typical fall climate. He could feel the tremors of his heavy heart. The darkness of the night offered no comfort to hide the nearly shivering body of this lonesome traveler. There were no stars in the summits; instead, only the cold emptiness of a hovering column which had forced the dates of romantic strollers to wishful warm days of cloudless but starry nights of tomorrow.

Richard sensed he was alone. He'd exiled himself from a society that hailed him and also from a community that adored him. He walked alone along the trenches of the complexities of life. Daybreak might have been four or even few hours away, but he had no longing for it. Every day would still birth out stories from pregnancies of yesterday, and tomorrow would rush the offspring's again to do the dictates of the wheel of time. Dawn must wait; must take her time and must not be induced into laboring the birth of his adultery story and stories of coercions by other Palate personnel into the intrigues of Palate power politics. They must wait, perhaps not birthed at all. Richard was dreading the gossips, the rumors, the discussions, and the phone calls.

Indicted for treason for disobeying and maligning his conscience, by the ruling maverick dynasty of his mind, Richard knew that he had no power to wield over the struggles for his mind. Although as a proven and distinguished attorney, the enormity of the task to defend his name, his profession, and his job, had estranged him to an abandoned terrain of despondency.

The streets were too quiet for him. The hollow volumes of silence could only be filled by empty imaginations of cinematic haunts. His sight, which wasn't as keen as the nocturnal eyes of the owl, was prone to interpret swaying tree branches as shadows of lurking men with fiendish intents brandishing weapons to ward off his prowl on their turf. His plight led the way; his imaginations haunted him, his fate guided him, his name spurred him on.

Richard was aware that he wasn't sleepwalking. He reminded himself. He was simply hearing the crackling steps from the hard soles of his shoes. They sounded like the feet of an approaching platoon advancing in steady stomp towards him. He made a logical turn to the right and that opened up a view as far as his eyes could carry him. He saw a sleeping city with pockets of lights in the distant homes. His home wasn't within reach, about twenty miles away, where his son Josh might be coiled up in bed. Josh, as usual would wake up with the daily question on his breath: "Mom, did Dad come home last night?" The answer might be the same, the same disappointing expression: "No, he will be home perhaps tonight." Apphia knew her answer was far-fetched.

However, she'd put faith in hope and each day a chip of that bold stake and the value that she had put in the tenacity of that hope dropped. Without any physical closeness, that night Richard was hearing a loud reecho of his son's question. It grew louder in the hollow halls of his heart: "Did Dad come home?" It was even louder still, reverberating in his aching head that it exploded into Richard's oral scream: "Ye-e-e-s-s-s!" But it didn't silence his mind. The war raged on. Worry had raised its standard; the walls of worry seemed to have evolved into a condition that was adaptable to his conscience. No pangs, no cares, the long walk home had just begun. It was well, he thought. "He knows I love her, I do, I truly do – love them." He tried to resolve his dissonance; his family was in his mind's eye.

CHAPTER 26

The cold breeze that continued to hit his face had rendered his eyes watery. His steps were weary. The sound from each step said it all. He would concede that they had slowed; they were irregular. Richard must have known where his feet were carrying him for he was a stranger on the quiet streets. He slowed his pace as he thought he heard a strange noise which might not have come from him, very different from his crackling feet. A coyote perhaps, he thought. He turned and an object from the foliaged landscape behind the street lanes froze on impulse of Richard's reaction. He fixed his gaze on the object; then there was partial movement.

Crouching behind the bulrush was a young boy with very active and engaging eyes, even in the dark. The sight of the boy frightened him. His immediate thoughts raced from fantasy to reality. He might have been surrounded by young villains, perhaps spirits or a lone adventurer-in-training for nocturnal activities by a supervising adult. Richard thought he was facing an armed miscreant on a prowl for any worthy prize or prey.

After few seconds, the boy emerged from behind the bulrushes and the overgrown landscape. He was about five feet tall and stood a distance of twelve feet away from Richard. He looked up at the towering Richard and opened his mouth with a confident greeting.

"I come in peace. I bear no arms; I seek peace with my fellow man."

Richard was taken aback by the seeming scripted nature and tone of the greeting. He wondered whether he was dreaming or was experiencing a live reality. His response equally, was of a classical bearing.

"Peace I do seek and no arms I do bear, but who, if I may ask, am I speaking with on this cold early hours of the morning?"

The young boy cautiously drew closer and stood in full view maintaining a ten-foot distance between them. He was handsome, but seemed to have been toughened by the rough dictates of life.

"I don't know you well enough to tell you my name." The response was brusque and was enough to convey to Richard that he was standing before a smart boy.

"Well, my name is Richard."

"That's not enough. I would like to address you by your last name. You are Mr. ..."

"Bridges, but just call me Richard."

"I'd rather not. I try to accord adults of your age with the 'mister' respect. I am taught to do that." Richard was beginning to be comfortable, but was yet to come to grips with the oddity of an early prowl by such a youth.

"And who taught you that, your parents?"

"My parent, yes - can you help a dying man?" The request was abrupt and it stemmed from desperation. Richard acknowledged his desperation, but realized he had to approach his decision gingerly. He reweighed his doubts about the young boy and concluded that an assailant wouldn't have the patience to encourage a lengthy dialogue, so he might not have really been in danger.

"What's your name?" Richard asked.

"Call me Robert. Mr. Bridges, my father needs help, please." Richard was touched. The frantic request made his shivering dissipate, but wondered what he could do since he had no First-Aid training, not even the basics or knowledge about any health assistance.

Robert led the way through a bushy path and through a small wooded field to finally arrive at an old van location. He opened the side door and he entered in with Richard. Before his eyes could adjust to the darker indoor of the van, an unusual sound emanated from the van, a voice of an older person.

"Did you get help?" In an involuntary reaction, Richard turned towards the direction of the voice. He saw a movement on the floor, an object in parallel positioning right behind the driver's and the front passenger's seats. The voice came from the floor; Richard observed after his eyes had eventually readjusted to the new environment. The van had no seats. It seemed the seats were intentionally removed to make for a greater floor space. The person groaned his words: "Robert, are you here?"

"I have brought help." Robert responded.

"Who is the help? Is the person, somebody I know or somebody who knows me?"

"I am not sure." Robert turned to Richard. He pulled the sleeve of Richard's coat to urge him to say something. Richard was reflecting on how he'd thrown himself into such a bizarre situation and wondered if there was an escape for him from a labyrinth of this kind. He didn't anticipate a world in an old van; and neither anticipated the queer behaviors of his new acquaintances. With a measure of qualmishness, he tried to introduce himself.

"I'm Richard Bridges. I was hoping to get a taxi by the street when Robert approached me with a request for help. How can I help you?"

The sprawled figure pulled itself to a sitting posture on the floor. There was no light in the van room to reveal the faces of the voices. His voice gave him away as a thirty-something or a slightly older person. He heaved deeply and exhaled a strong windy sigh – probably from the straining effort while gathering his strength to squat.

"Mr. Bridges, you may not know me, but your name is familiar. You may be the answer to what I have wished for or what I may say, or my answered prayer. Robert is my brother. He is young. We share the same father but different mothers. He calls me "Dad" because my age suggests I could be his Dad. His mother, my father's young wife died when Robert was only two years old. Our father died a year later – all from complications of drugs. I believe genetically we have this drug thing in us. I take no pride in what I have allowed myself to be. I think more of Robert and I don't want him to end up the way I am now."

Richard turned around on hearing Robert's attempt to snuffle in his dripping nose. He'd been sobbing. Richard wrapped his arms around young Robert for an assuring sympathy. He felt Robert's cold fingers and began to rub them. Robert sensed that Richard was acknowledging the gravity of his plight and that moved him even more. He felt an assurance of care. His sobs were louder; they drowned the heavy breathing of his brother the 'father' figure. There was silence.

"I'm still breathing, but my breath is shallow." Richard heard the whispery utterance. He moved closer to hear him better. Richard felt a touch by a trembling hand and he reciprocated the touch. He felt he had touched a hairy, but very skeletal frame.

"Thank you. Please, don't be too close. I am in very poor health."

The words brought memories of his street encounter with Seth. It also reminded him about how he and his wife Apphia planned and successfully lured Seth to their house for the first time. He was hearing Seth's protest - refusing to sit in their chair because he was concerned that he might contaminate it. The memory was still fresh about their corporate effort to help Seth overcome his sickness; he remembered how Apphia tactically set the chair behind Seth to deny him the option of refusal. The dark environment was presenting a ghostly mimic of that event; the characters were different and so were the voices.

"My name is Cannon Jetteh. Time is running out on me." Cannon moaned his self-introduction. He turned and cast a dismal glance at Robert. "I try to teach Robert, and to guide him to - not follow my drug-abuse path, the path of our father, Doug Jetteh. Robert – O – Robert, my brother who I consider my son at the same time. He is a good boy. Yes, Robert Jetteh is a good boy. He chooses to listen to me."

All was quiet around them, in and outside the van. At every interlude of Cannon's parting words, the depth in sound of his breathing filled the van and Richard wondered if fate was also counting down on his life's tenure also on earth, especially due to the unprepared situation he had walked into. Sure, he was witnessing something he had not at all anticipated. A sound of sniffling was heard. It was Robert's, very emotional, while Cannon still bemoaned his past indulgent mistakes.

"Robert is young, too young to watch this unfold before him. I'd rather let him observe my peaceful farewell than to leave him unprepared for a future he cannot imagine - in a van. We've been talking a lot tonight. I see his fears. But, Robert has promised me. He will be good. He will grow into the man people will be proud of."

The vehemence in Cannon's retraction suggested his detachment from the swaying appeals of modern society. How long had he been a hermit? Richard wondered as Cannon continued. Then Cannon reached out into a wooden box which looked like a tool box, and fetched out a book. It was an old Bible. It had been kept well. There was silence – it was a long pause, about ninety seconds. Cannon became emotional as he unfurled a piece of cloth that his Bible was wrapped in for preservation purposes.

"I introduced Robert to the Bible two years ago. There are many things we don't understand, but one thing I do know and believe, is that every part of me; my body was engineered and structured for a particular functioning. If it is so, then somebody might have intentionally crafted me; crafted you, and crafted Robert. Please, don't go far, think about the parts of your body; think about how each part is purposely designed and engineered for and to function as it does."

The words arrested Richard's attention, but found them hard to reconcile Cannon's transient bearing with the telling attractiveness of the wisdom in what he was saying. As a result, Richard swayed his head involuntarily towards his shoulder in subjective response to Cannon's claim. Richard tried to speak, not to necessarily question Cannon's beliefs, but wondered if that was Cannon's artful ploy of religiosity to win his favor. Nonetheless, the alcohol smell on Richard's breath was overpowering in the van. It couldn't escape a comment. However, as he tried to respect the solemn atmosphere in the van, he still gave himself away with his ambivalence, and by trifling with the solemn moment of Cannon, a very broken and dying man. Cannon spoke softly; his spirit remained docile while his eyes rested on Richard Bridges.

"Mr. Bridges, I am mentally sound. Any new thing that challenges popular opinion is often branded crazy. I am sure you'll find out one day." It seemed it was a direct response to Richard's unexpressed remark, and it surprised Richard.

Cannon chuckled, but the sound in that chuckle commanded a peaceful confidence and an irony of pity for his listener. "D'you know, they even called Jesus crazy – crazy for speaking and declaring truth against the popular opinion of that age?" Richard looked keen.

"Mr. Bridges, sometimes my mouth gets very dry, and it makes chewing difficult. I wouldn't attempt to chew anything with my dry mouth because there will be bruises all over my tongue and the walls of my mouth. But, it's funny, when I am hungry and I see food or smell food, saliva begins to build up in my mouth. The mouth becomes more watery. Our maker has created a system, a way to make the mouth produce more saliva before the food gets into our mouth and to eventually moisturize it for mastication. The teeth have their roles; to beat down the food and crush it so that it can be swallowed soft without bruising the chambers of the mouth. It's a simple thought. Don't you think a master mind must be behind that? I am not ashamed to declare this truth. I wonder even more about the idea that the creator had a ready provision, a fountain of milk, food for a baby before his or her arrival. A very caring maker did plan it all out. Would you say this systematic procedure was by accident? It is sad if anyone ignores the truth about creation and the creator, either by arrogant refusal or by ignorant rejection. Definitely, the maker knew what he was doing. He planned it all. Even so when I pray, and call on him I expect his response."

The serene silence of the surroundings and the ignored orchestra of chirping crickets all conduced to a tranquil keenness of attention to a crying heart that was bearing itself out to Richard, the heart of Cannon. He spoke very passionately and at this point he became very emotional. Richard and Robert sensed the emotion in his voice.

"O, my friend - for all these years I didn't give this a thought. I do now. I'm not ashamed to declare that I believe it now. O, I know I have wasted my short youthful years with pleasure, pleasure, and pleasure. You know, there comes a time in a man's life when the glamor will be gone and man will begin to ask: What next - when the looks fade or go away? What next when your great voice could no longer hold a simple note, or could not be heard? What next when the sensation fades, the charm wears out and the popularity fizzles? What next when the taste is gone and the appetite goes dull, when wealth loses its worth; when demand does not determine value; when daily strength fizzles? Where is the answer; where is the solution, the cure? I don't know."

"One thing I know; there is hope. If my body is the engine of my life and runs on gasoline, but I choose to refuel it with salt water, I must take the blame for my disobedience and folly. It meant, I failed to follow the manual which had the instructions from the maker of the engine. I have no excuse. My next step is to approach the maker and to apologize and petition him to repair me again. Then he chooses to remake me, to make me anew. He tells me his word is sure. He'll replace the broken engine with a new one. It's in the book, I mean in the manual, the Bible. Mr. Bridges, I'm at peace."

Cannon heaved a loud sigh. His right hand seemed to be groping around the floor, perhaps to reach Robert's. Robert sensed it and he reached out to him in the dark. Cannon was not done yet.

"Mr. Bridges, when the music was loud, we all danced to it. The drinks – O - we all drank to our fill. Hmm, the loud boozers would feel denied if the music stopped, but then there would always be a soft voice that would say 'Good night.' It would. It always did. The question is: what 'good' could we make out of the 'night' when the music stops and the lights go out. They call it 'late.' My friend, I hope the light continues to shine in us and through us, and we'll still be alright in the night – even when the light is out."

Richard couldn't fully comprehend the distant discourse of his strange acquaintance. He was convinced that Cannon's hermitic ideologue and allegories must come from the Bible and seemed to make sense, but then he wondered, without visible and audible expression: 'Why would he like to live like this?' He felt, however, that Cannon had earned his sympathy. Cannon had told him much about himself and Richard hoped he'd spare him the ordeal to not request reasons for his lone escapade on the streets.

"My friend, I've told you all of this because my behavior or how I lived my life, has been shaped by my perception of God, our Maker. As I reflect on my life, I realize that the conditions of this world offer us appetites to do the wrong things, even when we know those things are wrong. They are seductive. They offer appealing appetites through desire and influence and a craving for instant pleasure. They satisfy the appetite, and then abandon the person to face the consequences of his decision. However, God meets us where we are. He reaches out to us, to help us. He came to live with us, to help us by showing us how to live. Our failure is that we doubt that he's real. We fail to recognize him for who he is and shun his help. I've accepted his offer; he's been working in me and I am at peace. That's the love of God."

Cannon's words were poignant. Richard wondered if he was inferring that he himself was literally a God-sent to them. No, that could not be. His conscience continued to indict him every moment and Cannon had just hung his affair on that flagstaff of his conscience. Richard could not trivialize the words he was hearing.

"Our kindness and our goodness do not present us as people without sin. How often have we disappointed ourselves with things we've sworn we would never do but ended up doing those very things? Man needs help. That's why it rains on both the good and the bad." Richard had heard the words which were beginning to give him a different take on life; strange words from a strange source.

"Sir, my breath is fading." Cannon began to feel weak.

Richard began to panic. Robert brought the half-bottle of water that he'd been dispensing earlier to his 'brother.' Richard got Cannon to incline on multiple pillows which he'd been using earlier and placed the opened bottle to his mouth. They heard a couple of sounds of subdued throat activity. There were long seconds of silence and Cannon broke his silence again.

"I have been active in three wars and God has saved me from all three wars, but perhaps, not this time. As a veteran I know the culture of the battlefield."

Richard became more confused. He felt like calling for emergency help, but wondered what answers to give should the medics arrived and began questioning. Robert and Cannon were new acquaintances and Richard was yet to know them. Then a voice volunteered itself out through Richard's lips.

"Cannon, God saved you on the battlefield; he will save you again on this hustling field of life. Did you say he has reasons for the things he does? Then he must have a reason for your life. I'm told prayer helps. Have you asked him to reveal that to you?"

There was another long pause. Cannon sighed. "I haven't thought of that request. Huh, I need to think hard about that."

As time wore on, weary Robert was beginning to feel sleepy. Nonetheless, Cannon was not done. Richard began to contemplate on his next move from his hermit-like environment. He heard his name and this time with a solemn plea. It arrested his attention.

"Mr. Bridges, please, if you may, please, take Robert as your son. I have rushed you into a commitment, but there is something you must know. As Robert and I were talking, it struck me to ask him, if I died in this van, where he would go from here. His answer was: 'Don't worry. I believe after knocking on few doors around here, somebody will eventually say yes.' Then we strangely heard

355

a scream from the streets 'Ye-s-s-s!' We couldn't believe our ears. I heard it; Robert heard it, we all heard it. He rushed out to find out who yelled the response. I was actually surprised at his bravery and determination. Mr. Bridges, he met you. Did you scream 'Yes'? We all heard it; somebody did; I am sure you heard it too. Please, you were the screamer, were you?"

The rather persuasive questioning had Richard cornered between truth with responsibility and denial with regrets. He thought for a moment and concluded that he would not want to add anymore guilt to the haunting past he was fleeing from. Again, he thought for few minutes and admitted that he did scream. "But that makes me no better responsible person than anyone else."

"Man is from the rough of the soil." Tired Richard felt he was hearing a still whispering in the ears of his mind. "The cloudy, rainy days of life wash the rough out to reveal what manner of a man a person really is. He may be as smooth as a pebble, but sometimes he had to be conditioned among the rough, like a shiny stone suppressed and oppressed by the trampling of the surface of the rough. May be you are the shiny dust that cannot pull itself together unless rainy circumstances reveal the hope in your glitter or allow a careless stream of events to sadly wash you away to deeper roughs. What drove you to yell on the street? Perhaps, it's something that is trying to reveal the rough-type of soil that you are. Whatever it is, allow the texture of your goodwill be revealed."

Evelyn tossed in her bed again. She'd just been stirred out of bed by a rather unusual very early morning call. She'd had her days of anxieties. Her position as a career attorney of Milo, Grady and Strong hadn't leveled the field for her to be what she had always wanted to be. Within the early few months of her association with Richard, she had benefited from his good-naturedness by encouraging her to reestablish her relationship with her mother, Dorina; she witnessed his selfless commitment to helping his friend, Seth; rescuing him from the brink of suicide while defying the danger of potential infections. Richard's moral resume had molded the heart of Evelyn into a trophy chest of his accomplishments. To her, Richard could never go wrong. He always triumphed.

When the rumors began to move around the office that Richard's board membership at Palate was being challenged on grounds of abuse of trust and misconduct, as her team partner and friend in the Firm, Evelyn explored every pore to access any legal prudence that might help whitewash the actions of her friend. She found none. Then she heard the heart-breaking news; Richard was being relieved of his position with Grady, Milo and Strong. She'd suspected that Richard might have had wind of his plight. Indeed, when Richard stopped getting phone responses from Sally, his administrator, his intuitional conclusion was that there had been a mutiny behind him, and Sally might have been told to not administer any responsibility in the office on his behalf. In view of these developments, when Evelyn's phone rang and she saw the caller's identity, she shuddered to take the call. She wouldn't want to be the source to confirm the bad news to him. She ignored the second call. She yawned and the more she thought of Richard's rumors the more the early chills drew yawns. Her phone rang again. It was Richard.

"I need a favor, Evelyn. I'm at a Bus Stop. Could you come over to see me, please?" Richard appealed in a very somber tone. Evelyn hurriedly pulled herself together and she was on her way. She wondered what she would tell him or what he would tell her that she did not know.

Evelyn pulled up at the bus stop as she was directed, but didn't find Richard. She saw three people waiting. She decided to drive off; she had barely covered few yards when she saw from her rear mirror that she was being flagged down by a person at the bus-stop. It was foggy and was difficult to identify the face that came to the car window. He had a tired face and the eyes were sleep-shot. In a not-decent suit, the man looked haggard. It was Richard.

Evelyn lowered the car window and hysterically commanded her instruction.

"Get in. It's freezing."

"I can't leave without these two; I'm with them."

"What do you mean? I don't know them." Evelyn turned off the engine, got out her car for a closer and better look at the figure on the bench. After treading stealthily and bending to observe Cannon on the bench, Evelyn's figure imposed its frame over the bench-sleeper. It startled the bench occupant and he woke up to see the face of a young lady. Cannon thought he had met Richard's wife. Richard interrupted Evelyn's curious snooping by pulling her aside for a talk with her. They returned in a minute to the car; Richard took the front seat and the two occupied the back seats.

"Evelyn, this is Cannon and his young brother, Robert. We'll get acquainted better later. Please, I can't go home looking like this."

"No. I'm not taking you to your house. I'm taking you to my mother's. I'll discuss the situation with her." She suggested.

"I'm very grateful, Evelyn; very, very grateful." Richard expressed.

"There are two extra rooms; you can use one to get some sleep. I will let your family know where you are. Cannon and his brother may use the other room. Honestly, Richard I don't know these people; with all due respect, I hope, as a lawyer you know what you're doing."

"Miss, that makes us appreciate it even more; thank you. Please, we're a very peaceful people." Robert spoke softly. His soft and surprised mellow remark instantly wooed Evelyn's favor that it prompted her to take a look at him again from the rear mirror as she drove on. She couldn't resist a smile.

Richard felt comfortable to discuss their office.

"Evelyn, where is Sally? She hasn't been returning my calls."

"Sadly, she was fired when they found out that she had brought you some files from the office. I guess the Palate files." Richard was quiet after hearing the fate of Sally. A feeling of guilt and responsibility overtook him.

"Any word of her after that ...?"

"Yes. She expressed there were some items that she personally wanted to hand them to you. I am sure she's been trying to get hold of you."

"I appreciate that very much."

Richard and the group eventually arrived at Dorina's house. Dorina looked very different from Richard's last meeting with her; she looked younger and healthier.

CHAPTER 27

The day was young and Richard's mind was still a crowded field of frets of care. As he sat in Dorina's car at the parking lot of the neighborhood's grocery store waiting for Seth to show up, he was preoccupied with how to retrieve his car from the kind bartender, find what to do with Cannon and Robert, return to his family and to reshape his plans for the future. He needed Seth to be the bridge between him and Apphia. Seth was a willing go-between, but was very concerned about Apphia's state of mind. Richard's actions had completely wiped out any vestiges of trust that she had in him; in fact, to her, no man was worthy of any trust.

It was midweek and the brisk activity of cars in the full parking lot suggested an unusual atmosphere. He witnessed a lady who was grappling with her uncontrollable crying daughter and her heavy laden grocery cart that she had yoked to her small frame. The lady continued with sheer determination to push the heavy grocery cart to her car. Upon noticing that, Richard stepped out of Dorina's car and walked to help her. She yielded the cart-control to Richard as she transferred more attention to her crying daughter. She felt relieved and was very thankful to Richard.

"That's a lot of shopping for today." He expressed as he unloaded the items unto the lady's car.

"I know. My in-laws are arriving tonight for Thanksgiving tomorrow; my husband is serving at overseas so they're coming to keep us company as we cook together."

"How nice, well, have a Happy Thanksgiving." Richard wished her warmly as he headed back to his car with a betrayed conscience. He'd forgotten that Thanksgiving was near and evidently at Apphia's table, he would be an absentee husband and father. The thought didn't leave him. He opened the driver's door and unconsciously curled himself into the seat. Seth had seen him in the distance and was walking to him with a surprise. He had Josh with him. Josh had been counting down the minutes when 'Uncle Seth' informed him about a trip to his Dad. His excitement brewed every minute with countless questions fueled by his imaginations of the Dad he had not seen for weeks. Then he saw his Dad. Richard had just gotten out of the car upon seeing them in the distance. He waved to them. They waved back. Josh's excitement was unrestrainable. He left the hold of 'Uncle Seth' and started running excitedly to meet his father. Then a car screeched. The onlookers gasped. Josh was on the ground.

His father and Seth rushed to him while the crowd gathered.

Josh wasn't moving; and there was blood.

The ambulance arrived early at the hospital with Josh's eyes' still open, but he was struggling to communicate. He tried; his father couldn't stand the sight of the blood that appeared to line across his lips.

Apphia came rushing into the waiting room. Bearded Richard could not easily be recognized by his wife and he could neither recognize his wife. Her extreme weight loss was a natural disguise. Apphia looked sickly. She passed by her husband but instantly stopped and acknowledged Seth. It wasn't an act to spite her husband, but Apphia simply didn't recognize the changes on the Richard she knew. After a long look from a distance, dispirited Richard joined them. After many weeks, husband and wife for the first time, looked at each other in silent surprise.

In no time the physician walked in.

"The x-rays reveal non-displaced rib fractures; it means the ribs aren't completely broken. He couldn't talk to you because he was finding it difficult to take deep breaths due to extreme pain. So far, we haven't seen any damage tissues or organs. No head trauma. He has been stabilized and is sleeping. We will continue to monitor his response to the treatment."

"Does he know we are here?" Richard asked.

"Yes, he does. I sensed he was trying to ask for you and I told him you are here. He will be fine. You can go in and see him, he is sleeping now - please let him sleep."

The group walked in and found Josh sleeping peacefully. Richard stepped away for a brief word with the supervising nurse.

The nurse returned shortly and uncovered the legs of Josh for a brief inspection by his father. Then Richard saw it. His son was fulfilling the pact he had with him. He was wearing the socks his father had specially purchased for them which they had covenanted to be wearing anytime they would go walking together. The son had been faithful; the father had not been. The sight and the thought of his unfaithfulness tore Richard's heart as he imagined the worst in picturing the still but sleeping body of his son. He, instantly and very emotionally, withdrew from them to a quiet corner. Apphia saw the pain and agony in her husband's eyes so she followed him with a shared heart of anguish for a gripping moment of reconciliation.

Thanksgiving Day came. Richard and Apphia met at the bedside of their son again. They heard Josh talking faintly and smiled at them. He tried to make a hand wave, but had been restrained by multiple intravenous lines that covered his arms and body. The doctor had assured them that their son might be discharged early if he continued with his rate of recovery. Although the words of the doctor were assuring, they didn't serve to placate the outraged guilt that continued to attack Richard's. He'd concluded that if he'd been home, there would not have been any cause for a meeting at a grocery parking lot. That claim had quieted him into a simple muted walking life. He hardly shared words with his wife, but she knew him well and she understood his struggle. They parted again on another melancholy note.

However, Seth's assignment as emissary of peace for his friend, Richard seemed to be far from over. His new assignment was to reconcile himself with the Bridges. Since the accident, his actions of self-deprecations had held him away unsociably; he considered himself unworthy of the favor of the extended stay they had granted him. He'd imposed upon himself the overall blame for Josh's accident. His former student and friend, Eloquenter who had been an encourager and had always been there for Seth, hadn't been seen for some time. As the evening wore on, and as Seth sat lonely on the stool by the kitchen bar stand, he retraced his thoughts to the time when Richard and Eloquenter rescued and brought him from the park to rehabilitate him in the Bridges' home. He wished his young friend Eloquenter was with him. Actually, Seth's muted wish was a prayer. He wanted Elo to pray for Josh and the Bridges.

CHAPTER 28

A typical morning at Dorina's house had always remained quiet. There was no morning rush nor a quick breakfast bustle. Her guests, Cannon and his brother, Robert were still sleeping, but Richard was up. His son's accident had kept him up through the long hours of the night. He would hear Cannon and Robert engaging in long chats and games with Dorina into the late hours of the night. Dorina also seemed to be benefiting from their stay with her. She'd become livelier and Evelyn's father was considering to move back in with her. As Richard looked across his window, he saw Dorina on an early inspection of her plants and flowers. Dorina had also noticed that Richard was surprisingly up early for probably some coffee. She didn't want to pry into his affair, but she had followed with great empathy and concern about the fate of his son.

"Well, autumn the fall season is here; winter is near." Dorina expressed as she saw the dew on the brown leaves on the ground. "And sure enough, spring will also bring new life into these shedding plants."

"That's right, Miss Dorina. They say Spring always springs new life and hope. I need some words of encouragement; I haven't been myself lately." Richard admitted.

"It's interesting you say that. It tells me you have hope in spite of what's going on in your life right now and that's the right attitude." she said confidently.

"Thank you." The words hardly escaped his lips when a swarm of police cars filled the driveway and blocked the garage area of Dorina's house. He turned and looked with surprise at what was beginning to unfold. His mind instantly rushed to Cannon and Robert and wondered what they'd done. In no time, he began to upbraid himself quietly for his association with them. Then the word rang out, "freeze!" Dorina "froze" in obedience. Her past had haunted her for many years and she was convinced that the law had levelled with her. Shocked by the unfolding development, Richard rushed out.

"What has she do-o-ne?" The question died in his mouth.

"Mr. Richard Bridges, you are under arrest for suspicion of murder."

One of the gun-drawn policemen asserted his duty as they approached him cautiously. In bewilderment, Richard threw his arms impulsively in the air in conventional surrender. He thought he was dreaming because the night had been less kind, and had been wishing he would get some sleep before heading out to his house and then to the hospital to see his son, Josh.

"You have the right to remain silent." The officer maintained.

"Are you sure about your actions? Why am I being arrested?" The officers offered no response while Richard's arms were being cuffed behind him.

They forcibly turned him around to face the police cars and the shocked faces of Cannon and Robert watched on from a window. As they lowered his head and forced his shoulders into the police car, Richard saw a shy hand and a shocked face, waving feebly at him. It was Evelyn's hand. She'd followed the police to see what would become of her friend and mentor. They'd earlier questioned her but she was under strong orders to not call Richard.

Before they drove off with him, Richard turned for a quick glance at her. His spirit was saying: "I know I have betrayed your trust, but I am innocent." She saw innocence in his eyes, but she saw fear in them too. So she looked on, very nonplused while every element in her screamed "Richard, no – no – not Richard." But, the words could hardly be heard. Her Richard was out of her reach.

Richard could determine from the sound of the approaching steps to his window that they were Evelyn's as he waited for his first meeting with her after the arrest. She was emotional upon seeing him, but he gave her an assuring and settling smile. With his arms resting by the jail window desk, Richard commanded a confident demeanor.

"They're preparing for a hearing appearance for a first degree murder – double homicide. The bodies of Bruna Dhahl and Shazzy Spicer were removed from Bruna's residence later this morning. Richard what do you know?"

"Nothing – absolutely nothing"

"What do you mean by 'nothing'?"

"I didn't know they were dead; I didn't know they've been killed and I don't know who, what, when, where, how and why. I'm in shock like everybody else is. Did you see the bodies?"

"No"

"Pictures?"

"Yes, but they're not willing to release the pictures till tomorrow." Evelyn explained. "Please, tell me what you know; what happened on the Tuesday before Thanksgiving Day." Richard blushed instantly at the question. He threw his head back in deep thinking - trying to recapture the events of that night.

"How many minutes do you have?" Richard asked.

"It doesn't matter. I'm representing you." The answer surprised Richard because MGS policies wouldn't allow its employees to represent a non-MGS client, especially concerning him, since he'd fallen out of favor with MGS.

"Did MGS approve of it? Evelyn, you could lose your job."

"They've already told me that; conflict of interests, yes, but I'm going ahead anyway."

"No, you can't do that. I wouldn't want you to. MGS holds a lot of promise for you and I wouldn't want you lose it."

"Richard, I've done things for people but none of them came with sacrifice. Please, for the first time, let me taste the value in the virtue of self-denial. It may taste like the virtue you valued. If MGS fires me, the taste of virtue will still be in my mouth."

Richard smiled at her response and was touched by her ardent conviction to stand with him. He cleared his throat and explained that there were a lot of things going on at Palate International which he wasn't particularly happy about. Palate, which was known for its high credentials about the choice of wines, was venturing into other fields.

"I spoke against the idea and dissented on a number of decisions. They weren't pleased with me and got Milo to pressure me to go along with Palate plans. I refused."

"How did Bruna play into this?" Evelyn asked.

"Hmm. It's a long story, but I'll make it short. There was a subtle mutiny against the outspoken Shazzy Spicer, because it

371

seemed he was behind the scheme that created the problem for Palate. During my investigations, Bruna invited me to her house; that was the first time."

Richard paused and was choked with emotions. Evelyn had heard various versions of the rest of the story. It was worth her while to hear it directly from Richard, but Richard couldn't restrain his emotions. After a long emotional pause, he continued.

"Bruna went to her bedroom to fetch me documents to substantiate Palate's claim for blaming Shazzy Spicer for Palate's problems. She returned empty and promised me the documents the next day. There was police activity in the area. She decided to turn her lights out to ensure her privacy. To while the time since I couldn't leave, she brought her famous ageless Medoc La Grand, as she claimed. We drank some; we ended up in her bedroom."

Evelyn smiled. She seemed anxious with a comment, but checked herself. Richard wondered why her sudden change of mind, but he chose not to press her. Evelyn took a notepad and recorded a point. She smiled again and it led to a brief laughter.

"Now, on a serious note, did you think you were drugged then or do you now assume you were drugged? Please, think about it and take your time to answer the question."

"Evelyn, I've been underrating you, but I tell you, you beat me to this. Let them seal that wine and request that into evidence." Richard was concerned and it showed.

"Richard, you've not answered my question. Remember, I'm in charge now. Your excitement won't help us. Please, answer the question."

"I think you've brought my mind to that night. I strongly think I was drugged. I assume now that I was. She gave me a generous amount to take home, but why would she do that?" Richard wondered. "Do you remember you once asked me why I don't drink and I assured you that I would tell you one day? Well, this is your answer."

"Richard, listen, whatever theories you have won't fly because you continued with your affair with her. You liked her. You slept with her again and again."

"I liked her, yes, but not as repeatedly as you think." Richard replied in a somber tone.

"Wha-a-at!" Evelyn exclaimed in utter disbelief. "Richard Troy Bridges, you know better than that. You're lying to me. You can do better than this. What's wrong with you?"

"Evelyn, I'm not lying and please don't call me a liar." Richard expostulated.

"I talked to your wife before walking in here. I told her to not make statements to anybody, not even to the press. I've counselled Cannon and Robert to stay from public view. Josh is fine. He's alert and even playing. I'm told he'll be returning home today. Now, Richard, for all these nights that you've been sleeping out, where have you been sleeping? Tell me. I don't have to be in your personal life but, remember I'm almost a family. Apphia says the two of you haven't been intimate since your affair with Bruna began. You and I know that's crucial to our argument. Tell me, what has been going on?" Evelyn's long remark was deliberate – to calm the argument atmosphere. It worked.

"I stayed working late, researching and exploring every justification that I could find to dissuade them from pursuing that venture, and I've been sleeping at the Palate Club House. I hope we aren't being recorded, but I hope they bring Palate's venture in court."

"They assured me they wouldn't record." Evelyn reassured Richard.

"Good, you see, Shazzy Spicer had always maintained that Palate's business would always be about appetite. He was suggesting a venture that would increase children's appetite to video games of heroism. He coined the name PAL, Palate Avengers League. The idea was to introduce violent video games that would involve kids in league with other kids to fight anything that challenges their will."

"It sounds like fun, what's the big deal?"

"The idea is more ominous and worrying than it looks on paper. Evelyn, the prospects are very tempting, but reek of something diabolical. You should read the concept, the FAL Project."

"Imaginary, if it's a game, I don't see anything wrong with it."

"Perhaps not, but wait until the PAL games begin to desensitize and transform the kids into ignorant villains. When scoring is based on the number of so-called 'enemy eliminations' at the minimum time per the task rate, and you see a demonstration of the game, you'll understand my concern."

"Are you seeking a cure for social ills too?"

Evelyn refused to acknowledge Richard's apprehensions. She was more focused on how to get him out of his mess than to argue with the self-imposed chief urban moralist or doctor. Her mind was saying 'shove it Richard.' She changed the subject.

"Were you at Bruna's house on the night of the murder?"

"When was the night of the murder?" Richard reposed the question inquisitively, and answered himself: "I don't know; how would I know?"

"They think you were, around midnight or the very early hours of Tuesday morning." Evelyn replied.

"Conjecturing?"

"Yes, they're conjecturing. Richard, were you there, at Bruna's?"

"I was, yes, about one in the morning." Richard admitted.

"But why, Richard why?" Evelyn asked in frustration.

"I was kicked out of the club house, and I didn't have anywhere to go."

"What do you mean? You could have gone home, to your wife."

"I didn't want to, for many reasons. I was wrong with my spurious affair, but please, I will not discuss Apphia." Richard's response silenced Evelyn. She became pensively quiet. She wondered why on earth somebody like Richard would cheat on his wife.

'That's it for now." Evelyn got up and was ready to leave. A few strides away, she turned for a quick glance at her friend behind bars. She saw him gesturing her to come back; so she made a quick turn back to him.

"When a witness tries to evade an implicating question, the witness or the accused feigns angry and mimics the face of feeling hurt - from an insult. Don't fall for that. You fell for mine. By the way, I had no reason to evade your question."

Evelyn, with her right open palm, jokingly slapped the glass that shielded Richard's face. It's her way to say: "How dare you? I got it." They exchanged smiles and she was on her way.

CHAPTER 29

The ironies of life quite often depicted the reality of the uncertainties of life and how the fortunes fluctuated with ever changing trends, beliefs and even gossips. The entrée into the courtroom of the famous former defense attorney Richard Bridges on his day of appearing was a portrayal of a fall of a mighty puritan, shackled in heavy chains on legs and wrists to reveal a live specter of an irony of life. Many in the filled courtroom thought it was a poetic error to humiliate the good with a miscarriage of normalcy. The accused was not a convict, but was on display like a felon. That gusto of Richard to always defend the innocent was on trial, but not for the alleged evidence gathered against him. As anticipated, Richard pleaded not-guilty at the preliminary hearing. He'd earlier refused to be cajoled into a plea bargain that would consequently suppress the truth.

So, a step at a time he took as they led him away. Each tread was a tread that beat the marching drums of fate, signaling his life or death, and with the rhythmic clinking of his wrist and ankle chains, Richard made percussions beat discordantly with his heart heavy in fear. He dragged the weight of his shackled steps to the confines of his uncertain future and to the wintery walls because of Palate palaver.

As they led him away he heard a whisper: "Jesus felt the same way, even far worse," the whisperer said. Richard turned to catch a glimpse of the whisperer. It was a face he knew, Miguel, better known as Eloquenter. He smiled strangely at Richard's misfortune and discomfort but Richard found it comforting.

The whisper had thrown Eloquenter back into the life of Richard again. He wished he would see him again preferably earlier than his next court appearance. The praying kid who had been helping his wife and Seth in their challenges was now sought-after by Richard. He would have a lot of questions for Elo. He remembered the lines, "What is good May be crude." He tried to read a meaning to it and to ascribe the unexplained meaning to his situation in his cold cell.

His bones began to ache in the cold cell. Richard called out the warden for an extra blanket. The tall and almost three hundred-pound built warden returned with one. His built was intimidating but he appeared to Richard as a gentle giant. The impression gave him courage to attempt a question.

"Officer, please, could I ask you a question?"

"What do you want again?" The warden asked Richard impatiently.

"Please, have you heard the name 'Eloquenter' before?" Richard asked submissively.

"Yes, Elo, he comes visiting folks here every Sunday. He'll be here this Sunday." The warden chose to walk away while delivering his response, and to avoid further questions.

Richard felt shunned and the reality of jail life set in for him. He felt lonely and miserable, but it gave him the opportunity to reflect on many things. Among them was why Bruna was anxious to medicate him on the night of her encounter with Apphia and his fall-out with Bruna. His thoughts also travelled to the grapevine inspection event. Richard recalled how sick he felt. The nausea feeling, his hallucinations, and the strange experience of talking to himself were all beginning to make a strange puzzle meaningful. Richard instantly tried to reach into his pocket for his cellphone. Another instant reality set in; his clothes had no pockets and his aching hands could actually do very little to help him. He looked forward to his next meeting with his lawyer Evelyn.

Since Evelyn's reconciliation with her mother, she'd been spending more time with her. She loved her cooking and Mom Dorina's kitchen had never disappointed her. On that afternoon, Evelyn didn't finish her lunch when her phone began vibrating again in her purse. She reached into her purse and tried to answer the call with her mouth full. Her mother urged her to try to finish her food, but she shook her head in disagreement. She had to take the call. Evelyn stepped away to a corner where there would be less noise for greater voice and line clarity. The voice was Sally's.

"They've come to impound all the files which Mr. Bridges had me keeping for him."

"Who were they?" Evelyn asked with a strong presumption that it was MGS effort to subtly intimidate Sally.

"I don't know, the police I guess and two other men." Sally replied.

"Are you speaking from your cellphone?" Evelyn asked again.

"No"

"Good, I'll talk to you later."

Evelyn hurriedly kissed her Mom on the cheek and was on her way to see Apphia. She arrived just in time to meet her. Apphia had been told that Josh's condition was changing to what the doctor described as 'not happy about.' She'd become very worried and the arrival of Evelyn instantly alarmed her more. But Evelyn immediately went to business; she called out Seth.

"Do you know how to copy files?"

"Yes, I do." Seth's reply was followed by a strange incoherent remark as his eyes seemed to have transferred the focus off from

Evelyn to the main door. Typically Evelyn got impatiently frustrated, but then she picked Seth's clue. There was policemen and a detective at the door and Seth smartly changed the subject.

"Yes, I do and we'll carry few of Josh's favorite toys to him. I'm sure he'll like them. How you're doing officer?" Seth addressed the police officers and the few civilian-clothed men at the door. Evelyn requested to see the search warrant and any document that warrant their presence in the house. After inspecting the warrant, Evelyn walked to Richard's office and made a copy.

"I won't stand in the way of the law, and I won't forbid you to exercise your responsibility, but I must tell you, any iota of material you glean out of anything you touch will be illegal and will not be admissible in court. And I will fight this with all my might; the law is on my side. It's an illegal search, not a judge authorized search. Your warrant did not also stipulate the number of persons assigned to this job, and here we stand with a troop of so called agents, and your document fails to validate who is and who is not part of this."

One of the men decided to rebuff Evelyn's legal claim.

"Ma'am, are you saying we forged this document?"

"Those are your words, not mine. How do I know who is not supposed to be among you, perhaps somebody you might have picked up from somewhere or who may be or may be not remotely implicated in this case, I don't know."

Evelyn then brought out her handy camera, very handy for pictures in case of road accidents, and took three different shots of the group at the door. The action spurned a fiery reaction from the leader of the group. Charged by his disdain for being outdone by a woman, he tried to physically and forcibly seize the camera from Evelyn. Seth stepped in to shield her from the rather ingenuous onslaught of the assumed officer from District Attorney's office.

"Miss you have no right to take a picture of me without my permission." The officer fumed as he panted heavily.

"You're on private property, my client's property. My client and his interests have every right to pursue any action deem legal or without bodily or physical harm to any uninvited guest who attempts to perpetrate any unwelcome action in my client's house." Evelyn was furious. "I expect you to know the law. I will sue you, your person, your office, the city, the state and anybody I can think of. By the way, I have a video of every nook and cranny of this house with the things in them before your visit."

"Guys, don't listen to her. Collect every file, the computers, anything of interest, evidence worthy, just sweep up and let's get out of here."

Evelyn, Seth and sad-faced Apphia looked on as Richard's office was ransacked. Evelyn took pictures of the boxes, in their hands as they exited the house. Apphia's worry was very visible, although Evelyn tried to allay her fears.

"I'm concerned, what about, about, I don't know." Apphia expressed resignedly.

"By the way, Evelyn, I have copied the entire files on his computer. I anticipated this visit." Seth remarked to Evelyn's elation. She hugged Seth gratefully with a peck on his cheek.

"Apphia, don't worry. I've planted confusion among them. I made up some of the claims to get them thinking. It's not lying. It's a psychological punch against a litigating rival. Guess whom I learnt this from – from a brilliant lawyer called Richard Troy Bridges." Then Evelyn winked at Apphia and she smiled back

CHAPTER 30

Sally was a bundle of nerves when Eloquenter showed up at her house. She didn't know him and he didn't know her. They'd never met before and that fit well in Evelyn's plan for an unknown choice to be the contact person with Sally. At best, that would secure communications between Sally and Evelyn. Eloquenter was to act as Sally's boyfriend and Sally's son was to address his mom's friend as Uncle Elo.

Sally explained to Elo that Richard had instructed her to carry the files out of the office to her house. She said her intuition drove her to make copies of each sheet in every folder and had them stack in her mother's house. However, there was something she found in one of the folders which worried her. She described two small plastic snap seal-lock bags, about six-one quarter-inch by five and half-inch bags containing some herbs in them. The plastic bags were stapled to two folders.

"Do you have them?" Elo asked nervously.

"No, I mean uh, no."

"C'mon, you can trust me. I've told you I'm working for lawyer Evelyn Hedge. You know she is representing Mr. Bridges in the murder case. Whatever we find at this stage is very important."

"I told you I don't have it." Sally did not relent.

"Look, we're all in this thing together for Mr. Bridges. I visit his wife Apphia and their friend Seth. I don't know what else to do to convince you."

"I'm telling you I don't have them."

"Who has them?"

"They were in the files they carried away."

"You will blame yourself if Mr. Bridges is nailed in for life for failing to prove his argument. Remember, it will be your fault. I've got to go." Elo got up and walked to the door. His bluff worked; Sally called him back when he got to the door.

"Where are you taking the herbs to?"

"…To his lawyer, Evelyn, of course." Elo was getting frustrated.

"Please, you may have to hide them well, and let the labelling and everything remain intact. There shouldn't be proof of tampering, please."

"Trust me. I know what I'm doing. Maybe they're watching us and if I should leave right now they will be suspicious that I came to just pick something up from you and they will wonder what it is. So relax, I have to hang here for at least an hour like a normal visit, if you don't mind."

"Well, if that works for you, I don't mind."

"Are you married or have boyfriend; will he be offended?" Elo asked; he was being cautious.

"Boyfriend, he will understand if I explain the situation to him."

Elo settled in a small couch in the living room and Sally's son engaged him in a chat. While Elo had the boy occupied with a drawing, he repacked the plastics with their herb contents in another Ziploc plastic container as a measure to prevent tampering marks. With Sally's permission, Elo left for his car while carrying Sally's son playfully on his shoulders. Immediately, they got into the car, the boy excitedly got behind the steering wheel while Elo quickly hid the Ziploc plastic container bag in the speaker cabinets by laying it flat at the back of the diaphragm to conform to the shape of the hind portion of the speaker's diaphragm, and then sealing it with the woofer in place. They returned to Sally's living room only to be joined by her boyfriend. A mixture of surprise and a frown was visible on his face. Sally stepped in quickly to clear any misunderstanding.

"So, what do you do?" Sally's boyfriend asked Eloquenter.

"I'm in Bible College. I'm studying to be a Pastor."

"Really? You don't look like a Pastor."

"I've heard that many times; I'm judged by my age and probably by my past."

"So, you know that?" Sally's friend derided.

"Yes, I do. People forget that the greatest preacher in the Bible used to be a murderer, and the man who became the greatest king of Israel was just a teenager when he became king. Could you imagine, God called him his friend."

"Dude, you're freaking me out; who were they?"

"The preacher was Apostle Paul, otherwise known as Saint Paul, and the king was King David who wrote many Psalms in the Bible including 'The Lord is my Shepherd.' So, I am getting there. I'm young but, I will one day."

Eloquenter's profound commitment to his beliefs and aspiration astounded Sally's boyfriend. He believed him. He'd learnt something he'd never heard before and Eloquenter's conviction translated well in his confidence. However, with the business on hand, Elo suggested that Sally's boyfriend must take the lead to part with Sally and he would follow thereafter. Thus, his longer stay would establish a standing relationship and not an overnight acquaintance which would play into any assumption that his quick visit was for a hasty pickup.

Eloquenter waited and followed a few minutes after Sally's boyfriend had left. Two blocks away, he saw a car that matched Sally's boyfriend's car that had been pulled over by the police;

Eloquenter drove by with non-interfering civility. His instincts were right.

Evelyn continued to build her evidence and argument in defense of her friend and alleged murderer. She knew she didn't have to overlook the importance of talking to Cannon and Robert who were in Richard's company on the day of the murder. She knew she had to talk to them before they made any statements to the District Attorney's office. It was imperative that Evelyn explored their backgrounds because they barely got acquainted. Cannon chose to go first.

He introduced himself confidently unlike how Evelyn had anticipated. She'd expected Cannon to have had a checkered past that might influence his reluctance to sharing his story.

"My name is Cannon Jetteh. I have two siblings, a boy and a girl born to Robert Jetteh senior and Lydia. I don't know my mother's last name."

"Why not"

"My father and my mom lived together, but they never married. I normally accord her the name Jetteh, that's Lydia

Jetteh, but that's not her maiden name either." Cannon tried to explain.

"If Robert is your brother, where is your other sibling, your sister?"

"My mother left with her, and we haven't seen them since."

"You see, Cannon, I'm asking you these questions because the prosecution will have to find out who you are – whether you'll be a credible witness or not. They will want you in a particular light that will be convenient for their case, so I really need to know everything. What is the name of your sister?"

"She was a baby when Mom took her with her. We all call her Dolly."

"Cannon, what can you tell me if I ask you 'What do you do for living?' What will be your response?"

"I will tell you, I proudly served in the US Army for nine years. When I got out, I wanted to go into farming but landed as a Trapeze artist for Circus Bonanza for seven years and currently, unemployed."

"Any criminal record …?"

"Ms. Evelyn, I'm sure they will do their homework before they take their chance to call me. Criminal record … clean, Drugs . . Yes. I did, but now I'm sober."

"Well, Cannon, I salute your valor for serving. You told your brother Robert that you were dying. Why was that?"

"I was feeling weak and was experiencing shortness of breath; seriously I thought I was dying but, thinking about it now, I realize it might have been something else."

Evelyn felt she might have had enough from him and turned to ask Robert if he would have something different to say from what he'd heard. He smiled and shook his head. There was a glow of innocence about Robert and it beamed admiringly before Evelyn. It was an endearing smile and it won Evelyn's heart. She smiled back and complimented Robert: "You are a handsome kid; be a good boy."

The questioning was interrupted by a gentle knock on the door. After a few seconds pause, the doorbell chimed. Cannon went to the door and peeped through the hole while Evelyn waited with engendered zeal to deal with any so-called investigator at the door. Cannon beckoned Evelyn to come to the door. Upon looking, she was relieved to find that the man at the door was a contractor in his working clothes. Evelyn left and Cannon opened the door.

"This is the home of Ms. Dorina Hedge, right?" The visitor sounded to be no stranger.

"Yes," Cannon replied carefully. "How can we help you?"

"Please tell her "Maunty's son is here." Cannon repeated the name 'Maunty' to familiarize himself with the sound before approaching Dorina. Dorina was frantic on her feet at the mention of 'Maunty' to the dismay of Evelyn. She hastened to the door and heartily embraced the young man; the man, time had stolen from her. She stood dwarfed under him. There were tears of joy in Dorina's eyes; the tears were infectious, and the rest teared up inadvertently with her but they knew not what their tears were about. Dorina held his hand and dragged him to the nearest couch by her favorite chair. Then she tried to catch her breath in her attempt to honorably introduce her visitor. She smiled and took a long admirable look at his visitor again.

"My friends, I want you to meet my friend Jimmy. Jimmy was my young neighbor when I moved in here years ago. I was very sick then; he would always come to help me with my dishes and …" Dorina was choked with emotion and struggled with the words. "The flowers, this garden you see around me, Jimmy did it all for me, for, for, for free."

James was feeling uneasy hearing Dorina splurge on her appreciation for him. "Maunty, it's enough. Remember, I did it for a very wonderful woman." He turned and angled his neck to catch the face of crying Dorina again, and they locked their eyes with a warm smile at each other. Evelyn looked on nonplused; her feelings were mixed. She'd never found her mother that happy since they mended their relationship. However, it did awaken the slumbering sense of guilt that tended to question where she was during her mother's crisis. She heard James describe her mother as "a very wonderful woman," something she'd been blind to see.

"So, Dorina are these all your children?" James asked with an itching impulse to be introduced particularly to Evelyn. However, the presence of Cannon and Robert was redefining James reference to 'children,' which Dorina couldn't own up to or say 'no' to because of the inherent responsibility of a lengthy explanation. She opted for the former with a stuttering 'ye-yess.'

"James, so what have you been doing?"

"I'm a landscaper. I decided to follow that as my profession. It's interesting; I love it. I was here some time ago to see you when I moved back from Seattle but, you were in a family meeting so I couldn't get the chance to talk to you."

"Do you still play guitar?" Dorina asked.

"Yes, I do, and now the piano too. I'm sure your daughter took your fiddling skills, did you?" Evelyn smiled for courtesy sake and tried to not embarrass her mother.

"No, I don't play the violin, I may one day."

"That will be nice. I must be going. Dorina, you bet I'll come again."

"Jimmy, when – remember you said you don't break promises." Dorina would have loved for him to stay longer, but she figured he had his reasons to leave.

CHAPTER 31

Richard wore a dark blue suit and sat between his two counsels, Evelyn and a last-minute volunteered defense attorney, Mr. Daniel Stein. Reputed for unearthing buried evidence, Dan's presence was to simply strike fear among the prosecution and their witnesses. He had a commanding look which often intimidated witnesses to even yield their leanings to his side. Both of them wanted a swift foray into the trenches of the prosecution and their legal hold that they had over Richard. The preliminary hearing had begun with Judge Terrance Manor presiding.

After a brief opening statement, the prosecution team led by Celia Cromwell called their first witness, Mr. John Mckle, a bartender. Mr. Mckle was led to introduce himself and to describe what his job entailed.

"Mr. Mckle, do you recall seeing this man, the accused in your bar?" Lawyer Cromwell pointed him to Richard.

"Yes, I do."

"What do you recall?"

"He walked in for a drink."

"What time was that, if you recall? Cromwell asked.

"About one in the morning, some customers were leaving, and he walked in when the place was almost empty."

"Are you sure about the time?"

"Yes, I was getting ready to close when he decided to purchase more drink."

"So, you did speak with him."

"Absolutely. I wasn't keen on selling him any more drinks, but I changed my mind and offered him one."

"Why did you change your mind?"

"He looked distraught and as he faced me on his bar stool, he struggled to empty his glass."

"Did he get drunk?"

"Yes."

"How did you know?"

"He couldn't keep his balance on the stool, and his eyes – he seemed he had been crying. Some men cry when they are drunk."

"How many were in the bar?"

"Eventually, it became just the two of us."

"And you wanted to close for the night? Did you wish to see him leave so that you could close?"

"Yes, I did, but he wanted more drink and this time I refused to serve him."

"Why?"

"He was too drunk. I decided to sober him up before his attempt to leave by driving."

Evelyn cut in and objected the line of questioning, because it was failing to lead and to address the crux of the hearing. Ms. Cromwell shot back that he was laying grounds that would lead to the defendant's motive. Evelyn didn't yield.

"Your honor, we are seeing sheer circumlocution, a deliberate endeavor to wear out the witness."

"I will grant the prosecution the opportunity to lay out their groundwork. I will also grant you the same when defense takes its turn. However, I may warn both of you not to abuse it." Judge Terrance Manor remarked.

"Why did you try to make him sober?"

"There was no way he could drive safely home."

"So, what steps did you take?"

"I prepared coffee for him and played a few songs. I suggested that a little dancing exercise would help burn out the alcohol in him and that would help him."

"Your suggestion was not to dance with him. Was it?"

"O – no, no, no, no, no – he was to dance alone. He needed the workout, not I, please." Mr. Mckle's reaction to correct the impression was loud and vehement that it generated a lot of laughter in the room.

"Did he dance?" The witness laughed in his attempt to answer the question. He looked at Richard and both smiled.

"He wasn't bad at all." The few in the courtroom laughed; the judge couldn't hold back his smile as well.

"A couple walked in around that time and impressed with his dancing, dropped him some bills." The bartender added.

"Having him sobered a little bit, did he tell you he was ready to leave?" The prosecutor asked. Evelyn got up and protested the wording of the question. She felt the question was influencing response from the witness and was, "putting words in his mouth." The judge requested for a rewording of the question.

"Mr. Mckle, Please tell this session what followed after the defendant's dancing."

"He wasn't sober enough and surprisingly requested for more drinks. I refused him; he was disappointed and he vented it on me. However, he apologized and explained that his comment was a bad joke and he actually was not good at jokes and further explained that somebody on the executive board at his work was not being kind to him."

"Mr. Mckle I may ask you, are you sure you heard the words: "Somebody on the executive board was not being kind" from the defendant's mouth. If you are, what makes you so sure?"

"I am. The defendant is not like the regulars who come to the store. He was very gentle and he made the statement softly; it touched my heart and I decided to get a cab for him. I didn't not want to see him drive in that condition."

"Thank you very much. You may cross examine the witness, Ms. Hedge." Ms. Cromwell was satisfied with the witness that she strutted back to her team with a smile. During that moment, Richard whispered into Evelyn's ears: "please go soft on him, we'll need him." Evelyn smiled and responded: "I got it."

"Mr. Mckle, you strike me as a very kind man."

Mr. Mckle smiled at Evelyn's compliment and responded, "Thank you."

"Well, Mr. Bridges wants me to express his deep appreciation for your kindness and apologizes for the delay to pick up his car from your property. I am sure you might have heard that on the day he planned to pick up his car, his son was hit by a car and is still hospitalized."

"Yes, I was saddened by the news. I hope his son gets well soon."

Ms. Cromwell was restless and angry at the defense's deliberate approach to emotionalize the testimony and she did not restrain her feelings.

"What is this? Your honor, defense is trying to turn this hearing into a crisis counselling parlor. What a cheap ploy."

"Ms. Cromwell, I am shocked at your heartless reaction. Mr. Bridges sees it relevant to thank Mr. Mckle. He appreciates him more because he could have rendered the same fate that has hospitalized his son to another person or even to himself had he driven drunk that night. Well, Mr. Mckle, thank you again."

Lawyer Cromwell regretted her move. She realized that the sympathy of the room might turn against her and especially when the judge remarked: "We are sorry about the news of your son and this court wishes him speedy recovery. And by the way Ms. Cromwell, I am sure you didn't mean this flare, and I want to believe that you share the graces of this court. Defense may continue."

"Thank you, your honor. Mr. Mckle, I want to bring your mind back to that night with Mr. Bridges. You said when you refused him the service of more drinks because he was drunk, he 'vented it' on you. What did you mean by 'vented,' did he address you angrily?"

"No, not at all, he joked with a statement which was not in good taste."

"So you knew the statement was a joke."

"Yes."

"You may not be able to produce it verbatim, but you can paraphrase the statement. What did he say?"

"I remember hearing him say if I was not going to serve him the drink I would eventually be out of business and out of job. I was hurt by that remark. It was in poor taste."

"If you knew it was a joke, why were you hurt?"

"We bartenders hear this joke all the time. It's like telling us we benefit from getting them drunk. I was tired and wanted to close and after being patient with him, and for him to say that at that time, I didn't take it well."

"So, what did you do?"

"I decided to throw him out."

"And how did he receive your action?"

"He was in shock. That was when he made the statement that somebody on the board did not like him."

"In your earlier testimony, you did say he made the statement 'softly,' and yet you heard him. What did you mean by 'softly'?"

"Yes, although he wasn't loud the tone was soft. He sounded like he was lamenting."

"So, he didn't appear angry. Did he?"

Ms. Cromwell objected to the phrasing of the question. She felt the defense was feeding the witness with words. The judge requested a rephrasing and Evelyn continued.

"Mr. Mckle, what was the defendant's mood?"

"He felt sad and sounded like nobody liked him."

"You said you called a taxi for him."

"Yes, I did."

"Have you, after that night, seen that cab driver again?"

"Yes, I did."

"Do you know him well?"

"Yes, for his business. He runs his service late so when a customer from my bar needs a service he is always available. He is reliable."

"So, when you met him after his service for that night what did you talk about?"

"We talked about our business."

Evelyn suddenly turned from a charming cat to a cajoling tigress. The room sensed her disposition as she took her stance closer to the witness seat.

"Mr. Mckle, I've been particular impressed by your candor and sincerity to this court but, I still want to remind you that you're under oath and your answers to these questions are very crucial. Please, did you – and - the cab driver – discuss - Mr. Bridges?" Evelyn delivered her question with the effort of pausing to choose her words to drive home her seriousness.

"Yes, we did."

"Did anybody ask you about the cab driver?"

"Like, at the bar for his service?"

Evelyn looked fiery and was like ready to pounce upon a prey because she was sensing an evasion.

"No, like about what the cab driver told you about the night when he went to drop off Mr. Bridges." Evelyn hinted.

"Yes, the cab driver said when he heard about the killing in that house on the news, it reminded him about something."

"Did you ask him about that 'something'?"

"Yes."

"What did he tell you?"

"He said he wouldn't want to discuss it. He begged me not to pressure him because he didn't really want to talk about it."

"Did anybody ask you about the cab driver?" The bartender hesitated for a second.

"Yes."

"Who did - anybody in this room?" The eyes of Mr. Mckle panned across the room and the focus settled on the Assisting Prosecutor with Ms. Cromwell. The patience of Evelyn was running out as Mr. Mckle continued to drag his feet with his answer.

"Mr. Mckle please, - answer the question." Evelyn implored softly but persuasively.

"Yes, the man sitting by Ms. Cromwell." The witness pointed to the Assisting Prosecuting attorney.

"He told me to not discuss with anybody my conversation with the cab driver."

"Your honor may I approach the bench?" Evelyn couldn't hide her anger.

"Absolutely, and now - with all the legal parties on this case, right now," Judge Manor did not hide his anger and frustration.

"Lady and gentlemen, what's going on here? Was the prosecution attempting to stymie an effort by the defense to acquire evidence?"

"Your honor, we were simply counselling the cab driver to refrain from spreading stories which may generate wanton speculations among the public." The Assistant Prosecutor explained, but wasn't enough to dissuade the incensed Evelyn who said she would prove to the court that the prosecution was deliberately keeping the cab driver away because of evidence in favor of the defendant – a total obstruction of justice.

"Your honor, we're talking about a cab driver with an expired visa who, because of his vulnerability, was threatened with immigration deportation by the prosecution if he failed to comply with their demand of silence and to not talk to us."

"Where is the cabdriver, Ms. Cromwell?" Judge Manor asked.

"We don't know - your honor." Ms. Cromwell answered.

"Do you mean you haven't served him to appear before this court? Defense must go ahead to serve the subpoena on the cabdriver immediately, until he is successfully served to appear I will adjourn this session for three days."

The parties parted with Judge Manor to their various seats to recalibrate for the next session. Evelyn knew she had an enormous task ahead of her. She'd just made various allegations against the prosecution which were partly true but, the rest were sheer conjectures and had no immediate or remote grounds for proof. She was simply driven by the fact, as Richard had mentioned to her earlier, that the cabdriver had a foreign ascent. However, to her surprise, the prosecution didn't question her assertions. She knew it wasn't time to celebrate, yet she carried her air with her. She walked confidently to the bartender witness and engaged in a brief chat with him and then returned to talk to Dan Stein. It was too late for her to speak with the defendant; Richard had already been escorted out. The courtroom was almost empty; Mr. Stein stood by the door and patiently waited for Evelyn

"I have news for you. It doesn't look good for Richard's son."

"My Goodness! Has he been informed?"

"No, we all thought he was doing better, but it took a worse turn this morning. We can't break it to him now. I don't know how to."

Evelyn reached for her phone from her purse and dialed a number. It rang five times without response. "I'm going to the hospital. I'll stay in touch. I'm working on getting the cabdriver served hopefully tonight." Evelyn expressed hastily as she and Dan walked out of the courtroom.

CHAPTER 32

Nothing had changed much for Richard, a day after the preliminary hearing. The weather outside his jailhouse was cloudy and he was beginning to feel it. He sat on his small bed, swathed himself in a small blanket which could only cover half his body. Somehow the cloudy outdoors were proclaiming the indoor silent groans of his overburdened heart. It had just begun to drizzle and a trickle indoor matched a drizzle outdoor. Richard had long bewailed his estrangement with his family in their warm walls. The last news he heard about his son was the hospital's unwillingness to discharge him. He drew his conclusions but refused to utter them, a foreboding that frightened him.

His cold walls continued to insinuate his guilt. If he'd avoided Bruna, those situations would never have arisen. He juggled blame and guilt but refused to find his posture in any. He was miserable, but with a heart not ready for failure in fatherhood. He heard the footsteps of the warden and wished they were coming his way. They did. It was an odd time to receive a visitor. He'd been given a special consideration to talk to a visitor. His visitors were two. He showed no excitement; he wondered why the late visit.

Apphia had lost so much weight and Richard assumed that she must be sick. The sight of her challenged his conscience: "O what so much pain I have caused her." The sound of Richard's pain crystalized in his voice.

"A-pphi-a, how are you?" Richard asked his wife in the company of Evelyn.

"I'm fine. My worry is Josh. He isn't doing well. The doctor says for some strange reasons, Josh is giving signs like his organs are beginning to shut down." Apphia expressed with a heavy heart.

"Why is that?" Richard asked with a trembling voice.

"I don't know." Apphia explained tearfully. However, Evelyn had been more informed by the doctor, because it had been difficult for Apphia to take them in.

"The doctor explained to me that Josh's extremities are becoming cool to a touch because warm blood isn't flowing into them at a normal rate, and his length of sleeping seems to be abnormal." Evelyn explained emotionally. "The doctor says all is not lost yet. They're still trying to find if it has to do with his kidneys or any other vital organs, but we should pray."

Richard broke down and wept; neither his wife nor Evelyn had ever seen him in such overwhelming show of brokenness. He tried to wipe his eyes and his wet nose, he succeeded but yielded to the unsightliness of brushing his wet hands of tears and his nasal slimy phlegm on his orange jail uniforms. His visitors cried with him and other prisoners who were overhearing them as they intoned their emotions, wept with them. The mood inside the jail reflected the mood outside; his was an outpouring of tears whilst the outside was a downpour of fears. Even nature was moaning with him. There was a long pause. Evelyn had come to know Richard – enough to know about what normally characterized his long pauses. She knew his long pauses were often a prequel to something outrageous – an outrageous statement or thought.

"What is it, Richard – what is it?" she asked.

"Have you heard from the court?" Richard asked.

"Yes, we're reconvening tomorrow."

"Put me on the stand." Richard demanded firmly.

"Richard, are you out of your mind? I know I can't describe how you're feeling, but please, with all due respect, Richard, you know it's the wrong thing to do."

"Evelyn, put me on the stand tomorrow. I demand it." Richard asserted his will. However, his attorney and friend countered in thundering terms that her voice echoed within the walls of his confinement.

"Richard, these people have a catalogue of your relationship events with Bruna and why they believe you would do anything to hurt Shazzy Spicer. Perhaps you forget you've been accused of murdering the champions of appetite, the champions of the appetite of this society. In other words, your words, you - you would not taste better in their minds' mouth." She yelled her concern to him.

"I care less of the merits or the demerits, put me on the stand tomorrow, otherwise you're fired. My son is dying, I'll vindicate myself early enough to see him before he breathes his last. If I fail, like Eloquenter said, the innocent Jesus had been treated this way before. And even so, it's noble to die innocent, or may be to die with my innocent son. Evelyn, promise me; you'll have me on the witness stand tomorrow." Richard spoke matter-of-factly.

Evelyn, who had had her head down, as he commanded his demands, lifted it up and shook her head in reluctant obedience. "What do you want me to ask you?"

"Anything, my answers will give you leads to the questions." Richard turned his attention to Apphia. He was seeing something he hadn't seen before. She looked dispirited and pale; there was no fight in her. He wished he could command words to cheer her up, but he didn't have any. However, she looked up in her husband's eyes and managed a smile. Apphia then turned and looked at Evelyn interrogatively.

"Why don't you tell him?" Apphia asked, but it was a prudent betrayal, because she felt Richard ought to know and could advise on that. Richard eyes travelled searchingly between the two faces that sat before him and wondered what they were trying to keep away from him.

"Evelyn, will you please tell me what it is?" Richard was confused.

"I will see you in court tomorrow. I will save it for tomorrow," Evelyn whispered as she got up and thus, hinting it was time they left. "It's beyond your persuasion. Have a good night." Evelyn wished him. "I love you." Apphia declared softly, but assuredly. That was music in its finest rendition in the ears of Richard.

The evening left and the night arrived unannounced for Evelyn. Her mind was racing and chasing after auxiliaries for the defense preparation for the next day's preliminary hearing. So far it had been like chasing a mirage. She was yet to get a word that the cab driver had been served the subpoena. She wasn't sure if he would appear or continue to stay in hiding. Her hopes had run dry and her preoccupations had rendered her appetite awry. She wanted to be alone and she chose to sit at the backyard of her mother, Dorina's house.

The rain had reduced to sheer drizzling. Aided by the lights in the back yard, she watched the drizzling over the little foliage that had survived the California Autumn. She tried to engage her mind in games with the drizzling drops and the leaves by trying to observe how the leaves on the little plants reacted individually to the raindrops. She saw the plants sway side by side with the wind as if they wanted to avoid the drops. Her attention was interrupted by a stranger's voice. He was the visitor who called her Mom, 'Maunty.' She heard her Mom's voice ring with excitement again at his appearing. She tried to ignore them, but not for long.

"May I be intruding if I request to keep you company?"

"No, but I'm afraid you may find me boring. I've had a long day and my thoughts are not here."

"Where could they be, unless they are resting in a distant cherished heart?"

Evelyn was surprised by James' poetic response and she reacted by instant involuntary turning of her head for a quick glance at the responder. James was equally surprised at her obvious sharp reaction.

"Which of these describes me: annoying, presumptuous, arrogant or contemptuous?" He followed up his claims.

She turned full angle and smiled. "None, can you come up with another description of this fleeting persona you just shared. And will you be kinder to yourself?"

"Very limited with words, but I may," he replied. "Pleasant, unpretentious, polite, confident – do these fittingly describe that persona, - wait, one more – 'kind?'"

"Yes, they do. You have a good sense of humor." She remarked with a broader smile.

"You're kind. May I ask you? Is it your choice to be alone here?"

"Actually, it is. I'm representing a special client in a case I can't afford to lose. So, I'm here doing all the thinking I can."

"You're a strong lawyer – as I see. Are you afraid?"

"Honestly, I am, but my client isn't."

"That's assuring. Try to build on his confidence." James advised, but he realized that Evelyn was very absent-minded to acknowledge his comment. He, therefore, chose to comply with her silence. James was eager to talk; after a minute he broke the silence.

"Evelyn, what are you looking at?"

"I'm simply watching the drizzling as they drop over the leaves and the reaction of those poor individual small plants." She responded.

"Interesting, and what are you observing? I daren't question your adeptness with words but, I'm sure you know what I'm trying to imply." James expressed humbly.

"As the wind blows and the plants sway, the drizzling drops end up touching the stems," She smiled in response.

"Strangely, I'm seeing something different. I see the small plants dance and sway to the whistling music of the wind as their stems move by the guiding touch of each drizzle."

Evelyn was speechless. She jerked her upper frame backwards in an instant dumbfounded reaction. The yawning gap of her mouth remained open for seconds. She was overly impressed by James interpretation of what they were both seeing. "He couldn't be a landscaper," she muttered.

"What are you – a poet or something?"

"I told you, I'm a landscaper. What else are you observing?" He asked again.

"The leaves of the plants seem to be avoiding the weight of the raindrops." Evelyn expressed and while making faces for a challenge, she was still wondering in anticipation, what else he might have poetically to confute her claim to extra mastery of poetic applications - also.

"Another interesting observation," He said. "Do you want to hear mine?" He asked laughing and seeing a prepared Evelyn with ready remarks to challenge whatever he might have up his sleeves. "I see little plants expressing playfully 'hit-me-if-you-can' in a dodging game with the little drops. It's simply fun, fun, fun for these little plants."

Evelyn heaved in suppressed disagreement. James laughed at seeing her yield to an exponent of positive perceptions. "You know, I heard someone say that in all things we should give thanks to God. We may not have immediate understanding for a situation and even the thought may not make an immediate sense, but with time or in the future, it will."

She listened and smiled. She was beginning to be fond of him. James smiled back; he'd liked her the first time he laid his eyes on her. To him, it was enough being Maunty's daughter. "I'll be routing for you tomorrow." He said and parted with her for the night.

While Evelyn was having her moments with James at her mother's house, a lonely figure sat under the low night lamps in the living room of the Bridges. She didn't have to perform her bedtime duty of story reading. Her sole audience lay sick in a hospital surrounded by multiple beeping lights from instruments with claims to keeping her son Josh alive. The weight of worry had oppressed Apphia so much that it had rendered her irresponsive to anything associated with hope. Her reservoir of tears had run dry. The same lingering questions kept coming – what if, how is it that, why is this, why me? These questions were the reasons of Apphia's jeopardy.

She still struggled with her active conscience that kept libeling her with shared blames for her husband's troubles. How could she be, she'd often asked herself? She was yet to come to grips with them when her doorbell rang. Since the raid on her husband's home office, Apphia had become nervous at each ringing on her door. She could hardly predict what else could lie in wait for her by the door and before she could get there, Seth had beaten her to it. He opened the door and Eloquenter entered. Eloquenter was a little wet from the showers outside. He'd come to simply encourage Apphia. The last report he heard about Josh wasn't promising, and he'd imagined its sheer devastation on the Bridges'.

"There must be an escape from this situation." Eloquenter sounded his usual hopeful note, but Apphia was beginning to resign to a fate that was defining even Richard's thorny predicament - the only hope so far for her family. Eloquenter held her hand. He knew Apphia would need every support anyone could offer.

It was still showering outside and Seth could see the once young and vibrant Apphia succumbing to the treachery of fear. Overwhelmed by empathy for his friend's wife he began to think if there really was any escape from the problems. Perhaps he should see what benefits were inherent in the outdoor rain against a backdrop of cloudy doldrums inside the walls of her house. If there was a story of hope, Seth was a living narrative of one.

However, in his lifetime, Seth hadn't heard anybody celebrate a season of drought when the streams of joy and life are speedily evaporating. In his pensive mood, and as he watched Apphia empathetically, he heard a still quiet voice in his mind: "Life begins in water and water sustains life. Water is a gift from God."

Suddenly a fountain of hope burst open in him. It was inexpressible, but he checked his excitement. He wouldn't want his momentary spurt of good feeling fashion him as an eccentric. He walked to Apphia and extended his hand in invitation to her to get up from the chair; he then clasped her hand into his, and on they walked to the kitchen; they passed by the kitchen and walked on through the den, and to the door facing them, the very door that led to the backyard. Apphia stopped and looked at Seth in surprise. "It's raining, what is he up to?" Apphia's mind spoke inaudibly.

"Yes, let's go," Seth nodded in a firm urge, and she was compliant. She stepped into the rain with him, hand in hand, and Seth began to sing. His voice overpowered the outside volume of whispering sound of rain on the rainy night.

"Many are the questions floating in the sky

Many are the answers, but with little truths to fly

Many are the choices hovering all about

Many are the decisions that shut all wisdom out"

Apphia remembered what Seth was trying to remind her about with that song. She looked at him and smiled. Yes, she remembered the ride in Richard's old yellow Volkswagen Beetle when Apphia was in "Mommy's" disguise and Richard was "Sonny" in their benevolent abduction attempt to their house to provide him with help. Yes, she remembered that very well as they rode home and were singing that famous song, The Dry Desert Rock. The memory was fresh, but Apphia seemed to have lost the urge to sing it again this time.

"Why should the skies cause the days of drought

O teach me to understand what's this all about

There's a flowing fountain in a dry desert rock

It takes the believing heart to take in the pleasant shock."

Elo sat by the window and watched Seth hand in hand with Apphia while Seth wonderfully bellowed the song very movingly in a slow and steady walk in the rain across the stretch of the backyard to and fro. He was wet; she was wet; and both were oblivious to any querying eye. The support with music and the walk in the rain were helping Apphia cope with her distress. Elo couldn't help it and decided to join the party in the rain. He took the other arm of Apphia and she found herself sandwiched by her two wonderful friends, as they walked the backyard in steady to and fro in the rain.

"Many are the achievements, boasting our skills to survive

Many are the attainments bragging our passions on how to thrive

Many are the influences testing the human will

Many are man's tendencies that pride our strength and zeal"

Apphia looked at Eloquenter and smiled; then the words came to her. It had always been Elo's theme anytime he talked to her. Apphia could not restrain the urge; her voice took over.

"Can we dare to lay a claim to things we did not create?

Can we ever shift the times to annul decisions of fate

Oh tell me – can we even change the spots from the leopard's scan?

Do we know the wonders that mock the minds of man?

There is a well of water hidden in a dry dessert rock

Fresh living water springing from the dry desert rock

Flowing fountain from the dry desert rock

It's the hope of all who believe

Taste and see; it flows from the rock

Many are the miracles waiting for the believing heart.

Miracles do wait for the thirsty trusting heart."

The rain continued, but eventually the three retired in doors. Eloquenter prayed with them and left Apphia with the thought that he once shared with her: "Sometimes the hunger, the rain, the injury, the hurt and the pain, they tell the nature of the road for the journey, the journey from nervous Worryland to sure Cherryville. It's anybody's story. It depends on the traveler. You have a story, because you're still travelling."

CHAPTER 33

Prosecutor Celia Cromwell sat flanked on both sides with her team of prosecutors. Her countenance was declaring a buoyant spirit. Her new beautiful hairdo was declaring it loudly. A member of her team got up and struggled to inch his way out behind the tight seating space of Ms. Cromwell. He whispered into her ears to make room, and she smiled in acknowledgement. He got out and proceeded to talk to a lady, about four rows behind them. The lady nodded in response and whispered back into the ears of the prosecutor. He responded with a chuckle and returned high-fiving his panel in a clear ostentation of overly pronounced confidence. To ascertain if their courtroom psychological theatrics were working, Ms. Cromwell stole a glance at the defense corner and her eyes met Evelyn's.

Ms. Hedge winked at her in subtle derision that implied: "Sure you're looking good." Then Evelyn brandished a smile that spoke of her greater psychological weaponry of the defense team. Her smile was a comfortable feeling of 'It is well with us.' She was winning the courtroom cold war and Ms. Cromwell hated that. She wouldn't lose to that untried defense attorney with very little experience. Evelyn admittedly had been nursing that hidden fear. The evidence she'd collected so far hadn't been enough to support an argument that would persuade the judge to not hold the case for trial. Richard's belief in his innocence wasn't enough, and

Evelyn was realizing that. She must find and must have more to outweigh whatever the prosecution might have against her client. Her heart pounded when the judge walked in, and took his seat. The hearing resumed.

The prosecution informed the court of their readiness to proceed with their argument that a crime was committed and that crime was by the defendant, Richard. Ms. Cromwell further informed the court that they'd shared with defense whatever information they'd requested. Then the prosecution announced their first witness of the day and Richard felt jolted.

"Prosecution would like to call Mr. Milo of the Milo, Grady and Strong Law Firm." Evelyn saw the frown on Richard's face. He was upset that she'd kept the information from him. She tried to offer an assuring goodwill touch on his hand, but he withdrew it in open protest before the surprised eyes that were on them. The reaction unsettled Evelyn and she was equally upset about his behavior. The activity in the defense corner didn't escape Judge Manor's attention. Evelyn had to explain that her client had had "some anxious moments last night, but he will be okay." Judge Manor had to announce a fifteen-minute recess to help the defense handle the anxiety attack of the accused.

"Please, Richard, help me to help you." Evelyn didn't hold back her frustration as she appealed to him privately."

"At least, you could inform me about Milo. That's not hard to do." Richard derided.

"You're a lawyer. Weren't you expecting him to be a witness? I didn't have to tell you that he would be a perfect candidate for a witness against you. What do you think? Richard, you know better."

Evelyn retorted sharply and that announced her claim to dexterity over the case. Richard felt humbled and was convinced he was in good hands. He chuckled in submission. After a few minutes the session resumed, and Milo returned to the stand.

"Mr. Milo, what has been your relationship with the defendant, Mr. Bridges?"

"I've been his boss, colleague, and friend. He's one of the finest any firm could boast of." Milo looked Richard's way, but found him with his head bowed.

"Would you briefly describe his current duties?"

"Well, because of his situation right now, he's currently under suspension pending the outcome of this case. I'm not sure how to answer your question."

"Well, prior to his present situation – please, tell this hearing about Mr. Bridges duties."

"He's been handling legal and public relations issues and affairs by means of counselling to Palate International. This responsibility gave him automatic membership of the Palate Board."

"Did Mr. Bridges have to handle your law firm other responsibilities vis-à-vis the commitments of Palate's?"

"Yes."

"Did he operate from your office or in Palate's?"

"Both."

"Mr. Milo, I'm going to show you an email copy addressed and sent to you few weeks ago. Please inform the court if you received it and if indeed it was sent by Mr. Bridges." Ms. Cromwell approached Mr. Milo in the witness stand with a sheet of paper. Milo handed the paper back to the prosecutor after a cursory look at it.

"Yes, I received it, read it, and it was from Mr. Bridges."

"Your honor, I intend to submit this as today's exhibit 'A' and humbly request an audible reading of this exhibit in the hearing of this gathering."

Ms. Cromwell again advanced towards the judge and handed him the paper. Judge Manor took his time to read the document inaudibly, and passed it on to the court clerk for a louder reading in the hearing of the court. The court clerk began:

"Mr. Milo, I waited futilely for your call to discuss my growing frustration with Shazzy Spicer's in-roads into the new projects of Palate. My official responsibility ends with counselling and not to meddle in or craft Palate business projects. However, I would not want to closely or remotely in anyway be associated with anything unsavory with Palate. Frankly I do not want to surprise you with my resignation announcement. Please call me." Milo replied:

"Son, you must learn to tolerate Spicer. You may find out soon that his shadow still looms large on Palate. It's unfortunate, but that's the reality." Mr. Bridges followed up with a remark:

"Oh, I could kill that fool. Honestly, I can't work with him." The email signed off *'RB.'* After the reading the prosecution proceeded with its questions.

"Mr. Milo would you say the responding remarks in the email were yours?"

"Yes, they are mine."

"For now, no further questions" Ms. Cromwell retired to join her team of prosecutors. Evelyn was already up before the words of invitation for cross-examination were yet to roll out of the judge's mouth.

"How're you doing, boss?"

The response could hardly escape the lips of Milo's when Celia Cromwell assertively shot out her disapproval of the defense's questioning approach.

"Your honor, this isn't an office party. We're seeing a propensity to making light-work of the proceedings by the defense and thus undermining the weight of seriousness of this preliminary hearing session." Judge Manor burst out laughing, and the whoop of the hearty reaction from him caught the room by surprise that it morphed into another hilarious moment. It even wiped out the festered seriousness on the face of Cromwell that she yielded to the infectious round of laughter.

"Don't you think I should be the judge of that? Thank you. By the way, Ms. Hedge, get straight to your point." The laughing lingered awhile in the room. Milo was still trying to compose himself when Evelyn launched her cross-examination.

"Mr. Milo, I'm sure you recall that with a warrant from the court and with your cooperation, we went onto your computer, and into the office email file, and examined your emails which we specifically narrowed to an anthology of categorized 'mails-of-interest.' They're quite a collection – all printed out and with the permission of the court, please tell us whether each mail is from your file." Defense handed the mails to the witness while the court waited for his certification of the mails.

Evelyn retired to rejoin her team while Milo examined each mail. After few minutes, she walked back to the witness to retrieve the pile.

"Your Honor, among this pile is another set of emails of interest, particularly highlighted due to the high bearing of importance to this hearing. One of them is from you, addressed to Mr. Phil Sawyer. It reads:

'Phil, If we lose this tournament, I'll kill you. You've simply relegated this to the ordinary and you know how much this means to us. As sponsors, we should not lose. Good luck.'

"Now, Mr. Milo, do you recall this note?"

"Yes, I do."

"Is Mr. Phil Sawyer still alive?"

"Yes," Milo smiled in his response.

"Did you attempt to kill him?" Evelyn tried to suppress her chuckle.

"No."

Evelyn fetched out another mail and appealed to have it read in the hearing of the court. It was from a Mr. Thompson to his admin and a copy to Mr. Milo. The wording of the mail as read by Evelyn was:

"Ms. Jordan, I am yet to receive the reservation confirmations for the .... hotel. Time is of the essence and Mr. Milo is waiting for a word from us. Please expedite action on it and don't forget to copy Mr. Milo on the response. Remember, if we miss it, I'll kill ya before Milo kills me. Best wishes 'J'."

"Mr. Milo, you've just heard me read this second email. Are you acquainted with that also? And by the way, who is Mr. Thompson - as addressed in this email?"

"Mr. Thompson is a lawyer with my firm, MGS; the addressee, Ms. Jordan is his admin."

"Thank you. Was the reservation, as discussed in that mail successful?"

"No."

"What happened?"

"We were simply late."

"Did Mr. Thompson kill Ms. Jordan?"

"No – Ms. Jordan still works with us. I would say, it's a loose expression which everybody uses. I know parents use it on their children."

"Mr. Milo, upon hearing the Defendant's email regarding his frustration with Shazzy Spicer, did you warn the Palate office about any danger awaiting Shazzy Spicer?"

"No."

"Why not?"

"Richard Bridges cannot kill a fly, it is not his nature. The term 'kill' is a lose expression with no weight."

"I assume that you did not warn Mr. Spicer either."

"No, I did not."

"You didn't consider that as a basic ethical standard obligation." Evelyn continued to press her argument against the 'kill' word that the prosecution was factoring in their argument to prove the defendant's intent.

"No."

"To your knowledge, has Milo, Grady and Strong Law Firm under any circumstance, ever been confronted with any form of civil or criminal liability on any theory of negligent supervision?"

"Negligence in what – I mean, what did I neglect to do? I don't understand the question."

"I mean negligent to advise the office about an imminent threat by MGS employee to a client and the subsequent need to offer counselling to that employee."

"No, as a lawyer I can provide copies of police transcripts on where and when even they, the police, expressed the word inconsequentially. There was no need for me to do that and MGS hasn't experienced any form of endangerment."

"No further questions. Your Honor, there's no valid reason why the defendant is being held in jail - for a crime he didn't commit. He was not at the scene during the crime, did not have the weapon, in fact, nothing points to him as the perpetrator."

"I will grant the prosecution their right to exhaust the line-up of their witnesses and I will then make my ruling. This hearing is recessed for one hour." Judge Manor dropped his gavel and exited the room.

Evelyn returned to the defense seat and was met by a very hysterical Richard. It seemed he'd been waiting impatiently for Evelyn to wind up the cross-examination and had wasted no time to unload the weight on his mind.

"What happened to the driver who hit Josh? Do you know?"

"Nothing - why are you asking this in a middle of a crucial hearing - like this? I know the police filed a report but no charges were filed against him – why?"

"Please, Evelyn, get hold of Apphia now. Please, ask her to request the hospital to discontinue Josh's treatment. She must impress them that she wants to try an alternative treatment at home. Please, do it. I will explain later. It's a long story. Please do it now." Bridges was panting in anxiety and almost emotional.

"Richard, look at me. Are you sure you know what you're doing?" Evelyn was convinced he was suffering from some psychological hysteria, seemingly a culmination of his problems. The flux of his actions had rendered her nervous. She would soon have to face the wrath of the prosecution who had been very bruised by the open ridicule by Judge Manor's laughing and comments on the earlier objection that Celia Cromwell raised. She began to think of a way to talk Richard out of his request.

"Please, ask Sally to fetch the purple disc for you. Please, I can't tell you much. I don't know who is reading lips out here." Richard was persistent.

Evelyn began to see how grave his requests were. Before the trial began, she was convinced the landline in his home had been bugged, and she wondered why. After all, they had him in custody. Evelyn was beginning to see things from Richard's perspective. She decided to drive to meet Apphia.

The visit was unannounced. She arrived and Apphia wasn't home. She must be at the hospital, Evelyn concluded. She made it to the hospital early enough to catch Apphia on her way out. Seth was with her.

"How well do you know Dr. Appleworth?" Evelyn inquired.

"You mean, Marlene – very well, patient and physician relationship."

"Please, see if she can continue with Josh's treatment in the house. Discuss all modalities, treatment and payment. It's crucial we get Josh out of here today. I'll explain later, and please don't act as if you are suspicious of anything although we have cause to. Seth, come to the session if you have time to and observe. It doesn't matter when you get there. I'll need Elo to get the purple disc from Sally. I don't know what's in it, but I know I'll need it."

Evelyn delivered her desperate demands and was immediately on her way to the court house. The traffic was light but few blocks away to the court, road work had forced few lane closures and had created traffic bottlenecks for pedestrians and motorists as well. Evelyn checked her watch, she realized she would be late and that would not augur well for her and the defense when the judge resumed the session. She called Dan Stein, her fellow defense counsel and the call went straight to his voicemail – an indication that his phone was off; he was probably already in the courtroom.

Judge Manor made his entrance and prosecution was ready, but the lead defense attorney was nowhere to be found. Richard became very worried, and his other Attorney couldn't offer any explanation for her lateness, perhaps absence. The judge announced he would offer the defense five minutes to get ready otherwise he would make his ruling based on the information he'd heard so far, and also on the unexplained reason of the absence of the defense counsel. It started to dawn on Richard that he might have to defend himself if Evelyn failed to show up. The judge cleared his throat amidst the tension of silence.

"Is defense ready now for the court to resume?" The silence was unnerving.

"Yes, your honor." Evelyn walked in with a muddied skirt and a jacket caused by a splash from a wet pot-hole. As she approached her seat in the courtroom she continued with her struggle to brush off the stain on her skirt. Her efforts were not good enough. Her defense colleagues were relieved to see her, but amused by the sight she commanded.

"Please, I would like to apologize for holding up the session. I had to contend with unforeseen traffic just around the corner. I'm sorry my dressing may not be kempt enough for this audience, and I do appreciate the indulgence." Evelyn submitted.

"Ms. Hedge, we're happy you are here," Judge Manor said and went on to ask prosecution to introduce their next witness.

They showed signs of surprise at the invitation of the judge. There were mute speculations about holding off with their originally planned witness; the grappling among them was validating the speculation. After a minute, Ms. Cromwell announced the prosecutions next witness, Mrs. Spicer. She was nervous and clearly had been in deep mourning of her late husband.

"Mrs. Spicer, again, we're sorry for your loss. We hate to subject you to this, but we believe you share with us that the murderer should be brought to justice." Mrs. Spicer nodded softly in acknowledgement. Judge Manor also seized the opportunity to express his personal and the court's condolences to her, and again, Mrs. Spicer bowed to acknowledge the judge's words, and the session resumed.

"Mrs. Spicer, how long have you been married?"

"For nineteen years."

"Any children?"

"Yes, two boys – fourteen, and twelve, and a five year old daughter."

"Any previous marriages?"

"No."

"All your children from your Spicer relationship, right?"

"Yes, but he had another son in an early relationship with another woman."

"How would you describe your family life?"

"Very good, warm, loving, he was - a wonderful - husband and a father." Mrs. Spicer stuttered in her response. She sounded unsure.

"I'm sure you miss him a lot."

"Yes, I do." Mrs. Spicer said softly – holding back her emotional choke.

"Now, let me ask you. Do you know Mr. Bridges, the defendant?"

"I've heard about him, but haven't met him before."

"Have you seen any pictures of him?"

"Yes."

"How did you come by that picture?"

"They were pictures Shazzy brought home, and of course from the TV news."

"Your honor, I will seek your permission to request the witness to disclose what she might have heard about Mr. Bridges, the Defendant." Prosecutor Cromwell implored of the Judge.

"As long as the defense has no objection to it," Judge Manor remarked with a solicitous brow-raising look at the defense.

"Your honor, the question strongly invites answers predictive of hearsays, but we shall allow it as long as prosecution will not flag objections over our follow up cross-examinations on her very answers, because we intend to pick needles from every haystack of answers."

"Fair enough," Judge Manor ruled with a very visible smile – seemingly amused by Evelyn's assertive remark and her subtle witness intimidation.

"Mrs. Spicer would you please tell this session what you've heard about Mr. Bridges."

"Well, I remember, my husband was saying, was, was…"

The words instantly froze in the mouth of Mrs. Spicer. Prosecutor Celia Cromwell was wide-eyed by what was unfolding before her. With her eyes seemingly transfixed on the witness, she moved cautiously towards her in the witness stand like she was approaching an apparition. In a strange and raw disbelief, she was observing that her witness was drifting off; did not seem to be alert and might be having a form of an attack, panic, anxiety or heart attack – something didn't look right with her. In the prevailing atmosphere of the anxiety-stricken courtroom, the prosecutor hysterically yelled out an open request for a 911 call to be placed. Her voice was resolute and conveyed all the urgency she could command. Judge Manor ordered everyone in the room to remain seated, and asked if any trained and licensed physician was in the room. The request yielded no response but, one of the court security personnel decided to offer immediate Cardiopulmonary resuscitation.

After several speedy chest compressions, Mrs. Spicer regained a measure of alertness before the arrival of the paramedics to the relief of everyone. Nonetheless, she was hastily wheeled into an ambulance and to the nearest hospital. Judge Manor found himself compelled to adjourn the session again and set resumption date after three days, at which time prosecution would have to call their next witness pending Mrs. Spicer's qualification to continue with her testimony. While prosecution scrambled to readjust and set their house in order for the next session, Evelyn was also scrambling for time to understand the puzzling Purple disc and the state of Josh's health.

It dawned on her that a few days before, Josh was playing and responding to jokes with his visitors and was ready to be discharged from the hospital. Those recovery signs were no fluke. What might have or could have turned the tables on Josh, Evelyn wondered. After a quick word with Dan Stein, she hastily walked out of the courtroom while Richard was being escorted into the jail vehicle. As she attempted to cross the street to her parked car, her eyes caught a waving hand in the air. Seth was attempting to catch her attention. She wasn't expecting him that early at the courthouse. He had reasons.

"I've just spoken with Dr. Appleworth and she's agreed to see Josh. Apphia feels she will be okay to handle the hospital assignment alone; it will reduce the level of suspicion – she thinks. Now, listen to me and don't look back. I'm seeing the driver of the car that hit Josh." Seth whispered.

"Where - are you sure?" Evelyn whispered back, but with excitement, and Seth had to restrain her again to prevent her from scarring off the prey. Seth took Evelyn's hand and strutted with her like a couple to her car. When they got to the car, she hastily reached into her glove compartment while their prey, the Josh-accident driver was still dialoguing. In fact, he seemed to be arguing. Without the use of the flash, Evelyn pressed the shutter and the prey was safe in her camera. The Los Angeles outdoor brightness was enough

"You're a genius," Seth flattered.

"Check my courtroom antics tomorrow." She winked and drove off on a mission to see Dr. Marlene Appleworth. Evelyn needed to be informed on the condition of Josh and be able to convey that to Richard the next day. Bound by duty as his retained attorney, it behooved her to recondition his state of mind for readiness and for a disposition to handle a grueling examination by the prosecution. Evelyn was foreseeing that.

CHAPTER 34

Dr. Appleworth wasn't happy and it showed. The presence of Seth had always reminded her of the death of Erika, Seth's wife. Erika was her patient and Appleworth had carried with her the stigma of the failure to save her. Ironically, she'd found herself in the clutch again and this time to reshape their opinion of her as a sounder steward to her calling. To garner back that favorable opinion she realized she had to be candid with her prognosis of Josh to her waiting visitors, Seth and Apphia. The physician still kept a worried look in spite of Seth's effort to attenuate that countenance by injecting light-hearted comments.

However, Dr. Appleworth was more professionally minded. "I'm not sure, but I can tell you that it doesn't look good. You see, a standard protocol for head injury or trauma is by lowering the patient's body temperature immediately after the injury. In other words, the patient is chilled to hypothermic level. That step may effectively help the brain chemicals to help the brain cells function rightly despite the severity of the impact. It's possible that the process might have been excessive for your child. I'm not sure. But, I can assure you, we'll keep an eye on him every minute and I'll do whatever I can for him."

Marlene Appleworth reached out to Apphia, took hold of her right hand and squeezed it gently to register an assuring pact and the warmth in her commitment. She turned to go back to her unit when Evelyn caught up with Seth and Apphia. They looked distraught and she figured that the news hadn't been good. It meant she had to face the mammoth task of breaking the non-heartwarming new development to Richard. So far, the unpleasant reminder that he'd shown less-strength to handle any news about his son's health, tended to undermine Evelyn's hopes.

She hastily whisked past them, and found herself in step with the physician who was approaching the security access door to the unit. She got her attention by steering her pleading eyes to the doctor's face and the doctor yielded.

"Dr. Appleworth, I have to convey a word to my client. You must know that he suggested, I mean – recommended you. He has huge confidence in you, and he's a huge fan of yours, what would you suggest would be safe to tell him."

"The truth."

"The truth – what do you mean? Is there something more than meets the eye?"

"The truth that his son's condition is critical and I will do my utmost for him." The doctor didn't mince her words and that was her mark whenever she dealt with lawyers. Evelyn was no exception, although her approach was submissive, both in tone and intent.

Dr. Appleworth had had her battles with lawyers who'd tried to paint her as less-empathetic to a patient's psychological anxieties. On one occasion, among the many depositions she'd testified in, a lawyer interpreted her matter-of-fact tone to answers as "arrogance" and went far to describe her as a "fox in a white coat." Since then, Marlene hadn't been a friend to lawyers. However, Richard had earned her respect and appreciation from the time he approached her about Seth's rashes. Richard would always remain a gentleman, a different lawyer, at least in her eyes.

"Assure Bridges," Appleworth said, "I will do my best for his son and he can count on it – even if it will take recruiting another doctor to assist, I will." Appleworth smiled, and Evelyn knew it was a very assuring smile, and she could count on it.

Evelyn walked back to her car with her head down, not because her eyes had to contend with bright rays from the sun, for a partial cloudiness of a December afternoon was beginning to form, but because a recurring echo of the phrase "son's condition" had lowered her spirits and her head had physically resigned to that docility. The words of the doctor were very assuring, but they were coming up against a reminder about the "condition" of a child who was left in a rain in a wooden box cradle, whose

440

helpless cries couldn't sail above the drowning sound of the rain. Condition, condition, condition - it took a lady with a righteous indignation and a heart for benevolent pilferage to rescue that child from her drowning condition.

Evelyn knew that story very well and the woman who carried out that feat. It was her story. It took her long to embrace her mother as a heroine. A feeling of indebtedness began to assail her conscience and she took a tacit vow behind her steering wheel that she would do anything within her power regardless of the merits or the demerits to save Josh from his condition.

Her car, which was heading towards her house, began to obey to Evelyn's will to rather head for her mother's house. She made a quick turn and was on her way to see Dorina. She missed her. She missed her Romanian air; she missed her walls and she missed her violin plays which, as a child, she rebelliously refused to learn from her. She was beginning to miss everything about Dorina, from her morning pastries to her dinner spaghettis. The inclinations of a hungry woman began to emerge and she told herself that she would settle for anything she would have on her table.

The timing was right; the aroma had stolen its way to the outdoors that it had fumed a neighbor's dog into a barking frenzy, and Evelyn into a burning impatience for whatever was being cooked. As she made her way to the front door, she could hear the sound of her Mom's violin. It puzzled her reasoning. How could she combine cooking and fiddling at the same time? The answer was the man by the stove, "Maunty's son," James.

They were surprised to see each other again. She was supposed to be in court and he was supposed to be at work. She wasn't sure if their meeting was a pleasant surprise. She was starting to become appreciative of him, at least for his show of concern during her lonely moments few nights before, but not this day. She wasn't sure she would be disposed this time to talking with him because she already had her plate full. Evelyn however, suppressed her indifference and flashed a spurious smile.

"What are you doing here?" she asked the surprised cook.

"I was going to ask you the same thing. I was expecting you to be arguing in court." Their voices drew her mother's attention and she came to join them.

"Today of all days, I wasn't planning to cook and James offered to cook for me." Dorina explained, however, Evelyn had observed that unlike her previous visits, her mother didn't look cheerful and she wondered why. She took consolation from the assumption that her mother wouldn't be playing her violin if she were not okay. Probably, it was just a moody feeling that had come over her, Evelyn hoped. The spread at the table was inviting and James could claim bragging rights for his work. It was sheer artistic layout intending to make a culinary expression, and James did that very loudly. When they settled at the table to eat, Evelyn realized that Cannon and Robert, the house guests weren't present.

"Where are the guys?"

"Cannon's at work. He's just got a job. Robert's at the library. He loves reading and he goes there every morning. He'll be home anytime." With those explanations from her mother, Evelyn felt at ease to eat. She heaped her plate with every item on the table. She'd just begun to eat, when she was interrupted by James with his request to bless the meal first. Evelyn smiled at his effort to impress her with a genteel bearing.

"This – is – good." Evelyn expressed emphatically after his first bite.

"Thank you. I feel flattered." He remarked. "But you may have to pardon my appearance at this table. My calling sometimes deprives me of dinner table propriety."

"So, about Cannon, what's he doing?" Evelyn asked; she was naturally concerned about their wellbeing. Dorina paused and turned to James hoping he would provide the answer for Evelyn, but when he wasn't not forthcoming, Dorina spoke.

"Cannon's been employed by a landscaping company and he works together with James."

"So, you're colleagues." Evelyn tried to seek a clarifying confirmation from James but he simply nodded for his mouth had been bridled with food. So far, he'd spoken very little. After emptying his plate James was on his feet and ready to leave. He packed a late lunch for Cannon and he was on his way. "I'll see you tonight," James expressed as he stood by the door.

"I won't be here." Evelyn responded.

"I'm sorry, but I meant your Mom. You take care, and I mean, both of you."

Evelyn was surprised at James's poignant show of less-enthusiasm and indifference towards her. She'd perhaps expected more sentimental overtures from him. Evelyn was beginning to feel humiliated. She turned to her mom for an answer. Dorina knew her daughter very well, and she tried to not encourage any discussion on James.

"How's the hearing going?" Dorina asked.

"It's going well, but Richard is fighting many people so it isn't easy. He's fighting an institution and the fate of many people depends on the outcome. By the way, what's going on with James? Is he alright?"

"Yes, he's alright. He'll be coming to see me this evening, whatever is bothering him I'm sure he will share it with me."

Evelyn wasn't very satisfied with the answer, but she chose to not press it. She had her theory but decided to wait for time to unfold it. In the meantime, she had work to do, but her mind drove her to James again. There were no showers, no poetic lines, but the company of a mother with a profound story of bravery that she witnessed and which she was also part of. She kissed her mother and was on her way to prepare for the morrow.

CHAPTER 35

Evelyn was among the few early arrivals at the court. Apparently she wanted to atone for her lateness at the previous sitting. And this time, she arrived in no muddied clothing. "Nice suit," Richard joked. "Thank you," she joked back with an ostentatious bow. She liked to see Richard in better spirits. It had always helped her to muster more confidence and she needed that as she approached the day's deliberations. Her team mate, Dan Stein wasn't present and she had to do battle alone that day but, she looked ready.

The Prosecution team also looked ready, but weren't. Clearly missing among them was Mrs. Spicer, the widow of Shazzy Spicer. Her testimony was deferred due to a sudden health emergency while she was on the stand at the previous hearing. Judge Manor had ruled at the last hearing that Mrs. Spicer would continue with her testimony when she felt disposed to. Mrs. Spicer hadn't arrived and the judge was yet to hear about her condition and ability to continue with the hearing from the leading prosecuting Counsel, Celia Cromwell.

"Is the Prosecution ready to resume the testimony of Mrs. Spicer?"

Celia Cromwell got on her feet and suggested she would like to approach the bench jointly with Evelyn. The judge beckoned

446

them forward. The prosecutor then presented a medical report from the Physician of Mrs. Spicer that explained her condition and indisposition to appear for the hearing. After reading the document, Judge Manor instructed the prosecution to return and call their next witness. Both lawyers walked back to their seats with a measure of pride and confidence in their gaits to their seats.

"Your honor, it was our intention to present our testimonies in an arranged fashion that would help in the flow of building our case effectively. It would also help us in building our case which would address the motive of the defendant very meaningfully. It's very clear under these circumstances that we cannot make that happen. We would therefore, like to cede this ground to the defense and to allow them call any ready witness of theirs if they're so willing."

Lawyer Cromwell's submission didn't come as a surprise to the defense, but they, in turn had a surprise for the prosecution.

"We empathize with the prosecution on their plight, but in view of the fact that this development had come as a surprise to us as well, we would also like to submit few conditions: that after our first witness we shall also have the latitude to make a pre-emptive request to call a prosecution witness to take the stand before the prosecution's normal turn to examine that witness. I believe it will help the court and all of us to expedite this hearing. Your honor we await your word." Evelyn sat down as a very gratified defense counsel.

The prosecution acceded to defense request and the Judge acquiesced with them all.

"Your honor, defense would like to submit a video recording of a deposition of a defense witness, Mr. Lomi Spicer son of Mr. Shazzy Spicer."

On that note, Ms. Hedge decided to approach the judge with the recorded video and took deliberate long strides to the judge to, again, simply advertise her confidence. The motive also was to plague the prosecution with uncertainties, and to raise their level of worry, if any, to a defeatist attitude level that would impel them to eventually throw in the towel. After presenting the judge with a copy of the deposition yet to be watched, she returned and started the video.

In his preliminary response in the recorded video, Mr. Lomi Spicer introduced himself as a twenty-four year old son, born out of wedlock to the late Shazzy Spicer. He'd been a chef since the age of nineteen and had credited his success to a commitment of deriving his satisfaction from seeing a pleased customer. In this early stage of the deposition Lomi revealed a gentle side of him as a young Spicer.

"Mr. Lomi Spicer, did you keep in touch with your father?" Evelyn led the questioning for the defense.

"Yes, but not frequently," Lomi Spicer replied.

"How often?"

"I think once in a year or two."

"When did you last see him?"

"About three months ago."

"Why? Was there a problem in your relationship?"

"I don't know. I realized I was better off when I stayed away from him."

"'Better off...?' That's very unflattering. Again, Mr. Lami Spicer, let me ask you, why did you choose to stay away from him?"

"He didn't like me. He said I wasn't aggressive enough; I was too soft, I guess for him. I feared him."

"You feared him. Did you ever think he would hurt you?"

"Yes."

"How, as an adult? Did you fear him even in your adult years?"

"Yes, he threatened he would have our restaurant closed."

"Why?"

"Because, we refused to sell beverages he was trying to introduce to the market."

"Who owned the restaurant?"

"It's a joint venture, my mother and I."

"And why did you refuse the beverages?"

"My father said they contained medicinal plants, herbs which we weren't sure of – we were simply not comfortable selling anything we didn't know much about."

"Did you try any of the beverages?"

"No, we did not."

"How then, could you determine if they were marketable or not?"

"Because they weren't FDA approved and we simply didn't want to go there."

"Didn't you consider it would be fair and wise to learn about those herbs before ruling out the market prospects of your father's product?" Evelyn pressed for answer.

"Actually, he lectured us more about the plants. He said a few were from Africa and others from Brazil and they had aphrodisiac properties."

"What do you mean by 'aphrodisiac properties'?"

"Well, my father claimed his wine, Palexir, is a sweet wine and with its low-level alcoholic content, a person may have to drink more. However, the big deal is its ability to increase sexual, desire and fantasies."

"So, you didn't believe him?"

"I wasn't sure about his claim."

"How could you have been, if you didn't try it?"

"My Mom is a sobered addict. She seriously advised me to stay away from anything that would affect normal conditions - I guess because of her past experience."

"I'm hearing, for this reason, you didn't try it. You were not fair to your father then."

"I was. I have the right to choose what I want to try and what I don't want to, although he tried to tell me more about it and to twist my arm, but I didn't want to."

"What do you mean by 'twist my arm?' What did he say to you?"

"He said the Palexir was tried in Africa and some other countries with great success. It's difficult to question his claims because I believe naturally the drink will prove itself. Perhaps people have experienced his claim. I don't know. But what got my concern was the suggestion that it was a high-end wine that would typically sell for about forty thousand dollars a bottle. He came up with stories to hype the drink, and I didn't want to be part of that. I guess I disappointed him again. "

On that response, Evelyn stopped the video. The short clip of the deposition recording didn't say much and the prosecution surprisingly declined their opportunity to cross-examine the witness during the deposition recording.

"The deposition video you've just seen is a precursor to the testimony of our next witness. The defense would like to call the Defendant, Mr. Richard Bridges to the stand."

A literal audible gasp went out in the courtroom at the announcement that the defendant would take the stand. Richard, wearing a dark blue suit, walked to the stand not only as the cynosure of all eyes, but also the cynosure of judicial prudence. There was no nervousness in his walk. The nervous one was Evelyn who had just braved her doubts to make her defendant the prime witness. She hadn't rehearsed him and wasn't sure if he would live up to expectation as the seasoned lawyer that he'd been. Evelyn knew that the weeks of incarceration had taken a toll on her client. And she feared that his son's, sickness would compound his anxieties. Evelyn was beginning to question her client's mental frame and readiness for this crucial moment. She tacitly questioned her action but, it was too late.

Richard pulled the front edge and the hem of his jacket, as his way to straighten it up and advertise his readiness. He held his chest and chin up as his eyes contacted Evelyn again. Their eyes spoke. Confidence was back. Crunch time had arrived. He was sworn to take the stand.

"Mr. Richard Bridges, do you know why you are being held in jail?" Evelyn asked amidst the utmost silence in the court?

"Yes, on suspicions of killing Mr. Shazzy Spicer and Ms. Bruna Dhahl." Richard replied.

"Did you kill them?"

"Absolutely not."

"You sound very confident. Do you know Mr. Spicer and Ms. Dhahl?"

"Yes, I had to work with them on a project which I was assigned to by the MGS law firm."

"What was the project?"

"A project to help resolve a public relations problem for Palate International, the employers of Shazzy Spicer and their contract sommelier employees of which Ms. Bruna Dhahl was part of and as a representative for the sommeliers."

"I take it that the three of you met in the performance of your assignment." Evelyn inferred.

"Yes."

"Mr. Bridges, I will cut to the chase, during this period, were there moments of agreements or disagreements with these unfortunate alleged homicide victims?"

"Yes, multiple times with Mr. Spicer, but rather spasmodically with Ms. Dhahl."

"What in your opinion would explain the cause of your disagreements with Mr. Spicer?"

The question brought Prosecutor Celia Cromwell to her feet. She looked and sounded angry.

"Your honor, defense is trying to create a framework to prejudge the intentions and actions of the prosecution. If this hearing is fed with disagreements in the light of the circumstances, defense will be establishing a measure of bias against the absent or silent plaintiffs, and I mean Mr. Spicer and Ms. Dhahl. They have no voice or voices to disclaim any disagreements, and assertions the defendant may try to make. His versions may be distorted or may not carry the whole truth. Whatever charge or indictment brought against them, prosecution may not satisfactorily meet the arguments on their own grounds because our best witnesses in this case are the silent Mr. Spicer and Ms. Dhahl."

Judge Manor gave an interrogative glance at the defense and Evelyn perceived his silent query.

"Your honor, prosecution will have their chance, to totally challenge any claim or claims the defendant may make. The only reason the accused is in jail is because, prosecution has been trying to build the motive of murder simply on grounds that the defendant in this hearing had differences and disagreements with the late Mr. Spicer and the late Ms. Dhahl. He's a suspect in jail with a strange accusation that he was capable of translating his disagreements into murder. Your honor, there's no better forum for my client's voice to be heard than this hearing; claims of the nature of disagreements and misunderstandings must be told and heard. Do they carry any vitriol or hate to even incense a non-violent person to commit such wickedness? We don't know. Please, I must inform this hearing that, for hours this defendant was held in jail without knowledge of who the murder victim or victims were. He did not even know about their deaths. It is not a far-fetched claim to sound that this defendant had been prejudged from day one, before he was even brought in here. Defense hopes to support every claim of Mr. Bridges' disagreements with Mr. Spicer and Bruna Dhahl with proofs – solid proofs, files, which are also in the custody of the prosecution. We intend to furnish exhibits, which the prosecution is already aware of, to this hearing. Your honor, nothing has changed."

Evelyn's frenzied tempo was more on display than the prosecution had anticipated. Judge Manor ruled, "Prosecution, you will have your turn. I will allow the question."

"Mr. Bridges, I implore you to spell out your disagreements with the fallen Mr. Spicer and Ms. Dhahl. And yes, we do mourn them." Evelyn expressed again.

Energized by her performance, Richard assumed a more confident stance while he faced the judge.

"Your honor, my future and my life are at stake here and at this very moment. I would therefore, crave your indulgence and the indulgence of this hearing to grant me sufficient latitude to explain my disagreements."

Judge Manor smiled and nodded to grant his request. Richard on his part, tried to keep a cool demeanor which stood in sharp contrast to the assertive presentation made by Evelyn.

"Your honor, this is a time I have to cast my mind back and to try to recall moments and events with Mr. Spicer and Ms. Dhahl. I see a man and a woman who were standing upon their convictions that they were offering something right, simply marketing their claim or brand and trying to bring in business and ultimately help the economy. I see also another party, a man with a greater conviction that with his knowledge of the law and the morals of the society we belong to, is trying to challenge the legal and moral principles regarding what Spicer and Dhahl were trying to offer.

Your honor, my lawyer has already in few words, presented my innocence before this hearing. Please, I'm not here to question the quality of lives these alleged murder victims lived. I would take no delight in that. I wouldn't relieve the mind of the murderer or murderers with a gratifying thinking that their alleged killings were just rewards for the alleged ill-wills that Mr. Spicer and Ms. Dhahl were planning to exact upon men. Your honor, I simply cannot indict the memories of Dhahl and Spicer. Doing so is like indicting the ambitions of the living and the unrealized dreams of the dead, no, I would not. Why, because I believe, there are still promising glimpses of virtuous nurturers yet to emerge into the glow of moral uprightness without any hindrances.

I did not kill Shazzy and Bruna. The murderer or murderers are out there with consciences that had timed themselves out of civilization and I would not appease those consciences with a stale condemnation of Shazzy Spicer and Bruna Dhahl. Nonetheless, I will still speak the light of my conscience.

Like everyman, they had axes to grind, their right to explore, right to create and the right to pronounce what is or what are acceptable to them. Our actions to explore or to create, quite often, are driven by our needs. And I'm steep in my conviction that many times the needs of a person does translate into the choices that the person makes. However, the needs of a person do not summarily reflect the person's outward decisions. In any effort to meet a need, society mustn't bear the brunt of the effort. Especially so, it mustn't affect the values of the society or the community the person lives in as a whole. So then, is it right for a self-gratifying need or ambition, even vile as it may seem to be, to be accommodated at the expense of the rest of the community?

No, it mustn't be. It shouldn't be, when the values and principles of the people stand in sharp contrast to the self-gratifications of an individual. However, if the people embrace the needs of the ambitious self-gratifying man, then there is no vile blood between the people or the society and the self-gratifying man.

Can the people then stop Spicer from carrying his dream business project?

The answer is no, because the people don't know his mind nor do they know his hand. Simply put, the people don't know what, or the nature of the project Spicer plans to present; they're uninformed about the letter and the spirit of his project. However, if people become aware of how vile his project is and the spirit of his project, how it stands in total affront to the civil and moral values of our society then the people have the right to protest Spicer's project.

How then do we know what the minds of Shazzy Spicer and Bruna Dhahl's reveal?

Here again, even steeper am I in my conviction that Spicer and Bruna's ambitions reflect their minds which give voice to their decisions and ambitions.

What was their ambition? We may want to know, but do we really want to?

Yes, we do, but we must offer them the right to explain their ambitions. If we don't, we shall be straying into the precincts of denying them the basic right to defend their ambitions. But then, how do they defend their project when their voices are silent?

Your honor, the ethos of their ambitions reflects their choice and their actions, and actions speak louder than words.

Even so, in their silence, I do hear a more silent voice. It is the voice of purpose. For every action is motivated by purpose or intent. Where then is the voice of purpose?

There must be this voice of purpose, simply put, there must be a motive or intent or a reason for creating their project or ambition, good or bad.

These different voices are roaring on the streets of conscience, the voice of moral purpose and the voice of ill purpose.

If self is denied for the greater good of another person then the purpose is good; the will is good. Call it goodwill.

However, if a person is denied or is deprived of for the greater interest of the depriving perpetrator, disregarding the effects on the deprived person or persons then the purpose is evil; the will is ill. Call it ill-will.

O – Sanity must prevail. Even steeper, steeper, steeper I do plunge my convictions that there is no greater voice of silence than the silence of the missing voice of goodwill, a choice that speaks greater volumes of goodwill towards men.

Was there any goodwill in Spicer's ambition?

We've just watched and heard Mr. Spicer's son.

Where do I place Spicer's will?

We may draw our own lines."

Richard turned and allowed his eyes to travel around the room to see if his words were making any impact at all on the crowd in the courtroom. He was seeing a mixed feeling of apathy and a very much suppressed ardor. He was seeing fear in some eyes – not of him, but for him. He seemed to have been affected by what he'd seen. He sensed his own spirit falling within him. He was in agony.

"O – My strange circumstances must not cajole me into meddling in vindictive hearsays.

Bear with me – I'm not here to indict the ambitions of Shazzy Spicer and Bruna Dhahl."

Suddenly, a loud yell broke the lifeless quietness of the courtroom.

"Tell us! You owe it to us. Tell us!"

It was a female voice. Judge Terrance Manor, known for his uncompromising courtroom protocols and discipline was surprised at the yelling in his courtroom. He roared the room to order while the Court Security rushed towards the heckler to restrain her.

"I will not tolerate any more of this. I will not be lenient with a charge of contempt. Do you understand? Madam, do you understand?"

The heckler who seemed to be in her fifties rolled her eyes in reluctant obedience. Richard knew the crowded courtroom was all ears. He also knew he had a tight-rope to walk on; he wouldn't want to offend the already infuriated Judge Manor.

Richard had begun to sweat profusely. He tried to wipe his brow with the sleeves of his jacket, a rather unsightly gesture. At that point, it didn't matter. He caught a glimpse of his lawyer. He saw pity in the eyes of Evelyn. That wasn't going to help his course; it rather imposed upon him a shadow of self-pity. Then his thoughts settled on his family and the living reality of his prevailing plight – his lonely sick child and his loyal wife that he cheated on. "They're worth more; they deserve pity, not me," his conscience reminded him.

He cast his eyes back on Judge Manor. He was trying to suppress his public heaving and puffing, the result of his emotional reaction to the heckler. Richard began to sense what was in the air for him. He recomposed himself and continued.

"Your honor, the ambitions of Shazzy Spicer and Bruna Dhahl may be right in their own eyes. However, if their ambitious attempt to deprive the people of their core moral principles and values, then the voices of their ambitions, after all, are not silent. Actions speak. They are actively declaring their ambitions in thundering terms even in the silence of passive response. They are simply proclaiming their ill-will. So, in reality, again, they are not silent.

When their ambitions suggest a worrying trend that will benefit them only as individuals, then their act of ill-will becomes an enigmatic stigma in the society.

Again, are their ambitions dictated by needy situations or circumstances that they find themselves in or are they dictated simply by desires they label as 'needs'? Where every man stands on this, I don't know.

I do know though, that a person tends to esteem one's need as greater than the need of others. We prioritize our needs and also weigh our needs in the scales of our perspectives. If these also influence our judgments, then there must be a line – a line to guide, and a line we must not cross. We may call them laws or rules or regulations.

Where do these lines begin and where do they end? Even so when do they begin and when will they end?

I may ask. Who is or are drawing the lines or who might have drawn them?

Your honor, I am alluding to the principles that constitute the moral values of our society. These are the values that must hold the foundations and the structure of the laws of this society.

I would not go stealing food because I needed food. That would not be the way I must meet my need. There must be a principle to guide me in my effort to meeting my need or in acquiring what I need. Theft is theft, even if it meets a need.

If these principles in very subtle ways are frowned upon by any influential opinion stirrer or stirrers then prudence begs our judgment.

If there is a moral compass that guides our needs or ambitions, then where is it? Where does it direct us to? Even so, who or what drives it?"

Judge Manor felt very uncomfortable with the question raised by him in his own defense argument. Richard noticed that his words had unnerved the judge. He paused briefly in anticipation of a comment from Judge Manor. Indeed, the Judge chose to hold not his breath this time. He came swinging.

"Mr. Bridges, may I remind you that the law dictates no expectations or what you esteem as 'values.' It dictates what it has. It dictates the minds of the people who wrote it, their opinion and their beliefs. It is like the rain. It pours on the good and the bad, the rich and the poor. The law will not tell you how to eat your salad. The dressing for your salad is your choice."

Richard got excited by Judge Manor's argument.

"Your Honor, this is exactly my point. We may have to eat the salad anyway, but what greens or leaves constitute the salad, the very salad we may have to eat. If the leaves are from poisonous plants, do we have to eat them? The choice is ours, but what happens to the greengrocer who mixes the good leaves with the visibly identical poisonous leaves?

Do we settle for morality or for legality – the right to sell salad leaves, come what the leaves may be, adulterated or not by any means possible, or the right to eat salad leaves simply because they are labelled salad leaves and we innocently purchase them as privileged buyers from an innocent grocer who receives them prepackaged by an ill-will farmer scheming for a greater gain with poisonous weeds and ivies in our plates?

Hear me hearers in this court. Should the farmer make his money taking advantage of the trust the innocent grocer placed in him or should we make ourselves sick by our silence when even the buck is passed on to us. Remember, as it was well put by our august judge: 'The law dictates no values. It dictates the mind of the people who wrote it.'"

At this point, Judge Manor hated himself that he had been intellectually impudent with his remark. And Richard seized the moment.

"What if the ambitious farmer and the writers of the law are like-minds? Again, remember, the law dictates no values. The law writers give us what they have, their mind, which is the provident goodwill or the flip side, equivalent ill-will salad. Nothing indicts them while the sick groans. Folks, let me ask you. What do you want in your plate?

"Mr. Shazzy Spicer never shied away from defending what Palate International had always stood for - appetite. His vision was to spell appetite in every sphere of life and to create a very lasting investment prospect for his work. To achieve this, Spicer targets very young people. He believes a younger generation strategically will trend his ambitions through many generations to come. Notwithstanding other previous appetites that he'd already introduced, his current creation of media and electronic games that recreate gun fights and violence for pleasure is very troubling. The project is called PAL, Palate Avengers League."

"The PAL project idea was to introduce new genre of subtle sadistic video games. In this case it would involve kids in league with other kids to contest in fights against anything that challenges their will. Through online social interactive schemes, kids team up with other kids, give their team a name and then settle on a time with the rival team; and the fight begins."

"Mr. Spicer admitted this in a letter. The court has a copy on file: that among the multiple benefits of his project, it aims at helping kids stand up for themselves. It is also meant to generate participation of all ages who also watch the Avengers fight."

"Your honor, this game is more than it meets the eye. The children may find themselves learning how to plan and to administer physical pain in the visual electronic, video or sound media forms. The project makes light-work of violence and euphemistically describes the actions as 'defending themselves'. A team is rewarded with higher scoring when a successful self-defensive action eludes the enemies. Other higher scorings are generated by the Avengers' ability to handle the level of the avenging tasks in the shortest possible time. The weapons for the fights include guns, knives and any means accessible."

"The climax of the games is the Palate Individual Encounters, the PIE series which Mr. Spicer dubbed the 'dessert.' This part of the game is an open brawl to determine the last man standing, a survival feat. He did not mince his words to declare it as his favorite part, the dessert – PIE. What's in a name?"

"Your honor, a fight is a fight and words cannot lessen the steamed feeling of the ultimate goal in fighting; that is to destroy the opponent."

"The concern is that, the children are going to be gradually desensitized to cruelty by the subtle exposures to diverse bloody entertainment schemes that are beginning to woo parents as well. A major component of morality, found in forgiveness and kindness is being replaced by vindictiveness and guile. To sum it up, the children's games may culminate into violence on our streets energized by subtle elements of ignorant ideological or political or spiritual or social beliefs. Your honor the thought is frightening. The unhealthy appetite may prevail. We need a cure. Mine is a plea for a total healing for the minds that align with Mr. Spicer's strange appetite.

Hear me my people, please, I plead for your ears, for, fearfully, the stream of compassion will even run dry in the milky bosoms of women.

Children may form innocent attachment to wicked persons and cruelty may laugh to scorn the tenderness of caring hearts.

'Sorry' may no longer even be a cliché, but a sordid absentee in our daily dialogue.

"Your honor, the PAL project is ingeniously insidious, crafted to fly innocuously under the radar of witty detection.

"Who is a pal? Pal means a friend, of course. And that's how Spicer's Palate International packages its offer. It always comes with a covering with the most delectable friendly appeal.

"The very name Palate Avengers League, PAL, beguiles people into thinking that they have found a pal; they have found a friend in Spicer and his projects.

"PAL is no friend. PAL is a chameleonizing cheer-leader, cheering the colors of hypocrisy that are pleasing to the young ignorant spectators.

"Palate's PAL is no friend.

Your honor, I am being held in jail on grounds that my opposition to the late Mr. Spicer and the late Ms. Dhahl suggests probable reasons to have a motive to murder. In other words, any voice of dissent to Spicer and Ms. Dhahl makes one allegedly culpable of this alleged crime.

Hear me O hearers in this court. This preliminary hearing must hear the active claim of goodwill. Any person with a heart for the purpose of man's goodwill is on trial here today.

Hear me hearers, please do not be hoodwinked by the wink and smile of the game makers into believing that it's all about fun. That's their game. They are good at it. Spicer and Dhahl intends to feed you through the mouth, the eyes and the ears, sometimes at the same time. It's a bombardment.

There are different types and forms of fun. Brothers even wrestle each other for the fun of it, but no - not Spicer's type of fun.

His fun wrestles away the sunny youthful years of the young while fiddling his strings of fulfillment as the children kill themselves with idle lethargic pleasures. Indeed, the sun will set one day. Then, these untapped great minds with their unrealized great dreams, ideas and inventions may unfortunately idle into unproductive years and eventual eternal sleep.

Yes, the sun will set one day; dreams will go sleeping; a new era will dawn and dreamers may still be sleeping while new offspring's may be yawning.

Hear me hearers. Think about what Spicer is offering you. I stand accused for being in the way of a project that Spicer attempts to introduce. Does that qualify me as a murder suspect? If it does then that calls into question the probity of the law.

I must submit that if the law is silent about Spicer's plans, then silence suffocates morality. It chokes the very purpose that gives life to the prudent law, the spirit of its essence, the breath of love for one another. Your honor, if laws and the regulations do not promote the presence of peace as the main purpose, then they are promoting the absence of it.

Good-naturedness or love keeps us within the boundaries of respect for one another. Outside these boundaries, you and I know, it will be total disorder. Again, without the ethos of love in the law, the law justifies malice, packaged in the splendor of self-indulgence. 'I did it because it pleased me,' one would say."

Richard, at this time raised his arms to try to touch his right ear in a demonstrative gesture to depict a person straining his ears to hear something.

"What am I hearing – O what am I hearing?"

Richard was beginning to succumb to his emotions that he'd tried to suppress throughout the hearing sessions.

"Your ears O – you hearers, your ears;

O – I must not insinuate. For the indolent are prone to insinuate by hiding the tough truth behind a curtain of words. I must make it plain. Indeed, I promise, I do not intend to attack their memory, no, I will not.

Your honor, I could go on and on, but I shudder at whispering this to this court – another of Mr. Spicer and Ms. Dhahl's schemes. Perhaps, this trumps all the schemes. In fact it is actually the brainchild of Bruna Dhahl. The concept is called the PLAY project, Palate Live Art of You. The idea as described by Bruna is about expressing live lifelike art, that is, instead of nude statues, it will bring to life a vivid world of nude art. The project intends to reveal in live form, nude strollers on a twenty-acre grove orchard, the Eden Grove Garden Strollers to be known as the EGGS. This large park is meant to be an outdoor recreational ground where adult couples pay to have picnics in the nude, stroll in the nude, and relax under the festoonery setting and atmosphere of the EGG. The concept argues that it's simply bringing to life nude art sculptures.

Your honor, the California Penal Code Section 314 states and I quote:

'Every person who willfully and lewdly, either. 1. Exposes his person, or the private parts thereof, in any public place, or in any place where there are present other persons to be offended or annoyed thereby: or, 2. Procures, counsels, or assists any person so to expose himself or take part in any model artist exhibition, or to make any other exhibition of himself to public view, or the view of any number of persons, such as is offensive to decency, or is adapted to excite to vicious or lewd thoughts or acts, is guilty of a misdemeanor.'

Your honor, yes, EGGS offers attractions for television shows, and recordings, but are there other persons present who will be offended or annoyed thereby?

I mean, if television producers lift these scenes and sceneries onto our television screens, by way of developing programs around them, are they not making these persons who willfully and lewdly expose themselves in a public place, offend or annoy other persons present?

Yes they do. And I am not limiting the reference of the offended party to only be the cinematographers or camera men and the recording crew. I mean the viewers at home and the broad spectrum of viewers will be offended or annoyed for having been made to be present in the public place through the means of television or any electronic medium that support watching person or persons who willfully and lewdly expose themselves to public view.

Perhaps, television networks may see a potential harvest in this and may not care about the merits or the demerits of its effects on society.

Please, your honor, viewing EGGS scene from a TV at home is not different from watching live nudity in a public place since they all have a common effect. For, if we can accept an incident on a video as evidence in court to validate an occurrence of an incident or crime, why can't we accept similar role of the video in another real situation? It will simply be replaying the incident before the eyes of the viewing public at home or at a public square?

In other words, an incident in a public place has equal weight of substance like the video of the public place incident. So any form of nudity in a program or programs or in any adapted form has the same telling effect of being offensive to decency and will equally excite to vicious or lewd thoughts or acts.

Policy makers may not talk about this because of its economic viability; after all, the laws are their opinions.

The EGGS project may boast of economic prospects, but how low do we go if morals are sacrificed on the altars of economic gain while we encourage the laws to remain silent to this?

Can we imagine what it will be like if the minds of our society are held captives to licentious appeals of nudity.

Indeed, nakedness rules over the eyes of the beholder. It strikes enticing urge in the mind of the tempted, and sends a sensuous seductive appeal to the salient Saint. In other words, these elements that nakedness commands are the elements that create the offensive circle of indecency, exciting lewd thoughts, vicious thoughts, vicious acts, creating broken homes and eventually, society, community, cities and it ripples on to chaotic extremity.

Morals will be absent. The fruits of propriety borne from a life of decency will not be able to bequeath any will of peace and moral consciousness.

It reminds me of a judge who had an elegant judicial robe. She wore it only when she was adjudicating in court. When she spoke in court, she spoke the law. She spoke the life of our jurisprudence. This judge received so many praises for the elegance of her robe that she chose to wear it everywhere, in ceremony and out of ceremony. She wore it to do groceries, shopping, to the gym and even to the beach. In other words, she wore it everywhere, and for many times. Yes, she was proud of it. Yes, but, she over wore it.

With time, this robe that defined this judge's intellectual bearing, her judicial authority in court, her social prominence, faded into the cold doldrums of street ordinariness and casualness. With time when she gowned on her elegant robe, she failed to turn eyes, and captured no ears. The very robe that extolled her wisdom and knowledge of the law, lost its worth and its symbolic strength. It cast a shadow of the judge's relevance even on the bench. That judicial robe was meant for the bench while adjudicating in court, and not for all over the place.

Your honor, we all, like that judge, have our individual birth robes, robed in the natural elegance of our nakedness by our creator. But in principle, we do not have to wear these robes of nudity everywhere. Whereas the judge's robe is for the bench in the courtroom, ours is for the bedroom in the chamber. And by the way, when we open our mouth, we may strike a note of sensual harmony to or with the heart that is in harmony with ours. However, when we wear it - all over the place, the effectiveness of its relevance fizzles into bland lifelessness. I mean, we cheapen it.

It's all we have from birth. When we bare it all - the entire glow, the glow fizzles before it reaches the eyes of the valued promised, beloved beholder.

Hear me O – hearers. This is the stock in the trade of Shazzy and Bruna."

Judge Manor fidgeted in his chair. It was a clear show of uneasiness and displeasure about the subject Richard was discussing. Perhaps he was seeing the irrelevance of the figurative allusions he was trying to make. He broke his long silence and patience.

"If I were you I would stay within the boundaries of trying to prove that you didn't threaten Mr. Spicer and Ms. Dhahl by any means possible. And you have never had any violent encounter with them or anyone. So far, what I have been hearing has been a razzle-dazzle of your virtuous self and your hatred for the ambitions of two deceased entrepreneurs in the persons of Mr. Spicer and Ms. Dhahl. And yet you claimed you wouldn't indict the memory of these former colleagues of yours."

Judge Manor reproached Richard. Apparently he had run out of patience for him. However, Richard's voice surprisingly rang out again.

"If I may your honor, allow me to publicly express my gratitude to you for your magnanimity. Please, my accusers are holding me in jail for simply being in opposition to these schemes. I do think I have to express that I have held nothing against their persons, and I'm simply divulging their ambitions that I had opposed to, and I am convinced that any farsighted person who loves people and esteems the law will equally oppose the ambitions of Mr. Spicer and Ms. Dhahl without encroaching into their private lives.

Your honor, as a father, I seek the betterment of children and their future - that all children may steer away from the dangers of ignorant and naïve criminalities. Unfortunately, there is a child out there who may not hear my plea."

Richard became emotional. His voice began to betray him.

"But I hear his heart every day, the prayers of his heart.

I wish I were a child again. O - I need to be birthed again, and allow innocence to grow with me."

"Enough!" Judge Manor yelled above the quietude of the attentive court audience. The words froze in Richard's mouth. The judge had had enough - enough of the sharp gobbledygook of Richard that otherwise was dissecting the core of the judge's own ambivalence to social values. He dropped his gavel to announce the adjournment of the hearing. He looked clearly angry; Evelyn was convinced her case was in peril.

"I will give my ruling tomorrow."

He got up with little ceremony and began his walk out of the room. The unpredictability of his ruling remained more unpredictable.

The audience filed out leaving a very visibly worried Evelyn in the empty courtroom. Her tired head was resting on the briefcase as the events of the hearing session were reeling in her mind's eye. She was hearing herself asking, "where did we go wrong?" The answer was equally elusive like the mirage from the heat of the day's uncertainties. She had no word for her client. She simply stared unbelievably as they drove him away.

Richard's fate was in the balance. His prosecutor, Celia Cromwell might have reasons to celebrate. The strange reaction of Judge Manor was the most visible signal. But Ms. Cromwell wasn't celebrating. The fervor for celebration had been gloomed by the defendant. She might hate him for that, for ruining it. But she couldn't. She was beginning to see how revealing the defendant's closing words were for her. They were casting shadows over her childhood years which had always haunted her.

She could still hear her mother screaming behind the closed bedroom door while being battered by her drunken father. She was recalling the numerous occasions after her mother's battery, nonetheless, in a show of support and loyalty, her mother would come up with a litany of excuses for her abusive husband. As a child, Celia even wondered why her mother continued to stay with her abusive husband, the late lawyer Campy Cromwell, her father. The intellectual showing of Celia's father had walled her father's fierce inner conflicts that they were indiscernible to the world, and Celia knew that.

She remembered an incident when being urged by her father to take a sip of beer from his bottle, and her mother realizing the stupidity and gaucherie of her husband's action, came rushing in to restrain her, from that stupid bidding of her father. Celia remembered how her mother was greeted with a fiery onslaught by her father for her thoughtful interference. Those childhood events were lasting incidents, and were as clear and vivid as live unfolding before Celia's eyes. She cringed at each thought of them.

While she continued to wait outside the building, Celia began to see a divergence of fate and how fate had played her into this drama. There were mother-and-daughter moments that she wouldn't forget. However, Mrs. Cromwell lived with a sad commentary about the life of her husband Mr. Cromwell: "Your father followed his appetite all the way to the grave. There was no measure of temperateness in him. I married a spoiled child, of a rich fool." She once confided in Celia.

Mrs. Cromwell's verbal stance was a voice too late.

Providentially, it could be an indirect counseling to a daughter who never thought 'appetite' could be a fate decider in a case of another father. Was her mother right; why not blame the appetite champion? She frowned at her own answer. Then she remembered that for the past two years she was yet to win a case for the district office. Was she about to blow it again?

Unable to clear her mind, Celia continued to wait for few more minutes, having her eyes glued to the main door which she expected Evelyn to emerge from. She eventually decided to leave, wondering what she might, in actuality, say to Evelyn should she emerge from the door. Perhaps she might announce to her about her escape plan from the conscience of betrayal about her sentimental moments with her mother - if that was not too late.

CHAPTER 36

The courtroom was packed to its capacity. Mrs. Spicer had braved her health condition to be in court. She looked frail, and if looks could speak, then her shroud of empathy was spelling doom for Richard. She sat with her sons in the front row behind Prosecutor Ms. Celia Cromwell. Her strategic seat choice would render the convenience of eye to eye contact between her bench and the judge's. A sense of somberness hanged in the air as every second drummed a marching moment to the decision time.

Richard was wearing a formal black suit and was flanked on every side by his able attorneys. Evelyn had her small hand over Richards's for an assuring support that Richard might need. She however, looked more like the person with morale deficiency. Evelyn's eyes were giving her away. She looked tired but had been trying to keep a smile which Dan Stein kept fostering by whispering silly things into her ears to keep her spirits up and awake. It had been working and sleepy-eye Evelyn encouraged it.

Her night had been rough. On the eve of decision day, the lights were low when she showed up in her mother's house. She hoped she would find it a haven of rest and to escape the torments of doubts on her mind. Her mother had very few lights on to depict her vigil expression of empathy and support for their friend, Richard. Evelyn assumed that the low lights might provide the atmosphere to lull her to sleep, but just when sleep was beginning to softly descend on her, she heard the loud ringing of her mother's home phone. She heard her mother pick up the phone with a whisper, and then silence followed. Dorina trod softly to her window; peeped and waved the phone-receiver to signal to Evelyn an invitation to the phone.

Under those strange circumstances any phone call meant something to her – perhaps a possible positive development in the case. Evelyn grabbed the phone enthusiastically, but her expectations dropped when she heard James' voice.

"You sound disappointed." James sensed it. "I'm sorry if I did. I've been trying to call you, but I guess you have your phone turned off."

It was a welcoming reminder for Evelyn who had turned off her phone earlier during the court session. She placed James on hold and rushed for the cellphone only to find multiple missed calls awaiting her response. She was apologetic and as usual, James was gracious.

She spent hours trying to respond to some of the calls. One was from Richard from the jailhouse. Very distraught, he'd left an emotional message for her. Apparently, he'd made futile attempts to speak to his wife, and Evelyn his perfect contact for his wife was absent. His son, Josh was on his mind. He feared he might not see him again if the Judge pronounced him to stand trial. A justifiable fear as it was. If his case were to go to trial, he would find himself with many limitations. He was aware of that and she was, as well. The reminder was haunting and it was too late for Evelyn to act on Richard's requests. She was upbraiding herself for that breach of commitment. She replayed the message.

"Eve, I need a favor from you. I've made futile attempts to reach my wife. I assume she might be in the hospital with Josh. I don't think she's avoiding me. I strongly suspect my son's condition might have gotten worse. Please, ask my wife to say repeatedly to him 'Dad loves you.' Let it be an anthem in Josh's ears until I see them again. I believe I will. Truth always prevails. Please, tell Apphia I love her. I will see you tomorrow."

That was Evelyn's night, but she had to be very awake enough to hear the outcome of the hearing.

With his back to the audience, Richard could hardly tell if he really had sympathizers among the crowd. Prominent among them was Stan Eavesderry, the one-time client of Richard, charged with sexual assault; Eloquenter who had hoped for a seat that would get him closer to Richard and wished to be seen by him during his escort to the room. Phil Sawyer sat few seats away from a familiar face. While everyone waited for Judge Manor to be announced in, Phil spent his time trying to figure out who owned that familiar face. Eventually it dawned on him. The face was Seth's; the black college friend of Richard who Richard had been trying to help with a cure for his strange skin rashes or disease. Phil was realizing that he looked different. Perhaps Richard was able to discover the cure for him after all.

Sally Sanchez, the giggling happy go-lucky admin assistant for Richard was content with her back seat. Melancholy had replaced her sunny and vibrant spirit. She was yet to come to terms with the allegations levelled against her former boss. She scorned the allegations but continued to nurse a fear for any misconduct and other situations that might adversely affect exoneration prospects for her boss. The thought had driven her more worried and to emotional lengths. She blotted a tear from her right eye. Her immediate seat neighbor offered her a facial tissue from the bundle he carried. Sally sensed that he had a hearing problem so she whispered closer to his ears: "He's a good man. He didn't do it."

His response was rousing. Due to his hearing problem, her seat neighbor ignorant of his loudness blared out his response: "O — we all know he didn't to it. They just want to get him because he's under their skin." The hushed courtroom couldn't resist the invitation to laugh. Surprised Sally couldn't resist the invitation as well. The chorus of laughter attracted a court security personnel to Sally's seating area, but the court security could not pinpoint the culprit.

Hush fell again in the courtroom. Reality was near. Evelyn continued to warm Richard's hand. Dan Stein was behaving himself with his jokes. Evelyn didn't need his whispering anymore. The jostling at the door hinted of the judge's readiness to walk in, and the announcement went out.

Evelyn, for the first time, felt Richard's nervousness. His hand, his fingers began to restlessly shake, and Evelyn's also began to shake in a shared response of concern. Judge Manor's voice went forth. He tried to summarize the arguments of both sides.

"So far, I haven't heard much of an argument that …."

Then a voice in absolute contempt to the court loudly stilled the judge's address.

"I did it; I mean we did it, my brother and me." Judge Manor readjusted his reading glasses to behold a spectacle of weeping juveniles. He was flabbergasted. He was seeing sincerity in a confession that had stifled his prepared decision which would otherwise be at variance with the spirit of the confession, he had just heard, the truth. His nonplused disposition had suppressed his ability to wield his gavel authority to silence the room. He couldn't turn his eyes off the crying juveniles, Shazzy Spicer's children. He launched his huge upper frame forward in a partial sprawl over his desk, in a move that communicated the body-language: "What-did-I-hear-you-say?"

The weeping timid voice reiterated, "We did it."

Evelyn's eyes and Celia Cromwell's locked in a sudden glare of surprise at each other, and sharply also, they looked away in synchronized precision to listen to, or perhaps follow Judge

484

Manor's reaction. The judge requested an immediate conference with the prosecution and the defense lawyers, and ordered the court's security to escort the boys into his chambers.

The mood was very sober in Judge Manor's chambers. Mrs. Spicer requested to join her children in the meeting chamber. Upon Judge Manor's approval, she wheeled herself in in her wheelchair. As she approached the door, one of the lawyers had it propped in readiness for her, but as she passed through the door, her handkerchief fell off from her lap in the doorway. In an eager and more desirous state to reunite with her children before the judge, she moved on ignoring the liter of handkerchief she had caused. Sitting with her children and having them flanked on her sides, she portrayed a flagrant show of solidarity with them.

Fourteen-year old, Flag as he was called, told the audience of invited prosecutors and defense lawyers that their plan was to kill their father's girl-friend, Bruna Dhahl. He gave an account of their arrival time at the house and hiding from view upon seeing a man leaving the premises of Bruna Dhahl. The front door wasn't bolted and Flag was able to sneak in when Bruna arrived in attempt to lock the door. Flag recounted when Bruna fell and how his father tried to talk him out to hand the gun over to him. He told the quiet audience in Judge Manor's office that his younger brother came to his aid when his father launched forward at him in attempt to wrestle the gun from him, and in the ensued struggle their father fell when the gun went off accidentally.

The cold chambers of Judge Manor became colder. There was no reason to doubt Flag's recount of the event, but Judge Manor was yet to understand the reason behind the action of the two boys. His silence begged many questions. Why would he question the confession?

However weak as Mrs. Spicer was, she tried to summon strength and courage to declare a less-flattery assertion response to challenge Judge Manor's unexpressed decision.

"I will tell you why. My husband always used to say if he could control my appetite he could manipulate what appeals to everyone. Shazzy was offering more than wine. His obsession with appetite was to dominate not only the desires of man but also the needs of man.

"I typed out his projects; I mean, those he tried to keep away from his office. He boasted of his influence in high places and declared arrogantly that he didn't care whoever suffered from his work. And really, he didn't, because Snazzy tried to kill me. Bruna was serving her wicked will by dispensing to me her special wine."

Mrs. Spicer paused and waved a piece of paper to the chamber audience. It contained a text dialogue between Shazzy Spicer and Bruna Dhahl. It read in part: "The elixir is working on her. She's down, but not out."

Mrs. Spicer continued her tearful story.

"What did they mean? That night, I drove my children to Bruna's house, and by the way, my children had never trusted Ms. Dhahl. The rest of the story you already know."

A gasp went out from the courtroom and was heard in Judge Manor's chambers. It betrayed the courtroom audience and instantly the Judge's office audience became aware that their proceedings in the office were being overheard by the courtroom gathering, much to the disdain of Judge Manor.

Mrs. Spicer's handkerchief that littered the doorway had helped to maintain the door partially propped and had helped words escape the chambers. Infuriated Judge Manor got up to personally close the door, but then, he froze upon what caught his ears.

"Honorable Judge, you know as I know when you give care, you give cure. Unless, you don't know as I know, deny care and you've denied the denied."

Judge Manor blushed and stuttered for words. "Mrs. Spicer I don't seem to understand; I don't know what you're talking about." He turned and took a hard look at Mrs. Spicer. Yes, he knew as she knew, but he would rather be in her face for an awkward professional posturing than to be defrocked by amok-running lips of Mrs. Spicer.

Judge Manor remembered when as a child his parents arrived with him at a small and old clinic that served a small desert town. His fever was running so high that the worst was very predictable. They'd arrived early enough to beat the crowd and had met a young Spanish-speaking teenager who was tidying up the main reception area. As a child, he and his mother could hear him whistling and see him working from the partially opened door. That young worker was under strict instructions not to allow anyone inside until the clinic officially opened. Manor remembered very well the exchange between his mother and the cleaning boy who feared he would lose his job if he allowed them in from the chilly wind outside.

"Young man, sometimes you take risks to help, to care."

"I lose my job, my whole family suffers." The young man replied.

"You will not lose your job; save life first and life will reward you and your family."

Manor's mother pleaded. Timidly, the young man opened the door and allowed them in. He even allowed them to place young Manor on the single examination bed in the clinic.

Judge Manor recounted this story in his scholarship application essay. Few years later a young college grad, single and who later became Mrs. Spicer was hearing this story retold by Mr. Manor at her school's commencement program.

However, betrayed by her sound perceptions of life, she'd just realized that time and place could often rule and dictate tone and tenor of choices that people often made. She loathed it as a reality. She hated hypocrisy. She determined not to cower to it. Unflinchingly, the lingering glare from the eyes of Judge Manor rather refueled her determination. She strengthened her facial muscle and returned the Judge's look with a more heated glare.

The Judge remarked mockingly: "Could words of care come from a killer?"

"Yes, from a killer whose purged conscience has returned, and with a change of heart. Words could be weapons too, you know. You were my husband's friend. You knew him well and you know what I'm talking about. Both of you belong to the nudists club. Remember, I called you 'honorable.' We've confessed. Our consciences have spoken. Let your conscience speak and the will of man will listen.

"You heard Mr. Bridges; he spoke, not as a felon, but like an honorable character. Please, speak like an honorable Judge who mirrors the law in the spirit of truth. Our confessions make it easier; your commitment to uphold the spirit of this truth. It makes it easier still. Remember, I called you 'Honorable.' You know he's an innocent man; let him go. You will be judged honorable. Be honorable."

Judge Manor returned to the courtroom, and in his trail were the lawyers he conferred with. The Spicer's remained in the chambers to await the reading of their Miranda Rights.

Conscience did speak. It had many voices, but one language, the savoring language of honesty that is so tasty. Richard became a free man; nonetheless, he still remained a captive of his shirked call to paternity.

CHAPTER 37

A cheering crowd greeted Richard as he stepped out from the main front door of the courthouse. The noise was thunderous, more than he'd anticipated. Within view in the crowd was a waving hand. The hand belonged to a young man with a humble spirit, but was rather adamant in his pursuit to heal the heart of Apphia with hope. This young man was faithful to his commitment to mend the broken spirit of Seth and was graciously tolerant to dismiss Richard's ignorant profile of him, Eloquenter. His right hand was up in the air and it towered above the heads of the happy crowd and waved vigorously to arrest the attention of his freed friend. Richard's eye caught him and he led his escort towards him. The embrace was long. It spoke volumes - the unuttered "Thank you."

Richard loosened his warm grip eventually and Eloquenter had the chance to whisper into his ears. The eyes of the crowd were on them. Eloquenter had planted questions on their minds. "Who is he that has the ears and the hug of their folk hero?" He might be his brother, a plausible assumption. The crowd's chant "Bridges, Bridges, Bridges" was drowning and Richard had to bend and return his ears to Eloquenter's less vociferous mouth for a second whispering attempt. He straightened up. His face looked grim and allowed Eloquenter to lead the way to his car.

Evelyn kept her distance to reward her client with the non-tedium and social informalities that come with celebrations. She chose to watch from the distance her client's interaction with their common friend, Eloquenter. She began to follow them in her car and with a keen suspicion of where they might head to. She was right; they were heading towards the hospital where Josh still lay in critical condition. Evelyn felt the vibration of her cellphone and nervously, she picked it up.

"Turn on your radio." Eloquenter's voice instructed excitedly without the norm of phone courtesies. Evelyn obeyed. Her ears were greeted by a talk show host who was listening to a caller express his opinion about Judge Manor's ruling. The caller didn't hold back his disdain for the judge's premeditated decision to rule against Richard, even when an open confession was established. "It clearly shows how screwed some of the Judges are." The caller expressed angrily.

Another caller came on and was full of praise for the defense team. He joked he would like to marry Evelyn if she were single. However, not all the calls favored them. A caller ranted, calling Richard a clever demagogue.Evelyn had learnt through the year of her association with Bridges that not everyone would chorus his tune. However, if she could find one juror to side with her in her argument, she would have a better chance to have the scales swing to her favor. She began to reflect on the dramas in the courtroom for it had become apparent that she was going to lose

Judge Manor's decision no matter how aggressive she might have argued. Richard's sincerity that aimed at the heart was what brought out the confessions of the Spicers. It went without doubt, that honesty and sincerity could root out the better part of a person.

Through these moments of reflection, Evelyn began to question Judge Manor's posturing for interposing Richard's remarks with his furtive comment.

The Judge had said, "If I were you I would stay within the boundaries of trying to prove that you didn't threaten Mr. Spicer and Ms. Dhahl by any means, and you have never had any violent encounter with them or anyone. So far, what I have been hearing from you has been a razzle-dazzle of your virtuous self, … Dhahl, yet you claim you will not indict the memory of your former colleagues."

Evelyn realized that the comments were at best, a sinister motive to derail Richard's pursuit to win his hearers to stand for laws inherent in love and sincere values. Judge Manor's remark, coming at the heels of Richard's strong appeal to the heart of his hearers, did indicate how unnerving Richards's testimony had been to a malign-opinionated Judge Manor. Evelyn tried to clear her mind. She smiled as she thought aloud, "Richard Bridges always wins." However, the smile instantly faded; Richard's most contentious fight was yet to unfold.

Eloquenter pulled his car into the available parking space. The car hardly stopped before Richard opened his door, ejected himself out; in no time, his legs were flying towards the main front door of the hospital. His frantic display of urgency caught the attention of guests in the lobby. They recognized him, but he was in no mood to bask in his legal battle triumph. His son was dying and he simply wanted to condition himself to receive the worst news.

In contrast to his frantic efforts in the lobby, he walked out of the elevator calmly like a patient reacting to a fresh dose of tranquilizer. Sedated by fear, broken by worry, Richard had lost strength in his stride. His steps were feeble and wobbly as he approached the door to the room where Josh lay. Richard was having an anxiety attack. He saw his wife. She looked like a stranger. Her posture told it all. She sat sprawled on the only couch in the room. Hopelessness defined her face and her stuttered speech prefaced the news Richard feared to hear. He took in a deep breath, and tried to relax. Gradually he edged his way to Apphia's couch and lodged his body beside her. Apphia had lost her voice from crying. She couldn't celebrate her husband's court victory. She hugged him and returned to her slouched posture beside him.

"Richard it's late." Apphia declared resignedly.

"What do you mean?" Richard asked - with the little strength in him.

"It's too late. He's been unresponsive. That's what the doctor is saying."

Eloquenter walked in while Richard tried to pull himself from his slouchy condition in the guest couch of the room. He drew nearer to Josh's bed. Josh's eyes remained close. Richard took a deep breath and exhaled his frustration under clinched teeth. He felt like screaming, but he was in a hospital setting. Then he yielded. The levees of his eyes couldn't hold the rising emotional flood. He wept; Eloquenter wept; Apphia sobbed; she was tired of crying.

Suddenly, Eloquenter froze and turned in a sharp frantic reaction to face Richard. Richard was seeing a different Eloquenter, seemingly possessed by the seriousness of the likes of a revolution champion.

"Talk to him." Eloquenter commanded.

"To whom?" Richard asked.

"To your son, Josh," Eloquenter's voice was firm. "Talk to him. Let him hear your voice. All we've been doing is mourning the living. He isn't dead. Mr. Bridges, talk to him."

Richard obeyed. He drew much closer to Josh. In a rare defiance of the hospital's officialdom and protocols, Richard took off his shoes. He climbed onto the bed, his head closer to his ailing son's ears.

"Josh, it's me, Dad. I've come to say sorry to you. I've been away for a long time. I'm here now. I'm wearing our favorite socks, the socks you and I plan to wear anytime we go walking together. I've always thought about you during the time I have been away. I thought about how you and I would play ball together and how I'll teach you how to hold the bat and hit the ball well. Uncle Seth told me about how he's trying to teach you how to play the guitar, and the song the two of you sing together. Josh, I want you to tell me the stories Andy told you."

Richard paused for few seconds. He'd been hearing words that challenged his conscience. However, one word stood out, "stories." As he tried to pull his thoughts together a nurse walked in. The smell from Richard socks hit her. Richard had worn them from Day One of his jail time. The nurse couldn't hide her feeling. She asked Richard to get off Josh's bed, because the policies of the hospital didn't encourage that. She didn't hide her fears either. "With this kind of smell, patients could easily pick up germs and get infected." The Nurse was unkindly or perhaps professionally blunt.

Richard felt insulted. The nurse had burned off the glow of triumph that followed him from the courtroom. He felt humiliated.

Richard reflected; a part of him was upbraiding himself for his insensitivity towards his family: "Where have you been when your son's health has been crying out for you?" The answer challenged his judgment. He'd come a long way, he was then very resolved. He wouldn't allow anything to come between him and his son. If insults on his judgment would be the element, for what it would take to foster warm relationship with his son, he would take them all. If insults on his person would be what it would take as the prime factor to restore his son to full recovery, he would take them all. He was ready. After all, he hadn't alienated himself from the feelings of society. He'd been in court defending an innocent father and arguing against the cunning wickedness being machinated on innocent humanity. That indeed was noble.

Richard had a firmer word – enough to challenge the empty assertion of the nurse. He was ready.

"I will get off the bed, but I'm getting off this bed with my son in my arms." Richard declared matter-of-factly to a very petrified nurse.

"Do you want to take the child off these monitors? Do you know what you're doing?"

"Yes," Richard replied. "I'm replacing my dirty feet with the warmth of a clean heart."

The nurse walked out of the room. Her voice in the hallway reached the nursing Station: "Call security, call security."

The mention of "stories" as Richard was speaking earlier to his nonresponsive comatose son, reminded both of them, even in their individual dispositions, about one of the stories that Josh had shared with them. It was a story that Andy told Josh having heard it from his mother. The story was about an old man who covered his live body over a dead child while praying for him, and eventually the child was restored to life.

Apphia looked on as Richard got off the bed with Josh on his father's chest, clasped in his arms with his head over his shoulders. Two clinical tubes dangled from Josh's arm; while the tension from the monitor lines dragged the mobile monitor machines behind them to the roomy hallway, meantime the son stayed in the warm embrace of his father. Apphia was getting nervous and becoming very apprehensive; she had cause to be. The spectacle was reminding her of Richard being in another confrontation with the law. Nonetheless, a greater reminder seemed to quench her fears, Andy's story of the old man and the dead boy. Apphia got up, spurred by fear, yet driven by hope; she joined her family, covering them with her thin outstretched open arms in a splendid show of warm oneness and love for her family.

Evelyn arrived. She was in a state of bewilderment. "What's going on?" She asked Eloquenter softly under her breath. Eloquenter was expressionless in response; he simply walked towards the Bridges, opened his arms and joined the growing hearty huddle or embrace of support symbol of care for Josh. Evelyn couldn't take her eyes off the sight. She might as well join them; they were her people.

Seth had rightly suspected that he would find his friend at the hospital on a visit to his son. His timely arrival therefore, wasn't a surprise. Something was in the air. He saw a group clinging to one another in one big embrace as Richard towered above their heads with his son on his shoulders. The sight was about hope in desperation, "I belong there." Seth told himself and cast himself to this loud symbolism of united love for Josh.

Within minutes, the sound of a clatter of activities drew curious visitors of other patients to the hallway. They saw a band of huggers in one solid embrace. The rushing hospital security personnel were anticipating an encounter with rough and disgruntled patient's family but, as the Security Officers drew closer, they observed an embracing group, humming a familiar tune, "Jesus Loves Me, This I know." The humming that Eloquenter started, had crooned the group into swaying side by side in a graceful movement to Elo's mellow humming. His solo humming effort rippled to the circle of embracers – crooning and swaying for Josh. The sight was moving. It drew an emotional response from a nurse who stood by the door and watched on from the nurse station. She felt impelled to join the group but debated with herself the peril of losing her job. The better part of her won. She joined the growing circle of embracers and was soon humming in harmony and swaying with them

Her action drew a gasp from the other nurses. The nurse supervisor was furious. She considered the junior nurse's action an insubordination and asked her to return to the station. Her fury was clear in her voice.

"I should remind you the consequences of your action," she declared loudly, but her threat met a more determined nurse whose louder opinion about caring was substantially heartily than the ploy about well-articulated professional handy caring.

"If we deprive this family their way of affirming love to their sick child, then we're failing in our calling of caring. It's better for that child to be in his parent's arms, that was what he was first introduced to, and that's what he knows. I stand with them."

The bold stand on rectitude of judgment by the junior nurse drew a line in the sand between her and the other nurses who also questioned the propriety of her action. Would it be right if they all abandoned their responsibilities and joined the group?

However, her action did embolden two other nurses, who left their desks while charting their reports, to stand with their defiant colleague. Their action broadened the scope of the circle of embracers, in the symbolic expression of love and caring for Josh. Soon, they were humming and swaying.

Notwithstanding the wonderful expression of love and support for Josh, a voice was heard from the outside of the circle that chose to address Richard in a more conciliatory tone, a complete reversal of the brash display by the nurse supervisor moments before.

"Mr. Bridges, congratulations on your court victory." Richard turned to acknowledge the voice that had addressed him, and nodded gratefully. He wasn't a nurse, but he sounded like one. He was one of the security personnel from the hospital.

"We understand that you miss your son very dearly and you want as much as possible to stay in touch with him as closer and as long as you can, but the hospital has important concerns for you and your son. We have concerns about contaminations because of the environment you've just come from and also from the different individuals that make the crowd around you. We simply advise that you return your son to his bed to be given the necessary immediate attention. Please, do it for your son."

Richard heard him; every embracer in the circle did. The circle chain of embracers broke as Richard took his first hard step of the long journey away from his son's bed. The son's right arm drooped by the side of the father's chest like a puppet that had lost the strings to its limbs. There were visible blood stains on the bed which were from his son's discontinued intravenous site. Richard tried to unload the seeming lifeless body of Josh off his shoulders to the white, but newly blood-stained linen spread on the bed. Hope had left him. The evidence was evident. Josh was holding on to his last breath in a solemn parting moment with his parents.

Richard decided to lie partially by his son with his arm stretched over him as his tears drenched the small sagged shoulder of Josh that had been covered with white linen. Apphia couldn't bear the sight. Richard's heart wrung out its last wish: "Speak to me, Josh; Speak to me." The sight was unbearable to his fellow embracers who had gathered around the vicinity of the door. Josh was breathing his last.

Richard's arm felt it. He readjusted that arm to facilitate his son's last respiratory activity. The father heaved in a deep breath to summon his emotional farewell message to his son, but his lips kept throbbing. His set of teeth, both the upper and the lower were in rapid rhythmic vertical collision with each other and that compounded his emotional struggle to release his parting words to his son. The father, who was a bundle of nerves, eventually spoke.

"Josh, I love you. I always will." A cold dew of silence filled the room.

"I love you too, Dad."

Richard heard it. His ears hadn't deceived him. He felt a touch of tiny fingers on his rough beard. The throbbing lips froze in stupefied gasp. "Josh, my Josh," Richard exhaled a cautious whisper. "Josh is that you?"

"Yes, it's me. Where's Mom?" The triumphant whispery expression was loud enough to generate a greater crowd than that was last seen of the humming, crooning and swaying embracers in the hallway. It created a festive scene of huggers.

Urged by the author of life, Eloquenter's obedience to suggest to Richard, to in turn talk to his son was a spark of faith for a fiery whisper of cure. The author of life had prevailed again – with a tenacity of purpose. His warm bodily contact had broken the walls of Josh's cold skin that hitherto was a frosted hope to human touch, but had now become responsive and even welcoming to a caring divinely-created human with warmth of heart and spirit. His father's touch was the perfect cure for a son who'd yearned for that touch.

An example of an irony of human judgment had just been unfolded before the eyes of nurses, patients and visitors. This irony however, had no room for discussion in the room where this plausible miracle had taken place. Perhaps it wasn't noticeable, or perhaps the excitement and the circumstances had hushed any glibber in the room, or simply perhaps in the hasty bustle of activity, it didn't attract any worthiness for recognition. Nonetheless, it struck a core. The warmth of a persevering human spirit pervades through the lives of willing well-wishers. Again, Richard attempted to pick up his skeletal and feeble son from his hospital bed. He carefully lifted up his fragile body again to his chest while his head rested on his shoulders. Josh hadn't eaten for weeks. Few tubes still dangled on his arm; this time contamination was a non-factor.

Eventually an enthused doctor rushed in while the beddings were being hastily changed. She demanded to talk to the patient's family alone. Apphia saw the excitement of the doctor; she recognized that her mood was different.

"I have no immediate medical or physiological explanation for what has taken place. You may call it what you want. By the way, we can keep your son overnight for observation unless you opt to take him home."

"I want to go home," Josh spoke again.

The feared contamination had ushered in the cheered cure. That was an irony.

CHAPTER 38

A new life awaited her friend, Richard. He might be done with Milo, Grady and Strong Law Firm, knowing what the firm had particularly subjected him to. If he chose to leave the MGS, life there would never be the same, especially for Evelyn. She thought about the time they shared together, her first day at MGS, their first meeting with Eloquenter at the park, and even a more-recent ride that she gave Richard from a bus stop in the company of Robert and Cannon. Consumed by those thoughts within that pensive moment, she heard the unique calling of her name, "Ms. Evelyn" which was always traceable to Eloquenter.

"You want to go for a bite?"

"Yeah, do you know any good restaurant around here where I can simply eat and relax?" Evelyn asked looking much wearied from the day's events.

"You're kidding me. Everyone will be on you for autographs. You know, you're big time now. They're watching you on TV, you know. You can't relax around here."

Evelyn blushed at Elo's remarks. He had a point that she had to acknowledge her new public figure image. As a lawyer, she'd just collaboratively with her client, skillfully engineered a successful legal design that involved the risk of making a defendant's testimony speak to the conscience of a silent murderer and to eventually siphon an honest confession. In that case, not only from a single murderer, but it siphoned the confessions from accomplices as well. The art was a landmark defense strategy, aimed at allowing sincere testimonies speak to the conscience of litigants as well as the conscience of the public. Formidable that it was, the testimony went far to weaken the gavel-wielding arm of the overly-strict Judge Manor. Evelyn had endorsed Richard's philosophy that a grain of honest and sincere testimony would appeal beyond a huge harvest of evidences.

However, her victory wasn't on her mind. After all, it was a shared victory. It was Richard's brainchild and not hers. What was on her mind was simply food and rest. She thought of her Mom. She was very sleepy and the thought of contending with traffic undermined her hopes of staying alert and driving safely to her mom's. She jumped at Elo's willingness to drive, but to his place where his mother had a special meal for him.

Evelyn parked her car at a grocery store parking lot and joined her friend in his old car; they were soon on their way to Elo's Mom's. The car didn't meet the luxury standards of her own, but she was comfortable in the company of a trust-worthy young-man.

"Ms. Evelyn, how long will it take a person to study and become a lawyer?" Elo initiated a dialogue with sleepy Evelyn.

She laughed. She knew the day's events would naturally spark a lot of interest in law for many young people.

"Why do you ask? Do you want to be a lawyer?"

"Yes, I think I can help a lot of innocent people like you just did."

"Well, you have to finish college and a law school. It depends on how much time you can put in your studies, but have you abandoned your plans to be a pastor?"

"No, I never will. I want to do both. I know the streets. It's rough out there and I know that will be very helpful. Ms. Evelyn, I'm my Mom's only child – no brother, no sister. I look up to you as my big sister, you know. I hope you'll consider me as your brother and I hope I can count on you for direction."

Evelyn was touched by his request. She considered his request as an honor, because she'd always observed and considered Elo to always portray a mark of good-natured deportment. Elo truly reflected his beliefs.

"Yes, I feel honored. You're kind and very helpful; In fact, I feel you're already my brother." Eloquenter then turned and acknowledged her remark with a quick smile. His car pulled up at a parking place where the graffiti on the walls spelt the nature of the neighborhood where Evelyn was fearfully entering. Few walls were partially cleaned, but few inscriptions were stubbornly indelible. Elo led the way and used his key to unlock a door which led straight to a living room. A lady who could have been in her late fifties was busy cleaning the kitchen and was frightfully surprised to see her son bring in a friend without any notification. Elo allayed her mother's fears with immediate lively introduction of Evelyn.

"Mom, this is my friend; I call her my sister, Evelyn. You'll get to know her more. She's the smart lawyer on the TV who was defending my other friend, Lawyer Richard Bridges."

Elo's Mom presented her hand for a handshake while taking a keener look at their visitor. Lost in her admiration of Evelyn, she forgot the courtesy to offer her a seat until Evelyn had to mention the request and which she elatedly addressed: "Yes, Yes, Yes," in affirmation. Evelyn felt as relaxed as she'd hoped - in a room which could not boast of glamor but could proudly declare its cleanliness and orderliness. The walls had few pictures including one on Eloquenter's High School graduation. It attracted Evelyn, especially, the one he jointly took with his mother. His mother was all smiles – the evidence of proud motherhood. But then, Evelyn's mind wandered away. The aroma of food had pervaded the walls. In no time the three were all seated and dining together. The meal was good, beyond Evelyn's expectations.

A cry of an infant from one of the rooms pulled Elo's Mom away. She returned with a crying ten-month old boy. Then Elo's Mom broke into a playful song:

"Baby don't cry,

Yours is to smile

Smile and I will smile

Wave and I will wave

Light your face like the smile of rose

And you'll blossom,

You'll blossom,

Yes, you'll blossom.

Yes, you'll blossom.

Blossom, blossom throughout the year"

"That's a beautiful song. I didn't know you had a little child." Evelyn probed with sharp curious interest.

"No, she isn't my child. She's a child of one of the few mothers who leave their children in my care to baby-sit for them while they're at work. I guess one day I'll have the chance to take care of yours while you work."

"I hope so, but, I'm still single." Evelyn's remark drew sharp laughter from Eloquenter and an inquiring look at Evelyn.

"Mama, such a beautiful lady must have someone but she isn't giving him a chance." Elo's pointed jovial opinion drew more laughter and Evelyn felt obliged for direct explanation of herself to Elo's Mom. She struggled in her effort to articulate her social life and how she wanted to walk that line.

"Please, what's your name?"

"My name is Lydia, but my friends call me Lily. In fact, I don't mind when they call me 'Lily.' The response drew sharp gasp of surprise from Evelyn. It reminded her of Eloquenter's rhyming riddle.

"So, you're Lily." Evelyn was convinced she'd met the "Lily" in Eloquenter's rhyme.

"No, no," Eloquenter attempted to correct Evelyn. "I wrote about another Lily – although many find it easier to affectionately call my mom 'Lily' instead of Lydia. Strangely, I didn't have my mom in mind. The line is meant for the only one who is fittingly and often described as the 'Lily of the Valley', Jesus Christ, period. This is actually the meaning of my rhyming riddle. I wanted people to actually ask me the meaning of the riddle so that I could have the opportunity to tell them about Jesus. You see, lily is a very unique flower, and very unique in many ways."

The expression of Eloquenter, both in countenance and words captured the attention of Evelyn. She was seeing a young man with an avowed conviction to even deny her mom of the credit label with which her friends had coroneted her. Evelyn wanted to hear more. She readjusted herself in the dining chair in which she had remained seated.

"As you may know, lily is a beautiful flower. It's interesting also to know that it has seven seeds within it which are beautiful and golden in color like seven golden grains. Lily is also a very fruitful flower that one root of a lily generates around it about fifty shoots of bulbs. Another strange thing about this flower is that it is the tallest of flowers yet carries its head low. Ms. Evelyn, ask any Pastor, and he will tell you that the whiteness of the lily stands for its purity. It has other colors, like pink and many others. Tell he gold stands for royalty, and its tall height represents the fact that it's above all, and like Jesus, it hangs its head low as a symbol of humility. This typically depicted the picture of Jesus while he was on the cross. You see, lilies in many ways are a metaphor of Jesus. His purity, royalty, his fruitfulness with the shoots of bulbs around him support the picture that Jesus once described that he 'will gather his children under his wings like a mother hen gathers her little ones under her wings.' Did I tell you about the healing properties, I mean the medicinal benefits from Lily? Did I also tell you about how lilies grow? Ms. Evelyn, that's your assignment. You'll be surprised with the findings."

Evelyn was astounded at Eloquenter's lucid explanation of his rhyme. She was particularly struck by the strange coincidences about the lilies – the Lily in the rhyme and the Lily in the room. Indeed, she was caring for children under her roof. It set her thinking. She still believed Elo, and as a lawyer, she found the explanation indisputable. Nonetheless, she still wondered what must be spinning the wheel of coincidences the literality of his rhyme into life in Elo's home. What else in Elo's rhyme awaited her? – "an herb for sure" she wondered, but tried to dispel the anxiety.

"Lydia, could I call you Ms. Lily?"

"Yes."

"Are there other children you're taking care of?" Evelyn asked.

"Yes, total of two boys, and a girl," Lily replied heartily.

"They aren't sick. Are they?"

"No, they're not, not at all. Come, follow me. One is up playing in her play pen."

Evelyn followed Lily to a room where the other children were. She was beginning to see elements of Lily being a fulfilling reality of Eloquenter's rhyme. She picked up a toy and began shaking it to call for a playful response from the playing infant. The baby girl giggled repeatedly. While Evelyn was enjoying her happy interaction with the babies, Lily returned the infant in her arms to her pen and withdrew herself to the living room. When Evelyn joined them she found Eloquenter consoling his mother with the words 'You're good. It's fine.' Evelyn tried not to pry, and also tried to convince herself that her questioning about the babies' health hadn't unsettled her.

Evelyn hugged her newfound friend and requested if they could take a picture together. She brought out her small camera which she always carried with her in her purse and offered it to Elo. He took a picture of his mother, Lily, standing side by side with Evelyn.

The sun was almost setting and Evelyn was ready to drive back to her mother Dorina's home. She was met by a happy crowd of well-wishers including her father, Tom, her Mom, Dorina and her guests, Cannon and Robert and her special friend, James. An announcement of her arrival went out and a loud cheering of clapping and whistling greeted Evelyn as she opened the door and walked in. The planned surprise worked. The happily-surprised Evelyn bowed to acknowledge their support and shook hands to everyone as she travelled through the random forest of people, mainly family and friends who had assembled in Dorina's small living room.

However, when she got to James, she turned her back in a deliberate show of rebuff of him and walked away. The crowd looked on with shock. They watched James smiling it off and they wondered what was going on between them. Evelyn turned around and walked back to approach her mother but, veered sharply away and sped her steps back to James, jumped and threw her arms affectionately around his neck in a dramatic demonstration of her affection. She kissed him for the first time.

The crowd applauded. They'd just witnessed a rare side of Evelyn. She was in love. Could there be another side of her?

CHAPTER 39

A very different life had sprung in Dorina's home, even nights held little darkness, for even souls that walked her walls beamed an inner glow. Tom waited patiently for Dorina to emerge from her room. Dorina was aware that they had to be on time, for James wouldn't start the party without them. The party was in honor of their daughter's legal victory for Richard. It would have been in bad taste if their lateness kept the guests waiting. Eventually, Dorina stepped out and deliberately stood by the door for recognition. She was elegant and the once bed-ridden old lady with rashes now boasted her healthier skin as she emerged with shiny radiance on her arms from the captivating lamp-glow. She revealed the sparkles in her eyes which shined through the heart of Tom again. Tom took notice and was stunned. They were yet to understand how Dorina got her cure for the rashes.

"I don't know you." Overwhelmed with admiration, Tom declared his pointed unbelief. They drove off and Cannon and Robert followed them in another car as they caravanned through the busy streets to James house.

A few minutes behind them were Evelyn, who was being chauffeured by Eloquenter, while Elo's mother rode along in quiet passivity. Unlike Dorina, who had been at James residence before, the trip was Evelyn's first to James' house. The imaginations

515

about a landscaper's home were rife and so were his deep expectations for a poetic modesty. The journey seemed long and the rough streets leading to his house began to foreshadow Evelyn's expectations. Elo covered a few more miles on the hilly strip and stopped. Evelyn wondered why he had stopped and Elo's response was firm: "This is Mr. James's house," he pointed to a red flag on a flagstaff, in front of the house.

"Wow!" Evelyn wasn't discreet with her excitement. An attendant approached them when she stepped out of her car. "Ms. Hedge, please, the gate will open for you to drive in and park." They drove in and parked. The home was a mansion. The landscape architecture was breathtaking. The flowers were laid out to design a path with bouquets. The mini waterfall was greeted on descent by beams of varying lights. They were meant to achieve a kaleidoscopic beauty against a backdrop of suspending rainbow created by a blend of active waterworks and lights. James waterfall design was a masterpiece.

Evelyn reinstated her mood for celebration. She raised her right arm to Elo as a request gesture for escort. Lily followed her son, watching him arm in arm with "big sister." The lights were on them; the eyes were on them; the applause was for Evelyn. James met them halfway and took over the escort role for Evelyn to the reception hall.

Other special guests were the Bridges family. Josh sat between his parents around their round table. Seth was in the company of

Dr. Marlene Appleworth, Eloquenter and his Mom, Lydia. Tom and Dorina shared table with Dorina's former nurse. Thelma who had formed friendship with James during his frequent visits. Cannon and Robert shared a table with two landscape employees of James. There were many other guests, all ready for a wonderful night.

James welcomed the invited guests and requested few words from Richard. Evelyn was surprised that James and Richard knew each other all-that-time. Richard had been quiet about it because he didn't want his acquaintance with James influence his business decision and plans for Evelyn.

Richard thanked all well-wishers for their prayers and support during his son's ordeal and his. He thanked Evelyn for her selfless support and bravery.

"Before I invite Ms. Hedge to say few words, our host has few words also."

James walked to Evelyn and beckoned her to walk center stage with him. The quintet jazz group struck a tune but upon James signal they stopped. Still holding Evelyn's hand, he turned to cue Josh and saw Josh moved away from his father's table. Josh looked weak and very lean. He walked slowly, but eventually arrived at James with a note. Readily, James knelt before Evelyn, opened the packet in his hand and made his request known: "Ms. Evelyn Hedge, will you marry me?"

Evelyn's response was loud. She didn't anticipate the proposal, but her mother Dorina and her father Tom knew the night was for their daughter. As the guests lined up to congratulate James and Evelyn, Cannon seemed impatient for his turn to speak with James. He couldn't contain his anxiety. Cannon had seen a familiar stranger. With his back against the party, he felt a tap on his shoulder. It interrupted the flow of the greeting traffic to James and Evelyn which affected the conversation and generated a fleeting anger from Tom. "Cannon, it's me - Mom."

Cannon turned to face the face of the voice – the face that had spurred him to rush excitedly to James. Missing mom Lydia who vanished on a rainy day from the life of her children was standing a whisper-away from her son. Canon could say no more. He was in shock. His mother pulled him to a convenient corner where the prospects for uninterrupted conversation were much better. She wept over her son's shoulders. Their speechless moment was a speechless oration delivered by conceding hearts. Cannon knew what his mother had been through. As a child, he looked on helplessly while his mother went through the long travail of abuse from his father. Those are memories both would like to forget, especially on a rather pleasant memorable night. Twenty-five years of drowned relationship was being resuscitated.

From the distance, Dorina looked across the stretch of guests present. She saw Cannon and his mother heading towards her table. Years ago, any imminent encounter with Lydia would otherwise drive her sick with fear as a baby abductor. She'd changed into a different Dorina. Now, she could pick her battles and still triumph without a fight. Lily approached the table with Cannon, and Dorina welcomed them warmly into the empty seats of Tom and Thelma.

"How beautiful, mother and son reunion," Dorina's greeting froze the torrent of tidings they wanted to bear.

"How do you know?" Cannon and Lily asked in unison.

"Does it matter? I rescued your daughter who almost drowned when you abandoned her in the rain in the improvised box cradle; saved your sons who were led by Providence to my door. Your other son, Eloquenter met a lady at a park, who he didn't know, but formed a friendship with and still does not know they shared a common womb. What do these tell you?" Dorina summed up her experience and posed her question in a resigned tone of peaceful disposition. The wheel of coincidences continued to spin with less predictable consequences.

Lily was tongue-tied. She wished Dorina knew what she'd also been through - the guilt, the agony, the fear, the denial, the hopelessness she felt when the man who eventually married her died and left her alone with their son Eloquenter. She wished she would know that Eloquenter's father was a God-fearing man who inculcated his moral values into his son, Elo. It was that thought that had refueled her hopes daily and brought her peace.

Notwithstanding that, the stance of Dorina had moved her. Lily sought to ingratiate herself to Dorina, having won her heart as a woman of destiny. They hugged and sobbed in each other's arms.

"For years I have prayed that my children would not come to harm. You are the answer to my prayers. I fled an abusive relationship. When I saw the clouds forming that evening, I knew it was my chance to flee from the house of abuse because he was drunk and I knew he couldn't drive in the rain to come after me. That was my only chance. Evelyn belongs to a better home. Thank you and thanks to you again for Cannon, and well, Robert also. He who made us all led them to you." Lily expressed."

Eloquenter could not hide his feelings. "God has a way of piecing up the puzzle if we allow him. It takes a Cradle in the rain to discover a cure and a safer shelter. The most important thing is knowing the heart of God. Through it all, we see his truth, his compassion, and his love unfold. No matter how difficult it might be, his peace abides with us forever. It's a wonderful feeling."

"Let me ask you, what does Evelyn know?" Sobbing Lily asked.

"She knows about her rescue account," Dorina replied. "Evelyn wonders about her strange resemblance to you, Lily. That's why Evelyn took the picture with you. Dorina is graciously grateful." She hugged Lily again.

As she reflected on the incident of the fateful rainy evening, Dorina began to assemble the pieces of the puzzling incidents all the way to their first historic meeting. She'd enjoyed the night. She knew her past would no longer haunt her. She'd met Evelyn's biological mother and her lips had declared her, Dorina, as a wonderful mother.

Parting handshakes were beginning to be the order of the night, especially when the music was low unlike it was three hours before. The majority of the guests were beginning to leave and the caterers were winding up with their service. Few close associates, relatives and friends of James, including Evelyn and Richard lingered behind. Friends had been made; interests were shared, hopes were built for merry minds on a merry night. Amidst all these, broken pieces of hearts found their puzzle pieces around the menders table. Many didn't know Eloquenter, but as always, he tried to piece hearts together with warm stories of love and stories of heroism in selflessness.

"Every day, God directs and guides in the affairs of men. However, many times, men choose to refuse to observe and see his hand. We are too occupied to listen. We always want an immediate satisfaction or gratification. Even so, when God is ready to help, we are too impatient to observe his hand pointing to the emerging sprouts of solution from the roughness of the soil, the earth. As a result, because he is not forceful, he had to go through our suffering with us and even then, some still fail to get it. God is love."

The words struck a chord in the hearts of the few that joined Eloquenter at his table.

Dorina, Apphia and Lily continued chatting together. They were on a common ground. Each had a story to share and their stories had a common theme – how their sprouts of blessings emerged from the roughness of the adversities each had faced.

James hobnobbed his way to Richard. The two had earlier wanted to talk but the partying atmosphere suppressed the prospect. James pulled a chair.

"Did you see the land on your drive up here?"

"Yes, I did. It was vast and very beautiful." Richard remarked as James continued.

"As you know, that was a gift from my father. I wanted to develop it into a wonderful architectural piece of landscape. It would boast of orchards, trees, flowers, lawn designs and waterworks. When Spicer heard of the idea, he chose to adulterate the concept to suit his corrupt, lewd and dirty mind. Would you believe, he was going to call it Eden too?" James complained.

"I knew Shazzy and Bruna's intentions had never been good and the name 'Eden Grove Gardens' was to mask the idea with the name you chose. The goal was to eventually mislead others into his insidious scheme and to ultimately derail your plans. Shazzy Spicer was good at that," Richard expressed.

"You see, that's what I feared," James remarked.

"Well, breathe easy; I was informed this evening by my friend Phil that Palate has filed a motion to dismiss. Many unsavory items have affected the dangerous brew of Palate and the last straw was the revelations at the hearing. Well, James, I would say with profound optimism, breathe easy, Eden is yours."

The two cheered and high-fived each other so loudly that it drew the attention of the lingering few guests. However, as the night wore on and with very few guests hanging around, it was apparent that there was little left to talk about. But, there was something on Richard's mind. It kept bugging him.

Richard withdrew himself to the quiet balcony that overlooked the vast land of the James estate, the very land that Palate International had their eyes on for their (EGG) Eden Grove Gardens project. He instantly turned around, and with his eyes escaping from the captivating aerial view and his imaginary picture of the new Eden Grove, rushed down through the flight of stairs and desperately started calling out loudly to Dr. Marlene Appleworth who was heading towards her car. Richard was panting and trying to catch his breath as he stood before his friend, the doctor that he had much respect for.

"Doc, I need your help before you leave tonight."

"You sound desperate." Appleworth said.

"Yes I am," Richard replied breathlessly.

"I don't know how I can be of help to a desperate man outside my clinic, but what is it?"

"Does stress have any impact on a person's fertility?" Richard asked with a bashful smile.

"How am I going to be paid? You're within my professional precincts," Dr. Appleworth joked.

"That's called trespassing and I'm not ready to break any more laws. Doc, then may I respectfully and fearfully flee," Richard clowned in his response to bring out a shared laughter on their faces.

"Yes, it actually does," the doctor expressed. "Our bodies are wired to hold off occurrence of conception during extreme times of stress. I'm sure you've heard about adrenalin, our bodies release that hormone during times of stress, as a way to signal to the body that conditions don't favor conception. What happens is the adrenaline suppresses us from utilizing the hormone called progesterone which is very vital for fertility. In the same vein, it makes our pituitary gland release greater levels of prolactin which in effect causes infertility. These conditions could subsequently affect ovulation and even sperm count. Basically, yes it does, but remember, not everyone is the same."

"Thank you, thank you, and thank you." Richard was excitedly generous with his gratitude, but just when he turned and was about to leave; Marlene Appleworth restrained him with a compelling question.

"Richard, what is your motive?"

Richard looked around to search for an answer; engaging his brains to outwit the cunning prying of his physician friend. "There you are," pointing to James and Evelyn as they sat in a classic garden-swing under the moonlight. Richard smiled, winked at Dr. Appleworth and headed off to meet Apphia and Josh.

Every stride he made was a happy strut. Seth had said he didn't know how and why the rashes left him, but Richard could now boast that he knew. Earlier, he had been trying to find meaning behind the coincidental and sequential flow of events which had culminated into the night's celebration at James house. He remembered - the words Elo shared with Apphia; "Acknowledge always that there are people greater than who you are, and that every person has a need with the exception of God, who has all things, and almighty. Our genuine needs can only be met by God, if we patiently allow him to meet the need."

Richard continued to walk his way back to his wife. He looked happier. Apphia noticed it and wondered what had gotten into him. Then it dawned on her. Once upon a time, Richard listened to his heart. It was a call for caring. It sparked a hope to prospect for that cure for his friend, Seth. The journey led him and his family through some alleys of life as he held on to hope.

Many times, it takes the still small voice of the author of hope and life to render whispers of a cure to life's situations and challenges for the hopeful ultimate. Apphia lived it; she believed it.

"It's strange to see you bushy-tail happier. What are you keeping from me?" Richard smiled. It was a coy smile. "Perhaps we all needed a cure, and we've gotten it. I am a happier person, because I think I have helped to restore happiness to some persons. Do you remember Mr. Stan Eavesderry?" He breathed out softly.

With a brief pensive expression on her face she eventually nodded, "yes, yes, I do. Your former client who was offering you the gift after you won his sexual assault case for him." Richard smiled and nodded his head: "I am meeting him tomorrow; this time I am receiving it, and nothing is obstructing it." Apphia smiled, and remarked in a tone of very merry appreciation, "You better, you better Richard."

The Bridges' cast a parting look at James and Evelyn. The night was meant for them. They knew it. It was peaceful, and the garden was very inviting under the silvery glow of the moon. Evelyn was feeling it.

"How will you describe love?" Evelyn asked James as they shared their classic garden-swing.

"It has many answers; actually, it's one word with many definitions, but many of the definitions are based on the definer's immediate feeling, past experiences and prevailing inclination. The person may spin the definition to suit the person's purpose."

"What is your definition?" Evelyn persisted.

"I'll say: Love is expressed kindly in what a person creates and the desire to care for it. I may also say love is the mode for friends travelling and persevering to support each other on the journey. They know not when their trip begins and know not where the trip is leading them to until they arrive. Because as travelers, they endeavor to surmount all obstacles and challenges of the trip until there is no recognition for a challenge-worthy situation on the journey any more. That's arrival and that's love." James expressed.

"James, you amaze me. Few weeks ago, it was more of a poetic air, now it's a fervor for philosophy. Was that how you charmed them?" Evelyn asked insinuatingly.

"Do I dare attempt to charm this smart lawyer? If I could, then I must have arrived." James explained and continued.

"For, who can see beyond the parapet of this brow?" James moved with his right reach to play with Evelyn's brow.

"Where to charm it's no good even with a flattering voice

As truth confirms her beauty and poise.

No, I cannot go there with this kind of air

I must not dare.

One thing I do know, though,

With abundance of care,

Prudence always reigns."

A feeling of overwhelming fascination, like a morning dew began to settle on the lawny greenery of Evelyn's mind. "Here he is." Evelyn exhaled a warm hearty sigh to proclaim her tacit adoration for her man. "O - He has a very sweeping lucid way with words." Then she yielded. She could no longer hold her admiration, "Mr. James Adams, do I know you?"

"Yes, you do. I am a life inviting you into my life." James responded, but Evelyn persisted with another question.

"And who is this 'life?'"

James's response was simple.

"Life is a parable. We choose the characters; time writes the didactic plot. Whether we choose to read it or not, we are still choosing the characters for a parable in progress."

About the Author

George R. Swaniker is an author and playwright in the literary style of poetic prose, producing such works as *Shades of Umbrellas* and recently, *Cradle in the Rain*. He was born in Ghana, on the western coast of the African continent. George began his career in journalism and quickly climbed as a radio producer and broadcaster for the largest media conglomerate in Ghana at the time, the Ghana Broadcasting Corporation. There he pioneered several original radio dramas, game shows, and award-winning news pieces. In 1990 he transitioned to Los Angeles, California with his wife where he began his work in writing for the theater. An admitted news junkie, George feeds his addiction to his first love, journalism, by staying avidly connected to the political media circuit. George spends most of his time writing, cooking, dreaming, and spending time with his overly energetic grandchildren.

www.ingramcontent.com/pod-product-compliance
Lightning Source LLC
Chambersburg PA
CBHW071336020726
47502CB00001B/113